I0578509

THE HARMONY OF HOLLY

Shiloh Ridge Ranch in Three Rivers, Book 5

LIZ ISAACSON

Copyright © 2020 by Elana Johnson, writing as Liz Isaacson

All rights reserved.

No part of this book may be reproduced in any form or by any electronic or mechanical means, including information storage and retrieval systems, without written permission from the author, except for the use of brief quotations in a book review.

ISBN-13: 978-1-953506-34-4

The Glover Family

Welcome to Shiloh Ridge Ranch! The Glover family is BIG, and sometimes it can be hard to keep track of everyone.

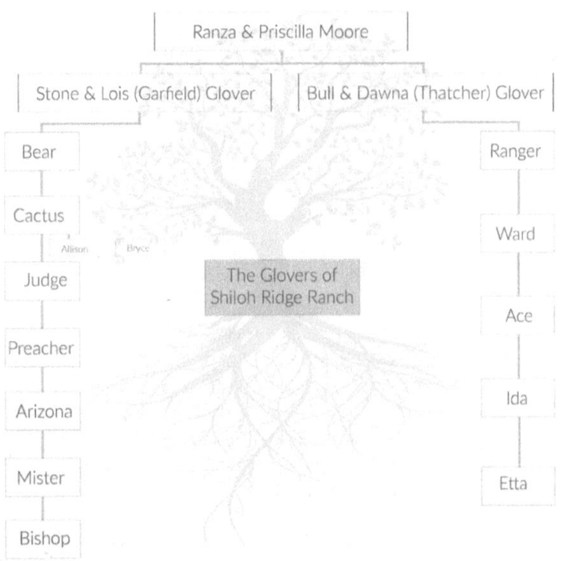

<u>There is a more detailed graphic on my website.</u> (But it has spoilers! I made it as the family started to get really big, which happens fairly quickly, actually. It has all the couples (some you won't see for many more books), as well as a lot of the children they have or will have, through about Book 6. It might be easier for you to visualize, though.)

HERE'S HOW THINGS ARE RIGHT NOW:

Lois & Stone (deceased) Glover, 7 children, in age-order:

1. Bear (Sammy, wife / Lincoln (9), step-son, Stetson (new-born), son)

2. Cactus (Allison, ex-wife / Bryce, son (deceased))

3. Judge

4. Preacher

5. Arizona (dating Duke Rhinehart)

6. Mister

7. Bishop (Montana, fiancée / Aurora (16), step-daughter once they marry)

Dawna & Bull (deceased) Glover, 5 children, in age-order:

1. Ranger (Oakley, wife)
2. Ward
3. Ace (Holly Ann, fiancée)
4. Etta
5. Ida (Brady Burton, fiancé)

Bull and Stone Glover were brothers, so their children are cousins. Ranger and Bear, for example, are cousins, and each the oldest sibling in their families.

The Glovers know and interact with the Walkers of Seven Sons Ranch. There's a lot of them too! Here's a little cheat sheet for you for the Walkers.

Momma & Daddy: Penny and Gideon Walker

    1. Rhett & Evelyn Walker
    Son: Conrad
    Triplets: Austin, Elaine, and Easton

    2. Jeremiah & Whitney Walker
    Son: Jonah Jeremiah (JJ)
    Daughter: Clara Jean
    Son: Jason

    3. Liam & Callie Walker
    Daughter: Denise
    Daughter: Ginger

    4. Tripp & Ivory Walker
    Son: Oliver
    Son: Isaac

    5. Wyatt & Marcy Walker
    Son: Warren
    Son: Cole

Son: Harrison

6. SKYLER & MALLERY WALKER
Daughter: Camila

7. MICAH & SIMONE WALKER
Son: Travis (Trap)

THE GLOVERS KNOW AND INTERACT WITH THE SEVERAL OF the cowboys and their families at Three Rivers Ranch too... There's a lot going on in Three Rivers!

You'll see:

1. Squire and Kelly Ackerman

Mother / Father: Heidi (owns Ackermans bakery) / Frank

Son: Finn

Daughter: Libby

Son: Michael

Son: Samuel

2. PETE AND CHELSEA MARSHALL (CHELSEA IS SQUIRE'S sister)

4 sons: Paul, Henry, John, Rich

3. REESE AND CARLY SANDERS: THEY'RE THE ADMINS FOR Courage Reins, Pete and Chelsea's equine therapy unit at Three Rivers Ranch.

Chapter One

Cactus Glover put on his left blinker and turned into a cul-de-sac. The teenagers in the back seat had fallen silent a couple of minutes ago, and he wasn't sure what to make of that. He couldn't believe he'd allowed Aurora Martin and Oliver Walker to come along on this little expedition in the first place.

He glanced over at Lincoln, who sat in the front seat. The boy pointed up ahead. "It's that one on the left. The blue house."

"All right." Cactus pulled into the driveway of the appointed house, which stood two stories tall and could easily fit three of his houses inside. His brother, Bishop, and his fiancée, Montana, had started construction on the Edge Cabin. It would be another few months at least until the expansion and remodel finished, but Cactus had made peace with the dust.

Sort of. As much peace as Cactus could make with

anything, he'd made it with the constant film of dirt in his house.

He worked all the time, so at least he didn't have to be home with the hammering, sawing, and loud music Bishop liked to play while working on a project.

Their birthing season at Shiloh Ridge had extended into March this year, and Cactus frowned just thinking about it.

"You're still gonna get the dog, right?" Lincoln asked.

"Yes," Cactus said.

"We're just sittin' here," Link said.

"We're waitin' for Grandmother," Cactus said. He caught movement in his rearview mirror. A black truck eased in front of the blue house, kissing the curb as Cactus had taken the driveway. "There she is. Everyone out."

He opened his door and got out of the sedan he'd bought so he could take Willa Knowlton to dinner. Aurora and Ollie got out on his side, and the teens immediately locked hands again. He swallowed back the pinch in his chest, as well as his annoyance, and stepped down the driveway.

"Donald," he said, reaching to shake his mother's boyfriend's hand. "Mother." He gave her a quick kiss on the cheek, noting they reached for each other too. He turned away, telling himself that he'd see Willa soon. Hopefully.

He exhaled out and faced the white front door. "All right. Let's go check out these dogs." He reached for Lincoln so he'd have someone's hand to hold, even if it was a nine-year-old's. He also told himself he was thrilled his mother had found someone to spend good time with. Donald made her laugh and smile in a way Cactus hadn't seen for a while, and he'd spent so much time observing everyone in the Glover family, he felt like he would know.

"Jace says they're so cute," Link said, trying to dance ahead of Cactus. "Are you gonna get the gray one or the black one?" He looked up at Cactus, pure wonder in his wide eyes.

Cactus loved the boy with his whole heart, and he smiled at him. "I'm not sure yet," he said. "I want to see 'em both again."

"But we're taking them home today, right?" Link asked. "And you said I could sleep over, remember, Cactus? So I can help with the puppy."

"I remember," Cactus said, trying to keep the dryness out of his voice. Lincoln had asked him about fifty times if he could sleep over to help Cactus with his new puppy, as if he couldn't do it himself. Cactus had had a few dogs over the years, and he knew what to do with a pup, but he'd told Lincoln that of course he needed the boy's help.

Cactus was almost forty-four years old, and if he didn't have to take the dog out in the middle of the night, he was all for that.

Besides, Sammy and Bear—Lincoln's parents—were expecting their baby any day now, and Cactus had agreed to be in charge of the boy. He could feed a child and make sure he got his homework done. Lincoln loved to come out to the edge and read to Cactus anyway, and he came almost every day as it was. Driving him to school would be the only thing Cactus wasn't currently doing that he'd have to add to his plate.

That task got him to town, and he'd asked Willa if she might be able to go to breakfast next week.

Since Christmas Eve, when he'd gotten his cousin's message and hurried to the barn because Willa was there, they'd been out a few times. Her schedule had changed, as she'd picked up her sermons again, and she'd taken a long-term substitute teaching job at the high school, leading all three choirs there.

Cactus had heard the woman sing, and she could take that position permanently and take the music department into the stratosphere. She possessed the voice of an angel, and her soprano voice melded well with his deep, bass tone.

He didn't always get to sit next to her in church, but when he did, he sure did like it. She let him hold her hand—at least until she had to sign to Mitchell. Her son.

Since she'd regained custody of him, Willa had grown exponentially busier. Cactus still had cattle to monitor, and then branding sat right around the corner. Then he'd spearhead the breeding at Shiloh Ridge, and after that, he'd have to administer all the antibiotics for the year before they drove their cattle out into the nearby hills and wilderness.

If Mother Nature kept the rain to a minimum, summer was actually his easiest time. He worked a lot once birthing season started, and from about November to May, he seriously wondered why he loved maintaining a healthy herd so much.

He reached the front door first, and he rang the doorbell. It warbled on the other side of the door, and more than one dog began to bark. He looked down at Link. "I'm not takin' one if they yap all the time." That was the last thing he needed.

"We can train 'im up real good," Link said. "Benny doesn't bark, because Bear trained him not to."

"Yes, well, I'm not Bear." Cactus had been living in his older brother's shadow forever, and he normally didn't mind. Bear wasn't perfect by any stretch of the imagination, but there were very few people or beasts who dared to defy him.

Cactus put on a spiny skin and barked out mean things to protect himself and keep others away, but he really had a heart of marshmallow. If he got a puppy and it wanted to bark, well, he'd probably let it.

The front door opened, and a little boy Lincoln's age stood there. He looked up at Cactus with wide, round eyes, and then he looked at Lincoln. "Heya, Link."

"Hi, Jace." Link let go of Cactus's hand and went inside the house. "Can we see the puppies? My uncle says he's not real sure which one he wants."

"Come in," Jace said. He turned and walked away, Link skipping along with him. Cactus stepped inside, everyone he'd brought with him filing in after him.

A woman wearing an apron over her clothes stepped out of the kitchen, drying her hands on a towel. She grinned at the crowd. "Hello, come in. You're here to see the puppies?"

"Cactus Glover," he said, reaching to shake her hand.

"Emily Butler. Come in."

"My mother," Cactus said. "Her boyfriend, Donald Parker." He let them shake hands, and then he introduced Aurora and Ollie.

"How many dogs are you thinking of getting?" Emily asked, tucking her short brown hair behind her ear.

"I'm considering one," Donald said. "I'm going to retire soon, and I need something to fill my time."

That was news to Cactus, but he said nothing.

"I honestly don't know," he said to Emily. "The kids are just along for the fun this afternoon."

"We've got three boys and two girls left," she said. "The multi-colored ones are taken, but we've got solid black and solid gray." She led them past the kitchen and into the back of the house, which was one big living room connected to the dining room.

A low fence kept the puppies in the living room, but they all crowded over by it, as Jace and Link already stood there, reaching in to pat the pups.

"Come on, Cactus," Link said over his shoulder. "Come look at this one."

Cactus joined the boy, and he had a gray puppy licking his hand. "He's so cute, Cactus. I like the gray ones better. You can see their faces."

"You sure can," Cactus said. He twisted back to Emily. "Can I pick them up?"

"Go ahead. Handle them. Get in there with them. We want you to pick the one you like best." She smiled and turned to Aurora as the girl asked her something.

Cactus bent and picked up the gray puppy. The animal was a beast already, easily weighing twenty pounds. The dog licked his face, and Cactus chuckled. Yes, this dog was cute. Cactus could easily see him coming to live out on the Edge, and he scrubbed the dog's back, his skin wrinkling up the way a mastiff's did.

"Look at this one," Link said, grunting. Cactus caught him trying to heft a black puppy up and over the gate, and thankfully, Donald stepped in and took the dog from Link's skinny arms.

"I think I like the black ones," he said to Lincoln, crouching down so Lincoln could get all the puppy's love without having to hold the animal. "You don't like them?"

"I like 'em," Link said, looking from the dog to Donald. "I just think you can see the eyes better on the gray ones."

"That's probably true." Donald cuddled the puppy and then lifted it over the gate again. He stepped inside and started interacting with all the puppies, but the one in Cactus's arms had settled right down. He rested his head against his chest, right above his heartbeat, and Cactus knew he'd be taking this dog home with him.

He stroked the canine, a perfect calmness filling him. He probably should've heeded Dr. Thompson's advice about getting a dog months ago, but he hadn't believed something as simple as a puppy could rid him of the anxiety and anger he'd carried for so long.

One of the pups kept barking, and Cactus would never pick him. Donald passed by him too, and Cactus turned to Mother. "What do you think?"

"I think that puppy has you wrapped around his paw already." She smiled at Cactus and patted his shoulder. "You're just going to get one?"

"I don't know." He slid the dog he held into his mother's arms and joined Donald in the pen. Several of the puppies came up to him, and Emily told him the ones with collars had already been claimed.

He wanted a dog that liked people, not the one that shied away from him and stayed in the corner. He didn't want one that was too aggressive, like the one who'd jumped up on him. Or one too vocal, like the one still crying at Donald's feet.

There were plenty of other choices, and he bent to pick up a black pup without a collar. This one went right for his face too, and he turned his head. He thought he'd like a pair, and he had the money. Two dogs weren't really more work than one, especially if he was taking them at the same time. He'd be going out anyway. He'd be feeding them anyway. He'd be leash training anyway.

"I like this one too," he said to Emily.

"That's Rosa," she said. "The gray one is Louis. You can name them whatever you want, of course. But you've got a black girl and a gray boy."

"I want them both," he said.

"And I want this one," Donald said, that black pup back in his arms.

Emily grinned at them and said, "Let me get the paperwork printed. You guys are ready to take them today?"

"Yes, yes, yes!" Link said, jumping up and down. Mother laughed and drew him away from his friend to hold the calm, gray dog she held. Cactus stepped out of the pen with the black dog, and he handed it to Ollie so he could sign paperwork and pay for his new puppies.

Back in the car, Aurora giggled in the back seat as the puppies kept climbing all over her and Ollie.

"You two okay back there?" he asked.

"Yes, sir," Ollie said, laughing with Aurora. "I'm going to ask my dad about getting a dog. These are *so* cute."

Cactus said nothing, but he hoped Tripp Walker wouldn't be too upset. If someone didn't have a dog, there was usually a reason why.

His phone rang, and Ranger's name came up on the screen. Cactus reached out and tapped the phone icon to connect the call, giving the car a moment to allow the sound to come through the speakers. "Hey, Range."

"Sammy and Bear just left the ranch. Her contractions are four and a half minutes apart, though they're not lasting a full minute. They want you and Link there."

Cactus's pulse went nuts, and he pulled to the side of the road, trying to think. "Okay," he said. "Do you need me to call anyone?"

"I'm putting it on the family text right now," Ranger said. "I just called you, because you have Link."

"Right." He started nodding, the landscape beyond the windshield blurring. He got thrown back almost twelve years, to the birth of his own son. This panic felt so familiar, and he pushed against it so he could think clearly.

"Ollie, can I drop you and Aurora at her place? Or yours?"

"Either," Ollie said.

"My mom will probably go to the hospital," Aurora said. "Should I just go with you?"

"If you want," Cactus said. "Oliver?"

"I can call my dad," he said. "But I'm sure I can come along."

"We have two puppies," Cactus said, his mind whirring.

Who could he call for help? He didn't have time to get back up to Shiloh Ridge and back to the hospital. Maybe he did. He didn't know how long it would take for Sammy to deliver.

Allison had been in labor for hours, and maybe he did have time to get to the Edge Cabin and back. He didn't want to leave the pups alone in the house. He could only imagine the nightmare he'd come home to.

He picked up his phone and tapped a couple of times. The line rang, and he started praying that Willa would answer.

"Cactus," she said, her voice bright and cheery. "I got your text. I just needed to look at the sub schedule first, but then Mitch wanted to make banana pancakes." She laughed lightly, and Cactus grinned at the sound of it.

"I have a favor to ask," he asked.

"Go for it."

"I just picked up two puppies, and Ranger just called to say Sammy went into labor. I've got Lincoln with me, and we need to get over to the hospital...." He let the sentence hang there.

"You want me to babysit your puppies," she said, her voice slightly less enthused now.

"That I do," he said, sighing. "It's fine. We could be hours at the hospital. I can take them to the ranch." He could leave them in the barn with the horses.

"You don't have time for that," she said. "I can take them, Cactus."

"You sure?"

"Of course." She sounded sure then. "We're just at home."

"I'll be there really soon," he said. "I'm only a few minutes away." Cactus eased back onto the road and made the next left turn. Only five minutes later, he turned into Willa's driveway.

She rose from the front porch, and Cactus couldn't help staring for a moment. She wore jeans and a red collared blouse with white polka dots on it. Her son stood too, and Lincoln said, "I wish I could play with Mitch." He looked at Cactus. "Do I have to come to the hospital?"

"Yes," Cactus said firmly. "Your mother is having the baby, Link. You can play with Mitch another day." He got out of the car and opened the back door.

Oliver got out with one puppy in his arms, and he handed it to Cactus. "I'll get the other one."

Cactus took the gray pup toward Willa, whose gorgeous hair called to him. He needed to touch it and slide his fingers through it as he kissed her. The past ten weeks had been a bit maddening to him, but he'd coached himself to be patient. Willa had several new things in her life right now, and she was juggling a lot.

"Look how adorable," Willa said, her smile bright and her eyes locked on Cactus's.

"I'm sure you're talking about the puppy," Cactus said with a grin.

"Maybe." Willa stepped right up to him and pressed her lips to his cheek, the wiggling dog between them.

Cactus's mind blanked, and had it not been for Oliver, he probably would've stayed staring at Willa, her touch burning through his face and down into his neck.

"You could probably put them in the back yard," Oliver said, and that got Cactus to thaw.

"Yeah," he said. "They'll be fine back there."

"I know what to do with a puppy," Willa said, taking the black puppy from Oliver. "You can give that one to Mitch." She turned, and Mitchell stood right behind her.

Cactus swallowed, because he hadn't spent a lot of time with Mitchell. He was a year older than Lincoln, so they weren't in the same grade, though Bear had told him to take him to Willa's so the two boys could play together.

That'll give you a chance to see her, Bear had said.

Cactus had suggested it once, but Willa had said Mitch had not had a good day at school, and he'd never brought it up again. She hadn't either, and he wasn't sure what to do with that information.

He'd been learning and practicing sign language, texting with Willa, and employing every ounce of patience he had. They'd seen each other a couple of times over the weeks, but Cactus wouldn't necessarily call them dates. He wanted a proper date with the woman. Badly.

Now, faced with her son, he decided he needed to practice his sign language. He shifted the puppy to his left arm so he could say hello.

Mitch's face burst into a grin, and he signed the same word back.

Cactus could sign *dog* and he spelled out the name he'd chosen for this one. *T-a-n-k*. He raised his eyebrows, and Mitchell signed something that Cactus didn't get all of. He needed real, live practice, and he told himself he wasn't going to let Willa put so much distance between them for much longer.

He cocked his head and signed for Mitch to slow down. *I'm new and don't know everything.*

Mitch slowed down, and Cactus got the gist of the question. He shrugged and signed, *I don't know. I thought I'd only get one dog, but I got two. It's a girl. How about you think of a name for me, and when I get back, we'll talk about it?*

Mitchell's face lit up, and he reached for the gray puppy. He vocalized something, but since he'd been born deaf, he didn't know the sounds he made, and Cactus couldn't understand what he'd said.

He watched the boy head back toward the front porch, and his eyes lifted to Willa's. She stood at the bottom of the steps, a shocked look on her face.

"What?" he asked.

"You just signed with Mitch," she said.

Cactus pulled in a breath, but he didn't know what to say. So he just shrugged again. He signed, *I've learned a little. Call you later?*

She nodded, and Cactus turned away from her before he closed the distance between them and told her he'd go to any end of the earth to be with her, and that of course that included learning sign language so he could converse with her son.

She'd know without him saying it out loud anyway, and his face heated as he ducked behind his cowboy hat so she wouldn't see him blush.

Chapter Two

Willa Knowlton watched her son take two dogs inside her house. That alone should've set her every nerve on fire, as those canines weren't potty trained at all, and her home had plenty of carpet to get ruined.

Not only that, but she didn't own the home, and her landlords had a way of popping by at the most inopportune times. In that moment, she remembered that pets weren't allowed here, and that was why she'd re-homed Abe, her springer spaniel, with Patrick for the time being.

She'd had to move from the one-bedroom where Abe could live with her to this two-bedroom rental so Mitch would have a bedroom. Giving up a dog to gain a son had been well worth it.

Mitch giggled from inside the house, and Willa absolutely loved the sound of it. She'd missed her son terribly, and there had been countless nights where she'd laid awake, praying with everything she had that she'd see Mitchell again in this lifetime.

The Lord had answered her prayers, and she couldn't believe all that had happened in the past three months.

She turned back to the road as Cactus revved the engine and drove away. Her heart jumped over a couple of beats, reminding her of the sexy cowboy she'd seen signing to her son.

"Signing," she said, her voice quiet to her own ears. She'd shown up at the Glover family ranch on Christmas Eve, a deaf ten-year-old child in tow, and Cactus had taken it all in stride.

"Right." She scoffed as she went up the steps and into the house. She needed to corral these puppies in the kitchen so if any accidents happened, she could easily wipe them up. She also needed to find a way to cage her thoughts about Cactus Glover.

She didn't think for a moment that he'd taken her reappearance in town with a deaf child in stride. The man held everything so tight—*so tight*—and he'd probably been lying awake at night too.

"Let's keep them in here," she said as she signed the words to Mitch. He sat on the floor as the puppies played with him and each other. He caught the end of her sign, and she repeated it so he'd bring the pups into the kitchen.

"You could also take them outside," she said. "The back yard is fenced."

I'll do that, Mitch said, and he pulled open the sliding door that led down four steps to the yard. Early March had brought more sunshine to the Texas Panhandle, but Willa still pulled on her jacket before she joined her son outside.

The sun wouldn't reach back here until afternoon, and Willa sat in the rocking chair on the small deck and pulled up her sermon on her phone. Pastor Summers had spoken to her and Patrick after church last week, and he'd be announcing his retirement in the next month or two.

She and her brother had been preaching on a regular schedule for about nine months now. She'd taken a break over the holidays, but she couldn't wait to share the responsibilities with only Patrick. Right now, she stood behind the mic about once a month, and she'd gone back to leading the choir.

It had been plenty because of her long-term substitute job, but that would end in another five weeks.

Willa read what her thoughts had been this week, as she never really taught from a script. She made notes all week about what came to her mind, what struck her, things that had happened, and somehow a message came from all of that.

She had another twenty-four hours to tie it all together, and she typed in a couple of things about being available to help a friend in need.

Out in the yard, one of the puppies yipped, and Willa glanced up to find Mitch rolling in the grass as the dog leapt over him. "He needs a dog," she said aloud to herself. That was one thing she loved about having a deaf child—she didn't have to censor the way she talked out loud to herself, something she'd done since childhood.

His birthday would come before summer, and she opened

a new note and started a list of things she might be able to give to him. She wasn't sure she could handle a puppy, but the animal shelter had to have adult dogs that needed a good home. She'd heard of some deaf people getting a hearing dog, and Willa wondered if such a thing was out of her reach.

Mitch had never been anything but a cheerful, happy child. Even when she'd woken up at the scene of the accident, with pain and panic pouring through her, she'd found Mitchell charming the EMTs who'd arrived while she'd been passed out.

She toed herself back and forth, using her good right leg, because teaching all day, every day, had really put a strain on her injured body. She front-loaded with painkillers at breakfast, and she took them when Patrick picked her up every afternoon too.

Her phone chimed, and she swiped on the message that popped up at the top of the screen. Martha Webster, her landlord, had said, *We have the doorbell light now. Can we come install it tomorrow?*

Sure, Willa responded. She didn't anticipate Mitch being home alone very often, but he could easily answer the door when someone came over. The child was very astute, and he responded well to vibration too. He could read lips, so he could at least understand what someone wanted from him, even if he couldn't communicate back without writing. His alarm clock vibrated and flashed, and he never tried to stay in bed when he should be up and getting ready for school.

She knew that would all change in a few years when he hit his teens, and Willa couldn't wait. She'd missed enough of his life, and she didn't care if it was hard, easy, or in-between. She wanted to be there.

Her phone rang this time, and Willa grinned at Cactus's name. His picture came up too, and it showed a long-haired cowboy with a growly look on his face she'd never seen before. The Cactus she knew had trim, neat hair and plenty of life in his deep, dark blue eyes.

She'd have to tell him he needed to update his profile picture, but right now, she just swiped up to connect the call. "Hey, stranger," she said, wondering if that counted as flirting or not.

He chuckled. "Would you believe me if I said I may have dropped my wallet at your place?"

She got to her feet and signaled to Mitch. He sat up and she signed quickly that she needed to run out front for a minute. "Stay here," she said as she signed.

"I can go look." Inside the house, she glanced at their breakfast dishes, deciding to ignore them for the day. "You were only here for a minute."

"It's not in my pocket," he said. "It's the only place I can think it would be. I paid for the puppies, and we got in the car. My cousin called about five minutes later, and I came to your house."

Willa reached the front door and went back outside. She held onto the railing as she went down the steps, a soft grunt coming from her mouth.

"How are you feeling?" Cactus asked.

"I'm a little tired," she admitted. "Teaching is hard work, and I'm on my feet all day long."

"I'll bet it is hard," he said. "You need one of those soaker tubs that athletes use."

She laughed, because such a thing was laughable. "Right," she said with a hint of sarcasm. "This house is bigger than my other one, but it's still only one bathroom. Surprisingly, it doesn't have a soaker tub."

Cactus chuckled too. "Listen, if it looks like Sammy isn't going to have this baby any time soon, I'll come get the dogs."

"Okay." Willa walked down the sidewalk, and sure enough, a brown leather wallet sat in the grass. "Your wallet is here."

"Perfect," he said, a measure of relief in his voice. "I'll come grab that from you at some point too."

"All right." Willa found she didn't want him to go. "How's Sammy doing?"

"They're not even here yet," he said with a sigh. "I should've just taken the dogs up to the ranch."

"It's fine," Willa said. "I'm happy to help, Cactus." She didn't mention that she technically couldn't have dogs here. And technically, she didn't. They weren't her dogs, and surely she could have friends come visit who owned dogs. "You should see Mitch. He's in heaven."

"He can come see them anytime," Cactus said. "Or I'll bring them down to him."

Willa made her way back to the steps with his wallet in hand. She sat down, groaning as she did. "You're learning to sign?"

"Yes, ma'am."

"How?"

"Believe it or not, I have the Internet up at the ranch." His voice held plenty of teasing, and Willa sure did like the sound of his voice in her ear. "How did you learn?"

Willa exhaled and remembered the day she'd learned Mitchell was deaf. "I took a class. A lot of classes."

"When did you find out Mitch was deaf?"

"When he was about three months old," she said. "I immediately started learning sign language, and as he grew and got older, I was able to teach him."

"That's amazing," he said. "You know what? I'm going to leave Link here with Aurora and Ollie and come get my wallet and dogs. Sammy's not going to have the baby in the next hour."

"Probably not," Willa said. "Most births take a little longer than that."

"Especially first babies," he said, and Willa heard something in his voice. Something that said he knew what he was talking about.

Before she could ask, he said, "I'm on my way, and I think I'm gonna stop at Meat, Pray, Eat. Do you guys want hamburgers for lunch?"

"Is the sky blue?" she asked with a laugh. "Anything without mushrooms for me," she said. "Mitch likes cheese and bacon on his. Nothing else."

"Nothing? No mayo? Ketchup?"

"Ketchup," she said.

"I'll be back in a few minutes." Cactus exuded confidence, and Willa did like that. She held her phone in her lap, the wallet on the step beside her, and waited for him to return. She didn't live that far from the hospital, but she decided to return to the back yard and Mitch. He didn't usually call if he needed help, though he did have working vocal cords. That was why listening to him laugh brought her such joy.

He still ran in the back yard, letting the puppies gallop after him, a smile on all of their faces. That made Willa smile, and the wattage of that only increased when she heard Cactus call, "Willa?"

"On the back porch," she called back to him, and a few moments later, she heard his footsteps. The sliding screen door screeched as it opened, and she looked over to him. Her pulse started acting erratically, and a man hadn't affected her like this for many, many years.

"Hey," he said gently, and she watched him lace so many things back where he wanted them. She wanted to unravel them one string at a time, and she wondered how hard she'd have to pull. What secrets she'd have to tell. What ghosts he had in his closets.

"Here's your wallet," she said with a smile.

He came closer and took it from her. "Thank you." He looked out to Mitch and the dogs. "Oh, he loves them."

"He really does," Willa said.

"Has he had a dog before?" Cactus asked, barely glancing at her again.

"No," she said.

"You had a dog. Abe. Where is he?" He turned toward her fully, curiosity in his expression.

"This rental doesn't allow pets," she said. "Patrick has Abe."

"Oh."

"You can sit if you want," she said, noticing the paper bags of food. "Or should we go inside?"

"Let's go inside," he said, nodding out to the yard. "How do you get his attention?"

"Stand at the top of the steps there and raise your hand. Wave a little. He'll see you." She'd told him before that Mitch could read lips, and that was why she said everything out loud to him as well as signing it. She'd explained that he needed to look at a deaf person when speaking to them, as they relied so much on facial expressions and eye contact to even know someone was talking to them.

Cactus moved over to the top of the steps leading from the deck to the yard and did what she said. Mitch did notice Cactus and came racing toward him. Cactus chuckled as the boy flew up the steps and into Cactus's arms.

He might be prickly with his siblings and cousins and everyone at church, but he was nothing but a marshmallow when it came to kids. Just the fact that he'd had Lincoln, as well as Aurora and her boyfriend, with him to pick out his puppies spoke of that.

They'd probably asked if they could come, and he didn't have the heart to tell them no. Watching him laugh with her son as he held him made Willa's heart pinch. She realized what she'd been missing all this time, and she pressed her eyes closed and said a quick prayer that she and Cactus could find their way through the maze in front of them to a happy ending.

He looked her way, and Willa knew then that she'd have to go backward in order to move forward—and that she'd have to bring Cactus with her.

She immediately balked at the prospect and wondered why she'd let this man into her life as far as she had. She also knew now that she'd been keeping him on the outskirts of her life since her return to Three Rivers, and that he likely knew that too.

So while she wanted the happily-ever-after and to set sail into the sunset with a good man at her side, she wasn't sure she could weather the storms it would take to get her to that place. Perhaps it would be better for her—and Cactus—if they simply didn't try.

"Come on, boy," he said, looking away from her and right at Mitch as he spoke so he could read his lips. "I brought you a hamburger." He put the boy down and led him inside the house, whistling for the puppies to follow him.

And of course they did.

They had a hard time getting up the stairs though, and they both whined up at her. Willa giggled as she went down to gather their warm bodies into her arms. "Come on, you two," she said under her breath once she had one settled in each arm. "Let's go eat with the sexy cowboy."

Chapter Three

Cactus didn't bother with plates. It wasn't his house, and he didn't want to root through Willa's cabinets. Plus, why dirty a dish when it wasn't necessary?

Instead, he laid out the burgers and fries, pushed a small cup of soda toward Mitch and waited for the boy to look at him. *Eat*, he signed as Willa came in the back door.

"They can't get up steps," she said. "Just so you know."

He turned back to her, finding her arms filled with dogs. A smile burst onto his face, especially when the gray one licked Willa's cheek, causing her to flinch away and giggle at the same time.

"They'll learn," he said, moving toward her to take one of the pups. He set the gray male on the ground. "But not if you carry them around."

"They were whining," she said, their eyes meeting.

Everything slowed to an instant stop. Cactus could only hear the booming pulse of his heart, and he wondered what

Willa saw when she looked at him. Did she see someone she wanted to get to know? Did she feel the arcing, crackling electricity he did? Did her thoughts scatter and her mouth turn dry?

Probably not, as she simply gave him another brilliant smile and stepped past him to the table. By the time he'd regained the ability to move, he found her seated across from Mitch, unwrapping the burger that had come in the white wrapper.

He took the seat next to her, because he wanted to be able to talk to her and Mitch, and the boy needed to be able to see to communicate.

"By the way," she said after she'd taken a few bites of her meal. "I can't go to breakfast with you. I have to teach."

"I thought you had a day where you had a late start," he said, glancing at her. "No?"

"That was just a one-time thing," she said. "For a teacher development thing the school was doing."

He nodded, his disappointment cascading through him like river rapids. His first thought told him to let it all go. Once Willa wasn't teaching anymore, he could bring breakfast to her and they could eat it right here at her kitchen table. She still didn't have a car, and the questions he had for her had been piling up on top of one another.

They'd texted a little bit over the past several weeks, but it was mostly about how things were going on the ranch or if she was preaching on Sunday. He'd run into her and Mitch at the grocery store once, and he'd been in a state of disbelief over it. That Two Cents app had been absolutely right—it was easy to meet women at the grocery store.

He'd only gone because he'd told Ace he was trying to get off the ranch more often by himself, and his cousin had been swamped with a field that had decided to spontaneously produce only weeds. So Cactus had done the weekly shopping for everyone in Bull House, as well as himself and Bishop.

"What about dinner?" he asked, employing his second thought. He didn't want Willa to put him off. He wanted to see her. It was almost a craving he couldn't curb, and he looked at her again.

She kept her focus on her fries, picking up a couple at the same time and biting off the tops.

"You don't need to get someone to watch Mitch," he said. "He's welcome to come."

That got her to look at him. "You want me to bring my ten-year-old son on a date with us?"

Cactus dipped his head slightly, concealing his eyes. "Would it be a date?"

"When a man asks a woman to dinner, it's usually a date," she said.

"I don't know," he said. "I think there's more to a date than just a meal. Otherwise, is this a date?" He gestured to the food on the table. "But we could go to a movie or the gardens or something after dinner." He looked up again, right into those dazzling hazel eyes that haunted him in the quiet seconds before he fell asleep at night. "*That* would be a date."

"Is that what you want?"

"What? To take you on a date?" His voice turned slightly gruff at the end of the question. She didn't confirm, and

Cactus looked across the table to Mitch. The boy reached down to feed a bit of hamburger to one of the dogs, and the sight made Cactus's whole world brighter.

He still hesitated, because he was well aware of his strong yearning to be a father. He knew exactly what he'd lost, and that he couldn't replace Bryce with Mitchell.

He'd tried to date a woman with a son last year, and that hadn't gone well. He'd liked the boy more than Violet, and he knew he couldn't do that again.

He looked at Willa, and plenty of desire shot through him. He liked this woman a whole lot already, though their encounters had been stilted and somewhat strange over the past several months.

"Yes," he said.

"Wow, Mister Glover," she said, plenty of coyness riding in her expression and her voice. "That took you forever to come to."

He ducked his head again, his hamburger suddenly the most fascinating thing on the planet. "I've got a lot to work through sometimes," he admitted to the meat.

Willa's hand landed on his forearm, sending pure fire through his skin and muscles. So much that he actually flinched, causing her to remove her touch.

"Sorry," he murmured. He tilted his head so his hat blocked his view of Mitch, but created a window for him and Willa to look at one another. "Sorry, it's just...you sent a little charge through me."

He wanted to die. Just close his eyes and drift away. Why had he said that? Who said that to a woman? He could never tell Bishop or Ace about this. Never.

At the same time, he couldn't wait to talk to them. They'd help him know what to do next time, and hopefully, he wouldn't blow up so much with only a few words.

Willa smiled, but Cactus told himself she was simply a kind person. She smiled at everyone. She liked everyone. She talked to everyone.

"I was just going to say I'd like to hear what you have to work through," she said. "I'm imagining it's not stuff you'd want to say in front of Mitch."

"Maybe not," he admitted. Ice moved through his veins now. He couldn't imagine telling anyone about Allison and Bryce. Heck, he hadn't even told his family for a long time. Not all of them anyway.

Don't be afraid of the past.

Dr. Thompson's latest advice ran through Cactus's mind as he bit into his burger. He tried hard to listen to his therapist and do the exercises he set for him. He'd done one uncomfortable thing every day for months. He'd put the pants on backward and left dirty dishes in the sink. He'd gone to family meals when he'd rather stay home, and he'd moved up to the front of the chapel with the other Glovers when he went to church.

Heck, the fact that he went to church was an uncomfortable thing that had become easier over the months.

"I'll talk to Patrick about babysitting," she said. "There are some things changing with the church, so I'm not sure when he'll be able to."

Cactus just nodded. He didn't need to know what was changing at church. He hated gossip, and he'd rather stay out of drama. "You have my number."

"That I do."

With that done, Cactus looked up at Mitch. Their eyes met, and Cactus put down his food. "What do you think for her name?" he asked as he did the signs. He signed *black* and *dog*, reminding Mitch that she was a *girl* too.

Willa watched him, her eyes heavy on the side of his face. Cactus didn't dare look away from Mitch though, as the boy had started signing. Again, he moved way too fast for Cactus to understand.

He signed for him to slow down again, and a hint of frustration filled the boy's eyes.

"He said she's really playful," Willa said. "She's bigger than Tank, and she's faster."

Cactus had gotten bigger, Tank, and faster. Mitch started to sign letters, and his mind linked them all together.

"Galaxy," he repeated. He didn't hate the name, but he wasn't sure about it either. Mitch's hands and fingers moved so easily, and Cactus really wanted to keep practicing his own signing so he could be as good and as fast as the boy. "Or Flash."

He looked at Willa. "Galaxy or Flash?"

"Flash is terrible," Willa whispered. "Plus, it's not a female name."

Cactus looked back to Mitch, whose dark eyes held wonder and hope. The whole world lay before him, and Cactus wished he was ten years old again, without heartache and unhappiness in his life. At the same time, he'd learned so much from what he'd been through.

"Galaxy," he said and signed. "That's brilliant." He made the sign close to his eye and lifted his hand up, and Mitch beamed at him with all the power of the sun. "You can come see them anytime," he told Mitch, and he looked at his mother with the biggest puppy dog eyes Cactus had ever seen.

Willa just smiled and shook her head, and Cactus realized he may have just made her life harder.

"Or I'll bring them down here," he told Mitch.

The boy nodded, peeled off another bite of burger, and fed it to Galaxy. Tank whined, and Mitch fed him too.

"Cactus," Willa said, and he turned his attention to her. "I don't have a car."

Translation: *I can't bring my son up to your ranch to play with the dogs.*

"Okay," he said. "I'll come get him or bring the dogs down here."

She studied him, the playfulness and smiling attitude she always had dropping from her face. "Don't you want to know why I don't have a car? I mean, how do I get Mitchell to school? How do I go to work? How do I get groceries?"

"Uh." Cactus swallowed, suddenly nervous. "I guess? How do you do all of that?"

"Patrick has to take me," she said, looking at her French fries again. "Pathetic, right?"

"No," he said quickly, thinking of the past ten years of his life. "No, it's not pathetic. You leave the house. That's more than I did for a long, long time."

She nodded, but she wouldn't look at him.

"Listen," he said, and he knew he was about to say something else that Bishop and Ace would groan about. "I'm forty-three years old. I have a lot in my past, and I can't tell you about all of it at once." He swallowed, remembering how she couldn't get in and out of a truck and the way she'd collapsed in the parking lot at the ice skating rink after a phone call from Maurice Maxwell, a lawyer out of Temple, Cactus had learned.

"I'm thinking you have several things in your past too, including something about a car accident, a ten-year-old son who I'm assuming wasn't immaculately conceived, and the reason you don't have a vehicle."

She looked at him with clear shock in those beautiful, beautiful eyes. He smiled at her, everything inside him softening. "I'm willing to learn about you one bit at a time. Whatever you're comfortable sharing. It's, uh—" He ground his voice through his throat, his brain screaming at him to *stop talking!* in the voices of his brother and cousin.

He couldn't stop himself though. Cactus had never been great at self-control. "It's going to be hard for me to share some things with you. It'll take me some time, I'm sure. But Willa, at the risk of blowing everything wide open, you're the only woman lately I've even wanted to try to share these things with."

He swallowed, his voice suddenly mute though he had more to say. He picked up his burger and finished it, waiting for her to say something. Only the crinkling of wrappers and the slurping of Mitch sucking on his soda filled the air, and Cactus suddenly wished he hadn't said so much.

"Okay, so dinner maybe one night next week?" she finally asked.

A smile burst onto Cactus's face. "Yeah, sure. You name the night."

"Tuesday?"

"Tuesday works for me," he said, glad she'd chosen a night early next week.

"You know what you're comfortable with," she said. "I'm happy to tag along with whatever you want to do."

Cactus nodded, slight foolishness moving through him. He dusted his hands and looked at her. He didn't say anything, though his mind moved through all the possibilities for what he and Willa could do in only three days. He needed to check the weather and figure out what to wear.

He could talk to Bishop and Ace at the hospital, and he suddenly remembered he needed to get the dogs up to the ranch and get back to town to be with his family. He did not want to miss seeing Bear's baby the moment he could.

He still took the time to reach over and put his hand on Willa's knee. She smiled at him and laced her fingers through his.

"I need to go," he said.

"Go ahead and go," she said, but she didn't remove her hand from his. Maybe he could just stay for a little while longer.

Across the table, Mitch started to sign, and Willa looked at him. "Yes," she answered. "He has to go. His brother's wife is having a baby. Help him get the dogs loaded up, Mitch."

Chapter Four

Bear Glover held his new son while a nurse took Sammy through the check-out procedures. He wanted to stay at the hospital, because he had no idea what to do with a baby at home. Here, someone would keep him alive should something happen. What, Bear had no idea.

But the nurses took the baby at night if Sammy asked them to, and no one would be doing that up at the homestead. Bear knew that.

No one would teach him how to diaper the boy, or how to get him to calm down when he started fussing and wouldn't stop.

Sammy kept nodding, though the information given to her was astronomical. Finally, the nurse finished and said, "If you have a car seat, all I have to do is process the final paperwork and you'll be good to go." She beamed like this was a great thing.

Bear frowned, though Sammy really wanted to leave.

They'd been in the hospital for two full days and most of Saturday. Bear had left exactly once to go up to the ranch and shower. He'd brought Sammy a doughnut the nurse wouldn't let her eat, and while he wasn't looking forward to folding himself onto the tiny couch for another night of sleep, he seriously doubted he and Sammy could keep this baby alive at home.

Other people do it, he told himself. Sammy sure seemed to know what to do with the infant, and Bear was determined to support her any way he could.

"We have a car seat," Sammy said. "Bear put it in the truck a week ago." She flashed him a smile, and Bear managed to return it. He had put the car seat in the truck a week ago. He just wanted to be prepared.

The nurse left, and Bear looked at Sammy. "You really think we can do this?"

"We haven't killed Lincoln yet," she said, smiling. She got out of the hospital bed and moved over to the couch. She began putting on her shoes, and Bear looked back at his son.

They'd named him Stetson Stone Glover, and Bear fully intended to pay close attention to the boy so he could choose a nickname that fit the child and the family naming conventions. Perhaps Stone would be sufficient, though only Ward used his middle name and didn't actually have something different.

Before he knew it, the nurse had the paperwork, and Sammy took baby Stetson with, "Can you get our stuff, Bear?"

"Yep." He collected his backpack and her tote, and he followed her down the hall and out of the maternity wing.

He increased his pace, saying, "Let me go get the truck. You wait in the circle drive, okay?"

"Okay," she said, and once she stepped outside, she moved over to a bench and sat down. She'd been brilliant in labor, and while it seemed to take forever, the doctor had been pleased with how quickly Stetson had come. The boy had wailed the moment the doctor had him all the way out, and Bear could still hear his son's tiny, angry voice.

He'd gone with the baby to give him a bath, and then he'd taken the boy out to meet Mother. She'd been at the hospital the most besides him, and Bear fully expected her to be at the homestead tonight too.

"Probably with a five-course meal," he said to himself as his truck came into view. He quickly tossed everything in the back and headed toward the doors.

Sammy looked ashen, and Bear jumped from the truck before she could get up. "Hey, are you okay?" he asked, jogging toward her.

"I'm just tired." She got to her feet and let him take their son. "How many people do you think will be at the homestead?"

"It doesn't matter," he said, though he suspected everyone would be there. "I'll handle them. If you want to take a nap, you can take a nap."

She looked up at him, such hope and adoration in her eyes. "Could I?"

"Of course." He cradled the baby in one arm and steadied her with his free hand. Once she sat in the passenger seat, he opened the back door and carefully placed Stetson in the car seat. "There you go, bud," he said. "Now, it's kind of a long drive, and Momma's tired already. So you just take a little snooze. Then you'll be ready to meet Grandmother and Uncle Bishop, and Aunt Zona...." He smiled at the tiny infant, who'd actually weighed just over nine pounds at birth.

Such love overcame him, and Bear fell mute. He finished buckling the baby into the seat, tucked his blankets around him, and hurried around to the driver's door.

Once behind the wheel, he asked, "Doughnuts?"

Sammy gave him a smile made of joy and sleepiness. "Doughnuts would be amazing."

ALMOST AN HOUR LATER—THE DRIVE-THROUGH LINE AT Hole In One, the newest doughnut-only bakery in town had been forever long—Bear pulled up to the homestead. Baby Stetson had done just what he'd suggested and slept the whole time.

"Stay there," he said to Sammy before sliding from the truck and going to help her down. She stepped a little gingerly, and Bear wasn't quite sure why. She'd been so eager to leave the hospital, and he hoped she really was ready.

He collected their baby while she waited at the hood, and then he passed Stetson to her. Slowly, step by step, they went up to the porch, where Bear heard someone say, "They're here," right before Cactus opened the front door.

Everyone had been at the hospital too, but Bear wouldn't have them stay away from the homestead either.

"How'd everything go?" Cactus asked.

"Swell," Bear said. "I have five dozen doughnuts in the back seat."

"On it." Cactus paused to peer down at Stetson, pure love on his face too. He had a date with Willa that night, but Bear knew there was no way he'd be able to stay up late enough to hear about it once Cactus returned to the ranch. As it was, he felt like he could go to bed right now and not get up until tomorrow morning.

He guided Sammy through the front door while Cactus's boots made plenty of noise on the steps leading to the graveled parking area in front of the homestead. Oakley, Mother, and Ranger all stood just inside the door, and Sammy started weeping at the long line of people behind them.

Everyone had shown up. Absolutely everyone.

Bear's voice stuck way down deep in his throat, and the only thing he could do was step into Mother's arms and hug her. When he turned, he found Sammy passing Stetson to Oakley, who gazed at the infant with glassy eyes.

Ranger stood right behind her, and Bear could not fathom his agony despite the smile on his face. He took Bear into a hug, the same way he had at the hospital, and they clapped one another on the back.

"Doughnuts," Cactus announced, and he took the boxes through the foyer and under the arched doorway into the kitchen. Bear started after him, breaking up the party. Everyone surged into the kitchen, where Bear found three pots of soup, three bowls of different salads, and a basket the size of a bucket filled with rolls.

His stomach roared, despite the raspberry fritter he'd eaten on the way home. Aunt Dawna stood behind the counter, her joy beaming from her. "Welcome home, Bear," she said. "Sammy, come get something to eat. You look pale."

Bear put his hand on her lower back and brought her in front of him. "She does need to eat, and then she's going to lay down and take a nap."

The noise hadn't swelled the way it normally did, and everything felt different in the homestead now that there was a baby here. Oakley took Stetson into the living room and sat right in the middle of one of the couches. Ida and Etta crowded in around her while everyone else loitered around for food.

"Will you say grace?" Bear asked Aunt Dawna, as she had such a powerful voice and spirit.

"Of course." She looked at Ward, who started getting everyone gathered around if they weren't already. When they were ready, Aunt Dawna said, "Dear Lord, we thank Thee for Thy bounteous blessings. There is nothing better than a baby straight from heaven, and we're all so grateful Sammy was able to bring Stetson Stone Glover to our family."

She paused, and Bear's heart filled with love again and then again. When Aunt Dawna continued, her voice wavered with emotion. "Bless any in this company that need a special favor at this time, according to Thy will. We especially ask Thee to bless Holly Ann with her party tonight, and bless Cactus on his date with the preacher. Bless Oakley and Ranger with peace and comfort, and bless Bear, Sammy, and Lincoln that they will know what to do with Stetson and how to do it." Another pause, and then she said, "Amen."

The crowd chorused it back to her, and Bear's eyes went to Cactus first. He smiled softly at Aunt Dawna, and Bear turned back to his aunt when Ward said, "Thanks for praying my date would go well, Mother," in a dry, sarcastic voice.

"You have a date?" Bear asked. Ward seemed to go out with a new woman for a date or two every six months or so, and he hoped he could find someone who made him want to see her every night, night after night, forever.

In fact, Bear prayed for it right then. He just took a moment amidst all the hustle and bustle, while Judge and Mister jostled for first position in line, and while his brand-new baby gave a little cry, to pray for Ward and the clarity of mind he needed when it came to women.

Bear opened his eyes, and everything in the homestead seemed brighter. He found Bishop standing down by Ace, the two of them chatting about something. Bishop would be married in a little over a month, and Bear already missed him though he hadn't moved out of the homestead yet.

He and Montana were racing the clock to get their house finished before the wedding, and Bear said a mental prayer for the two of them too.

Ace had asked Holly Ann Broadbent to be his wife, and she'd said yes. They were planning a wedding for the upcoming autumn, six months from now, and he'd asked Bear to get on the agenda for an upcoming Friday morning meeting to discuss his housing situation too.

Aunt Dawna refused to let Preacher or Mister go first, and she guided Sammy to the front of the line, detailing the creamy corn chowder, baked potato soup, and Texas lawman chili available for lunch.

Bear loved his aunt's lawman chili, and he knew what he'd be eating. He watched his wife take the potato soup, as he predicted she would, and she met his eye as she piled salad onto the other half of her two-bowl platter.

He couldn't help the way his heartbeat jumped and his smile lifted his whole countenance. He'd loved Samantha Benton for such a long time, and when he'd finally decided to get serious about dating, he'd gone straight to her.

He hadn't had to hunt around like Ward was, or deal with women who hadn't wanted him the way Bishop had. Ace too, as Holly Ann had tried to break up with him twice before they'd made a relationship stick and work.

Cactus had been married before and suffered great loss, and even he was out there, trying to find someone. Bear hadn't had to try. He'd only had to figure out how to tame his inner wild animal and somehow convince Sammy he was good enough for her.

The doorbell rang, and Mother said, "That should be your parents, Sammy. Your father had a doctor's appointment that made them a little late." She strode toward the foyer and the front door as fast as her aged legs would take her, and Bear smiled after her too.

He went to join her as well, because Sammy's parents meant the world to her, and that meant Bear loved them too.

"Bear," Lincoln said, racing through the door and down the foyer. "Guess what? Guess *what?*"

"What, buddy?" Bear scooped the boy into his arms. Cactus had taken him to school the past few days, and Rachel and Vaughan had obviously checked him out to bring him back.

Link put his hands on either side of Bear's face. "I got invited to a birthday party."

"That's great," Bear said. "Who is it?"

"This girl named Aberdeen," Link said, stumbling over the name. "She's gonna be nine like me, and the party is on Friday. I can go, right? Grandpa said he'd take me shopping because of the baby, and I have that five-dollar bill Uncle Ranger gave me for sweeping out the garage at Bull House, and—"

Bear started to laugh, cutting off Lincoln. The boy could talk and talk, that was for sure. Bear normally didn't mind, because Link's colorful stories could make an afternoon of chores go by in the blink of an eye. He got excited about everything, even a birthday party for a girl he saw every single day at school.

"Come see your momma," Bear said. "She missed you." He touched his nose to Link's and added, "I did too."

Lincoln hugged Bear around the neck, and he set the boy down on the ground to say hello to Rachel and Vaughan. "Thanks for getting him," he said. "It's good to see you." He leaned over and kissed Rachel's cheek and shook Vaughan's hand. "There's plenty to eat, and Sammy will want to see you."

He re-entered the kitchen just in time to see Cactus slip out the door to the deck, his phone pressed to his ear. He caught Bishop's eye, who shrugged, and Bear frowned at the door for several minutes while the line thinned.

Cactus never returned.

Chapter Five

Willa wouldn't be able to put Cactus off if he called again, and she pressed her eyes closed and prayed he wouldn't call again. She'd had a prep period that morning due to an assembly, and she'd spent the first half of it pacing.

Her leg ached, and she still had two periods to go. The teacher had a stool she could sit on, but Willa struggled to get on it sometimes, and she didn't want to embarrass herself in front of eighty students while wearing a skirt.

She'd sent a text to Cactus saying she couldn't go to dinner with him that night, and she'd prayed he'd be too busy to see the text right away.

He hadn't been, because he'd called almost immediately.

A sigh came out of her mouth, and Willa sat at the desk in the corner of the room. She liked where the teacher had put it, because it hid behind a grand piano, and if someone came into the classroom looking for her, they wouldn't be able to see her right away.

Her phone bleeped out an unusual chime, and she checked it to see her voicemail notification sitting at the top of the screen.

"He's not going to go away," she said to herself. "Although...." She had put him off after Christmas, and he'd let her. She hadn't entirely meant to then, though she knew exactly what she was doing now.

She'd been moving, adjusting to life with her son, preaching more, and starting this long-term sub job so she had enough money to pay her bills.

As she gazed at the phone, debating whether she should listen to the message or not, a text from Cactus came in. *I've been tasked with getting dinner for my brother, so I'll drop something off at your place around six.*

She didn't want to answer it, because then he'd know for certain she'd screened his call. She swiped down to tap on the voicemail notification, and she put the phone on speaker as it rang. She had one message, as literally two people had this number: Cactus and Patrick. Oh, and Pastor Summers.

"Willa," Cactus said on the machine, and her resolve wavered. Fine, it crumbled and fell. Which was why she couldn't speak to him. The moment he said her name in that sexy voice...she forgot why she couldn't be with him.

"I have a feeling you're putting me off for some reason. It's just dinner, not a marriage proposal." He paused, and he might have sighed but Willa couldn't tell for sure. "Will you please call me back?"

"How do I say no to that?" Willa asked, moaning as she rolled her neck from left to right. She reached up and rubbed the back of her neck next, her back throbbing from all the pacing.

"Lord." She looked up and closed her eyes. "How do I deal with Cactus Glover? How can I possibly tell him about David? About the car accident? About any of it? Why do I have to relive these horrible events of my life? Why must I face the woman I left behind?"

She wasn't the same person she'd been two years ago, and she did not want to open that door. Cactus would not only make her open it, he'd make her step back into that room, and he would go with her.

Two thoughts came to her mind, and she repeated them out loud. "Be patient." She tapped on her phone to type it into her notes. She wasn't preaching that week, but she could use any experiences she had in future talks. "Trust."

Trust, she thought as she typed in the five letters. "Trust who? Trust him? Trust You?"

The bell rang, signaling the end of lunch, and Willa flipped her phone over and got to her feet. Her knee nearly buckled, and she gritted her teeth to keep the cry of pain from leaving her mouth. She steadied herself against the desk as the first students started entering the room.

"Steph," she said when she caught sight of the dark-haired girl with a voice plated in gold. "I need your help today."

HOURS LATER, WILLA SAT ON THE FRONT STEPS, WHERE she'd been for the past thirty minutes since her brother had dropped her off. Mitch should be skipping down the street any minute now, and while she normally went inside and changed her clothes before he did, today, she'd been too tired.

She heard the air brakes of the school bus, and Mitch only had to walk about a half a block to get home. Willa's house sat back from the street, so she couldn't see him until he was almost to the house, and she kept her eyes trained down the road.

He finally appeared, and she lifted her hand when he looked toward her. He grinned and cut across the lawn at a dead sprint. She couldn't stay unhappy or angry when in Mitch's presence, though today rivaled his power more than any other.

"Hey, baby," she said with her voice and her hands. "How was school?"

Great, Mitch said. *I got all the problems right on my math test, and Aaron said I could play soccer with him at recess. It was great!* He jumped into the air after the last sign, and Willa laughed with him.

Her mother heart took flight, because he'd had a bit of a rough start to fourth grade here in Three Rivers back in January. The other kids didn't know how to deal with his disability, and they didn't know how to communicate with him. They didn't realize they didn't have to do anything different. It was only Mitch who needed to figure out how to talk to them.

He'd been doing it for a decade, and he was very, very good at helping others understand him. Willa had met with his teacher four or five times before Mrs. Aarons had smiled her most gorgeous smile and said, "Willa, your son is an amazing child, and we are having no problems communicating. In fact, he's taught me so much already, and I'm learning some sign language in the hours after school. We're *fine*. He's *fine*."

Things had been fine since then. Mitch reported school being *great!* every day she asked, and he'd settled into his schoolwork and his schedule. And now, apparently, soccer games too.

"I'm glad," Willa said. "Now help your old momma up."

Mitch extended his hand toward her, his grin infectious, and Willa managed to get to her feet. *Can we have cookies?* he asked before going up the steps in leaps and bounds, and Willa wouldn't say no to that.

She needed some cookies too, along with another dose of painkillers and one of those soaker tubs Cactus had talked about.

By the time she got inside, Mitch had the package of cookies on the counter and was currently buried inside the fridge trying to lug out the nearly full gallon of milk.

Willa stepped over to help him, because she knew from experience that plastic milk jugs could shatter when dropped, and the last thing she needed was to clean up almost a gallon of liquid.

Mitch climbed up on the barstool while she got down cups and filled them. She didn't drink milk with anything but cookies, and even then, it was really only good for dunking. She worked her way through four fudge-striped cookies before she told herself to stop.

She tapped Mitch on the shoulder and waited for him to look at her before she signed, "Last one."

His countenance dropped, but he nodded. Willa got up and resealed the package, put it in the cupboard, and slid the milk back into the fridge. When Mitch finished his cookie, she said, "Homework. We're going to Uncle Patrick's tonight."

Mitch got down to get his backpack while cowardice moved through Willa. If she could get over to Patrick's in the next hour, surely she'd miss Cactus even if he showed up an hour early with dinner.

She never had texted him back, and she'd stayed strong and hadn't called him either.

Be patient, she thought. She didn't know with what or with who though. Herself? Cactus? Something else?

Trust.

Again, she didn't know in who or in what, and her thoughts only frustrated her more than anything.

Patrick had gone to pick up his daughters from school, and he said he needed to stop and pick up the groceries he'd ordered. Then he'd swing by her house to get her and Mitch, and they'd all go back to his place.

He had a nicer house than she did, with way more room. He'd offered for Willa to move in with him once they knew Willa was going to get Mitch back, but Willa had declined. It probably would be easier for him in a lot of ways, and Willa's guilt punched her right behind the lungs.

Again.

She was so tired of feeling guilty. Didn't she stand up in front of a congregation of people and tell them to trust in the Lord? Didn't she tell them to go to Him with their problems? Hadn't she said a mere two days ago that the Lord forgave all sins for those who truly repented?

Hypocrisy swirled with the guilt, and Willa told Mitch she'd be right back. She went down the hall to change her clothes, the doorbell ringing as she pulled on her checkered pants.

With the new deaf doorbell, Mitch would see a flash of light, and when he looked around, he'd see it blinking above the door, indicating someone had rang the doorbell. They'd talked about how he should check with her before opening the door, and he appeared in the doorway, a question on his face.

"Go ahead," Willa said. "It's Uncle Patrick."

Mitch's face lit up and off he ran to open the door. Willa bent to get her shoes and started down the hall. The voice that met her ears was far too deep to be Patrick, and she came to a sudden and complete halt.

Cactus had come really, really early.

Her first thought was to back up slowly and barricade herself in the bedroom. But she wasn't six years old, and she couldn't hide from her problems.

Cactus wasn't a problem anyway. *She* was the problem. Her, and her choices, and the first thirty-five years of *her* life.

The door closed, but the energy in her house testified that Cactus had come inside. Mitch appeared at the mouth of the hallway too, and his signs indicated his excitement to see Cactus again. Of course he was. Cactus possessed the same powerful charms Mitch did.

No wonder Willa had been so attracted to the cowboy.

"I know," Willa said after dropping her shoes. "He said he was bringing dinner."

He has groceries, Mitch said. *Do we have to go to Uncle Patrick's? Cactus says he can make real Shepherd's pie, and I haven't had it for so long.*

"Willa?" Cactus called, his footsteps slow.

"Yeah," she said. "You can come in, Cactus."

He appeared next to Mitch, and he did have two brown bags of groceries in his arms. "I brought stuff to make dinner."

"I heard," she said, signing what Cactus had said and then her response so Mitch could be involved in the conversation.

The little boy bounced on the balls of his feet, his face so hopeful.

"You better call Uncle Pat," she said to Mitch, and he made a triumphant noise that sounded a little bit like an elephant trumpeting.

Mitch ran into the kitchen, where they kept his cell phone. Cactus tracked his movement, and then he looked back to Willa, surprise on his face. "How is he going to call your brother?"

Willa stooped to get her shoes, though she wasn't going anywhere now. "His phone is equipped with TTY," she said.

"What's that?"

"Teletype," Willa said. "The mode is always enabled, and Pat's phone will ring, but he'll get an electronic voice in his ear, reading Mitch's message."

"Fascinating," Cactus said, glancing in the direction of the kitchen again. He then actually stepped toward her. "Listen, I can really just drop this stuff off and go. Now that

I'm here, I can tell you don't want me here." He ducked his head, which was the most adorable thing in the whole world.

Did he have the Lord whispering in his ear so he'd know exactly what would pull on Willa's heartstrings?

She sure would like that right about now, and she concentrated, trying to see a way to keep her dignity and spare his feelings.

Darkness gathered on his face, and he turned away. He went into the kitchen, and Willa heard the crinkling of the bags as he set them on the counter.

"Help," she prayed, hating that the Lord had abandoned her in an hour of great need.

In that single moment, she knew why the Lord had gone silent.

He'd already answered her.

She darted down the hall, nearly colliding with Cactus as he moved toward the front door. "Oof," she said, her shoulder bumping into his and knocking her sideways because of his very solid form.

Because her legs were so tired, she lost her balance. Panic reared, because a fall could be disastrous for her. She thought of who would teach choir if the sub couldn't come in. She wondered who would take care of Mitch if she had to go to the hospital. Her thoughts raced like wildfire in a stiff wind, and her eyes widened.

Then Cactus's hands grabbed onto both of her arms, and he pulled her toward him, twisting as he went down so he could cradle her as she landed on his lap. Quite delicately too, if she did say so herself.

Her heart still raced, but at least she knew what to say and do now.

She turned toward Cactus, the scent of his cologne making her lightheaded and a bit woozy. Or maybe that was his close proximity. Or his strong hands on her hips. Or any number of amazing things about the man.

"Don't go," she said.

"Are you okay?"

"I will be if you stay," she said. She needed to take this leap...and trust that she'd be able to land safely on the other side. She reached up and ran her fingertips down one side of his face. "Tell me you'll stay."

Chapter Six

❧

Cactus couldn't get his thoughts to line up. Willa smelled like flowers and something fruity, and the touch of her fingers against his face had his heartbeat misfiring. He'd managed to catch her as she went down, and he'd pulled her onto his lap in the swiftest way he could.

"You just want me to make dinner," he said, his wit finally firing correctly.

She grinned and dropped her hand. "I am scared out of my mind," she said. "But yes, dinner would be great, and besides, I can't stand disappointing Mitch."

Fear crossed her face when she let the smile drop, and Cactus wished he could soothe it. "I don't think I can get up," Willa whispered. "I'm so tired, Cactus. I walked way too much today."

"No problem," he said, sliding her gently to the floor so he could stand. "I'll put you on the couch and start dinner." He bent and picked her up, which only made her face flush red. She closed her eyes as if that would prevent him from seeing her, and he set her on the couch.

He crouched in front of her and reached out to tuck her hair behind her ear. "Here's the deal for tonight, okay?"

She swallowed and nodded.

"You don't have to tell me anything tonight. Not one thing. We'll just eat and enjoy each other's company. The end. Nothing to be afraid of." He studied her, glad when her normal color returned to her face and she softened. "Okay?"

"Okay, Cactus," she said. "Is that your real name?"

He grinned at her. "What mother would name their baby Cactus?" He straightened, his knees protesting the crouch. He hoped the twinge of pain didn't show on his face, but he really was too old to stay in a position like that for longer than two seconds.

He turned back to Mitch, who'd finished his phone call and approached, his fingers flying. Cactus couldn't catch much, but he got Galaxy and Tank. "I didn't bring them," he said, maintaining eye contact. "Sorry, boy."

He truly was sorry too. He signed and spoke, "How about you help me make dinner for your momma? She's not feeling well tonight."

He wasn't sure he'd gotten all the signs right, but Mitch peered around him to his mother on the couch, and they had a conversation with just hands. Willa always spoke her half, but this time, she didn't.

Mitch turned back to Cactus, and said, *Okay, I'll help.*

"No knives for Mitch," Willa said. "I noticed he didn't tell you that."

Cactus glanced over to the beautiful woman on the couch

and then started opening cabinets and drawers to find a pot and a pan, wooden and measuring spoons, and a measuring cup.

He found a potato peeler and indicated to Mitch to get the ingredients out of the paper bags. The boy started to do that, and Cactus gave him the peeler and signed that he should get the potatoes de-skinned.

Cactus filled a pot with hot water and set it on the burner, then got busy chopping onions, carrots, and garlic. "Could you take tomorrow off to rest?" he asked Willa, and Mitch looked up at him, a curious look on his face.

Cactus wasn't sure how to sign what he'd just asked, and he quickly pulled out his phone and typed a note into it. *I asked your mom if she could take work off tomorrow.*

Mitch read it and looked over to her. He tapped on the phone and turned it to Cactus. *She won't. She feels too guilty.*

Surprise darted through Cactus, first at Mitch's observation and second that he knew what his mother felt guilty about.

"I don't even know how," Willa said.

"Surely subs get sick or whatever," Cactus said, pulling the peeled potatoes up onto the cutting board. He signed *potatoes* and *pot*, and Mitch started putting the cubed potatoes into the boiling water.

That done, Cactus reached for the chopped beef he'd gotten from the butcher at Wilde & Organic. He wasn't a whiz in the kitchen, but Mother had taught him a few choice recipes that he'd made dozens of times over the years.

Creamy chicken noodle soup. Sausage and orzo casserole. Shepherd's pie. Spaghetti and meatballs. French toast.

Anything with eggs, and Cactus could admit he ate scrambled eggs with diced ham and cheese at least three times a week. Sometimes for dinner even.

"I don't know," Willa said.

As he set the oven to four hundred degrees, Cactus considered looking up the name of the principal at the high school—it would be a single search on the Internet, which he could do on his phone—and calling her. He could get Willa out of teaching tomorrow in under five minutes.

He clenched his teeth when he distinctly remembered Bear telling him that Sammy didn't like it when he tried to step in and fix her problems for her. Cactus couldn't do that to Willa, though he wanted her to be able to sleep as late as she wanted tomorrow. He'd even take Mitch up to the ranch with him and drive him back for school in the morning.

Could he tell her that? Offer to call the principal? Take Mitch home with him?

"Willa," he said after turning on the flame under the pan he'd put on the stove. He could take a minute while the beef browned, and he quickly put it in the pan and headed into the living room. "I want to help you. What if I called the principal and just said you couldn't come tomorrow?" He sat down on the loveseat so she wouldn't have to look up at him. "I really don't think you're well enough to go."

"You might be right," she said.

"I can take Mitch up to my place tonight. I'll bring him down to school in the morning. That way, you can go to bed right after dinner and sleep as long as you want in the morning."

Her eyes widened, and Cactus felt sure he'd just made a

huge mistake. He'd told Ace, Ward, and Bishop what he'd said to Willa on Saturday, and after a discussion where Cactus had lost an hour of his life he couldn't get back, Ace had finally said, "Hey, it's working for you, Cactus. Maybe you should just do what you do and not worry about what we would do."

"You don't need to do that," she said. "Mitch is easy to have around."

"You'll still have to get up with him in the morning." He glanced over to where Mitch stood in the kitchen. The scent of steak filled the air, and Cactus needed to get back to the stove. "Think about it for a second, at least."

He returned to the pan and tonged the meat around. "Mitch." He signed the boy's name, which caught his attention. "Onions. Garlic. Carrots." He signed them all and indicated the pan. The boy put them in the pan, and Cactus stirred it all together to start cooking.

He added a couple of tablespoons of butter a few minutes later, and he asked Mitch to find him some flour. He salted and peppered everything, sprinkled flour over the meat and veggies, and then poured in the organic boxed beef broth to make the gravy.

Very last, he added the frozen peas and took the pan off the burner. The heat from the gravy mixture would thaw the peas and give him a moment to mash the potatoes.

With that done, he spread them over the meat and gravy mixture in the pan, then slid the whole thing in the oven to brown the tops of the mashed potatoes.

"Plates," he signed to Mitch, and he got busy putting all the dirty dishes and utensils in the sink. He wiped the counter and pulled out forks. "Dinner, Willa," he said, signing that for Mitch too.

She got up herself and limped into the kitchen. She sat at the table, and Cactus pulled the cast iron skillet out of the oven and placed two hot pads on the table before setting it in the center of where they'd eat.

"Bread," he signed to Mitch, and the boy brought the loaf over to the table.

They all sat down, and Cactus looked at Willa. She looked steadily back at him. "I texted Everett," she said. "I'm not going in tomorrow."

Relief flowed through Cactus. "That's great," he said, hoping he hadn't made too big of a deal out of it. "Do you two say grace?"

"Yes," Willa said. "Mitch, would you?"

The boy squinched his eyes closed and started signing, his hands moving quickly. Cactus didn't mind that he didn't catch everything the boy prayed for. He caught a few words like "food" and "mom." He saw him sign his name, and Cactus's heart grew another size.

"Amen," Willa said, but Cactus had had no idea Mitch had finished his prayer. The child knelt up on his chair, peering over at the Shepherd's pie with a glow in his eyes.

"You better help him," Willa said. "Also, did you call my brother and ask him what Mitch's favorite food is?"

Cactus took the boy's plate and scooped a healthy serving of the pie onto it. He set it in front of Mitch, who beamed like he'd just learned he wouldn't have to go to school for a year. "I didn't call Patrick," Cactus said. "I only know how to make five or six things, and this was my daddy's favorite meal. Mother taught me to make it when I was a teenager."

He served her too, and then he took plenty of Shepherd's pie for himself. "Oh, I bought a salad too." He jumped to his feet, but Willa said, "Don't bother, Cactus. You'll be the only one who eats it."

"You sure?"

"Yep."

He returned to the table and sat back down. His conversation topics had dried up, and his nerves returned. The food was perfectly seasoned, and Willa even told him how good it was. But he couldn't relax.

He'd basically forced this date to happen, and he needed to clear his conscience. At the same time, he needed Willa to understand he wasn't going anywhere. He also needed to respect her wishes, and if she didn't want to see him, he couldn't make her.

Not again, he told himself. He'd said she didn't have to tell him anything, and he'd stick to that. But he had a few things to say.

He cleared his throat, but he couldn't get the words out. So he finished eating, and he loaded the dishwasher while she sent Mitch down the hall to bathe.

When he finally faced Willa, the dam holding back his speech broke. "Thanks for letting me do this," he said. "I promise it won't happen again. Next time you tell me no, that'll just be it. Okay?" He took a quick breath. "I don't want to go anywhere. I want to see if we can make a relationship work. I really like your son, and I think you're the most beautiful woman I've had the pleasure of meeting in the past few years. But I won't force myself on you again. I feel foolish enough as it is. I'll respect your wishes next time, and I won't call you and I won't beg you to see me. I won't stop by with groceries, and I won't offer to fix anything for you."

Dear Lord, he thought. *What have I done?*

He ducked his head, embarrassment and horror filling him from boot to brim. He reached up and touched his cowboy hat and said, "Have a good night, Willa."

She let him walk out, and Cactus stepped onto the porch, actually surprised to see the sun well into setting for the day. He took a deep breath, went down the steps, and said, "Please forgive me," as he got behind the wheel of his car.

Misery accompanied him back to Shiloh Ridge, and he parked at Bull House and went inside.

"Hey." Ward sat up and dropped his socked feet from the coffee table in front of him. "You're back early."

"I left early," Cactus said. He sighed as he sank into the armchair next to the couch. "Just you tonight?"

"Mister's in the shower," Ward said. "Ace is down helping Holly Ann with the party."

Cactus nodded, his focus moving to the TV. It was just sound and light, and he didn't have a clue what it was.

"Do you want to talk about it?" Ward asked.

Cactus closed his eyes, trying to remember everything he'd said to Willa. His mind was a complete blank. He shook his head. He'd said enough for one night.

"Okay," Ward said. "You're welcome to stay here tonight if you want. It's a long ride in the dark."

"I've got the pups," Cactus said. In fact, he should leave right now, as they'd been in the barn for hours now. Once he got them fully potty-trained, he could leave them in the house when he had to.

He stayed for a few more minutes, until Mister came into the living room, and then Cactus stood. "See you gentlemen tomorrow," he said.

"No report?" Mister asked, popping the top on a can of soda. He groaned as he sat down, and Cactus heard the pain in the sound.

"What's with you?"

"Oh, I got thrown today." Mister waved his free hand and drank at least half his soda.

"Thrown?" Ward and Cactus said together.

"That new horse has an attitude," Mister said. "I'll break him though. I always do."

He did too, and Cactus told him to be more careful tomorrow. Then he left, swung into Hammy's saddle, and said, "Take us home, my friend." He didn't have to do anything else from there. The horse knew the way back to the barn, and the dark night gave Cactus plenty of time to think.

He hated that as much as he liked it, and by the time he got Hammy brushed down and his tack put away, he was ready to flip a switch and turn off his mind. He couldn't do that though, and he made the puppies use the bathroom before he took them inside.

He stalled on the threshold of his house, as the flooring had been removed that day. A note sat on the counter, and he stepped across bare plywood to get to it.

Cactus, Montana had written in her loopy handwriting. *We're knocking down the west wall on Friday, so you'll need to find somewhere to stay. Bishop suggested the Ranch House, as Preacher and Judge have three extra bedrooms. Sorry, we're ahead of schedule, and I didn't realize it would happen so soon.*

Montana

He looked around at the house, and it was time to get out of the way so Bishop and Montana could get it done. They were still working on their house too, and he should be grateful and glad they were ahead on his.

"Come on, pups," he said to the dogs. "Let's go to bed." The clock hadn't even ticked to eight yet, but Cactus stripped out of his clothes and put on a pair of shorts and a T-shirt. He put his favorite sitcom on his tablet, propped it up on his nightstand, and laid down. Both dogs jumped up onto the bed with him, one nestling behind his back and the other right against his knees. With their weight and company, Cactus finally relaxed.

A few minutes later, his phone chimed, and he reached for it.

He sat straight up, dislodging Galaxy and Tank, when he saw Willa's name.

Would you like to take me to dinner—without Mitch—on Friday?

Chapter Seven

❧

"Thank you for coming to get him," Willa said as Mitch preceded her brother out the front door. Patrick was proficient in American Sign Language, and he got along well with Mitch.

Once Cactus had suggested he take Mitch up to the ranch so she could go to bed early and sleep late, she hadn't been able to let go of the idea. She simply didn't want to impose on him. So after Cactus had left, she'd called her brother and asked if he could take Mitch that night.

Patrick had come, as he always did, and Willa's gratitude for him knew no bounds.

"So Cactus Glover came and made dinner?" Patrick leaned against the railing on her porch and watched as Mitch got in his car. The overhead light switched back off, and they stood far enough away that Mitch probably wouldn't be able to read their lips.

"Yes," she said.

"Are you two dating?"

"I don't know," Willa said. "We haven't gone out. He brought his dogs the other day, because his sister-in-law went into labor, and then he came by tonight and made dinner."

"Why didn't you go out with him?" Patrick asked. "I was ready to babysit."

Willa sighed, because she surely didn't need to explain it to him, of all people. "Since my divorce," she said. "I have not been interested in dating."

"Mm." Patrick hadn't dated since his divorce either, and Willa wondered if she needed to say more. "He must be different, then."

Oh, Cactus Glover was different than any man Willa had ever met. He had sparked something inside her that had gone dormant years ago, and she really liked that piece of her he'd reignited.

"He's different." She thought of him learning sign language from Internet videos, assuming he'd need to know how to speak with Mitch. She could see the intensity in the depth of his dark eyes when he asked if he could call the principal for her. She felt the very solid form of his body beneath hers after he'd rescued her from falling.

The problem was, she was falling in an entirely different way.

"You need to take care of yourself, Wills. I'm so glad you took tomorrow off." With that, her brother pushed away from the railing and gathered her into a hug.

"Thanks, Patrick," she whispered, clinging to him for a few extra seconds. "For everything. For helping me. For driving me everywhere I need to go. For taking Mitch tonight." Her voice felt strangled in her throat, and she pressed her eyes closed and sank into the warmth of the brotherly hug.

"Any time," he said. "Did you appeal to get your driver's license back earlier?"

She stepped out of his arms, nodding. "I did," she said. "They said I'd know by the fifteenth."

"Less than two weeks now."

"Yes." She blew out her breath. "I have no idea what they'll do."

"The accident was over two years ago," Patrick said. "You've been doing so well. I think the judge will see your side of it, especially now that you have Mitch."

Willa could only hope and pray that her brother was right. She'd love to get her driver's license reinstated. That meant she could get her own vehicle and drive herself and her son where they needed to go. Patrick's burden would be lifted greatly, and while he never acted put out when she asked him for a ride, she didn't want to keep taking advantage of him. Not only that, she'd rather be self-reliant and enjoy the freedom that came with that.

"You're a smart woman, Willa. Just keep your head on straight and trust in the Lord. You'll figure out what to do." Patrick grinned at her, and the bond they'd shared since childhood strengthened even more now. "See you tomorrow."

"Yeah, tomorrow," she said. How he'd known she was doubting herself and her choices, she didn't know. Sometimes Patrick just knew things even when she hadn't said anything.

What she needed to do was soak in a hot bath, turn off her alarms for the morning, and find some birthday cake frosting. She had a tub of the sweet stuff in her pantry, complete with the multi-colored sprinkles in the lid, and she took it down the hall along with a spoon. She started running the water in the tub, because the house carried quite a lot of years, and it took a few minutes for the hot water to come in.

While the tub filled, Willa pulled out her phone, her mind oscillating back and forth. Cactus had given quite the speech before leaving, and Willa had still been processing when she'd heard him drive away.

I think you're the most beautiful woman I've had the pleasure of meeting, he'd said. Along with, *I want to see if we can make a relationship work.*

Did she want that too?

Yes, she thought.

She let her thumbs fly then, and she hoped she wasn't being too hot and then too cold. She'd simply gotten icy feet that morning. She'd gotten too far inside her head. She'd allowed her doubts to lead her, and she hated that more than anything.

She read over her text—*Would you like to take me to dinner—without Mitch—on Friday?*—deemed it safe, and sent it.

Then she silenced her device, turned it face-down on the vanity, and got in the tub so she couldn't obsessively check for Cactus's answer.

WILLA'S FAVORITE DAY OF THE WEEK ARRIVED: THURSDAY. She loved that the weekend lingered around the corner, and she adored going to the chapel and leading the choir. They practiced every week from six to seven p.m., and Willa arrived early on Thursday to set up a table to hold the mini sliders she'd gotten from the leftovers at school that day.

Her day of rest on Wednesday had been absolutely amazing, and she'd spent a large part of it texting Cactus while she lay in bed. She wasn't sure if it was the bed part or the flirting with the handsome cowboy part that she'd liked so much. Probably both.

They had a dinner date for tomorrow night, and Cactus said he'd booked them on the Midnight Moonlight Train that left at nine o'clock. Because it was still early in March, it would be dark by then, and the ride only lasted an hour. So the midnight part of it was completely misleading.

He wanted to go to dinner first, and then take the train up to the top of the hill. Apparently groups could hike it with a guide too, but Willa knew he hadn't chosen that option because of her leg.

She thought of her injury as the first of the choir members arrived. Thankfully, Joey and her sister Lane chased away Willa's black thoughts, and she grinned at the ladies and gave them a quick hug.

"Joey, I really need you to sing with the altos on *He Is Risen*. They'll follow you." She handed the tall, lithe brunette the sheet music despite the face she made. She really was more of a soprano, but her pitch was so perfect that Willa moved her where she needed a strong voice. In that particular song, it was the alto part that needed help.

"Lane, you're on soprano." Willa handed her the music and leaned a bit closer. "Could you try to stand by Angie? She can't hold her own music, and your voice will even hers out."

"You got it, Willie."

Willa shook her head at Lane, but she didn't correct her on the nickname. Lane wore a line of earrings up her left lobe, and she didn't look like the type of woman Willa would find in a church every Sunday and Thursday. And yet, that was exactly where she could be found.

People like Lane reminded Willa of the Lord's love for all of His children. She epitomized the idea that judgments shouldn't be made from appearances alone.

Willa continued to greet the choir members as they arrived, giving them parts for *He Is Risen*, the hymn they'd spend their time with tonight. Easter sat right around the corner, and Paster Summers had requested several songs. Willa had been working on the program since she'd returned to Three Rivers at the end of December.

"All right," she said, lifting both hands above her head. "Everyone find your spots and let's get started." She watched as Lane slid over by Angie, the eighty-nine-year-old woman who lived right next door to Willa. She'd left Mitch with her once or twice when she'd had to run to the post office for a moment or when she'd gone to sign the long-term sub agreement with the high school.

Anything longer than twenty or thirty minutes, and Willa asked Patrick to help with Mitch. Tonight, he was down the hall with his cousins in Patrick's office while her brother worked on the volunteer lists for the highway trash pickup effort the church sponsored.

"Squire," Willa said. "Can you switch places with Beau? Mm hm, yes, like that." Willa sometimes fancied herself a matchmaker, and if Squire stood on the tenor row, that put Beau Peterson next to Candice Gallagher, and the honey blonde blushed a bright red the moment Beau looked her way.

He looked up and back at Squire as if he had no idea the effect he'd had on the woman, and Willa realized he probably didn't. She shook her head, finding the exact spot where Cactus would fit in this choir.

She could still hear his deep, rich, bass voice singing at her side from months ago. She'd tried to recruit him for her community Christmas choir, and that had not gone well. Therefore, she had not brought up the idea of him joining the church choir.

"Let's have Mave play through the introduction and first ten bars," Willa said. "If you would, Mave."

The pianist started to play, and Willa heard every missed note, every slip, and mentally held some notes longer than others. She missed having a piano in her home, and as the longing rolled through her, she reminded herself she could come here and play this piano any time she wanted.

"Okay," she said. "Tenors, did you hear that D? Mave?"

She struck it again, and Willa held up one hand, indicating the tenors should find the pitch. They did—well, most of them did—and Willa led everyone through a series of scales in the same key as *He Is Risen*.

They sang the first stanza, and Willa then separated them into parts and made them sing as single units. "Sopranos," she yelled above the altos as they sang. "Do you hear where you go?" She began to weave her voice above the lower female part, and Willa never felt as free as she did when she sang.

When she finished, the smile couldn't have been removed from her face without a chisel. "All right, sopranos," she said. "Your turn. Altos, I want you to hum your part. Feel where it goes among their notes. Tenors, you're up next, and you should be able to find your pocket while the ladies sing."

As the end of the hour neared, Willa thought they'd made excellent progress on the song. Once the notes had been discovered and found, it was just a matter of combining them in a way that wove magic with music. She loved harmonies, and nothing brought more relief to her soul than a good hymn well-sung.

After that, every verse was just different words. Willa did have a couple of ideas for this particular hymn, including an acapella verse, and one sung only by the men in the choir.

"All right," she called. "That's a wrap. Music to me, please. Thanks for your hard work." She beamed as the members came out of the choir seats to turn in their sheet music.

"Willa," Squire Ackerman said, standing off to the side so others could continue to pass her their music. "My son Finn wants to know if he can join the choir. He's a decent little singer. He says you're his teacher at the high school right now."

Willa glanced up at the dark-haired cowboy. "Of course.

Finn," she said with a grin. "He is a good singer, and I desperately need basses. You tell 'im to come next week."

Squire smiled back at her and tipped his hat. "Thank you, ma'am." He then nodded behind her. "If you need a bass, why don't you get that one to join up?"

She accepted another piece of music from Angie herself before turning to see who Squire meant.

Cactus sat at the back of the chapel, looking utterly relaxed and yet incredibly tense at the same time. Willa faced the front again as she needed to collect a few more pieces of music. "I think if he was interested, Squire, he would've come up front."

"Oh, he's interested in somethin'," Squire said.

Willa's whole body flushed, but she said nothing. She separated all the music as the chapel cleared out and clipped it all in her binder where it belonged. Mave had stayed back to ask a couple of questions, and Willa helped her make a few notes in her sheet music.

Finally, it was just her in the chapel, and she dared to look behind her. Cactus had gone, and keen disappointment cut through her. Sighing, she went up onto the dais and sat at the piano. Her fingers knew the keys so well. They'd played together for years now, and Willa had old melodies and harmonies embedded in her brain from countless recitals and practice sessions.

She let her fingers play what they wanted, and the tune came out slow and sad at first. It brightened after a few bars, and she smiled to herself at the beauty hidden inside the notes.

"You play well."

She looked up at Cactus, who now walked down the aisle toward her. Her fingers automatically came off the ivory, and he shook his head. "Don't stop."

She hesitated before putting her fingers back on the keys to continue the song. He came right up on the dais too and slipped onto the bench with her. Surprised he could fit, and yet feeling like he absolutely belonged right there beside her, she looked up at him.

"Do you play?" she asked.

"A very little," he said. "About like my sign language."

"You're quite good at that, actually," she said. "Mitch gets the idea, at least."

His eyes softened, but his mouth barely lifted into a smile that quickly flattened again. Willa focused on her fingers on the keys, and a handful of seconds later, Cactus used one hand to add a higher register of notes to the tune.

Harmony and melody, a swell up and then a few beats where Willa pulled back, slowed, barely pressed the keys down at all.

She loved the way music moved, and she loved the way it filled her heart and soul with sound, life, and light.

Somehow, she and Cactus took their hands off the keyboard at the same time, and the last note continued to reverberate through the chapel, finally dissipating way up in the rafters. "When I first found out Mitch was deaf," she said, her voice barely more than a whisper. "I cried and cried. Not because I thought I couldn't raise a deaf child. Not because I thought he'd have a harder life than other kids. But because he would never be able to hear music."

"It's in your blood," Cactus said softly, none of the gruffness he sometimes had in his voice.

"Before I became a pastor," she said. "I taught voice lessons and piano lessons from my home. I worked in a Montessori school and taught the choirs." She smiled at the good memories from her past. "It's why I jumped at the chance to be the long-term sub here."

He kept his head bent low as if studying the keys. "Do you have a teaching degree?"

"No," she said. "I have a Bachelor's degree in vocal performance and a minor in piano. But I didn't need a teaching degree for Montessori. The degree in vocal performance was enough to qualify me to lead the choir."

They sat together on the piano bench for what felt like a long time but only a couple of minutes ticked by. "I should get home," she said. "Patrick is probably done with his work."

"Could I give you a ride home?" Cactus asked. "You've got Mitch, I assume."

"Yes." She slid off her end of the bench and stood. She picked up her phone and saw she'd missed a few messages. "Oh, Patrick already took him home." She looked up. "They left several minutes ago. He said he'd wait with Mitch at my place."

Take your time, her brother had said, which meant he'd seen her sitting with Cactus on the piano bench.

So what if he had? Willa wasn't trying to hide her relationship with Cactus Glover.

"I guess it's just me and you then," Cactus said, his smile absolutely stunning.

"I guess it is."

He stood closer to the steps that led off the dais, and he extended his hand toward her. She watched herself slip her smaller, whiter fingers between his, and she closed her eyes to truly experience every contact point where her skin met his.

She felt like she was coming home. At the same time, nerves ran through her, and adrenaline screamed through her veins.

"Did you drive all the way down here to give me a ride home?" she asked.

"What if I said yes?"

Willa didn't know how to respond. Cactus hadn't hidden his feelings for her. Heck, he'd said them right out loud. She didn't know many men like him, and his candidness scared her a whole lot.

He held her door while she got in on the passenger side of the car, and when he got behind the wheel, he said, "How do you feel about stopping for milkshakes?"

"I could be persuaded," she said, sliding him a smile.

He returned it this time and fired up the car. "Listen," he said, and she was starting to realize he started serious conversations with that one word. "I wanted to tell you something."

"Okay," she said.

He gripped the steering wheel and kneaded it beneath his powerful hands. Willa looked away and out her window, so he'd calm down and just say it. Sometimes it was easier for her to say something if she didn't have any eyes on her.

After several blocks of silence, he finally said, "I've been married before too, Willa. A long time ago. I've been divorced for twelve years now."

"Okay," she said calmly. He'd assumed she'd been married to Mitch's father, and she'd neither confirmed nor denied the sentiment.

"And…that's all. I guess I just wanted you to know."

Willa nodded, her throat suddenly too tight to breathe let alone sip a milkshake. Speaking definitely wasn't going to happen, at least not right now.

Unfortunately, Cactus pulled into Sugar Love, and for the first time in probably the existence of the shop, there was no line for the drive-through. "What do you want?" he asked, and Willa simply had no voice to answer him.

Chapter Eight

Cactus knotted his tie and ran his palm straight down it, pausing for a moment as he looked at his reflection. "No more confessions tonight," he told himself.

He'd hoped that by him telling Willa that he'd been married before too, she'd feel comfortable enough with him to give him a bit of her story. That had backfired spectacularly, and all he'd done was introduce a new level of awkwardness to their time together.

It was already less than what Cactus wanted, and he hated that he'd made a beautiful moment on the piano bench into something tense. She'd ordered a peanut butter cup shake, and he'd gotten his standard huckleberry cheesecake.

She'd lightened the mood by teasing him about his choice, and he had learned that she only liked candy in milk-shakes. "No fruit, no graham cracker crumbs." She'd taken a long draw on her straw then, and Cactus could still see the shape of her mouth around it.

His whole body heated, and he watched his face to see if it turned red. Thankfully, it didn't, and he left the bathroom and went out into the living room where Judge and Preacher were both sprawled on a different couch, each with one of Cactus's dogs laying right on top of them.

He grinned at Tank and Galaxy, and both dogs started wagging their tails.

"Knock it off, Gal," Preacher said, but Judge remained silent. He actually had a pillow clutched to his chest, and neither of them moved when Cactus said, "I'm headed out." He took them in, wondering if he had ever acted as wiped out and exhausted as his brothers.

Of course, he hadn't been up since three o'clock that morning. A couple of coyotes had crossed onto the ranch through a hole in a fence somewhere, and Ranger, Judge, and Preacher had been tasked with finding the weakness in their barrier and getting rid of the coyotes.

"Are you guys alive?" he asked, moving into the living room between the two couches. He bent down and gave Tank a good scrub along his jowls. "Hey, bud. You keepin' Judge warm, huh?"

He straightened and stroked Galaxy too. "Guys, I need someone to tell me if the tie is trying too hard." He wore blue jeans with a light blue and white checkered shirt, and the tie had come from Bear last Christmas. He'd called it "trendy," and Cactus had never worn it before.

He wasn't really into floral ties, but he figured he could give it a go tonight.

Preacher sat up, gathering Galaxy into his arms. She tried to lick his face, but he dodged her attempts. His hair stuck out at odd angles as he scanned Cactus from head to toe. "If you took the murderous look off your face, I'd say you're pretty passable," he said.

"I'll keep that in mind," Cactus said dryly, looking at Judge.

"It's not trying too hard," Judge said, moving only his eyes as he took in Cactus's clothes. "It's real nice. Looks good with that blue, like it's the sky for all those flowers."

Cactus wasn't sure if that was what he was going for or not, but he supposed he'd take it. "As long as I don't look like an idiot," he said. "This is my first real date with Willa. I don't want to look like an idiot." He looked down at the tie. "Is it too skinny? It's too skinny, isn't it?"

"It's great, Cactus," Judge said with a smile. "Don't over-think it. She obviously likes you."

"She does?"

"*She* asked *you* to take her to dinner," Judge said, finally moving his head to angle it up at Cactus. "No one's asking me that."

Cactus had not told them about the way he'd refused to let her cancel their date on Tuesday. He hadn't told them about what he'd said to her before he'd walked out. Bishop and Montana knew, as did Ward, but Ace had been busy with Holly Ann. Cactus had finished moving all of his stuff from the Edge Cabin to the Ranch House basement yesterday afternoon, and he'd driven Aunt Dawna back to Nestled Oak, the assisted living center where she lived. So he'd already been in town before he'd stopped by her choir practice.

He knew Willa ran choir practice on Thursday nights,

because her brother had invited Cactus to sing with the choir at least a dozen times. Maybe more. Willa herself had not, probably because Cactus had gotten into an argument with her the last time she'd tried to recruit him to sing.

He didn't want to join the choir. He just wanted to be near Willa, and if that meant sitting in the back of the chapel while she instructed men and women about how to feel the music and find their pocket of sound, that was just fine with him.

"Okay." He took a deep breath and started for the kitchen, which had a door that led into the garage. He'd brought Hammy over from his stables, and of course, the puppies had made themselves right at home. "I shouldn't be too late. Maybe like eleven or so." He wasn't sure why he was reporting to them. They weren't Mother, and he didn't have a curfew.

"You guys are okay with the dogs?"

"Yes," Preacher said. "Go."

Cactus caught the impatience in his brother's voice, but he hesitated anyway. "You should really mention to Ranger that Two Cents needs a meeting room. Maybe on one of the threads about best first date."

"I know people who've gone out because of the comments," Preacher said. "Angus out at Britt's place saw someone's comment about how they'd love to go to some tulip festival or something, and he commented back that he'd take her. They've been going out for a while now, and the tulip festival isn't for another month."

Cactus would never do that, but he could see Preacher

doing it. "You should do that," he told him. Something passed over Preacher's features, and it wasn't pretty.

"Nah," he said, trying to play it off. But Cactus had seen the displeasure. His expression had almost been...angry. "Have fun on the train." He laid back down, and Cactus stepped outside.

He didn't particularly want to go on the Midnight Express, but the groups were limited to fifty across five train cars, and the seats had been assigned. The ride came with an ice cream sundae and one of those candied waffles, and Cactus had thought it would be a good dessert for their dinner.

For that, he'd planned to take her to Modern Bistro, which was a pop-up restaurant that moved around town. One night it would be in the comedy club when they didn't have a show, and the next, the chef operated out of the elementary school.

Tonight, Cactus had managed to snag one of the six-thirty spots for him and Willa at the park voted most romantic by Two Cents users: Swan Canal Park.

Cactus personally didn't like birds that much, especially swans. They were pretty to look at, but wow, they were mean. Swan Canal Park had a massive outdoor amphitheater and a pavilion that was enclosed on three sides. The chef for Modern Bistro would be cooking over open flame tonight, and the menu included ribeye steaks, smoked turkey, and braised lamb shanks.

Only four couples could dine every half hour, and Cactus hoped it would be something unique and romantic he and Willa could remember with fondness for a long, long time.

The drive took no time at all, and before he knew it, he approached the red-brick house with the quaint front porch. He rang the bell, and he expected to hear a child's feet running toward him.

Willa calmly opened the door a few seconds later, her beauty punching him right between the eyes. "Wow," came out of his mouth before he'd even looked away from her face. She'd put makeup on tonight—more than usual. He liked the shiny, glossy lips and the dark eyeliner around her eyes.

"You look amazing." He drank in her curled hair, which fell to just below her ears now that it wasn't straight. She wore a bright blouse with pink and white stripes and a pair of snow-white pants that billowed around her legs.

She was classy and sophisticated. Gorgeous. Stunning. Cactus couldn't come up with enough adjectives to describe her.

"Thank you," she said, maintaining eye contact. She did that better than anyone he knew, and he suspected it was because of speaking with Mitch. "You sure do look good too."

"Do I?" He flipped up his skinny tie. "The tie's kind of throwing me."

She reached out and ran her fingers down one side of it, putting enough pressure into the move to make him shiver. "I like it." She looked up into his eyes, and wow, Cactus could lose hours looking at her. "I wouldn't peg you for a floral tie kind of cowboy, but I think you're pulling it off pretty well."

Cactus smiled at her and reached for her. "Do you need anything? Ready to go?"

"You said we'll be outside," she said, peering up into the sky though the roof over her porch prevented that. "Do I need a jacket?"

"You can bring it," he said. "Leave it in the car if you want, and then you have it if you want it."

"Okay." She stepped back inside and collected her jacket and her purse before joining him on the porch. He took her hand in his, casting her a sideways look, and found a smile growing on her face.

Maybe Judge was right. Maybe Willa did like him as much as he liked her.

He did his gentlemanly duty and held her door while she got in. He made her wait so he could open it once they arrived at the park. She slipped her fingers between his this time, and they walked toward the check-in podium for dinner.

"This is spectacular," she said, gazing around. "It smells fantastic."

The park had been cleaned up already, and the grass was starting to green again. The air held a salty quality to it, as well as something sweet and something spicy. Cactus hadn't eaten for a while, and his stomach wanted all of the food right now.

Willa laughed when she heard the growl, and he joined in. "I guess I'm hungry," he said.

"I guess so."

They waited in line, and finally, he said, "How's Mitch?"

"Good," she said with a nod. "How's the ranch?"

"We had some coyotes yesterday," he said. "But we found the hole in the fence, and chased them off. So good." He nodded too, hating this brand of small talk. This was exactly why he didn't date. "What's your favorite snack?"

She looked at him, surprise in those hazel eyes. "Wheat thins," she said. Her eyes narrowed. "Favorite color?"

"Blue." He indicated his shirt with a grin. "Favorite pastime?"

"Watching movies."

He had to stop the game as he stepped up to the podium to check in. "Cactus Glover," he said, and the woman looked up at him. His heart dang near stopped, and he almost turned and broke into a jog.

"Cactus Glover," Tracy Jacobs said, her light green eyes sliding down his body. "Look at you."

He couldn't look at himself, and horror had stolen his voice.

Beside him, Willa said, "I'm Willa Knowlton."

"Of course," Tracy said, turning her attention to Willa. "The preacher."

Cactus knew Willa didn't like that term, but she didn't correct Tracy. She just smiled and nodded, looking at Cactus.

"Oh, uh, Tracy and I, well, we...." He had no idea how to explain this. He and Tracy hadn't gone out. She was twenty years younger than him.

Tracy grinned like she was part feline and she'd just caught a canary. "I'd really like to hear the end of that sentence," she said, cocking that hip that Cactus had once found so sexy.

"Me too," Willa said.

Cactus looked back and forth between the two women,

realizing why he never left the ranch. It was safe up there. He didn't have to explain anything to anyone up there.

You also weren't living up there, he told himself.

Besides, when he met with Dr. Thompson next Friday, he'd have something to tell him. Hopefully, something good.

"So I met Tracy at the Christmas movie a while back. Not this last year. The year before that." He looked at her for confirmation. "Anyway, I got her number after spraying myself with ginger beer, and we texted a little." He swallowed, waiting for her to jump in with the punch line. She just lifted her eyebrows and wore a cocky little smile on her face.

"We were gonna go out, but I mean, I just couldn't."

"Why not?" Willa asked, looking at Tracy.

"Yeah," Tracy said. "Why not?"

Cactus gaped at her. "What do you mean, why not?"

"I mean, we were texting. I suggested dinner on Sunday, and never heard from you again."

"That's not true," he said. "We talked after that. I distinctly remember agreeing to the date on Sunday, and then I found out how old you were."

Willa looked at Tracy, her eyes wide and filled with questions. "How old are you?"

"At the time, she was twenty-three," Cactus said. "I was forty-two. I'm forty-three right now, and I just didn't think I should go out with someone two decades younger than me."

A couple of beats of silence followed, and then Willa started giggling. The sound started out low but grew with every passing moment. Before he knew it, Tracy laughed too, but he just looked back and forth between the two women with a deep frown riding his eyebrows.

"What's so funny?" he asked.

"I mean, it's a valid reason," Willa said.

"If only he'd have *said that*," Tracy said, enunciating the last two words quite harshly. She kept the grin on her face as she shook her head. "Here's your table number, Cactus. Welcome to Modern Bistro."

He took the tag from her, still not sure what was happening. Tracy scanned him again. "You are good-looking. I think we would've had fun." She glanced at Willa. "But you two sure are cute together. I'm assuming she's not in her twenties."

"That she is not," Willa said with another laugh. "Nice to meet you, Tracy." She gently nudged Cactus away from the podium, and thankfully, his legs moved at her insistence. "She's cute. I like her."

"Yes, well, you like everyone," Cactus said darkly.

"What does that mean?"

"It means that was super embarrassing." Cactus released Willa's hand and looked anywhere but at her, wondering if he'd ever be able to have a normal date with her. With anyone. Every single one he'd been on in the past couple of years had been filled with tension, awkwardness, or had some random, embarrassing thing happen during it.

"Oh, it was not," Willa said lightly. "So you thought she was pretty. She *is* pretty."

"She thought I was a stalker," Cactus said, watching the chef toss something into a hot pan. Smoke lifted into the air immediately, and his stomach roared again. "And somehow she still wanted to go out with me."

"Must be the good looks," Willa said in a mock whisper, and that got Cactus to look her in the face. She wore pure joy in her expression, along with plenty of flirtation. "I know that's why I said yes."

Cactus's face heated. "Come on," he said.

"Come on what?" Willa asked innocently. "You think a woman doesn't want to be attracted to the man she goes to dinner with?" She took his hand in hers again. "I assure you, Mister Glover, that she does."

"So you're saying...." He couldn't finish. He didn't need to finish. He supposed he was handsome, especially now that he'd cut his hair and bought new clothes. "There has to be more than that though," he said. "Right?"

"Always," Willa said, her grin perpetual now.

Before Cactus could ask her anything else, the dinner bell rang, nearly deafening him. Someone literally stood in front of a triangle dinner bell, clanging around it for all he was worth. He grinned around at the people already seated, and the eight waiting to start their meal.

With the last of the bell's gonging still hanging in the air, Tracy's voice came over a loudspeaker saying, "The six-thirty group will go with Sarah, please. Six-thirty couples to the pavilion with Sarah."

Chapter Nine

"So let me get this straight," Willa said, feeling like everything around her was made of sparkles and sprinkles. Cactus ignited something inside her that simply glowed, and she sure did like the energetic feeling that came whenever he was near.

"You never did tell her she was too young for you."

"I suppose not," he said, chuckling.

The food had been fantastic—literally one of the best steaks Willa had ever tasted. The creamy pea salad had been cool, refreshing, and sweet. They were currently waiting for their dessert, and Willa thought she could wait all night if she had to.

The conversation had been stellar, and Cactus had told her about several other dating disasters—his words, not hers—he'd experienced in the past year or so. She loved listening to the man talk, and she could only imagine what a night around a campfire with him would be like. Along with a bag of marshmallows, a box of graham crackers, plenty of chocolate, and Cactus Glover, it would be heaven for Willa.

"What about you?" he asked. "Dating mishaps since you've been single?"

Willa let her smile linger. "Who doesn't have a few mishaps in their past?" she asked.

"Maybe not Tracy Jacobs," he quipped. "But only because she's not old enough yet."

Willa giggled again, looking up as a waiter arrived with their cast iron skillet brownies. He scooped vanilla ice cream right from the barrel onto hers, and then signaled for someone to come put the marshmallow coconut on Cactus's.

The woman who brought that set a tray of toppings in front of them and said, "Enjoy," with a bright smile.

"This has been incredible," Willa said.

"I agree," Cactus said. "I wasn't sure how it would be, but I'd heard good things."

"Oh yeah?" She dug into her ooey gooey brownie, the vanilla ice cream melting and making a delectable sauce. "From who, Mister Glover?" She held up her spoon with the perfect bite on it, the brownie steaming. "I mean, you claim to have been a hermit for the past decade. You didn't even speak to your family, let alone anyone else. You haven't driven to town alone until *very* recently."

She switched her gaze from the dessert to the cowboy. "You don't like crowds, and you don't seem to like people in general all that much."

His eyes sparkled like dark diamonds, and oh, Willa wanted to tell him everything. She simply didn't know how.

You like him too much, she thought. If she didn't, she wouldn't care what he thought of her once he learned the truth.

"So who told you about this amazing dining experience?" She put the brownie bite in her mouth, the rich, chocolate flavor making her eyes roll back in her head. The vanilla ice cream was cold and sweet, and with the bitterness from the chocolate, and the heat from the skillet, it was simply the best thing she'd put in her mouth tonight.

"It was actually my sister," Cactus said.

"You just have the one of those, right?" Willa asked.

"Yes," he said. "Arizona's the youngest, and her boyfriend brought her to this. I guess Duke's her fiancé now." A shadow crossed his face, but he cleared it quickly. "I heard about it from them." He flashed her a smile and added, "There's dessert on the train too, just so you know."

Alarm pulled through Willa. "Really?"

"Really," he said. "More ice cream and one of those stroopwafles."

"I *love* those," she said, looking down at her brownie. "But I love brownies too."

"It'll be a while yet," he said. "The train doesn't leave until nine." He scraped up the last bite of his brownie and stuck it in his mouth.

Willa wanted to tell him how incredibly good-looking he was, but that yes, there was more to him than that. "Tell me something you've never told anyone."

He froze. One-hundred-percent-encased-in-ice froze. He didn't blink, and he didn't chew.

"Oh, I struck a nerve," she said, the moment suddenly very sober between them.

Cactus continued to stare at her, and Willa grew increasingly uncomfortable under the intensity of his eyes. She took one more bite of her brownie and then said, "When I was twelve or thirteen, I stole a bunch of money from my mother's purse." Willa could still feel the thumping of her heartbeat against her ribs. "I was so nervous I'd get caught, but she never said anything. Now that I'm older, I wonder how she didn't miss so much money."

"What did you buy?" Cactus sounded like he'd gargled with frogs.

"What all twelve-year-old girls wanted at the time." She flashed him a quick smile. "*Seventeen* magazine and nail polish." She reached up to tuck one of her errant curls away. She hated how girlish the shorter hair made her look, but Cactus had assured her he liked it. Willa didn't have much choice when it came to her hair. It refused to grow much longer than shoulder-length, and it held absolutely no wave at all.

So she wore it straight and slick, or she curled it and accepted that it took four inches off the length.

"You've never told her? Even now?"

"No." Willa shook her head. "I probably should, but it's been what? Twenty-five years? What would be the point?"

"Maybe she's been trying to think of where she put it all this time," he said. "My grandmother used to store money in every little crevice and crack she could." He smiled, the memory obviously a good one for him. "After she died, we found money in the cellar, in Altoid tins, in the bread box. Everywhere. Cleaning out her house became a game. Whoever found the money got to keep it."

"Did you find any?"

"I found three hundred dollars in a box in the top of her closet," he said. "It was full of photos and love letters from my grandfather. Tucked right in there was an envelope of twenties and fifties." He chuckled, and the memory made him so much softer.

She reached across the table and covered his hand with both of hers. "I like your heart, Cactus."

He quieted, turned his hand over, and squeezed hers. "What do you like about it?" Anxiety swam in the depths of his eyes, and Willa wished she could make it go away.

"I like that you love your family and have a close relationship with them." She gave him a smile that felt shy to her. She lowered her voice, because they sat at the long picnic tables with another couple only a few feet away. "I like that you like dogs. I like that you're so good with children."

"I don't like people much," he said. "You were right about that." He glanced at the man sitting down the bench. "I try, but I...don't know. I think I'm impatient."

"You're smart," Willa said. "And if someone doesn't get things the way you do, or as quickly as you, you get a little annoyed. It's a characteristic of the highly intelligent."

Cactus shook his head. "I'm not sure about that."

"I am," she said, tilting her head to the side. "You said earlier that you work with the animals at Shiloh Ridge. Are you the vet?"

Cactus cleared his throat, which meant yes. "Most of the time," he said.

She smiled and gave him a single nod. "So besides incredibly handsome, you've got smart going for you. Kind to kids, which by the way, in case you didn't know, goes a very long way with women. I happen to be a dog person, so you tick that box. Let's see...." She pretended to survey him by looking up to his sexy, black cowboy hat.

"You've got the cowboy hat, which I also really like. You're family-oriented, which most women appreciate. And you can cook."

"It was one meal," he muttered. "That I've made a hundred times."

"Still counts," the woman next to Willa said. She and Cactus both looked at her. She shrugged and looked at the man across from her. "Cooking impresses women."

"And he included my son." Willa gently pulled her hands away from Cactus's and leaned away from the table slightly.

"Oh, honey, you should sew this up. Do you have a ring yet?"

Cactus choked, and Willa forced a laugh from her throat. "I think this is our first date, actually." She glanced at Cactus, who had his sweet tea glass at his lips. Willa looked to the man sitting next to him. "What about you two? Have you been going out long?"

"A few months," the man said.

"And he has never cooked for me," the woman said with plenty of coyness in her voice. She put her elbows on the table and leaned her face into her hands.

"It's now on my list," he said, smiling at her.

"Did you hear her list?" she asked her boyfriend. "Handsome, hard-working, smart, good with kids, family-oriented, cooks a little." She glanced at Willa. "Sorry, but I'm a cat person. Or a bird person."

"We all have faults," Willa said, and the two of them burst out laughing. Cactus looked like he'd been hit with one of the miniature skillets the brownies had come in, and the other man actually said, "Wait. You're a *bird* person?"

"We should go," Cactus said, standing up. He tossed a twenty-dollar bill on the table, which surprised Willa as much as the abrupt end to dinner. "We don't want to be late for the train."

He put his hand on her back as she stood, and he nodded to the other couple, who didn't even look at him. On their way out, Cactus tucked her further into his side, and whispered, "I think you might have just caused that couple to break-up." He chuckled, which sent heated shivered through Willa's whole body.

She wanted to ask why he'd left such a big tip. She wanted to tell him about everything in her past. She wanted to keep him in her life for as long as possible.

So she leaned into his touch and said, "Well, no one should be a bird person—and if they are, they shouldn't admit it out loud. Am I right?"

"*So* right," he said, and they laughed together.

<hr>

WILLA SIGNED HER LAST TIME CARD AND SMILED AT THE secretary she'd gotten to know well over the past three months. "I'll miss coming here every day," she said.

"We always need subs," Roberta said. "You're welcome any time, Willa." She picked up the card and put it in the stack with the others, her smile quick and professional. She knew where everything was in the office, and where everything was in Principal Collins' office too.

"I'll keep my name in the system," she said. "I need a week or two off though."

Everett Collins came out office with another teacher. They finished their conversation, and Everett looked at Willa. "The concerts were amazing, Willa. Thank you so much for your help these past few months. We would've died without you."

"Oh, you'd have been just fine," she said, dragging out the I in *fine* like a true Texan.

"We were blessed to have you." Everett handed a signed paper to Roberta. "I've got the Trustlands form."

"Thank you, sir." Roberta took that and filed it where it needed to go.

"Well, thanks again," Willa said, and she waved to the finance secretary on her way out. Cactus waited in the circle drive where the buses usually queued up, but they'd been gone for at least half an hour.

He got out of the sedan and came toward her, his smile genuine and picture-perfect. "How was your last day?" he asked when he still had a few paces to reach her.

"Great," she said, adopting one of Mitch's favorite words.

Cactus dwarfed her and enveloped her in his arms, his chuckle deep and delicious and making everything inside Willa bloom to life. "I missed you today," he whispered in her ear.

"Yeah?" she asked, holding onto his broad shoulders, her happiness greater than it had been since her car accident.

"Why? Did the boys get out of line during branding *again* today?"

"Always," he said dryly. "Not only that, but Bear's asking me all kinds of questions about when you're going to come up to the ranch and how I'm doing."

She stepped back so she could see his face. Cactus gave away so much in those eyes of his, and Willa liked to get as much information as possible from him. "Oh, you hate it when people ask you how you're doing."

"Tell me about it." He turned toward the car, and they started toward it together. "I know Mitch is going to be home soon, but I have an order waiting at the bakery for your last day. It won't take but five minutes to pick it up, and we'll be on the way."

"What did you order at the bakery?"

"Your favorite." He beamed down at her and opened the door for her. She slid into the passenger seat and set her tote bag on the floor at her feet. A tired sigh hissed from her lips. Yes, she'd fully enjoyed teaching the choirs and doing the concerts, but she didn't have the same physical stamina she'd once had, and she was looking forward to a few days where she didn't have to get up, get ready, and get out the door by a certain time.

"What would that be?" she asked.

"It was tough to pick just one," he said. "You've said about ten different things are your favorite." He gave her a dry look, to which Willa could only shrug.

"I like a lot of things."

"Mm hm."

They'd had a pretty great three weeks together. He

planned exquisite dates, and Willa enjoyed holding his hand, listening to him talk about his brothers and cousins, the ranch, and the animals. He'd told her about a renovation and expansion project on his house, but she hadn't been up to the ranch to see it.

She hadn't been up to Shiloh Ridge since Christmas Eve, and she could understand why Cactus got annoyed with his family when they badgered him about bringing her to their Sabbath Day dinners or other family events.

Cactus had told her he'd need to go very slow in this relationship, and she'd agreed whole-heartedly. In fact, just that morning, she'd considered calling him and saying he didn't need to pick her up that afternoon. She was fine, Patrick could do it, she'd talk to him later.

Much later.

Willa still hadn't told him anything about her past. Not even one little thing. She didn't have a large family to occupy the conversation, and Cactus had definitely shared more about his life—current and past—than she had. Much more.

She swallowed as he pulled up to Ackerman's and into a pick-up stall. He texted the number on the signpost, and a few minutes later, Heidi Ackerman herself brought out three pastry boxes, one stacked right on top of the other, in her arms.

"Cactus," Willa said, plenty of chastisement in her voice. "Three boxes?"

"They're your favorite," he said as he got out of the sedan to meet Heidi. "And they freeze. Hullo, ma'am."

"Cactus." Heidi smiled at him with all the love of a grandmother and handed him the boxes. He took them in one hand and hugged her with the other. She held onto him for several long seconds, and Willa could hear her saying something, but her voice was so quiet, she couldn't make out what.

"I know," Cactus said. "I'll let her know, and I'll come tomorrow, okay?"

Heidi nodded, sniffled, and stepped back. Cactus stayed outside while she walked back inside, and Willa's mind raced.

He sighed as he sat down in the driver's seat. He handed her one of the boxes. "Open it."

"What was that all about?"

Cactus looked out the windshield toward the bakery. "Her husband died a few months back. She's lonely and struggling. My mother knows how she's feeling, and they've become quite close since Frank's death." He seemed somewhere else for a moment, and only when Willa lifted the top off the brown bakery box did he tear his gaze from the front of the shop.

"Cactus Glover," Willa said, surprise and strict firmness in her voice. "You did *not* get me a box of raisin-filled cookies." She gazed at the wonderfully pale cookies in the box—a full dozen of them. They'd been crimped along the edges, just like a proper raisin-filled cookie should be. They bore a figgy glaze, which was Heidi Ackerman's specialty, and Willa absolutely loved these cookies.

"No," he said. "I got you *three* boxes of raisin-filled cookies." He kicked a grin in her direction, and Willa's emotions engulfed her so quickly that she couldn't control them. Tears slipped down her face, and a sob tore through her chest.

"Hey, hey," he said. "Don't cry. Why are you crying?"

She turned toward him, shaking her head because she couldn't speak. She couldn't explain. She just grabbed onto him and held him tight with the console between them.

"I'm sorry," he whispered, stroking his hands down her hair and shoulders over and over. "I didn't mean to upset you. I'm sorry, I'm sorry, I'm sorry."

Chapter Ten

B ishop Glover paced in the grooms' room in True Blue, more nervous than he'd anticipated being. The heavy door kept the chatter and buzz of the audience out of his ears, but he knew how many people had gathered to the barn at Shiloh Ridge for his and Montana's wedding.

Too many.

"It's fine," he told himself. "She's here, and she's all that matters." He still slicked his palms down the front of his slacks and took another deep breath, as if that would calm his pulse and make this wedding be over already.

He'd wanted the big wedding. Montana had been married before. He'd wanted to throw the party, because she deserved one, and he loved her with his entire heart. He wanted the world to know it, and the best way to show them was to bring them up to the barn he'd built and feed them.

Stress sat on his shoulders, though, because Montana's mother had come to Three Rivers for the wedding. They hadn't gotten along for much of the past several years, and Bishop knew having Ruby Solomon in town had caused Montana a great deal of heartache.

He checked the clock above the door, and he wasn't sure how he'd survive the next ten minutes before he had to go out to the altar. The door opened and Ace slipped inside. "I come bearing dessert." He held up one of the mini bundt cakes, a triumphant look on his face. "German chocolate."

Bishop started to laugh, and he took the cake and then hugged his cousin. "It's normal to feel like I'm going to puke, right?"

"I'd be worried if you didn't feel like that," Ace said. He stepped back and kept one hand on Bishop's shoulder. "But you've got this. The cake looks stunning. The food is ready. Everyone's here. Your mother has the perfect music playing, and she's practically glowing at how many people are praising the decorations."

Bishop managed a smile. Mother had planned the wedding for Montana and Bishop, and she had done a spectacular job. Bishop had put the finishing touches on the house where he and Montana would live once they returned from their honeymoon.

Montana's Aunt Jackie and Uncle Bob were keeping Aurora during that time, and then she'd come up to the ranch too. Bishop was going to be a father of a fifteen-year-old in less than thirty minutes.

His stomach swooped, and all of his anchors had sunk all the way to the bottom of the ocean.

"Bear's on his way," Ace said. "You're spiraling, bro."

"I know," Bishop said, looking around wildly. "I can't

help it."

The door opened, and Cactus entered. Bishop practically ran to him, and Cactus held him in a tight hug. "Hey," he said. "Hey, you've got this." He squeezed Bishop and let him go. "You love her. She loves you. The end."

"Right," Bishop said, swallowing.

Judge and Preacher entered the room, quickly followed by Ward and Ranger, Mister and Bear. "Let's gather round," Bear said, waiting while everyone did just that. He put his arm around Bishop's shoulder. "If Daddy were here, he'd say a prayer."

Murmurs of assent moved through the group, and Bishop looked around at the other men in the room with him. He looked up to each of them in different ways, and he desperately wanted each of them to find the happiness and peace they deserved.

"Will you say it, Bear?" Bishop asked, his voice nearly hoarse.

"Of course."

They all removed their cowboy hats, and Bear cleared this throat. "Dear Lord, how grateful we are to be here today, together, as brothers and cousins and friends."

He paused for several long seconds, and Bishop felt his last word way down deep in his soul.

Friends.

They were friends.

They were family too, and that bond kept people together, but Bishop didn't want to spend time with anyone else. He was *friends* with his brothers and cousins, and they were his greatest heroes.

"Bless Bishop to be calm and clear today, and bless Montana and her daughter, Aurora, to feel the love and joy we all feel at welcoming them to the Glover family." Another pause, and then Bear simply said, "Amen."

"Amen," they chorused, and the circle broke up as people stepped back and settled their hats back on their heads. Cactus kept his gaze on Bear, but Bishop couldn't look at his oldest brother. Bear meant so much to him, and Bishop wanted to talk to him alone.

He hugged Mister, then Preacher, then Judge. One by one, they wished him well and left the room, until it was just Ace, Cactus, and Bear remaining.

"You've got this, bro," Ace said. "Don't be late. Your mother might lose her mind." He chuckled and stepped out too.

"Bishop," Cactus said. "You've found yourself an amazing woman. You deserve her, and she deserves you." He curled his fingers behind Bishop's neck and bent his head until he touched his forehead to Bishop's. "I love you, my brother. You didn't give up on me when others did, and I can't tell you how much I appreciate that."

"I love you, too, Cactus." Bishop hugged him again, and Cactus nodded to Bear and left the room.

"Bear," Bishop said, his voice a little too high.

"You're my hero, Benson." Bear grinned at him, his presence strong and filling the room. He looked so much like Daddy, and Bishop missed his father so much in that moment. So very much it felt like a crushing blow he wasn't there.

"You're mine, Bartholomew," Bishop said, striding toward

Bear and gripping him in a tight embrace.

"Thank you for being you," Bear whispered. "Don't forget who you are, okay? Marriage is wonderful, but it changes a man. Usually for the better, but remember who you are." He pulled back and placed one fist against Bishop's heartbeat. "You're Benson Glover, and Bear's brother, and Cactus's rock, and Ace's best friend. You're Daddy's youngest son, and his favorite to have in the woodworking shop, and the apple of Mother's eye."

He paused, his smile wavering. "And you're brilliant with a hammer in your hand, and a kind soul to everyone who comes to the ranch. You're about to be Montana's husband and Aurora's dad, and those require things from a man you might not have done before. But you can do them. Just remember to bring you to every situation, and you'll know what to do."

"Thank you, Bear."

They separated, and Bear left the room with, "Two minutes, Bish. Let's start this thing on time."

Bishop followed him out of the room, because he was ready, and he didn't want to be alone. He paused at the back of the hall, where the beautiful sliding barn door separated the great hall from the bathrooms and dressing rooms at the back of the building.

The rows were almost all filled now, and Bishop searched for Montana's family. He found them on the front row, his left side, while his family took up several rows on both sides of the aisle.

While he watched, he saw Cactus lift his arm and settle it around Willa's shoulders, and he couldn't believe his prickly brother had chosen a wedding to initially bring Willa to the ranch. She had come for Christmas Eve, but this was the first time she'd been on the ranch as Cactus's girlfriend.

Her son sat in the chair next to her, but Bishop didn't know much about him. Cactus didn't even have the full story from Willa yet.

"Bishop," Aurora said, and he turned toward the girl's familiar voice.

"Hey." He smiled at her as he took in the pretty light blue dress she wore. "Wow, you look so great, Aurora."

She gestured for him to come with her, and Bishop turned back to the hall. "I only have a minute."

"That's all we need."

"We?" he repeated as he followed her. He rounded the corner and Montana stood there. His next question died in his throat as he drank in the curves of her body in that gorgeous wedding dress. "Oh."

She lifted one hand toward him, and Bishop moved quickly toward her to take it. "I know it's bad luck to see the bride before the wedding, but I don't care," she said, her voice little more than air.

"I don't believe in that kind of bad luck anyway," Bishop said, leaning down to create an intimate space between just the two of them. "You're so beautiful." He ran his hands up her bare arms. "I'm the luckiest man in the world."

She laughed lightly and looked up at him. "Are you nervous?"

"Actually, yes." He chuckled, and it was definitely a nervous sound. "You?"

"Only of tripping in this dress," she said, lifting a handful of the skirt. "But not of marrying you." She met his eye again. "Of us, I am quite sure."

Bishop's anxiety quieted and settled, and he leaned closer. "Is it bad luck to kiss the bride before the ceremony?"

"I won't tell if you won't," she whispered.

Bishop touched his mouth lightly to hers, not wanting to smear her lipstick. He wanted to kiss her for longer and deeper, but Aurora hissed, "Your mother is coming, Bishop."

"See you out there," he said, and he turned quickly to head off Mother. "Thank you, Aurora." He gave her a quick hug and met his mom at the barn door. "I'm ready, Mother. Let's start this thing on time."

She turned and signaled, and the music stopped and changed to something else. He linked his arm through Mother's, they smiled at one another, and she said, "You belong to me, Bishop."

"Thank you, Mother," he said. "For this wedding. For everything."

"Your father would be so proud of who you've become."

Bishop laced his emotions into a tight knot and imagined his father on his other side. That allowed him to take the first step into the hall. He and Mother marched up the aisle to the altar, which he'd carved from the trunk of a huge tree they'd had removed from up by the Top Cottage after it had rotted near the top and caused the fear of falling.

He'd left the outer bark on, so it was rough and rugged, black and gray. Near the top, he'd shaved off the bark and then stained the wood underneath a light brown to show the wood grain. He'd carved around the trunk to make it an organic shape, sanded the top, and stained that too.

He'd then cut a large G into the center of it, making it stand out by putting negative space around it. In that area, he'd rubbed in shoe polish to make the G darker than the rest of the altar. He'd sealed the whole thing, and he planned to put it in front of the home he and Montana had built together, for their life together.

He reached out and touched the altar, tracing his fingers along the G, as his brothers, cousins, and Arizona got up to gather around him.

The wedding march started, and Montana rounded the corner back by the big, barn door. Her Uncle Bob escorted her down the aisle, his grin so wide and infectious that Bishop's nerves didn't have a chance to come back.

He faced the two of them, and when Uncle Bob reached Bishop, he drew him into a hug, complete with loud laughter. "You take care of her," he said right out loud. "She'll take care of you. You two are perfect for each other."

"Thank you," Bishop said, and then he took Montana's hand in his. He blinked, and the past year passed through his mind. It had been the best year of his life, and that was solely because of her.

They'd come a long way together, in every way possible. Spiritually, emotionally, intellectually, in their work, in how much they trusted each other. Everything.

Together, they turned to stand at the altar, and she reached out and traced the G with her fingertips too.

"Welcome to the marriage of Benson Flint Glover and Montana Jewel Martin," Pastor Summer said, and Bishop stepped forward and into the rest of his life.

Chapter Eleven

Cactus hated living in a basement. The temperature was never right—always too cold or too hot trying to heat up the rooms when they got too cold. He woke up one morning, realized it was May, and yet his nose was cold.

Icy cold.

He hated being cold while he slept, because then he piled on extra blankets, got too hot, turned sweaty, and basically woke up in a bad mood.

"It's fine," he told himself. "Today's going to be a good day." It was too, because he and Willa had plans to take Mitch, Mariah, and Gigi to the splash pad. The weather had been steadily warming for weeks, and as Willa didn't do a lot physically, Cactus had kept their dates to indoor venues.

He told himself he wasn't going to live in the Ranch House forever, especially now that Bishop and Montana had returned from their honeymoon and were working around the ranch with renewed gusto.

The best part about the basement was that Preacher and Judge left him alone. His two brothers lived on the main level, and Cactus had free reign in the spacious underground. He did like the solitude and silence, as he hadn't anticipated dating to be this hard.

At the same time, he wanted things with Willa to move faster. Restlessness filled him as he showered, because he hadn't done much more than hold her hand. She hadn't told him anything, and while he'd been the one to say he wanted to go slow, he actually felt like he and Willa had come to a complete stop in their relationship.

Back in his room, he dressed in his usual ranch attire—jeans and a long-sleeved shirt. Sometimes he got really hot, but he bought the most breathable fabrics, and the long sleeves kept him from getting sunburned, protected him from insects and barbed wire, and as he worked with a lot of animals, helped keep his skin dry and clean.

He did need to check that the cattle he'd treated yesterday were responding well to the antibiotics, and he needed to catch up on the paperwork Bear and Ranger demanded to detail the breeding and preventative health measures Cactus maintained.

He hoped to be down in town by lunchtime, as Willa had promised him a bologna sandwich, and he hadn't had one of those since boyhood. He loved them, and she'd claimed to be able to make one as good as his mother's.

A smile touched his face as he thought about Willa, something that still surprised him. The length of their relationship also touched him with a hint of shock. He'd been out more with Willa than any other woman, and he still wanted to see her. More and more often, if he could.

He was tired of standing still, but he couldn't make her share her past with him.

Cactus reached for his belt, his eyes catching on the photo album he'd brought over from the Edge Cabin. He paused, expecting the tear in his heart to start to weep. His chest twinged, but he reached for the book with a steady hand.

He loved this book with every fiber of his soul, despite the pain it held.

Sitting on the bed, he traced his finger along the edge of the book, his eyes drinking in the gold letters that spelled out PHOTOS.

The book held less than a dozen photos, but they meant a great deal to him. He opened the cover and looked at the first one. He and Allison smiled out at whoever looked at the picture, and Cactus recognized pure happiness when he saw it.

This picture held all of the emotions he'd felt on his wedding day. He didn't recognize the man in the picture though, as Cactus had been someone completely different back then. Someone who'd never really endured a hard day in his life. A cowboy who had the world in the palm of his hand. A man blissfully in love with a beautiful woman, who also loved him, and whom he'd believed he'd spend the rest of his life with.

Only two years later, Cactus had already started what had turned out to be a decade of living alone, talking to only three people in his family, and working until his bones ached.

He'd come leagues in the past eighteen months, and he didn't want to go back to either man. Not the one he was when he'd married Allison, and not the one he'd been in the years following his son's death.

He looked at the other pictures in the album, all of them of him and Allison, or just one of them. Their first Christmas. Her birthday party. A few showing the stages of her pregnancy.

The last photo in the album had been imprinted on the backs of his eyelids for how often he'd studied it. This was the only photo of his son he owned, and while he disliked looking at his own face, he did love the sight of the tiny face showing at the top of the bundle of blankets in Allison's arms.

"I love you, buddy," he whispered, strange as such a thing might be. He'd never had a chance to get to know his son, but the child had come from him, and Cactus felt as though he'd lost part of himself so completely the day Bryce had died.

He turned the page, though there wouldn't be another photo. He'd tucked his father's letter into this album, because he knew he'd always be able to find it that way. Bishop had found the letters last year during the upper cabin remodels, and all of Cactus's siblings had received a letter from Daddy.

My Brilliant Charles was how Cactus's letter began, and he had most of it memorized by now. He did have an excellent memory, but he liked seeing the words in black and white too.

Daddy hadn't known the married Cactus, nor the hermit

he'd become after the tragedies in his life. His letter still spoke truth to Cactus's heart and soul, and when he'd first read it, he'd wondered if Daddy *had* somehow known what he'd have to go through to become the man the Lord needed him to be.

As he set his own schedule and was the only vet at Shiloh Ridge—except for when he needed extra help in a crisis—he had time to read his letter again.

My Brilliant Charles,

I have put off writing your letter the longest for a reason I cannot name. Perhaps it's because you already know more than I do about Shiloh Ridge, so I have no career advice to give you. Maybe it's because I trust you to continue to be the perfect companion to Bear after I'm gone. The two of you have always been the best of friends, and I know that won't change.

Remember when you lost your final paper for one of your last classes? It was large animal diagnostics, I think. Bear got in his truck, and he drove all the way to college station to help you find it. He found a lab that could recover things from a burnt up hard drive, and he got that paper back for you with hours to spare.

Your family loves you, Cactus, and they'd do anything for you. I know you like to do things your own way, and you don't need anyone's help. But that doesn't mean you need to hold yourself apart from them. If you'll just let them into your prickly heart, you'll find the joy the Lord has in store for you.

Grandmother loved you to bits and pieces, Cactus. She loved your saltiness, as it made her laugh and reminded her of her father. She loved your wit and sarcasm. She loved your fierce independence, your heart of gold, and your ability to weather all storms. For all of those, she called you Cactus, because a cactus can endure the harshest of conditions. They can stand strong and tall despite little resources, the heat of the strongest sun, and the lack of relief.

Native American culture believe cacti to be representative of unconditional love, because of how strong and enduring they are in such bitter situations. I know you like to joke that you dislike people, but I think that's untrue. I think you love everyone, but you don't have the energy and time you need to give every person the unconditional love they need.

So you pick and choose who you'll give that to, and I hope, my dear son, that you'll always pick your family. Find a good woman and pick her. Choose your children all the days of your life.

Remember Mother after I'm gone, Cactus. She will need your resiliency, your strength, and your unconditional love. Bear will need it. Judge will, and Preacher will. Mister will, and Arizona will. Cactus, I fear Bishop will need you most of all, so don't overlook him because of his bluster and insistence that he's okay.

Stay strong and tall for them. Provide the foundational rock for them. Remember who you are and dig deep into your core when things go wrong and threaten to drag you under.

That's what cacti do.

I love you. I loved you the moment I found out Mother was pregnant with you, and I've loved you every moment since. You taught me that books and studying were important. You taught me that I couldn't treat all of my children like Bear, because none of the rest of you were Bear. You taught me to be stronger than I thought I could be, and to love deeper than I thought possible.

Please forgive me for being upset that you wanted to leave Shiloh Ridge for eight years to become a veterinarian. Of course that's what you should've done, and I think you're an amazing man for sticking to your convictions and proving me wrong.

I will miss you so very much. I hope you will not miss me too badly, and that you'll find a way to help the others do the same.

With all my love,

Dad

CACTUS PRESSED HIS EYES CLOSED, THE BLACK LETTERS still swimming in his vision. Daddy had not been happy when Cactus had told him he'd be going to Texas A&M for eight years. Almost a decade he'd lived away from the ranch, learning and studying and expanding his horizons.

He didn't want to go anywhere else though. He'd always known he'd return to the generational land that sustained him, and when he had, Daddy had welcomed him back with open arms and plenty of love.

He'd passed away only fourteen months later. Cactus's guilt had known no end then. He'd missed so much of his father's life right there at the end, and he'd felt wildly removed from everyone who'd lived on the ranch for the eight years he'd been gone.

He drew in a deep breath and let it out slowly. "I love you, Daddy. All is forgiven, and all is well."

He closed the book, stood, and went upstairs to get to work, feeling strong, straight, and hopeful.

Now, if he could just figure out a plan to accelerate things with Willa, Cactus would be one step closer to once again holding that world in the palm of his hand.

A WEEK LATER, CACTUS RODE TO CHURCH WITH JUDGE AND Preacher though he usually drove himself. He'd been sitting with his family every week, so going with others was just the next step.

"Is Willa teaching today?" Preacher asked from the front seat.

"Yes," Cactus said.

"Good," Judge said. "I like her sermons."

"She does have a way of saying things that make sense to me," Preacher said.

Cactus said nothing, because Willa's sermons were the reason he'd started coming to church regularly. He still wasn't sure where he stood with God, but he enjoyed church more, and he'd kept praying through everything.

He walked into the chapel with Judge and Preacher, noting the row where Bear sat was mostly full. Judge took the remaining seat on that row, leaving Preacher and Cactus to slide onto the pew with Mister, Ward, Ace, and Holly Ann.

"Howdy, Mister," Cactus said quietly.

"Cactus." He looked up from his phone briefly, and Cactus surveyed the audience that sat closer to the front than he'd like. A woman caught his eye, and a smile appeared on her face. He sat up straighter, not sure what was happening.

She looked away, and relief filled Cactus. Surely everyone knew he and Willa were seeing each other. They weren't keeping things a secret, and he'd taken her out several times in the past several weeks.

He glanced over to the woman, and she was staring at

him again. She raised her eyebrows and looked to Cactus's right. Everything made sense now. He looked at Mister and back to the woman, and she grinned fully.

Cactus's heart pounded. "Mister," he said. "There's a brunette over there who's eyeing you."

"What?" He looked up, obviously annoyed Cactus was interrupting whatever he was doing on that blasted phone.

Cactus ducked his head so his cowboy hat concealed him from the woman. "There's a woman over there looking at you," he whispered. "Big time checking you out."

Mister searched his face, and then shook his head. "I'm sure that's not true."

"Oh, it's true." Cactus was used to watching people, and he'd gotten very good at reading faces and intentions. "You should talk to her after church."

Mister scoffed. "I am not doing that."

"Okay, whatever." Cactus straightened and looked up to the dais. The choir started to sing, and a few people in the audience clapped along. Cactus never did, but he sure did enjoy the rousing opening number.

Willa got behind the microphone, and Cactus beamed up at her. She was glorious and gorgeous with the light coming in from the windows behind her, and she grinned out at everyone.

"Welcome, my friends," she said, and she absolutely meant she wanted to be friends with everyone in the congregation. "Today, I want to talk about turning to the Lord for help when you feel so buried that you don't know which way to turn. I think we all find ourselves there at some point in our lives, and if you haven't, you should probably get down on your knees tonight and thank the Lord for all He's given you."

She paused, and it seemed like even the babies knew to be quiet.

"I'm not one who's talking abstractly either. I have been in a position where I felt six feet under. I once found myself in a relationship that was dangerous to my health, and not just physically. Mentally, spiritually, and emotionally too. I made choices to stay in that relationship that led to some of the worst moments of my life. I ended up pregnant without a husband, and there are so many complications to a situation like that."

Cactus stared at Willa, his heartbeat pounding and pounding and pounding. It thumped through his whole body, and he could barely hear her next words.

"You might be wondering how someone as sinful as me dares to stand up here and teach you how to be better. I've wondered that myself, but I think it's a true testimony of the goodness of God. He is merciful and kind, my brothers and sisters. If you repent, He will forgive you. I know this with ultimate certainty, because I have experienced it. I know He will do for you what He did for me."

She continued to detail the steps of repentance and the beauty that came into one's life when they did.

Cactus heard her voice. It had often soothed him. Today, though, every word felt like a knife straight to his heart. Stabbing, stabbing, stabbing, because she had never told him any of the things she was currently spilling to the whole dang town.

After over two months of real dating. Not a word that

she'd not been married when she'd gotten pregnant with Mitch. Not a word about her ex-boyfriend and the dangerous relationship with him. Not a word about her transformation.

Nothing.

He'd gotten *nothing*.

He stood up and glared at her before stepping over Preacher and striding right out of the chapel.

Chapter Twelve

illa caught the iciness in Cactus's glare, and it
flowed straight into her veins, almost making her
voice stumble. He practically ran out of the chapel without
looking back, and Willa's mind blanked. She looked down at
her phone, where her notes sat.

She'd had several experiences this week that had shaped
this sermon, including Cactus's patience with her. They'd
enjoyed several amazing dates over the past few weeks, and
while he hadn't kissed her yet, Willa was okay with that. She
liked holding his hand and talking to him about anything he
wanted to say. She was good at starting small talk, and he
didn't ask her hard questions.

He didn't press her on anything, and she'd actually appreciated that.

"Be patient with yourself," she said. "It takes time to
change, but it's always worth it. The Lord will gently lead
you and encourage you along the way. His patience with you

is endless, and if you find yourself feeling impatient or frustrated, all you have to do is pray for more of what you feel like you lack."

Willa needed to do that, but with everyone looking at her, she couldn't truly identify what she was lacking at the moment.

Cactus, for one, she thought.

She managed to make it through the rest of her sermon, but it felt disjoined and she delivered it in a somewhat stilted way. She finally ended, and the choir got up to do their final number. She didn't direct them during Sunday services, which was a good thing as her face already felt like she'd stuck it in a microwave and let it run for an hour.

The service ended, and everyone stood to leave. She normally went to stand in the foyer to talk to the patrons. Today, she nearly fell down the steps, and she was late getting out to the door. Lots of people had left already, and Willa pasted a smile on her face as she shook hands and accepted praise for her honesty and advice.

As the crowd thinned, she found Cactus leaning against the wall near the hall that led down to the offices. He had his arms folded and his cowboy hat pushed low over his eyes.

Still, she could see him, and their eyes met. He pushed away from the wall and came toward her, causing Willa's pulse to scatter through her body.

"Interesting sermon," he said, but his voice didn't convey that he truly believed it was interesting.

"Thanks," she said, feeling about three inches tall standing in front of him. He'd always stood several inches taller than her, but she'd never felt so small in his presence.

His eyes blazed with anger, and Willa wasn't entirely sure why. He leaned closer to her. "How can you stand up there and say all of that?"

"Good sermon today, Miss Knowlton," Elaine Pike said as she passed.

"Thank you," Willa said, flashing a smile as the woman left the chapel. She swallowed as she looked back to Cactus.

"Your girlfriend is amazing," someone else said, and Cactus looked at Leon Houser like he'd fillet him alive. "So inspiring." He somehow got between Cactus and Willa and shook her hand. "I love listening to people who have real experience with their religion."

"Thank you," Willa said, very aware that Cactus was now fuming. She didn't know how to diffuse him when he turned into a bomb like this, but if she didn't, he was going to blow up.

Leon left, and Cactus glared at his back. When he turned back to her, she said, "I was just using my real-life experiences to help get across a gospel principle."

"I don't have a problem with that," Cactus growled. "I have a problem with you not telling me a *single* thing you just stood up in front of the whole town and confessed." He gestured toward the chapel doors, his voice growing louder and louder.

"You didn't ask," she said, hating the slightly accusatory tone and implication.

His chest heaved, and he drew in a long breath, calming down a bit. "I told you things I've not told anyone else. I've shared things with you no one else knows. That's what people do, Willa, when they're dating. You never said you weren't married to Mitch's dad. But your last name isn't Corning, which means you were married at some point. Or maybe not. I don't know. That's the problem, Willa. *I don't know.* You haven't told me anything about your past. We've been dating for over two months, and I've gotten less than every person who happened to show up at church this morning."

She searched his face, panic pouring through her. "Has it occurred to you that I'm not proud of my past?"

"Has it occurred to you that I'm not going to judge you? Or that I *want* to know everything about you—good, bad, and in between?"

No, that had not occurred to Willa. She'd been operating from a place of fear—and only fear—when it came to Cactus. She'd been *afraid* to ruin things with him by telling him anything. She'd been worried that he wouldn't want her if he knew about the misdeeds in her past.

"You comin', Cactus?" Preacher asked.

Cactus turned toward his brother, who stood with Judge. "Yep." He met Willa's eye again, reached up and touched the brim of his hat, and said, "Ma'am," before walking out.

"Cactus," she said after him, but his long legs just kept moving.

"Willa," someone said, and she turned toward Marvin White. "Excellent sermon, Willa. Simply excellent." The older gentleman wore a wide smile and shook her hand with both of his. "You remind me so much of my father. He was such a good man, who'd just stumbled a time or two along the way. He always righted himself though, and I admire that so much...."

"WHAT ARE YOU GOING TO DO ABOUT CACTUS?" PATRICK asked the next morning.

"What do you mean?"

"What do I mean?" Patrick looked over at her. "I heard your argument. I'm pretty sure everyone in the building heard what he said to you."

Willa looked out the window, pure embarrassment moving through her. The same feeling had kept her silent yesterday, and she hadn't called or texted Cactus. She should've. She'd known it the moment she'd awakened this morning.

She managed to put Mitch on the bus, and she'd put on her best dress for her hearing with the judge in only another forty-five minutes.

"I don't know what to do," she finally admitted.

"Why haven't you told him anything?" Patrick asked, making a turn onto Main Street.

"I'm scared."

"You've been seeing him for months."

"Just two."

"It's still plural," Patrick said. "And you want it to be three, then four, and then more. I know you, Willa, and I've seen the way you look at that man. I've seen how he looks at you." Patrick looked over at her, his eyes filled with wisdom and knowledge. "You have nothing to be embarrassed of. You've made mistakes, sure. Everyone does. You've turned them all around, and you've come out the other side where you need to be."

Willa noticed the buildings getting a little taller and a little older. "I just need to get through this hearing."

"Yeah, and if you get your driver's license back, you're going to drive right up to Shiloh Ridge to talk to that vet."

"I don't know, Patrick."

"I do, Wills." Patrick pulled up in front of the courthouse. "Just answer one question, okay?"

She sighed in an exaggerated way. "Okay, fine. What?" She looked at her brother, and he stared right back into her eyes.

"When you picture yourself in five years, living your best life, are you alone?"

Willa closed her eyes, thinking of her best life. "No," she said.

"If you're not alone, who are you with?"

Cactus's face floated through her mind, and she opened her eyes. "Fine," she said. "I'll talk to him today."

Patrick grinned at her, and Willa just shook her head, though she couldn't help smiling too. "Go on, now," he said, nodding toward the steps that led to the courthouse. "Go get your driver's license back."

WILLA DROVE DOWN THE DIRT ROAD THAT LED TO SHILOH Ridge Ranch. The arch over the road announced her arrival, and the looming homestead on her right reminded her of how many men lived and worked here.

Cactus had told her his cabin was getting remodeled and he was living somewhere else, but she couldn't remember where. He'd told her that there were enough Glovers up at the ranch to help her any time she should need it, and she certainly needed it today.

She gripped the wheel at ten and two, because she hadn't driven in a while, and she wanted to do everything by the book now that she'd gotten her driver's license reinstated. She only had a temporary permit on a printed piece of paper, but she'd never been prouder of something so thin and lightweight.

The hearing had been no more than twenty minutes, and the line at the DMV had been miraculously short. With the drive down the south highway, Willa had arrived at Shiloh Ridge just after noon.

"Lunchtime," she said, and her stomach pressed together and then flipped over. She crested the hill and came to the road that led down to the barn where she'd gone for Christmas Eve and Bishop's wedding. To her right sat the homestead, where a large gravel pad acted as a parking lot.

A couple of trucks sat there, and Willa pulled Patrick's car next to a large, black pickup. Willa got out before she could turn around and go home, and she held onto the railing as she went up to the porch.

Cactus didn't live here, but hopefully she'd run into someone who could help her find him. The windows had been opened somewhere, because she heard men talking, and then a round of laughter as she climbed the steps to the porch.

Gathering her courage, she reached out and pressed the button for the doorbell. She didn't think she'd have enough strength to knock on a door the size and width of the one here. Another rousing commotion of laughter filled the air, along with a few dogs barking, and she wasn't sure if the doorbell rang or not. This place had some good sound-proofing, that was for sure. Willa adjusted her purse over her shoulder as she waited for someone to answer the door.

"Do I knock again?" Willa asked herself after several seconds of standing there, looking up at the tall door. She'd come all this way…. She reached out and pressed the doorbell again.

This time, she heard the faint sound of the bell, as well as the dogs barking. The door opened, and Willa braced herself to have to ask for Cactus when someone said, "Hush up, now."

Instead, she found the man himself standing there, a joyful smile on his face. It dropped off his mouth instantly, and he said, "Willa," with plenty of surprise in his voice. Tank and Galaxy barreled out onto the porch, nearly knocking her down. They'd grown a lot in the past few months, and she stumbled backward.

"Whoa, whoa," Cactus said, darting forward to grab onto her. Another black and white dog came out onto the porch too, but he was calmer, with a doggy smile on his face. "Tank, Gal, sit. *Sit.*"

The two dogs obeyed their master, and Willa's heart crashed like cymbals against itself and her ribcage. Cactus steadied her, his eyes meeting hers and asking a silent question.

You okay?

She must have conveyed to him that she was, because he released her and stepped back, still holding one hand out to his hounds to keep them seated. Music played from inside the house, along with the unmistakable sound of a lot of people talking. It sounded like they were having a party in the middle of the day on a Monday.

"I'm sorry to interrupt," she said, smoothing down her blouse. "Do you have a minute to talk?"

"I suppose I do," he drawled even as someone called his name from further inside the house. He looked over his shoulder and then back to her. "You can come in." He retreated into the house, taking the dogs with him, and Willa followed him.

"Wow, this place is beautiful," she said, taking in the grand staircase that led up to the second floor. The foyer was a wide hall with a bookcase on the wall next to the stairs, and an arched doorway that led into the room where all the noise was coming from. Windows filled the front of the foyer, bathing everything in beautiful light.

"Who is it?" a man asked, and Willa tore her eyes from the fine craftsmanship of the house to look at Bishop, Cactus's younger brother. "Oh." His eyes widened with surprise. "Hi, Willa."

"Hello, Bishop," she said, falling into her professional, pastoral voice. Foolishness filled her, first at thinking she was anywhere near Cactus Glover's league. This house oozed money, and her face heated with embarrassment over her pathetic rental.

The man exuded charm, charisma, and power, and he could have any woman he wanted. Why would he possibly want her?

He'd walked over to Bishop and said something, then he turned back to her. "We don't bite, Willa. C'mon in."

"I don't want to interrupt," she said. "Perhaps another time would be better."

"Is your brother waiting outside?" he asked. He stood so far away, and Willa needed to bridge this distance between them.

Thankfully, Bishop patted Cactus's shoulder and left them by going back under the arch into the other room. Willa took a tentative step forward. "Something amazing happened, and I wanted to tell you about it." She swallowed back her nerves and her fears and all of her reservations. They were huge and sticky, and she could barely breathe past the lump in her throat. "There's so much I want to tell you. I just don't know how. I don't have the words, and I'm so scared you'll think so terribly of me."

She shook her head as tears filled her eyes. No. She had not come here to cry. She wiped at her right eye—the leakiest one—and shook her hair back. "First, please forgive me. I know I hurt you by staying silent on my past, and I'd like to fix that between us."

"Is that right?" He settled all his weight on his right foot and added, "Why's that?"

Oh, he was going to make her work for it. Fine. She could do so. She glanced down as Galaxy and Tank both circled and then lay down at Cactus's feet. The dogs looked at her like, *You'll have to go through us to get to him. Good luck.*

"You're quite important to me," she said, that ball of emotion and fear and humiliation rising up. "You've somehow integrated yourself into my life, and I like you there."

His eyes widened for only a moment, and then everything about him turned into marshmallow. He dropped his head and relaxed his stance. He came toward her, toeing the dogs out of his way, until he took her right into his arms.

Willa melted into him, held him with all the strength she had, everything trembling she clutched it so tightly inside.

"I like having you in my life too," he said, his voice that familiar gruff growl when he spoke with emotion. "But I feel like we're at a standstill, and it did hurt me that you told everyone things I didn't even know." He stepped back. "I had so many people asking me about you and talking to me about you, and I felt like a complete idiot, because I don't know anything about what you said yesterday."

Willa nodded, her eyes trained on his strong jaw, because she couldn't look him in the eyes.

"Hey," he said gently, but Willa's whole world wobbled with the kindness in his voice. "You're going to cry again, aren't you?"

"It's not a bad thing," she whispered.

"I still feel stupid, making you cry."

"It's because you're so nice," she said. "Just like with the cookies. It's not because I'm sad or upset—though I am upset with myself. I just...."

He placed two fingers under her chin and lifted it, making her look at him. "Hey, my beautiful." His smile had been painted by God Himself, because he was so gorgeous. He wiped that leaking right eye again. "It's okay. I forgive you."

"Thank you," she whispered. She drew in a deep breath, nearly intoxicated by the nearness of him. He smelled like fresh cotton and sweat, horses and dirt, home and happiness and health. "I do have a lot to tell you." She glanced past him as laughter filled the air. "You seem busy right now though."

"Have you eaten lunch?" he asked.

She shook her head. "No, I was in court this morning. I didn't even eat breakfast."

His eyebrows went up. "Court?"

"Cactus," someone said, and they both turned toward Bear, his oldest brother. "Oh, sorry. I didn't realize...Sammy's almost here."

"Okay," Cactus said. "We'll be right in." He faced Willa again, stepping to her side and lacing his hand in hers. "It's sort of a party today. We don't have parties every day. But there's a ton of food, and Sammy will be here with a cake in a minute."

"Must be someone's birthday."

"That it is," he said, grinning at her.

Willa knew that look. The man had a way of wearing mischief in his eyes, so it looked like a good thing. "It's *your* birthday, isn't it?"

"That it is."

She laughed, though a vein of frustration pulled through her. "Why didn't you tell me?" She wasn't a bad cook, and she'd have made him all the steak and eggs he wanted, followed by plenty of cake and ice cream. Oops, *cheesecake* and ice cream, as he'd told her once that he loved strawberry cheesecake more than anything.

He sobered, his dark eyes flashing dangerous fire her way. "You never asked."

The three words lashed at Willa's insides, but before she could say anything, the front door opened, and Sammy walked in. Bear's wife carried their baby in one arm and a brown grocery sack in the other.

"Praise the stars," she said breathlessly. "Take this, Charles. Hello, Willa." She handed the paper bag to Cactus and the three-month-old baby boy to Willa. "I hit Ranger's truck, and the blasted cake fell." At least half a dozen storm clouds swirled around her head as she strode into the kitchen, already yelling for help.

Willa hadn't held a baby in a very long time, but she easily tucked the little boy into her chest. He'd gotten rounder and pinker since his birth, and he was about the most adorable child in the whole world.

She beamed down at him and said, "Look at you, baby. You're the best thing ever, aren't you?" The tiny boy who wasn't really that tiny grinned up at her, swatted his hand forward, and babbled something that sounded suspiciously like, "Yep."

"Stetson looks just like your brother, doesn't he?" Willa looked up at Cactus, who stood there staring at her, his eyes wide and filled with an emotion she couldn't quite identify. "I mean, look at those eyes." She looked into them again, struck by them. "*So* blue, just like Bear's."

Willa looked at Cactus again, and he still hadn't moved. Other men started streaming out of the other room, all of them looking at her and Stetson. Cactus finally tucked the bag of groceries into his arm, and he faced Sammy as she came back into the foyer.

"Sorry, Cactus," she said, wiping her hand across her forehead. "I swear I've lost my mind." She looked like she might start crying too, and Willa's heart went out to her.

"You own a mechanic shop," Willa said. "You can fix Ranger's truck."

Sammy smiled at her, and she looked so tired. "Yeah, I'm not too worried about it. I was going slow. I just...I don't even know what happened. I pushed on the gas instead of the brake and rear-ended it. That baby's made me lose my mind." She smiled at the infant though, stepping forward to reclaim him. "Thanks, Willa."

"Anytime," she said. "I haven't held a baby for far too long." She actually mourned the loss of the chubby human being, with the soft scent of cotton and powder and lilac he carried.

"Did you come for lunch?" Sammy asked, looking from her to Cactus. "I didn't think Cactus had told you about it."

"Okay," Cactus said, taking a couple of steps toward the arched doorway. "You already ruined my cake, Sammy. Maybe you should quit while you're ahead."

Sammy grinned at him, but since his back was turned, Willa couldn't see his expression. He continued into the other room, and Willa stood there, unsure of if she was invited to stay or not.

The cowboys came back inside, many of them talking to or over each other, and she watched Bear step over to Sammy and kiss both her and the baby before they went under the arch.

"Come on," Bishop said, linking his arm through Willa's. "Ace?"

"Yep," another cowboy said, stepping to Willa's other side. "We're goin' in there, Willa, and it's gonna be loud." Ace Glover grinned at her. "But my fiancée made all the food, and it's fantastic." He leaned closer to her. "Plus, Cactus has been downright prickly since yesterday, and we need you to smooth him out."

"*So* sharp," Bishop muttered, watching the doorway. "Spiny. Salty. Can you try to sweeten him up too?"

Willa had no idea what to say to either cowboy flanking her. She knew she'd probably have left had they not stepped to her side, and she had no choice but to walk with them as they moved toward the doorway.

"Salty, yes," Ace said. "He definitely needs that whole cake to himself."

"What are you two doin'?" Cactus asked as he filled the doorway, his eyes dark and hooded beneath that crazy-sexy cowboy hat.

"Nothing," Bishop said with plenty of innocence in his voice. He passed Willa to Cactus, and Ace slipped away silently as well.

Willa looked up at him. "I heard something just now... Charles? Sammy called you Charles."

He looked down at her, his spines retreating. "It's a long story."

"Oh, so we both have a couple of those." She smiled up at him. "I'll stay for lunch and the party if you want me here. And I'm prepared to tell you several long stories if you have time."

He pressed his lips to her forehead, sending sparks and showers and tingles through her whole body. "I'm yours today, Willa," he whispered before stepping back and leading her into the nicest, biggest kitchen she'd ever laid eyes on.

Dozens of men and women milled about, and when Bishop yelled, "Okay, Mother. Hit it!" the house filled with deafening music, and everyone started to sing the most Texan rendition of *Happy Birthday* Willa had ever heard.

The best part? She joined her voice to the rest of the people in the room, easily integrating into them, into ranch life, into the party, and into Cactus's life, despite her mistake.

As the cheering and whooping happened, Willa grinned from ear to ear. Yes, because she'd been there to celebrate with her boyfriend for his birthday.

But mostly the smile belonged to the deep gratitude she had for Cactus's forgiveness, his willingness to try again, his patience with her, his kindness, and his friendship.

The smile belonged to the gratitude in her heart for the Lord, and His loving kindness, His forgiveness, and His gentle guidance that had led Willa to this homestead on this ranch on this day.

Chapter Thirteen

Cactus had prayed for a miracle that morning, and God had delivered. He'd delivered in the form of a gorgeous redhead, a birthday cake, and his family.

He couldn't stop smiling, though he really didn't like the look Mother wore on her face, nor the way she kept glancing at Willa as if she'd start interrogating her at any moment.

He hadn't liked Sammy's comment about him not telling Willa about today's luncheon. Heck, he hadn't even known about it until an hour ago. His birthday wasn't actually until Saturday, but Zona and Duke's wedding had trumped his forty-fourth birthday, just as it should have.

"Okay, okay," Holly Ann yelled. "Quiet down."

Bear whistled through his teeth, and that got everyone settled enough for Holly Ann to talk. "I know how y'all like to hear what's on the menu."

"Really, just Ida and Etta care," Cactus murmured to

Willa, who stood at his side. He'd put his arm around her and tucked her right against his body, in fact. He wanted her there, and he wanted her to know he wanted her there.

"So we've got steak bites with a spicy aioli," Holly Ann said. "Because Cactus loves steak." She smiled at him, and he nodded once back at her. She was a pretty woman, with long, dark hair that Cactus knew his cousin really liked. Ace had had a rough patch with Holly Ann there for a while, but they'd worked things out fine and fixed them and had been together for over a year now with hardly a break.

Cactus had known Willa for a year too, but he wasn't anywhere near the stage of Ace and Holly Ann.

He pictured Willa with that baby boy in her arms again, and everything male inside him fired, and fired hard. He wanted a child of his own so badly. One that would live and grow. One he could nurture and teach about horses and dogs and spend time with.

When he thought of that child, it wasn't the four-day-old infant he'd loved and buried. It was a brand-new baby, with pearly skin and reddish hair.

Stetson did look almost exclusively like Bear, but Cactus hoped any child of his would look absolutely like Willa Knowlton. The woman intrigued him. Interested him. Haunted him. He wasn't in love with her yet, but the moment she started sharing real, personal things with him, he knew he would be. Maybe that was why he'd been so upset she hadn't done that yet.

You didn't ask.

She'd said that to him yesterday, and he'd wanted to rage

at her. Tell her he didn't want to pry, that he trusted her to come to him when she was ready. But he'd been thinking about it for twenty-four hours now. If he wanted to know something, he better ask.

"And Sammy got a vanilla and chocolate cake from Acker-mans," Holly Ann said, finishing up. Cactus had missed most of the menu, but he knew what potato salad looked like for crying out loud. "It fell in the car, but it'll still be delicious." She gave Sammy a warm encouraging smile, and Mother stepped up to the counter.

"I'll say grace," she said, folding her arms and beaming at Cactus.

He loved his mother with his whole heart. When he'd retreated from the family, she'd let him go. Whenever he came up to the Top Cottage, she let him in, day, night, dawn, or midnight. When he'd gone to college, she'd calmed Dad and encouraged Cactus to be who he needed to be. Mother had always done that, and she had a unique way of seeing people and connecting to them.

Cactus tossed a quick look toward her boyfriend, Donald Parker, as Mother started the prayer, and then he hurried to get his cowboy hat off his head and pressed over his heart.

"Dear Lord, we thank Thee for our bounteous blessings. Thou hast always smiled on the Glover family for one reason or another, and we acknowledge Thy hand in our lives completely. We know Thou has protected us, saved us, healed us, and blessed us and this land we love." She paused, and Cactus felt that healing power of God moving through him.

"We're grateful for miracles, Lord," Mother said. "For having Charles here today is truly a miracle, and Thou art a God of miracles. Please bless this year for him, that he will continue to heal, that he will continue to be Thy servant, and that he will continue to be the incredible influence over all of the men and women and animals here at the ranch that he's always been." She cleared her throat, and Cactus opened his eyes and looked up.

Mother had tears running down her face, and that made Cactus's throat swell and narrow at the same time, choking him.

He met Bear's eyes, and his brother put his fist over his heart, the silent acknowledgement that he would say everything Mother just had. Cactus repeated the gesture back to his brother, their silent language powerful and very real in that moment. They'd always had a bond like no other, and Cactus had never been more grateful for the loving influence of a good man like Bear in his life.

Ranger stood next to Bear, nodding along with everything Mother said, and Ward stood next to him. As the second-oldest, Cactus and Ward shared a special friendship too. Ward met his eyes and nodded, his smile small but real.

"Amen," Mother said, and everyone in the room repeated it, some louder than others. Usually pure chaos broke out after that, but today, everyone stood quietly for a moment. All eyes moved to him, and Cactus almost felt like he needed to give a speech.

Anxiety itched beneath his skin, because he did not like having the spotlight on him. He did not like being watched.

"All right," Mother said. "You're going to drive him away. Let's eat."

The eruption happened then, and Cactus actually stepped back out of the way, his preferred position at family gatherings. Mother approached, and Cactus removed his arm from Willa's shoulders so he could embrace the woman who'd given him life.

"I'm sorry, Charles," she whispered. "I know you hate that."

"It's okay, Mother." He pulled back, and she cupped his face in her hands, pure love in her expression.

"You are my favorite second son," she said, grinning. "I love you more than you could ever know."

Cactus returned the grin and shook his head. He'd had a child once, and he had some inkling of the power of parental love. "I love you too."

"Now." Mother stepped back and looked at Willa. "Can I sit by you two at lunch? We need a spot for Don too."

"Of course," Willa said, giving his mother a quick hug before she joined her boyfriend and they got in line to get food.

"You have no idea what you just got yourself into," Cactus said, bringing her right back to his side. "My mother seems nice on the outside, but she'd got quite the bite when it comes to asking questions."

"Well, I can handle you arguing with me in the chapel," Willa said. "I think I can handle her."

Cactus looked at her, surprised by her quick wit and biting words. Then they smiled together and both started to laugh.

Yes, Cactus had been granted a miracle for his birthday, and it all had to do with Willa Knowlton.

CACTUS PUT UP WITH ALL THE HAPPY BIRTHDAYS AND well-wishes for long enough to eat and then stuff himself with cake and ice cream. Really, he couldn't wait to get Willa away from Mother, Zona, Sammy, Oakley, Montana, and Holly Ann. They'd all managed to crowd in around her and Cactus, and he hadn't known it was possible to have a six-sided conversation.

Willa fit with them as if she'd been friends with all of them for a decade, and Cactus had tried to stay out of the way more than anything else. Willa loved people, and she was very good with them. Her eyes shone like diamonds when she spoke, and she had a way of asking questions and then listening to a person's answers as if she were truly interested.

He'd realized that she actually *was* interested in what other people had to say. She was interested in their lives. She was interested in knowing them and helping them.

Finally, he thought he could get away with leaving the homestead—leaving his own party—and he stood up and took his and Willa's dishes to the sink. He rinsed them and loaded them into one of the two dishwashers in the kitchen.

"Leaving?" Bishop asked.

"I'm about to blow," Cactus muttered, looking out the window above the sink. The sky only held blue today, without a single cloud to break up the color. The tree branches across the road waved in the breeze, and he really needed some of that fresh air to keep living.

"Go," Bishop said. "You can stop by for the leftovers later. Or I'll send them with Judge."

"Send them with Judge," Cactus said, because he had no idea when he'd be done with Willa, and then he had all the horses in stable B to attend to. He was checking their teeth, eyes, and ears this week, along with their hooves and legs.

He'd arranged for studs to come to Shiloh Ridge next week, and he needed to make sure all of his horses were healthy, and his mares ready for breeding.

"He's not feeling well today," Cactus said instead of detailing how busy he'd be for the rest of the day. "He'll appreciate it."

"How are things at the Ranch House?" Bishop asked. "I swear we're getting close to done with your place."

"I hope so," Ace said, joining them. "Or Holly Ann and I are going to have to live with Mister and Ward." He frowned, and Cactus didn't blame him for not being happy about that.

"Whatever," Bishop said with a scoff. "The Top Cottage will be available by October."

"Maybe," Ace said darkly.

"We're meeting about it this week," Bishop said. "Don't worry."

Cactus mentally reminded himself of the Friday morning meeting and stepped away from the still-squabbling younger men. He returned to Willa and put his hand on her shoulder. She looked up at him, and he didn't have to say anything for her to know what he wanted.

A blip of fear crossed through her hazel eyes, and then

she stood. "Thank you for lunch," she said to Holly Ann. "It was great talking to all of you too."

"Cactus," Sammy said, and he paused though he wanted to fly from the homestead. "You bring her back now, okay?"

"We'll be busy," Cactus said, and Sammy grinned at him.

"I bet you will," Oakley said with way too much suggestion in her voice. Cactus just glared at her, and then everyone else before leading the way to the door that went out onto the deck. No sense in taking Willa back through the lion's den just to leave the house.

He leaned his palms against the railing across from the door and took a deep breath. The clicking of the door gave him even more relief as the laughter and chatter faded to almost nothing.

He closed his eyes and blew out his breath, immediately taking in another lungful of air.

"You don't like crowds," Willa said, stepping to his side. "Not even your own family."

"That I do not," he said. "Sorry about that. You'd probably like to stay for a while."

"We need to talk," she said very quietly. "I want to be with you."

He adored those six words, especially in Willa's voice. He opened his eyes and took her hand in his. They went down the steps to the yard, and he took her back up the hill beside the shed Bishop had built for Ranger to store his ATVs in.

"Yes, I think you said you had some amazing news," he said. "Or something that had happened."

"Yes," she said, and Cactus simply minded his footing and gave her time. "I had to go to court this morning, because I'd petitioned the judge to lift the restrictions on my driver's license. He did, and I'm able to drive now."

Cactus had to look at her, because he had to have somewhere to put his surprise and happiness. She wore a truly beautiful smile, and she seemed like she'd managed to do something fantastic.

"That's great news," he said. "Congratulations."

"Thank you." She sighed and brushed her hair back on her right side. "I haven't had a driver's license for about two and a half years now. They took it away from me after the accident."

He'd heard her say she'd been in a car accident. He hadn't realized it had been her fault. To him, she was lovely and innocent, and of course it would've been someone else's carelessness that had caused her great harm and injury.

He swallowed at his assumptions, knowing he shouldn't make them about anyone in any situation.

"The car accident is also why I lost Mitch," Willa said. "It's why I became a pastor. And why I'm here in Three Rivers at all." She looked up into the sky, seeming to gain strength from it. "I guess I'll start there, though there are other stories."

"I don't need them all," Cactus said. "Right now." She'd mentioned not being married to Mitch's father in church yesterday. So yes, she had other stories to tell still.

"I was texting and driving," Willa said. "I was distracted, and I caused a four-car accident in Temple, on the highway there near this really busy intersection."

Cactus started praying, because he needed divine help to know how to respond to her in a way that would keep her in his life and let her know that her past mistakes didn't make him like her less.

"I was injured the worst, as my car had been hit three times. I didn't wake up until most of the other people had been taken away. Two cars had been cleared. Mine was still fused to this truck, and I was in a panic over Mitch."

"I can imagine."

"Can you?" Willa asked, looking up at him.

Cactus's throat itched, and he didn't want to steal the story time from her. He simply nodded.

"Mitch was okay," she said a few moments later. "Charming the EMTs with his sign language and playful personality. I had a shattered right leg and hip, and I needed back surgery. I still have quite a bit of pain from those things, depending on how hard I push myself."

"I'm so sorry," he said, though he knew some mistakes did have consequences that lasted a lifetime.

"I lost Mitch to his father," she said. "He claimed I wasn't fit to care for him, and custody had been an on-going battle anyway. Me texting and driving put him at risk. I was fined for reckless endangerment of a minor child. I could've gone to jail if Patrick hadn't gotten me a good lawyer."

Cactus didn't know what to say, so he said nothing. He kept the prayer going in his heart and mind, hoping the Lord would guide him.

"I lost my job at the Montessori school," she said. "I was the choir director. I couldn't teach voice lessons anymore. I couldn't sit on the piano bench for longer than a few minutes, so I couldn't teach piano." She sighed and studied the ground now. "I'd lost everything because I thought I needed to send my ex-husband a nasty text."

She paused, and Cactus came to a stop too. "I wasn't a very nice person, Cactus. I had Mitch out of wedlock with a man named David Knowlton. We never married. I did marry Trenton Wendell a few years later, but we fought all the time. We didn't have any children, and our marriage lasted maybe a year. Mitch was six. I decided we had each other, and that would be enough. Then I lost him too."

Cactus took both of her hands in his and squeezed them. "Why isn't your last name Wendell then?"

"Because Mitch's isn't," she said. "I wanted us to have the same last name." She shook her head. "It's stupid, I know. It might not make sense, but in my head, at the time, it did. I changed my name, and now we match."

He nodded, though he wasn't sure he could ever understand that. A voice in his mind whispered that *he* didn't need to understand it. He only had to allow Willa to do what she thought was right.

"I lost everything that day. It took a very long time to recover. I moved in with Patrick and his wife, but they were having problems. I moved into a care facility, because my parents are elderly and couldn't really help me. I started taking classes from the online ministry, and I started changing. I started learning about God and the Savior, and I started reading the Bible for the first time in my life."

She gave him a smile that lit his whole world. "Patrick was a minister, and he helped me become one too."

"That's great, Willa," Cactus said, and he truly meant it.

"That's what I meant yesterday when I said I know what

it's like to be buried under shame and sin. I personally know what it takes to dig out from that. I've done it. It's hard, and I wouldn't want anyone to have to do it, but the repentance process is there for anyone who's willing to do the work."

Cactus nodded and then pointed to the hay loft. "Are you tired? We could go over there, and there's a bench around the back. I sit there to watch the sun set sometimes."

"Sure," she said, and they started walking north. "Anyway, I couldn't get a job in Temple. David wouldn't let me see Mitch. Patrick called when I was mere seconds away from a break-down, and he said there was a job in Three Rivers and would I like to come along. I said yes faster than anything I've ever said before." She laughed a little, and Cactus marveled at how easily she seemed to be able to speak of such hard things.

"I've been here for a little over a year," she said. "It's been wonderful, and I don't plan on leaving." She nodded like that was that, but then she continued. "I'm still healing, and I'm still learning. I have Mitch again, and that's a whole new ball-game too, especially with school ending next week." She sighed, and this time it carried more happiness. "But I'm a completely different person than I was three years ago. I gave up all the hate in my heart. I gave away all the bitter-ness and all the anger. I don't have much—or anything really—but I'm happier than I've been in a very long time."

Cactus slipped his arm around her waist and pulled her close to him. They walked the rest of the way to the bench in silence, and as the sun had passed high noon, it bathed them in light and warmth. He let his mind replay all she'd said, and then he lifted her hand to his lips and kissed the back of it.

"Thank you for telling me."

"That's all?" she asked. "No questions? No you should've's?"

"I have no idea what you should've done," he said, looking at her with some measure of surprise at her question. "I wasn't in your situation."

She nodded and looked out over the fields in front of them. "What are you growing here?"

"Ace has hay and grass everywhere he can," Cactus said with pride in his voice. "We have corn down the hill from the homestead and Bull House. Wheat up by the Top Cottage and down on the Kinder Ranch."

"How big is this place?"

"Oh, big," Cactus said with a sigh. "We all help with planting, the cattle drive, and harvesting. Our cattle is all grass-fed for the most part, though we supplement with hay in the winter if we have to."

"How big is big?" she pressed.

"We have thirty thousand head at Shiloh Ridge," Cactus said. "We practice rotational ranching, which means we move cattle every single day. Ward, Mister, Judge, and Preacher do a lot of it. We have seven full-time cowboys that live up here with us."

"What's rotational ranching?"

"We put sheep out onto the pasture first," he said. "Then the cattle. Then chickens, actually." Cactus smiled, because he did love chickens. "Ward added turkeys a few years ago. If you put them on the grass in the right order, you can get your grass to grow faster, feed more animals per acre, and sell them for more."

"Fascinating," Willa said, those eyes bright. "So you take care of sheep, chickens, horses, cattle, and turkeys."

"And pigs," he said. "We have about a dozen pigs."

"What kind of diseases do pigs get?"

Cactus grinned at her, because she was so darn good at asking questions that got other people talking. "A variety of diseases," he drawled. "Do you still talk to David?"

She flinched slightly and then looked away. "I have to," she said. "He's my son's father."

"How did you get Mitch back?"

"David got arrested," Willa said. "Drug possession and distribution. My lawyer in Temple filed for an immediate transfer of custody and a protective order, and we got it. I had to stay down there for a few weeks to get everything ironed out; that's why I was gone."

Cactus nodded. "And David?" he prompted again.

"He's in jail," she said. "He got four years. Who knows if he'll actually be in that long? Either way, I don't have to deal with him right now, though he can call if he wants to, and the judge said I better let him talk to Mitch."

"Has he?"

"No, sir." Willa studied her hands, her whole body radiating tension. "He's a loser, Cactus. I'm so embarrassed I ever saw something in him."

"Hey, hey," Cactus said, lifting his arm around her again. "People change, Willa. I know that better than anyone."

She looked up at him. "Yeah, your mother's prayer said a few things."

"Yeah." He closed his eyes and leaned back into the bench, letting the sun warm him from head to toe. "I'll have to tell you my story another time, beautiful. I'm tired from that birthday party."

She giggled and curled into his side, and the two of them simply breathed beneath the sunshine, and Cactus once again thanked the Lord for a pretty perfect day.

Chapter Fourteen

Ace Glover glanced at his phone, checking the time again. "Is Cactus coming?" he asked. Everyone else had already arrived in the conference room in Ranger's suite. They all seemed utterly unconcerned that the meeting should've started fifteen minutes ago, and they'd busied themselves with something else.

Ward and Ranger sat behind a giant screen, discussing something to do with Two Cents.

Bear and Bishop had their heads bent over a blueprint, their voices low as they talked about the Kinder Ranch.

Aunt Lois and Zona had been reviewing something for the wedding tomorrow on Zona's phone, and they looked up and met Ace's eyes.

"He's coming," Ward said, glancing over. "He texted me twenty minutes ago that he'd just gotten out of therapy. He'll be here."

"Okay," Ace said, but his mood didn't improve. He'd been

trying to meet with everyone for months now, and he honestly felt like they were all putting him off. Shoving him into a corner because he wanted the same thing Bishop had already gotten.

It's not a competition, he told himself. Yet he sometimes couldn't help competing with Bishop. In this case a beautiful wife, nice house, and a loving marriage. *If it was a competition, he's already won. Let it go.*

The door opened, and relief hit Ace square in the chest. But Montana walked through the door, a red folder in her hand. Ace frowned, not because he wasn't happy to see Montana, but because she wasn't Cactus.

The man didn't drive fast, and he seemed to operate according to his own timetable.

"Hey," Montana said, sliding into the seat next to Ace. "You want to see what I've been working on?"

He looked into her sky blue eyes, hope filling his heart. "Yeah, show me."

She smiled and flipped open the folder and put it in front of him. "This is what I tell everyone I show my designs to. You might not like something you see, and that's fine. Sometimes I can move elements around. Sometimes I can't." She licked her lips, and Ace had seen her do that before when she was nervous.

"I'm going to like any of them," he said, his pulse picking up speed. "I'm just glad someone seems to know I need a house to live in."

Bishop looked up and across the table to where his wife sat next to Ace. He grinned at them and said, "I can't wait to see which one he likes."

"You knew she had these done?"

"I live with the woman," Bishop said, rolling his eyes. Bear tapped something on the papers in front of them, and Bishop returned his attention back to the blueprint.

"Okay," Montana said. "In this one, you have less bedrooms, but that massive gourmet kitchen you said was a must-have." She spread the papers out in front of him, and Ace had to blink to be able to tell what he was looking at.

The door opened again, and Cactus walked in with, "Sorry I'm late. Dr. Thompson had an emergency appointment before me." As if Cactus's arrival ran the world, Bear rolled up the blueprints and Ranger emerged from behind the big screen.

"Let's get started then," Bear said, and Montana looked at Ace.

"We can talk after," she said.

Ace nodded, pressing his teeth together so he wouldn't say anything he'd regret. It wasn't Montana's fault his cousins and brothers did what they wanted, when they wanted.

He schooled his thoughts, because he loved his family. From time to time, he got a little annoyed with them—like right now. But overall, he wanted to be at Shiloh Ridge, and he couldn't imagine raising his family anywhere but right next door to Bishop, Ward, Ranger, and everyone else, so his children could play with their cousins the way he'd done.

"All right," Ranger said, standing up. "First, we want to welcome everyone who doesn't normally attend our weekly meetings. Ward is going to start with a report on the cattle, and Ace has something to say about the grass pastures, and then we'll get to the reason y'all are here—his proposal to build on the ranch." He nodded at Ward, who turned the screen around so everyone could see it.

"The rotational ranching is going well with the new meat birds," he said. "Our layer hens saw a huge decline this spring because of those pesky foxes, but because we got all those meat birds, as well as a dozen new turkeys, they're turning the fields over just as quickly as we need them to. That means we'll be able to keep eighty percent of our cattle as completely grass-fed, which increases our profit on those cows by thirty-seven percent."

Ace's mind started to wander with all the figures. He didn't care about data and percents, but both Ranger and Ward thrived on such things. The only time he cared about numbers was when treating soil, which he tried to do as naturally as possible.

Ward droned on about the scheduling of the semi-trucks for market day, and then he said, "I want to propose that we hire a cowboy or cowgirl dedicated purely to sales." He looked around the group. "I can't do it as the foreman. It's too much for me to oversee the sales and the whole upper ranch."

"Why's that?" Bear asked.

"I was overseeing sales before I started as foreman," Ward said, throwing Bear a look tinged with irritation and yet respect. "It's a full-time job for about five months out of the year, and I can't keep up with it and monitoring and overseeing everything else on the ranch, from breeding, to health, to agriculture, to watering, to building, to road maintenance, to the blasted birthday parties and weddings that we do here."

Silence fell over the group, and then Cactus started to laugh. "Hey, I tried to get out of having a party for my birthday."

Ace grinned at him, because he did know how to break the tension in a room. Sometimes he was the source of the tension, but he was really good at diffusing situations he caused and then some he didn't.

"I agree with Ward," Ranger said quietly. "It's a ton of work to get temporary cowboys to the ranch to bring in the herd. It takes a dozen phone calls to schedule all the trucks we need to haul the cattle. Then payments have to be made for all of that, and the sales manager does all of that."

"He's dealing with the sale of hay too," Ace said. "And we always have a surplus of that. So there's ads that have to be put out, or calls to be made. Deliveries organized." He shot a look in Ward's direction, glad when his brother acknowledged him.

"Not only that," Ward said. "But we don't just show up on market day and collect hundreds of thousands of dollars. Buyers have to be found for the cattle, and sometimes we get lucky and sell the entire population to one company, but sometimes we split them into three or four. It's a lot to coordinate, a lot to document, and a lot to follow-up on."

"And it's the main way our ranch continues to make money," Cactus said.

"Well, kind of," Ranger said, glancing around. He steepled his fingers in front of him. "Our investments outpace our sales now, which is why I can't be out on the ranch as much as I once was."

"We hired another full-time cowboy for you," Bear said. "And we moved Ward into the foreman position."

"Maybe it's time to pull Preacher over too," Ranger said.

Ace didn't come to many meetings, and he really liked how respectful they all spoke. They bounced ideas around and came to conclusions without getting upset, and he reminded himself to cool his hot head.

"Probably," Ward said. "Ace planted an additional seven hundred acres down on the Kinder Ranch, and I know he's working fifteen and sixteen hours a day to keep up with it all."

"So is Preacher though," Ace said. "And Judge. And Mister. The four of us can barely keep the animals rotated in the grass fields—Ward helps a ton with that still—and the sprinklers moved on the agricultural ones. If you pull Preacher from the team, it won't keep happening."

They couldn't take Preacher from him. He worked like a dog, and he never complained. In fact, Preacher didn't say much of anything. When he did speak, it was usually in some sort of riddle or parable, or a quote from a scripture. He showed up on time, and he did the job. Always.

He was reliable and strong, and Ace should probably let him know how much he appreciated the work he did for the agricultural side of the ranch.

Not that Ace was his boss or anything. They just happened to all work together, and Ace had the training and know-how to deal with the fields. He often found himself with a wrench in his hand too, to make sure the equipment they owned could plow, plant, pollinate, and then harvest their crops.

"So are you saying you need another body too?" Bear asked, the frown between his eyes deepening.

"If you take Preacher from me, for sure," Ace said. "Probably even if you don't, yes."

"I didn't know this was going to be a hiring talk," Bear said. "Two more people?"

"We have the cabins for them," Bishop said. "It's just a salary, and Bear, come on. We've all lived that life for a year. It's not much."

"It's fifty thousand dollars," Bear said. "How is that not very much?"

"Ranger," Ward said.

"We made fifty thousand dollars on the sale of ten percent of our stock in VanCorp," Ranger said. "Yesterday."

Bear blinked at Ranger, and Ace experienced a slip of victory. There was no reason they couldn't hire more men. This wasn't a case of reuse or recycle. This was the fact that they'd taken Shiloh Ridge in a new direction with the rotational ranching Ward had introduced five or six years ago, and they were simply too big now to keep everything as it was.

"How many head do we have this year?" Ace asked, drawing every eye to him.

"Thirty-one thousand," Bear said.

"How many did we have six years ago?" He looked at Ward and Ranger, as they had the computer in front of them. Ward's eyes immediately lit up, as he'd followed Ace's train of thought.

"Let me see," he said, sitting back down and tapping on

the keyboard. Bear glared at Ace, but Ace just waited for Ward to look up the information.

"Twenty thousand," Ward said.

"So we've grown by over thirty percent," Ranger said, and Ace could've done that math too.

"With the same amount of land," Ace said. "Ward did that with his new method of grass field rotation. We're doing thirty percent more work with the same manpower. We can afford two more guys."

"Or girls," Montana and Arizona said at the same time.

"Yes," Ace said. "Men or women."

"We have the cabins," Bishop said again.

Everyone looked at Bear, who finally waved his hand. "Make it happen, Ward."

"Thank you, Bear." He sat down, and everyone looked at Ace.

He swallowed and stayed in his seat. "I don't have a presentation prepared," he said. "We basically covered the grass pastures. They're doing really well this year, thanks to a lot of rain in February and March, and Ward getting the meat birds in plenty of time. The chickens are integral to making sure the grass pastures turn over faster."

Cactus stared at Ace, and he cleared his throat. "So we're good there. As for my house, I'm the one who knows every inch of farmland and pastureland on this ranch. Bishop got a little over half an acre up against a rise where we didn't lose hardly any pasture or field capacity."

He sat up a little straighter. "I like being at Bull House, because it's central and close to all the stables, which I also work in a lot."

He took out a single piece of paper, and it felt woefully inadequate compared to the blueprint Bear and Bishop had been looking at earlier and the huge monitor Ward had used.

"The homestead is here," he said, pointing to the square he'd drawn. "Bull House is here, and down around the curve but back up on the bluff is the Ranch House. Down the other way, there's the barns and stables, and True Blue, and now Bishop's place." He deliberately didn't look at his cousin and best friend. "There's a bit of land across the lane from True Blue, just after the road goes up toward the south cabins and the Top Cottage."

"It's next to the cemetery," Aunt Lois said.

"Kind of," Ace said. "It's not on the same level. There's a little meadow there, and we don't plant there. It's about three-quarters of an acre, and I do put a few cows on it every few weeks, but it wouldn't cut into our rotations at all."

"I know where you're talking about," Bishop said. "It's private too. A little secluded." He gestured to Ranger, who started tapping and clicking. "We'll have to test it to make sure it's stable enough to build on. It hangs over a cliff a bit, doesn't it?"

"A tiny crest," Ace said, and Ranger turned the monitor again.

"It's here." He clicked, and the meadow where Ace wanted to build his home came into view, in green and brown satellite view.

"Yes," Ace said. "That's it."

"Good spot," Cactus said.

"It's perfect," Bishop said.

"We need whole-family approval," Bear said. "But based

on what I'm seeing here, I don't see why you won't get this, Ace." He grinned across the table at him, and Ace smiled back.

"Can Montana and I take a minute?" Bishop asked.

Ranger gestured for him to go ahead. Bishop looked at Montana, and they had a whole conversation without saying a word.

"I guess I'm up," Montana said with a nervous smile. "Cactus's rebuild is almost finished. He should be back in his place in the next four to six weeks. We've hit a snag because the roofers are so far out, and that's something that Bishop and I have hired out so we can move forward with the other projects on the ranch." She glanced at Ace. "Namely, Ace's house and the remodel on the Kinder Ranch. The re-fencing put us behind on anything that wasn't our house or that, and then Cactus's project took over."

"I need another barn too," Ward said.

"I was just going to say that," Montana said. "And if we want that before the harvest...." She swallowed and looked at Ace and then away again. "I don't think we'll have Ace's place done before October."

Ace's stomach fell, though he'd anticipated exactly that. "It's okay," he said, making his voice as jovial as possible. "I think that's why Zona and Aunt Lois are here."

"I'm getting married tomorrow," Zona said. "Duke and I have a house on the Rhinehart Ranch." She reached over and took her mother's hand. "With Bishop gone, Mother's going to move into the suite here at the homestead. Then she won't be alone up in the Top Cottage, and she'll have main floor living."

Aunt Lois smiled at Zona, and no one at the table looked the least bit surprised, Ace included.

"So Holly Ann and I will live in the Top Cottage until the house in the meadow is done."

"Right," Montana said. "Bishop and I think it'll be done by Christmas, Ace."

"The perfect Christmas gift." Bishop grinned at him, and Ace couldn't stay mad at him. He was the one who'd brought him food last year and told him not to let Holly Ann break up with him. It was because of Bishop that Ace had her in his life at all.

"I don't think Mother will be in the homestead for long," Cactus said, and everyone looked at him.

"Is this on the agenda?" Bear growled.

Cactus flicked a look in his direction, clearly unconcerned about Bear's grizzly attitude. "Nope." He didn't say anything else, and Ace quickly looked at Aunt Lois.

She squared her shoulders and looked only at Cactus. "Nothing has changed in my life."

"Yet," Cactus added in the exact right spot so that it fit in the sentence.

"Charles."

"I'm simply saying you and Donald Parker have been dating for what? Almost a year now? What are you waiting for?"

Aunt Lois gazed evenly at her son, but Ace's pulse had started to skip. She said nothing, and it seemed no one was going to move until she did.

Finally, Montana said, "I'm sure Lois can and will make her own decisions when the time comes. She's seventy-eight years old, after all." She stood up. "Are we done? I have a tile supplier I have to call before lunch."

"We're done," Bear said, standing too. He held Cactus's eye for a moment and then he left the room first.

"Montana," Ace said as she moved around the table toward Bishop. "I want to see the designs."

"Give me fifteen minutes," she said with a placating smile. "Sorry, Ace. Really. Fifteen minutes." She already had her phone out, and she strode from the conference room.

"Come on, bro," Bishop said, clapping Ace on the shoulder. "Let's go get some lunch. She'll be at least twenty minutes, but it's going to be worth it." He grinned, and Ace could only laugh and go downstairs with Bishop, who got to work in the kitchen.

Chapter Fifteen

Arizona Glover's pulse had been elevated for seven solid days. She hated it. She hated feeling out of control, and a sprinting heartbeat made her feel wildly out of control.

"Zona," Sammy said from the doorway, and Zona turned around at the sound of Sammy's voice. She blinked out of her thoughts, because she hated being in there as much as she hated being out of control.

"Is that the dress?" Sammy came toward her, baby Stetson in the sling strapped to her chest.

"Yes." Zona had the garment bag with her wedding dress clutched to her body. It would probably take an act of God to get it out of her hands. Her fingers ached from how hard she gripped the hanger.

"Are you ready to go?" Sammy asked, pausing and peering into Zona's face.

Zona couldn't speak, and that really said so much. She'd

grown up with six brothers, and she'd developed a loud voice by the time she was six months old just to be heard. She never had a problem voicing her opinion—and she had plenty of those.

"Sweetie." Sammy took her into a hug, her baby fussing between them. She giggled at Stetson and said, "Sorry, baby," as she stepped back. She repositioned the pacifier in the baby's mouth and met Zona's eyes again. "Cold feet? Or just nervous?"

"Aren't they the same thing?" Zona asked.

"No," Sammy said slowly, her eyes firing questions at Zona. "They're not the same thing. It's normal to be nervous on your wedding day. You're doing something huge. Amazing, but huge. It's a massive life change. You're leaving the ranch where you've grown up. Moving out of the house you've shared with your mother for years." Sammy took Zona by the shoulders, her smile so real and so perfect.

She was the sister Zona had never had, and she loved her with that same bond. She trusted Sammy completely.

"It's a big change," Sammy said again. "It's normal to be nervous and a little afraid of what tomorrow will bring. But having cold feet? That means you have some serious doubts that could prevent you from becoming Duke Rhinehart's wife."

Zona looked down. Before she could answer, Mother entered the room. "Zona, if we don't leave now, we'll be late."

Zona nodded and turned toward Mother. "Let's go."

"Zona," Sammy whispered.

She didn't turn back. She didn't have "serious doubts" about marrying Duke. She loved the man; he loved her. She was ready to step out of the Glover family shadows and be her own person. She was.

She'd still work on the ranch. All she had to do was take the service road over the property line and then the same road down from the Top Cottage she'd always used. Duke would work his family's ranch, and they'd live happily-ever-after.

The only thing Zona worried about was losing her family. Bear had assured and then reassured her that only a couple of people knew about what Duke had done almost twenty years ago. Him, Cactus, Mother, and Ranger.

Zona had refrained from pointing out that four people was more than two, and four more than Zona wanted to know. When Duke had told her about the theft and embezzlement of funds from Shiloh Ridge, she'd been horrified.

At the same time, she believed people could change. She believed everything Willa Knowlton had said last week about repentance, that the Lord had the power to wipe the slate clean, and that God could change a heart so completely that the person it belonged to had become someone radically different.

She hadn't been through that particular experience herself, but she'd heard her boyfriend's agony. She'd seen his regret. She knew his change had been complete.

And the bottom line got her every time. She loved him. She'd fallen for him quickly, because he was quiet where she was loud, and he was steady when she felt wild, and he was calm when she got upset.

They both loved the Lord, and they both loved ranching,

and Zona had spent beautiful afternoons on horseback laughing and talking with Duke.

She smiled at her mother as she passed. "Sorry, Mother," she said. "Scottie will work her magic on me, and we won't be late for the wedding, I swear."

Mother said something Zona didn't catch because she'd gone by so fast. Now that she was moving, she couldn't slow down. Outside, she found Bear sitting on the steps at the Top Cottage, and she collapsed beside him, the garment bag with her wedding dress in it still clutched in her hands.

"I got the box with the shoes and your veil," Bear said, reaching over and slinging his arm around her shoulders. "You ready for this, Arizona?"

"I don't know, Bear. How do you know if you're ready for this?" She looked up at her big brother, needing and wanting him to tell her everything would be all right. He always had before, and Zona had worshipped Bear growing up. He'd practically been an adult by the time she had started voicing her opinions, but he'd always listened to her, the same way Dad had.

Bear smiled at her, his eyes crinkling the same way Mother's did. "You just know, Zona. The same way you knew you loved him, and the same way you knew you wanted to be his wife when he asked you to marry him."

Zona nodded, reflecting on those instances. "I do love him, Bear. I'm sorry that complicates things for you."

"It doesn't," Bear said, the porch squeaking behind them as Sammy came outside. He twisted and groaned as he stood. "Ready, sweetheart?"

"Your mom has a basket of brushes and hair supplies," Sammy said.

"I'll get it." Bear walked off to do that, and Sammy extended her hand to help Zona stand. The two women looked at one another, and Zona had no words. She was four years older than Sammy, but Bear's wife held infinitely more knowledge about life and love.

"No cold feet?" Sammy asked.

Zona shook her head. "Just nervous."

"Nervous we can deal with," Sammy said, looping her arm through Zona's and guiding her down the steps. "You should've seen me and Oakley on our wedding day. I swear, if she hadn't been in the brides' room with me, I might not have made it down the aisle."

"Really?" Zona asked. "You were nervous to marry Bear?"

"You've met your brother, right?" Sammy asked, giggling. They reached the truck, and she started unstrapping Stetson so she could put him in the car seat. "The man strikes terror into the heart of all who see him."

Zona held the door for Sammy. "Not you, though, Sammy. The man worships the ground you walk on."

"No, I know." Sammy handed Stetson to Zona, who cuddled the baby and kissed his cheek. "I was still nervous. It's normal."

Zona stretched into the truck and tucked Stetson into his car seat. Bear and Mother joined them in the truck, and they made the trek down to the homestead. Duke had agreed to be married at Shiloh Ridge, and Mother had hired a hair stylist and a makeup artist to come up to the ranch to help Zona and all the other women get ready for the wedding.

The sun bathed the world in warmth and light, and the perfect breeze blew through Bear's open window as he drove. Zona caught sight of the party planning van at True Blue, and Mother said, "Everything is going to be perfect, Zona."

"Thank you, Mother," she said. Mother had planned Bishop and Montana's wedding, and Zona had been working with her for six months to pull off the perfect wedding. She had no doubt it would be too, as Mother left no stone unturned and no detail unattended.

At the homestead, she finally relinquished her grip on the dress, and Mother whisked it off somewhere while Scottie ushered her into a chair. "Right here, honey." She snapped her gum and stood back, taking in Zona from top to bottom. "Lovely hair. Great length." The woman barely topped five feet, and she had ten years on Zona. She had a sharp look in her bright blue eyes, and Zona thought they'd be great friends if they had the opportunity to hang out.

"Your mom says you want an elegant up-do," Scottie said, coming closer and running her fingers through Zona's hair. Someone had brought in a full-length floor mirror, and Zona faced it. Scottie rounded her and their eyes met in the glass. "I think that's going to do just fine, but I have something a little more modern in mind. You have beautiful, thick hair, and I know this will be spectacular." Scottie smiled at her. "If you're willing to live on the wild side a little."

"Oh, didn't you know? I'm the wild child of the Glover family." Zona grinned at her. "Do what you want."

Sammy, Oakley, Holly Ann, Montana, and her daughter,

Aurora, sat at the long island, individual mirrors in front of them. The makeup artist, Birdie Newman, instructed them in how to put on the foundation, the blush, then eyeshadow.

They chattered like the best of friends, which of course, they were. They didn't work the ranch the way Zona did, and she'd spent so much time with Duke and his family, she hadn't been around here as much.

She felt left out, but she didn't know how to rectify that. She knew that if she needed something, she could call on anyone at the island, and they'd all come help her—even the sixteen-year-old girl.

She kept her eyes closed, because Scottie told her to, and she listened to the conversation happening on the other side of the couch.

"Is Oliver coming to the wedding?" Oakley asked.

"No," Montana and Aurora said at the same time.

"Really?" Sammy asked. "He came to Bishop's."

A silence followed, and then Montana said, "Aurora is thinking she might want to date other boys."

"Sort of," Aurora said, and if Zona had been able to see her, she'd probably find her glaring at her mother. Zona knew, because she'd often had conversations like this with Mother.

"What does that mean?" Oakley asked. "Sort of?"

"It means my mom thinks we're too serious."

"You are," Montana said. "And you're going into eleventh grade, and your whole future is out there somewhere."

"Maybe it includes Ollie," Aurora said.

"And maybe it doesn't, but you won't know it, because you're so wrapped up in him."

"Your mom could be right," Sammy said. "I dated this guy in my mechanical program when I was younger, and it was Brandon-this and Brandon-that. I missed family parties and very nearly didn't finish my training." She sighed. "He was handsome, but the moment he broke up with me, I could see everything I'd given up to be with him."

"Ollie doesn't ask me to give up anything to be with him," Aurora said.

"He kinda does though," Oakley said.

"I thought you'd be on my side," Aurora said, clearly put out.

"There are no sides," Oakley said. "Not for me. I just want you to be happy."

"Oliver Walker makes me happy."

"You don't even know if someone else—or something else —will make you happy," Montana said. "That's the whole point."

"How does he ask me to give things up?" Aurora asked.

Zona tilted her head as Scottie tugged on a piece.

"Everyone knows you two are together, right?" Holly Ann asked.

"Yes," Aurora said.

"So by being his girlfriend, you can't go out with anyone else," Oakley said.

"You can't just go to a dance with friends," Sammy added.

"You spend all your time with him, which means you're not spending it doing something else," Holly Ann said.

"Like FFA," Montana said. "Or taking that horseback riding teacher training this summer."

"Mom," Aurora said sharply.

"You're not doing that?" Zona asked, adding her voice to the conversation. Her eyes flew open. "Aurora, that training is spectacular. You could make money for the rest of high school with it, and we have horses right here at the ranch."

"See?" Montana asked.

"Maybe I don't want to do it," Aurora said.

"Mm hm," Oakley said as Sammy said, "Oh, girl, you're a liar," and Holly Ann said, "Yeah, right," and Zona said, "You were so excited about it."

The conversation stalled there, and Zona closed her eyes again. The front door opened, and Ida called, "Sorry we're late," and she and Etta came bustling into the kitchen with Aunt Dawna. "We'll be so fast getting caught up. Mother already has her makeup done."

Chatter broke out as everyone welcomed Ida and Etta, and asked Ida about her upcoming wedding. When a lull in the conversation happened, Aurora said, "Fine," in a burst air. "I'll do the dumb class."

"I'm not paying for it if you're going to have an attitude." Montana sounded like she wouldn't too.

"I'll just ask Bishop."

Oakley burst out laughing, and Zona couldn't help smiling too. Aurora knew what to do to get what she wanted, because Bishop couldn't tell the girl no. That, coupled with the fact that he literally had billions of dollars, and what was the two-hundred-dollar fee for a riding class?

Zona could pay it thousands of times over too—and she would, because knowing how to teach horseback riding to someone had changed her life. It had given her a skill and provided the confidence Zona needed to hold her own with all of her brothers on the ranch.

Montana started lecturing Aurora about asking Bishop for money and how she better not be late for work out at Bowman's Breeds on Monday morning.

"If I break up with Ollie, then what?" she asked next. "We were planning to drive to work together every day."

"Whoa," Ida said. "You're breaking up with Ollie?"

"We missed so much," Etta said. "I told you not to miss your alarm."

"I didn't," Ida said, her voice tight and furious. "I had to help my neighbor this morning."

"You have a truck," Montana said as if the twins weren't bickering.

"Yeah, that Bishop bought for me," Aurora said with plenty of sarcasm in her voice.

Zona laughed with the other ladies, and a few minutes later, Scottie said, "Open up, sweetie. Let's see what you think."

She opened her eyes. Her dark mahogany hair had been loosely plaited along her forehead, creating a crown of sorts. Scottie held up a mirror behind her, and Zona tilted her head to see better.

Her hair had been swept back in big chunks and looped into an elongated bun. "It's perfect," she said. "It'll hold the veil perfectly."

"We can add some flowers too," she said. "For when you take the veil off after the wedding."

"Yes, please." Zona had never considered herself a girly girl. In fact, she'd worked hard over the years to prove to everyone that she could do everything her brothers could. But this wedding had brought out every feminine quality she possessed.

She wanted a lacy dress. She loved flowers, ferns, and ribbons. She wanted delicate, delicious food. She loved shoes and fingernail polish.

She looked down at her nails as Scottie started tucking some blooms into her hair. "These are lily of the valleys," she said. "They smell incredible."

"I can smell them," Zona said, admiring her light blue nails. She adored blue, and she'd chosen it for her main wedding color. Peach accompanied it, along with ivory and a darker, burnt orange.

Mother had sewn ties for all of the men in the family out of a gorgeous dark orange silk, and Zona had asked the women in her bridal party to wear blue or ivory. Since most of them had periwinkle dresses from Montana's wedding, they were re-wearing those.

Zona didn't care. She wanted her sisters-in-law to feel comfortable and beautiful today, because they were gorgeous.

"Okay, you're done," Scottie said. "I need Sammy next."

"Right here," Sammy said. Zona took her spot at the counter, and Birdie pulled her kit over and glanced at Zona.

"You have great bone structure," she said with a smile.

A couple of hours later, everyone was properly made up, with their hair done.

"Time to move over to the barn," Mother announced, and the party moved down the road.

They unzipped bags and started stepping into their

dresses. Zona waited, because she needed help shimmying into the gown and buttoning up the back of it.

Once all of her bridesmaids were dressed, and Mother had put on her sparkly, rose-gold gown, one more garment bag got unzipped.

Zona stood in her slip while everyone gazed at the wedding dress.

"I love it so much," Sammy said. "Where did you get it?"

"It's Grandmother's," Zona said.

"The grandmother who gave everyone their nicknames?" Holly Ann asked.

"Yes." Zona gazed at the eggshell-colored dress as Mother hung it on the high hanger and smoothed it down.

"It's stunning," Oakley said. "You did a great job modernizing it."

"Thank you," Zona said.

"What did you do?" Montana asked, stepping forward and touching the bodice.

"The old lace on it had turned gray," Mother said, admiring the dress.

"I removed it," Zona said. "That took the longest, honestly." She stepped over to the dress too. "Then we cleaned it to remove the yellowing, and then I stitched on the new lace over the top here." She fingered the flowered lace in a bright white. The two shades of white played well together, despite being quite different.

"I had to take the waist out, because I'm a little bit more of a barrel than Grandmother was." She smiled fondly at the memory of her grandmother. She hadn't ever gotten a nickname besides a shortened version of her real name, but she'd loved her grandmother deeply.

She'd taught Zona how to braid hair and how to properly prepare a sourdough starter. She'd shown Zona how to repot plants one morning and then reupholster a chair the same afternoon.

"The train was too long, so we shortened that," Mother said, bringing Zona out of her head. "Aurora helped." She beamed at the girl, who smiled back at her.

"Right," Zona said, also grinning at Aurora. "She gave me the idea to make the hips swell a little bit so I'd have some shape."

"I like adding some flair to clothes," Aurora said, ducking her head.

"It's lovely," Holly Ann said.

"Let's get you in it, dear," Mother said briskly. "You can't be late for your own wedding."

"Duke's here, right?" she asked. Mother had timed and coordinated everything down to the minute.

"Yes, Zona," Holly Ann said. "Ace texted a few minutes ago to say all of the Rhinehart's had arrived, and they all went into the grooms' room with Duke."

"It's going to be fine," Sammy said, giving Zona a smile in the mirror. "Come on, sweetie. It's almost time to get married."

Chapter Sixteen

Willa stood behind the altar, a sleek piece of furniture that looked like someone had taken a bar-height, free-standing island with tall chrome legs and padded the top and then pulled a piece of robin's egg blue fabric over it.

Lace covered that, and Willa pressed her palm into the top of it, and it was soft and plush. She caught Cactus's eye in the first row, and she smiled at him. His intense gaze made her blush from fifteen feet away, and she wished she'd be walking down the aisle with him.

Zona was more traditional than the other Glovers had been, and she was having everyone in the family walk down the aisle in her wedding party. Cactus would have to go into the back soon, and Willa would be left to stand in front of the crowd.

She reminded herself that she stood in front of a crowd of people and preached the gospel all the time. Performing a wedding was the highlight of her job, and she kept her smile on her face.

Soon enough, all of the Glovers got up as if they'd all set a simultaneous alarm and it had just gone off. They buttoned jackets and adjusted ties and cowboy hats as they walked out, and wow, what a sight that was.

Tall, broad-shouldered men wearing tuxedos and midnight black cowboy hats?

Delicious.

Willa swallowed and met her brother's eye. He sat with his girls and Mitch and gave her an encouraging smile.

Willa absorbed it and used it to strengthen herself. A few minutes later, Bear and Sammy appeared at the front of the line, baby Stetson cradled in Bear's outside arm. Sammy clung to the other one, and they wore large smiles as the music began.

They came forward, followed by Ranger and Oakley, and then Cactus, who walked with his cousin Etta. Ida and her fiancée Brady followed them, and then came Ward, who escorted his mother.

Judge walked down the aisle with his mother, followed by Preacher, who escorted Aurora. Ace and Holly Ann followed them, along with Bishop and Montana.

Duke Rhinehart came last, and he walked alone.

As each person came forward, they removed the flowers that had been pinned to their clothes. Bear pushed his boutonniere into the padded altar, the blue and peach flowers matching the fabric and lace perfectly.

Sammy did the same, but her flowers were a darker orange with an ivory accent flower. One by one, they all pinned their flowers to the altar, creating a gorgeous center-piece for Duke and Arizona.

Once that was done and the family had made a rainbow behind her, once Duke had hugged his parents and taken his spot on the right side of the altar, Arizona and Bear appeared at the back of the hall. The wedding march began, and the audience stood.

Willa adored weddings, and the ones up here at Shiloh Ridge seemed to carry a special cadence to them she'd never felt before. The love that permeated the air here didn't exist anywhere else, and she felt honored to be the one to perform this wedding.

Thank you, Lord, she prayed, her eyes locked onto Arizona's as she came forward. She looked radiant and full of joy, and when her eyes met Duke's, the love between them streamed into the air, filling the barn all the way to the rafters.

Willa had never felt like that about a man before, and her eyes darted to the front row where Cactus had sat. He wasn't there now, and she refused to turn around and find him. The sight of him in a tuxedo was enough to give her heart palpitations, and she didn't need to be passing out moments before she was supposed to marry his sister.

Bear and Zona arrived at the altar, and Bear leaned over to say something to Duke. The two of them hugged, and then Duke touched his lips to Zona's cheek, they linked arms, and faced Willa together.

She beamed at the two of them, her thoughts coming together in that moment.

"Welcome one and all," she started. "I don't know if I'm

the only one who can feel the profound love here, but I hope not. Love is one of the most beautiful things in the world. It can be the very foundation for all other things. When a relationship is built on true, unconditional love, forgiveness can be found. Mistakes will happen, but they can be overcome when you remember the feeling you have here. The feelings you had that led you here. Life is hard, and the one thing you can always fall back on is the promises you make to each other here today, and the love you have between you."

Willa finished her talk quickly, got all of the right things said in the right order, and Duke tipped Zona back to kiss her. The family behind her erupted into cheers and applause, startling Willa though she should've been prepared.

She'd eaten meals with this family, and she'd attended a previous wedding with them. The Glovers surged forward to offer hugs and congratulations, and Willa braced herself against the altar.

Cactus's hand slid along her waist, and she looked up into his face. "Beautiful," he said, and she wasn't sure if he was talking about the wedding, the talk she'd given before the ceremony, or her. He called her *beautiful* sometimes, like other men called their wives and girlfriends *sweetheart*.

"How was my speech?"

"Exquisite." He pressed his lips to her temple, and Willa's blood burned like liquid fire.

"You look exquisite in that tux, cowboy."

"Will you dance with me later?"

Willa sure did like that he asked, as if it wasn't implied that they'd dance every song together later. "Yes," she said simply.

"Can I come over for dinner tomorrow?"

"Yes."

"Should I bring Tank and Galaxy down for Mitch sometime soon?"

"Yes."

"Can I see you every day this week?" He grinned at her, and Willa swatted at his chest, giggling. "Hey, I figured I'd try," he said. "You were just saying yes, yes, yes."

"Here comes Mitch," she said, returning his smile. "Let's see how good your signing is."

"I've been working hard at it."

"So you've been saying." She stepped away from him as Mitch arrived, and he asked if he could go into the kitchen with Aurora and get a cookie.

"Go ahead," Cactus said. "Get me one too."

His signs were immaculate, and he'd understood everything Mitch had said too. The child ran off again, and Willa turned back to Cactus. "Pretty good, cowboy. Pretty dang impressive."

"Wait till you see me dance," he murmured, taking her into his arms as if he'd twirl her around the floor right then. He didn't, but actually stepped away to help set up the tables so people would have somewhere to sit and enjoy their refreshments.

The family was having a private dinner later that night, and Willa had brought a dress to change into so she didn't have to wear her robes all day. She headed toward the back of the hall and the brides' room, where she'd hung her dress when she'd arrived.

She found Sammy there, sitting in a chair in front of the windows, nursing her baby. "Sorry," Willa said.

"You're fine," Sammy said, adjusting the blanket over herself.

"I can change?"

"Go right ahead." Sammy faced the window again, and Willa quickly switched her robes for a cute party dress reminiscent of the fifties.

"How are things with Cactus?" Sammy asked, lifting her son up onto her shoulder and patting his back. The baby grinned at Willa, his chubby cheeks absolutely adorable.

"Good," Willa said, smiling at the baby.

"Just good?"

"*Really* good," Willa said, taking the chair next to Sammy. "Can I?"

"Of course." She passed Stetson to Willa, who settled the infant on her lap and bounced him. He burped, and Willa told him what a good boy he was for doing so. Funny how in ten years, he'd be disgusting if he burped like that.

She tried to imagine herself with a baby like this, a chubby little chunky thing with a quick smile and eyes made of sapphires. She'd teach him how to sign so he could communicate with Mitch, and while they'd be years and years apart, they'd have a great relationship.

Her fantasies grew and morphed, and in all of them, she ended up at this ranch, in a cabin she hadn't seen yet, with a beautiful man who'd been nothing but kind and caring with her, her son, and the situation as a whole.

A soft sigh came out of her mouth, and Sammy said,

"Ohhh, things must be going *really* well with our dear Cactus."

Willa met her gaze, gave a little shrug because she couldn't deny it, and the two of them giggled together, Stetson joining in at the perfect moment.

"Is that baby laughing?"

Willa turned to find Cactus' mother approaching. She wore a wide smile that went with the sophistication and charm of her sparkling dress, and Willa lifted her grandson toward her.

She took Stetson and cooed at him, giving him a big, sloppy kiss on the cheek. The baby babbled and smiled, and she settled next to Willa with Stetson on her lap.

With bright eyes, she looked at Sammy. "I know what his name should be," she said.

Confused, Willa watched Sammy too. She seemed excited, and she leaned forward to put Stetson's pacifier in the diaper bag. "Yeah?"

"I suppose the naming will fall to me," she said, her face aglow.

"Naming?" Willa asked.

"My husband's mother gave all the grandchildren alternate names," Lois explained, looking down at Stetson. "She named her two sons Stone and Bull, so I should've expected it from the start." She smiled and shook her head, the warmth and love pouring from her touching Willa's heart.

"But you didn't," she said.

"I did not," Lois said. "When she first starting calling my oldest son Bear, I wasn't very happy."

"I haven't heard this story," Sammy said, crossing her legs.

The Glovers were steeped in tradition, and Willa found herself eager to hear it too.

"Priscilla was a firecracker herself." Lois gazed out the window too, most likely imagining the woman who'd been her mother-in-law. "She grew up right here in Three Rivers, and she married Ranza Glover when she was only nineteen years old."

Willa loved old stories, and she loved the sound of Lois's voice as she continued.

"Was Ranza his real name?" Sammy asked.

"Surprisingly, yes," Lois said with a light laugh. "But I'm sure you won't be surprised to learn he went by Roper."

"Oh, wow," Willa said, chuckling.

"Priscilla noted that his other brothers seemed to have these other names too. Victor worked in the very earliest stages of the space program down in Houston, and he went by Velocity. Carlton worked here at the ranch, but he went by Captain. And Seth went by Spike."

"Dear Lord," Sammy said. "Do not tell me you're going to call my son Spike."

Willa could connect dots, and she said, "So the assumed name always starts with the same letter as the given name."

"Always," Lois said. "How Priscilla came up with them to fit so perfectly baffled me a little bit." She looked down at Stetson, who yelled. His mother dug in the bag and handed him a pair of plastic keys to play with. They went straight into his mouth, where he started gumming them to death.

"He's teething already," Sammy said, sighing. "Don't say you're going to call him Slobber either."

They all laughed, and then Lois said, "His name is

obvious to me. Perhaps this is how Priscilla did it. Grand-mothers just have a special connection to their grandchil-dren, and they just know. I knew the moment I entered the room and heard him laughing."

She looked earnestly at Sammy and then Willa. "What three-month-old baby laughs like that?"

"He's always been such a happy baby," Sammy said, smiling at the boy and brushing his dark, wispy hair to the side, as if combing it.

"Right," Lois said, cuddling into him closer. Stetson waved the keys, causing a bit of clatter, and then they went back into his mouth. "That's why his name is Smiles."

Willa watched Sammy, who obviously wasn't so sure about the name. "It's actually kind of perfect," Willa said after a moment or two of silence.

"You know what?" Sammy asked. She reached up and brushed at her eyes. "It really is."

Willa wondered if step-grandchildren got special names too, and she couldn't decide if she hoped they did or didn't. After all, what would they call Mitch? Mute?

No, thank you. That term was offensive, but Deaf or Non-Verbal didn't start with an M.

"What about someone like Aurora?" she asked carefully. "Do you give them a special name?"

Lois looked up in surprise. "You know what? We prob-ably should. I haven't thought much about it."

"Hers is easy," Sammy said. "She's an angel."

"What about Lincoln?" Lois asked. "He's as important to our family as Stetson. Don't you think he'll feel left out if his brother has a special name and he doesn't?"

Sammy looked down at her hands, which suddenly twisted over and around each other. "Probably."

She knew worry when she saw it, and she loved Sammy. "What is it?" she asked gently, reaching over and touching her hands so they stilled.

Sammy looked up, her eyes bright and shining with tears. "Lincoln has struggled since Stetson's birth. He's been in trouble at school, and Bear and I are relieved there's only one more week." She swallowed and glanced at Lois. "We've been taking him to see a therapist, and Cactus is going to take him out to Courage Reins this summer."

Willa wasn't sure what Courage Reins was, but she could ask Cactus later.

"Sammy," Lois said. "I'm so sorry. Has the therapy been helping?"

"A little, I think," she said. "I still go to the shop a few days a week, and I'm thinking of pulling back completely." She looked so torn and so concerned. "I should be here for my son, right?"

Willa's throat closed, as she'd had plenty of experience with nights filled with worry and days full of indecision. She knew exactly what it felt like to not be there for her child, and she squeezed Sammy's hand.

"Lincoln is a light to everyone who meets him," Willa said. "He'll find his way back, Sammy, because he has you and Bear to help him. His grandparents, and a whole mess of cowboys who won't let him stray for long."

Sammy nodded, her smile quick. There then gone. "Thank you, Willa."

"You know," Lois said. "Light is actually a really great way to describe Lincoln."

"Oh, no," Sammy said, sniffling even though she smiled. "We are not calling him Light." She shook her head and reached for Stetson as he kept fussing in Lois's arms.

"No, that's not quite right, is it?" Lois mused. She looked out the window again, her thoughts obviously somewhere else. "We'll find something that fits him perfectly, don't you worry about that." She smiled at Sammy and then Willa. "I'll get Dawna on the case too. She's really good at this kind of stuff."

She stood as if she'd go do that right now, and she leaned down and kissed Willa's forehead and then Sammy's before leaving.

Willa marveled at the touch. At the love Lois obviously already had for her. At how easily everyone here at Shiloh Ridge, and in Three Rivers, had accepted her.

She closed her eyes and listened to Sammy sniffle and Stetson babble as she poured out her gratitude unto the Lord for bringing her to this special part of Texas.

Chapter Seventeen

"Make it happen, Ward," the cowboy told himself. As if hiring two people—full-time positions too—was so easy in the middle of the summer.

Well, it wasn't, and he had half a mind to march out onto the ranch, find Bear, and tell him to do the blasted hiring himself.

It wasn't easy, not if they wanted quality people that wouldn't quit come September—right when they needed them the most.

Ward stared down at the papers he'd printed for the applicants that had come in that week. Only five, and none of them felt like a good fit to him. Ward did so much based on how he felt, and he tossed the papers on the desk in the office at Bull House and went into the kitchen in search of something sweet.

He needed to call and order more gravel too, as the roads up here hadn't been redone in a few years. He had hay to deliver to Gavin Redd, and the new quarterly budget to complete before he met with Ranger and Bear on Friday morning.

Ward's work never seemed to end, and he mourned the days where he got up, got dressed, and got a job done outside. "Just tell me what to do," he muttered as he opened the cupboard and reached for a box of snack cakes.

He took the whole thing back into the office and unwrapped a package. As he munched through the waxy chocolate to the dense cake beneath, he pulled up the website for From the Ground Up.

He could make a phone call while he tried to figure out where to find good help. The job boards he'd been using had yielded poor results so far.

"Good morning," a woman said after he'd dialed the landscaping company. "How can we help you build your yard from the ground up?"

"Yes, hi, Wendy," he said. "This is Ward Glover up at Shiloh Ridge."

"Oh, Ward," the older woman said, though she didn't infuse any happiness into her voice. "I know what you need."

"Gravel," he said anyway.

"Yes," she practically snapped. "Let's see...Last time you ordered—that can't be right."

"It's right," he said, pinching the bridge of his nose. He hadn't actually ordered the gravel years ago—Bear had done that. Bear had done everything, it seemed. The man still worked a lot on the ranch—way more than Ranger now—but he'd pulled back quite a bit too. Ward estimated that he probably carried seventy-five percent of the load he'd once shouldered. Ward had picked up the rest, and he felt like he couldn't take a single step without great effort.

Something has to give, he thought, but he didn't know what.

"Twenty truckloads of thirty-five gravel?" Wendy asked. "Come on, Mister Glover. That can't be right."

It sounded right to him. "We're redoing our entire entry roads," Ward said.

"It's thirty thousand dollars," she said. "Plus delivery, as you guys are so far from us. And spreading, unless you're going to do that yourselves."

"How much is spreading?" Ward asked. In the past, yes, they'd call in every cowboy they could find and spread the gravel themselves. That was the way at Shiloh Ridge. Everyone worked, and they worked hard.

They fixed things. They repaired. They reused. They recycled, right down to the grass pastures Ward had been cultivating carefully with Ace for the past half-decade.

Why pay for a new truck when the one they owned could be fixed? Why pay to have someone spread the gravel when they could do so themselves, for free?

But right now, with everything Ward had going on, he just wanted to pay to have the gravel spread.

"For twenty truckloads?" Wendy sounded like Ward was putting her out, and annoyance sang through him. She didn't want his thirty grand? No problem. He'd call somewhere else.

But that only created another problem for Ward Glover, because From the Ground Up was the very best landscaping company in Three Rivers. They had the biggest and best assortment of barks and gravels, and they'd graded and prepped the roads and driveways here for the past several years.

"And we'll need a couple of new places done," he said. "With the rebar and then the three layers."

"Do you need three layers for the whole road system?" Wendy asked, something tapping on her end of the line.

"I think we just need...." Ward sighed. "You know what? I better get out there and make sure I know what I need. Can you send someone up to help me? Walk around with me and make an assessment of whether I need just the fines, or if I need the crushed stone? Or any of the roadways rebuilt or strengthened."

Wendy sighed as if such a thing would be so terribly hard. Ward gritted his teeth and told himself this was how Wendy Roberts was. Easily into her sixties, she simply wore a frown everywhere she went.

"I can get Dot out there in a couple of weeks."

A couple of weeks. Ward pressed his eyes closed. "Sure," he said as brightly as he could. "What day can Dot come?" He opened his eyes and clicked to get over to his calendar. Assorted colors to signal various people, events, and appointments assaulted his eyes, and it took ten minutes of back-and-forth with Wendy before they found a time that worked for him and Dot to come to the ranch.

It wasn't for five more weeks.

"Whatever," Ward said after he'd hung up. "It's just a blasted road." He picked up another cupcake and bit off half of it. It was just a road. Just a pasture. Just a horse. Ward needed to slow down and remind himself of why he loved ranching and why he'd wanted to be foreman at Shiloh Ridge.

A sense of newfound calmness came over him, and he closed his eyes, determined to pray—but only talk about what he was thankful for. He was not going to ask the Lord for anything. He just needed to count his blessings and express his gratitude, something he hadn't done for a long time.

As he did, he settled further, and the increased comfort and assurance that he was okay, that God was mindful of him and had him securely within His arms, only gave Ward one more thing to be grateful for.

He opened his eyes when Cactus called, "Ward?"

"In the office."

His cousin's footsteps came closer, and he filled the doorway with his tall frame a moment later. He took in the messy desk and the jackets Ward kept tossing on the arms of the couch next to where he stood.

"What's up?" Ward asked.

Cactus sighed and entered the room. He fluffed up the pillow on the couch and lay down, putting his boots right up on the armrest. Ward could only smile at the man. "Therapy?"

"Someone needs to tell me how to kiss Willa Knowlton," he said miserably. "I can't seem to get the job done, and I'm afraid I'm going to combust if I don't do it soon."

"You haven't kissed her yet?" Ward asked, realizing as the words left his mouth what a mistake they were.

Cactus growled and folded his arms, but he didn't turn his head and look at Ward. "Help me."

"Why did you come here?" Ward asked. "I haven't kissed a woman in years." He wished that weren't true, but facts could be sad sometimes.

"You've been out a ton."

"Not to kissing stage," Ward said. "I'm not Preacher. I don't kiss on the first date."

That got Cactus to chuckle, and Ward relaxed a little more too. "Let's start with why you haven't kissed her yet."

"I don't know why," Cactus said.

"You like her."

"Immensely."

"You want to kiss her."

"Terribly."

Ward had no idea how to advise Cactus. "Are you not alone? Is Mitch around?"

"I can get her alone easily," Cactus said. "When we are alone—like I was over there last night. Mitch was in the back yard with Gal and Tank. Willa's making pancakes, and we're talking, and it's easy and fun. I could simply walk over to her, take her in my arms, and kiss her." Cactus paused, this time turning to look at Ward. "I can *see* myself doing it. I *want* to do it. Then I don't do it."

"Mental block?" Ward suggested in a quiet voice.

"I'm not hung up on Allison," Cactus said. "What mental block would there be?"

"Maybe you're scared you won't do it right?"

"That's not a maybe," Cactus said miserably. "I know I'm scared, but I was scared to go to church too. Scared to go to town, even with someone. I've been scared to go to therapy, and scared to go out to Courage Reins. I do all of those things now. I do things that scare me."

"Then you've just gotta view this the same way," Ward said. "You can and do all these hard things you don't want to do. Kissing Willa is just another one."

"But I *do* want to do it." He sighed and looked up at the ceiling. "I hate that I'm so messed up. Why do I have to be so messed up? Why can't I just be like Ace and laugh about things, and get all the pretty women, and be happy?"

Ward stood up and took the box of cupcakes over to Cactus. He took a package and said, "Thanks," in a muted, tired voice.

"Cactus," Ward said on his way back to the desk. He sat in the chair with a groan. "You are not messed up. I know you think you are, but you're not. You're human, and you've been through some really difficult things. You've learned from them, and grown, and you've gotten plenty of pretty women in your life."

"I'm falling so fast for her," Cactus whispered. "What if it's too fast? What if I'm not ready? What if *she's* not ready? What if part of why I like her is because of her son? What if I can't make this work, and I'm already in love with her, and my heart gets ripped out all over again?"

He pressed his eyes closed, and Ward's heart tore for him, the answer plain now. He'd just said it. "There's your answer, my friend. You've just summed up why you don't cross the room, take her in your arms, and kiss her."

"I'm afraid."

"No, it's more than that," Ward said. "You don't want to give her your heart, and you know that when you kiss her, it's over. You'll be in love with her then, and your chest will be open, and she'll be able to reach right in and pluck out your heart if she wants to."

He took a moment to unwrap another treat, trying to find the words that would help Cactus but not push him away. It was a delicate dance Ward had been perfecting for a decade. "You have been guarding your heart for twelve years, Cactus. You buried it in that grave with Bryce. You're not just afraid. You know that if you give her access—real access —to your heart, you'll have to take it back from Bryce first, then dig it up, dust it off, and hand it to her. You'll be admitting that you're ready and willing to lose everything all over again should she squeeze too hard or throw it back in your face."

Cactus sat up and met his eyes, something intense in his.

Ward tried to smile, but he couldn't quite pull it off. "That's not just hard or scary. For you, Cactus, it feels impossible. You've put chains around your whole life for a long time. Past the chains was a twenty-foot fence, filled with barbed wire from top to bottom. If someone somehow made it beyond that, you then had a deep moat for them to cross. Then they *might* get to you. And you're prickly and salty, and there was *no way* they could get to your heart."

He looked down at the cupcake, the perfect white frosting swirled across the top of it. "She's gotten to it, and you're clinging to the very last thread of defense you have: your kiss."

"Maybe I'm not ready," he said.

Ward watched him, but he didn't agree with him. "You can tell yourself that if you'd like."

Cactus sighed and hung his head, showing Ward the top of his cowboy hat. "What do you tell yourself?" he asked.

"That I just haven't met the right woman," Ward said. "And Cactus, I think you have, and you know it, and *that's* what scares you. You're scared of surface things like being out of practice when it comes to dating and kissing. You're scared of making a mistake with Willa that will push her away. But deep down, what you really don't want to do is lose your heart again."

Cactus looked up and nodded. "I think you're right."

Ward took a small bite of his cupcake and Cactus even finished his. "What are you going to do?"

"I'm going to have to figure out how to find my heart so I can give it to her," he whispered.

"Start out at that grave," Ward said as his cousin stood up. "I think it's out there."

Cactus nodded and gave Ward a quick wave before leaving as quickly as he'd arrived.

Ward finished another cupcake and let a few minutes go by. "I lied, Lord," he said. "I am going to ask for one thing today, and that's a blessing on Charles Bryce Glover. He's a good man, with an amazing heart and a fierce spirit. Help him to know what to do and say. Guide him right where he needs to go to find happiness, joy, and peace. Protect him, and let him know that *You* will guard his heart, and that *You* will take care of him no matter what happens with Willa Knowlton."

He drew in a breath, held it, and then released it. "Oh, and it would be great if I could somehow meet the one right woman for me. I wouldn't say no to that."

Chapter Eighteen

C actus pulled into Willa's driveway and looked over to Bear. "You ready for this?"

"Yep." Bear twisted and looked in the back. "Ready, Link? You've got the cookies?"

"Yep." The boy opened the door first, and that gave Cactus the courage to do the same. He'd taken Lincoln up to Courage Reins with him over the weekend, and they'd had a good therapy riding session together.

"Get the dogs, boy," Cactus said to him, and Lincoln said he would. The truck shook as Link lowered the tailgate and Galaxy and Tank jumped to the ground. The three of them went down the sidewalk and up the porch. "He's a good boy."

"He is," Bear agreed.

"He'll come out better," Cactus said.

"I just worry about him," Bear said. "I love him so much, and I just want him to be happy."

"He'll find his way, and he'll be happy again." Cactus reached for the door handle. "Come on, brother. Let's go get this talk out of the way so I can enjoy my night with my girlfriend."

Bear chuckled, and Cactus collected the pizza from the back seat before joining his brother on the sidewalk. Willa waited in the doorway, her smile genuine and pure. Cactus saw himself crossing the porch and kissing her hello, but in reality, he crossed the porch and said, "Hey, beautiful," and handed her the pizza boxes.

Self-loathing hit him square in the chest, and all he could think about was his talk with Ward a couple of days ago. He'd gone to his son's grave, walked through his remodeled and expanded house, and tried to find his heart.

He wasn't sure he had, because it felt like he'd been operating with a stone in his chest for so long. Even now, he thought maybe he had half a heart, but certainly not the whole thing.

"Come in," Willa said, stepping out of the way. She wore a pair of navy blue shorts that fell to her knee, and a pink and white flowered blouse. She always wore blouses, and Cactus wanted to have a peek in her closet to see if she owned any T-shirts.

"I don't see a car in the driveway," Cactus said as he stepped past her.

"Oh, um, no." Willa followed him into the kitchen, and he checked out the back door to make sure Link, Mitch, and the dogs were okay. "I couldn't get the financing." She set the pizza boxes on the countertop and sighed. "I need a job."

Pastor Summers had retired a couple of weeks ago, and

Patrick Corning had become the full-time pastor. He'd kept Willa on part-time, but it obviously wasn't enough.

"School's out now, so I can't sub." She shot a glance in Bear's direction, who'd sat at the kitchen table, and he simply looked at her with those open, blue eyes. "There's really only two choices for me right now. Something in the tourist industry...or ranching."

"Willa," Cactus said, taking her hands in his. "I told you I'd finance the car. You can just make a payment to me."

She folded herself into his chest, wrapping her arms around him and holding him tight. "I know," she said. "But I can't do that."

"You can come work at Shiloh Ridge," Bear said, and Willa stepped away from Cactus.

"Thank you, Bear," she said with a smile. "I don't think I can. I can't even get in a truck. How am I supposed to get on a horse?" She shook her head, and Cactus could see the anxiety right there in her eyes. He hated it, and he'd do anything to get rid of it.

"If Mitch is coming up there anyway," Bear said. "It would probably be good for you to come with him. Only Cactus knows any sign language at all."

Cactus had discussed this at length with Bear already, and his jaw muscle jumped as he pressed his teeth together.

"Lincoln knows some," Cactus said. "I've been teaching him." Bear switched his gaze to Cactus, who stared right back. They both possessed powerful personalities, just in different ways. "The two boys would work with me this summer." He returned his attention to Willa. "I think you should call Heidi or Whitney. I know you could get a job at the bakery or the grocery store."

"I did," Willa said. "Heidi said I could come by any time and she'll talk to me. I just don't have a car to get there."

"I can take you once we talk to Mitch," Cactus said.

"I don't see how standing and walking around the bakery is any different than the ranch," Bear said.

"It's inside for one," Cactus growled.

"Heidi said she'd put me in charge of the gift baskets," Willa said. "And I can do that at a table."

"So that's taken care of," Cactus said. "I'll come get Mitch in the mornings, and he can come hang out at the ranch. Or Patrick can take him," he added quickly as Willa opened her mouth. "I know Link's grandparents take him sometimes too, and perhaps Mitch would like to tag along there too."

Willa's eyes filled with tears, and she turned away from him. "Thank you." She got down plates and plastic cups. "Thank you both."

"Don't thank me yet," Bear said, plenty of grumble in his voice. "We have to talk to that boy and make sure he understands what working on a ranch is. I'm scared, Willa, and I'm not going to lie about that."

Cactus had told her all of this already, and he looked at her somberly too. "I can admit it makes me nervous as well. I did call about a hearing dog, but there's only three organizations in the whole country who offer them for kids, and they're four months out."

Willa nodded, her throat moving as she swallowed. "Did you—?"

"Yes," Cactus said, because he hadn't discussed all of these details with Bear. Yes, he'd put Mitch's name on the list. Yes, he'd paid the five-thousand-dollar deposit. The woman couldn't even get a loan to buy a car; there was no way she could afford the down payment for a hearing dog. "I'm working with Galaxy to stay with Mitch," he said. "That's why I need him every day, beautiful. If he goes with Patrick one day, I still need to have him work with Gal. She can help him until we get a real trained dog."

She still didn't speak, and he suspected her emotions wouldn't allow it. She moved over to the sliding glass door and called to Lincoln. Bear and Cactus had lectured him the whole way here that he had to get Mitch's attention before leaving him behind or talking to him.

Cactus looked at Bear instead of watching Lincoln through the glass, and they had another hour-long conversation in the time it took for the two boys to run to the back door.

"Get them some water, boys," Cactus said, signing the words as he spoke them.

Mitch gestured that he would, and he grinned at Cactus as he climbed up on the counter to get out a bowl. Cactus's heart filled with love for the child, and he wanted to help him. *You should help others who need it too.*

The thought filled his mind, and Cactus made a decision right then and there to do just that. There had to be other single moms who needed help. Other deaf children who needed a hearing dog and couldn't afford one.

Kids with cancer, and kids who needed life-saving surgeries. Cactus had plenty of money in the bank; he could help more kids.

A part of his heart started to beat with new life. A part he hadn't known had been so damaged.

He realized now, a dozen years after his son had died of congenital heart failure, that he should've been donating money to heart research and to a fund for children with the same condition that had stolen Bryce from him.

Inadequacy filled Cactus for all the time he'd lost, but that new part of his heart beat right against it, whispering that it wasn't too late. He could still do something good.

"Let's eat," Willa said, and everyone picked up a plate and filled it with pizza. The five of them sat down at the table, and Bear tapped out a couple of texts and then asked Lincoln if he was ready to start on the ranch the next day.

"Yep," Lincoln said, and Cactus could hardly believe the boy could even make trouble at school. He was so sweet and so innocent, and yet, his teacher had been calling for the last five or six weeks, almost every week. When Cactus had found out, he'd offered to find someone for Link to talk to through Dr. Thompson, and he'd signed him up for therapeutic riding lessons at Courage Reins.

"I wanted to talk to you about Courage Reins too," he said to Willa, signing for Mitch. "And you too, boy." He smiled at Mitch, who smiled back but looked a little surprised.

Me? he asked

"Yeah," Cactus said. "The horses and riding are for anyone. You two should come with me."

"We can't afford that, Cactus," Willa said quietly.

"They have grants," Cactus said. "I know Pete and Reese real well."

What do you do there? Mitch asked.

"I'd like to know that too," Willa said, and she'd hardly touched her pizza. She settled away from it and folded her arms.

"You work with horses," Cactus said. "Real calm ones. You take care of them, and you talk to them. You talk to a counselor too. They're trained for kids with autism, who have cancer, who can't walk." He looked back and forth between Willa on his left and Mitch across from him. "They serve veterans—men and women who've served our country in the military—and help them with PTSD, trauma, physical ailments." Cactus picked up his pizza and waved it. "It's a great place." He let Mitch read his lips on that last part and took a bite of his pizza.

Mitch turned his eyes to Willa. *Can we go, Mom?*

"I don't know," she said.

"I liked it," Link said, and Cactus's eyes flew to his. "You don't have to stay by Cactus. I got to go off by myself with this huge horse named Ophelia."

What? Mitch asked, and Willa signed what Link had said for him. *Did you get to ride her?*

Cactus repeated the question for Link, and he nodded. "And you brush them down, and you teach them to kick a ball to you. All kinds of stuff. It was really fun."

Once Willa finished translating that, Mitch's eyes had grown wide and animated. Willa sighed, and Cactus knew exactly why: No one could say no to that face.

"Let's call Reese and talk to him," Cactus suggested.

"Maybe he'll have some grants." He exchanged a look with Bear, who'd cautioned him against solving all of Willa's problems for her. Apparently, Sammy hadn't taken kindly to that, and while Willa wasn't exactly the same person as Sammy, she wouldn't want to take advantage of Cactus or feel like he had saved her.

So Cactus would donate their fees to Courage Reins. No big deal. She couldn't get mad at an anonymous donation with her name on it.

"Okay, Mitch," Bear said a few minutes later. "Let's talk about you coming up to the ranch."

Willa signed for him, and Mitch said, *Okay*.

Bear looked at Cactus. He lifted his hands and started talking. "The ranch is not a playground, Mitch. You have to pay attention all the time. You can't hear a truck coming, or a tractor. You can't hear horses' hooves or someone yelling to watch out. We don't have things that flash out there. So you have to be consciously looking all the time. Looking to make sure you're safe, and that you know what's going on around you."

He glanced at Willa, who nodded. "You've gotten most of the signs right." She made a couple of other ones and nodded at Mitch.

I can do it, Mitch said. *I'm used to watching at school.*

"You'll be with me and Link," Cactus said. "If you don't know something, look up and ask us. If you need help, get my attention. I will always get yours before I leave you or talk to you." He drew in a breath. "I just don't want you to get hurt, and if you can't promise to watch—*really* watch—out there, you can't come to Shiloh Ridge with me."

Bear was going to make Willa sign a safety release no matter what. The truth was, Mitch *could* get hurt on the ranch, and everyone would feel terrible about it, but Bear didn't want a lawsuit.

I promise I'll watch, Mitch said, his hands moving fast. Too fast for Cactus to keep up, though he'd gotten markedly better in the past several months at reading Mitch's fast fingers.

He looked at Willa, who started to translate for him. "I'll look around all the time. I can keep Galaxy and Tank by me, and they'll help me. Link will help, and you can always bang on anything to get my attention. I can feel the vibrations."

He slapped his hand on the table and nodded.

I can feel it, he said. *Stomp your feet or hit the side of the barn. I'll be so good at watching and feeling and listening, I swear.*

He looked like he might cry, and Cactus glanced at Bear. He nodded, just once, and Cactus signed, "Okay, boy. You can come up to the ranch with me tomorrow."

Mitch yelped, the sound a strange mix of high and low, and jumped out of his seat. He threw his arms around Bear, who wasn't expecting that, and then raced around the table to Cactus.

He caught the boy in his arms and held him right against his chest. *Thank you, Cactus*, Mitch said. *I'll be so good. You'll see.*

Cactus couldn't wait to see, and he set the child back on his feet.

Bear stood up, a big sigh heaving out of his chest. "Okay, boys. Let's get our swim trunks on and leave your mom and Cactus to talk for a minute." He picked up their plates and took them into the kitchen. Sixty seconds later, at least it seemed that fast, they'd left.

Cactus's heartbeat had started flopping like a fish out of water the moment Bear had suggested Cactus would get to be alone with Willa for any length of time.

"Talk to me," he said when she hadn't started after several moments of silence.

"I know you're a good person," she said slowly and quietly. "I do not want to be your charity case."

"I know that," he said, meeting her eye. He reached for her hand and slid back in his chair. "Come sit with me."

She giggled but got up and perched in his lap. "I'm too old and too fat for this."

"You are neither," he whispered, the scent of her skin driving his mind into a frenzy. He had to kiss her today. He was sure he'd explode if he didn't. The only problem was he still hadn't found his heart.

"Listen, Willa, I just want you to be happy. If that means you get a job at the bakery, great. If it means I can help you with a car, I'm okay with that. If it means the two of us just sitting here like this, I'm absolutely fine to do that too." He ran his fingers down the side of her face, dangerously close to that gorgeous hair.

"I personally think you'd benefit immensely from the therapy at Courage Reins. The guy who's been running the office—Reese Sanders—was horribly injured overseas while he served in the military. He's stronger and better than ever, and he runs the office there, helping the owner grow the facility ten times over in the past decade."

"Riding a horse isn't going to fix my leg."

"No, it's not," he said, pressing his cheek to her shoulder. She wrapped one arm around his shoulder and one around the back of his neck. He hadn't had such a feminine touch in so, so long, and he ached for more. "But it can definitely make your leg stronger. Your back too. Your core. And when you're stronger, you don't ache as much."

"You're a good salesman," she teased.

He returned her smile, everything between them so easy now. "I think it would help you mentally too," he said quietly. "It does me. And I think it would help Mitch beyond belief with his confidence and social skills."

She sighed and met his eyes, searching his for something. "Fine," she finally whispered. "Let's call out there today."

Cactus grinned and reached up to cradle her face. "Willa...." He let her name hang there, and she was so very good at reading non-verbal clues. Her eyes drifted closed as she leaned toward him, and Cactus didn't need to know sign language to know what she was saying.

His pulse thumped painfully in the back of his throat, and he focused on her mouth in case he missed it. Somehow, his eyes closed too, and then somehow, he managed to match his lips to hers.

Color popped behind his eyelids, and everything male inside Cactus suddenly knew what to do. He knew where to put his hands, and he knew how to kiss a woman though he hadn't done it far, far too long.

Besides, Willa wasn't just any woman. He didn't move too fast, and in fact, kept her from accelerating the kiss too. She argued with him over it, and he finally let her speed things up.

He deepened the kiss, threading his fingers through her hair, and letting himself go.

He fell then. He fell down, down, down until he was all the way in love with Willa Knowlton.

Ward had been right. One kiss, and the woman had stolen his heart.

Chapter Nineteen

Preacher Glover removed the red, white, and blue tie and tossed in on his bed. "I need help," he called. Judge didn't come running into his room, but Cactus called back with, "With what?"

Preacher didn't answer, because he didn't want to tell either of his brothers that he had a date.

But he had a date.

He watched himself smile, and he wasn't entirely sure why. He'd never met Ellison Garfield, but she seemed nice. They'd been talking via text for a couple of weeks, and the day Preacher had asked her if she wanted to do anything over the Fourth with him had nearly knocked him out.

He hadn't dated much in his lifetime, ever. Talking to girls had been a chore as a teen, something that kept him from running or his debate practices. Not only that, but he wasn't good at it, and always ended up making a fool of himself.

"Like you will today," he muttered.

"Help with what?" Cactus asked, appearing in the doorway.

Preacher turned around and gestured to his clothes. "I have—I'm meeting someone in town. Do I look all right?"

"Do you look all right?" Cactus leaned into the doorframe and folded his arms. The man missed nothing, and Preacher hadn't particularly enjoyed having Cactus in the Ranch House. Judge at least left Preacher alone to do what he wanted. Cactus saw it all, and he had a way of making Preacher feel inadequate without saying or doing anything.

Preacher knew that was his problem, not Cactus's. He existed right on the edge of self-consciousness all the time. Funny how Bear always described him as confident and strong.

Ace had called him aloof when they'd gone to New Orleans over Christmas, and Preacher longed for another day when he could get behind the wheel and just drive until he decided to stop.

"You have a date," Cactus said, hitting the T hard. "Who is she?"

"Just someone I started talking to," Preacher said, not about to give him a name. Cactus was the smartest of them all, and he could use the Internet better than anyone. Well, maybe not better than Ranger.

"You started talking to her? How? Dating app?"

"No," Preacher said, turning back to the mirror. "I did what you said, and I left a comment on her comment on Two Cents."

Cactus started to chuckle, and Preacher allowed himself

to smile. "There's a ton going on in town for the Fourth, and she'd voted on a few things a few weeks ago, and I...we exchanged numbers, and I finally asked her if she'd like to meet."

"Incredible," Cactus said, stepping into the room. "First off, it's hot today. You're not going to work on the ranch, so I'd ditch the long sleeves. What are you doing?"

"I signed us up for the historic Three Rivers walk," he said. "It comes with lunch and dessert at the cider mill."

Cactus grinned at him and opened his closet. "Willa's mentioned that. She's worried about how much walking there will be, so you'll have to let me know how it is."

"Okay."

Cactus pulled out a bright blue shirt. "This."

"That's practically neon." It still had the tags attached too, because Preacher had gotten it as a gift and hated the shirt.

"It's blue," Cactus said. "And it'll look amazing with your dark skin and hair. It'll bring out your eye color *and* scream how patriotic you are." He shook the hanger, which rustled the shirt. "Trust me on this."

Preacher eyed the shirt like it might throttle him if he dared to put it on. He finally took it. "Fine." He unbuttoned the long-sleeved, black and white plaid shirt he'd chosen and tossed it on the bed over the tie.

"Why didn't you tell me you had a date?"

Preacher glanced up at Cactus, his pulse suddenly bumping a little harder. He shrugged into the shirt, all the answer he wanted to give.

"You and Judge sure do keep your secrets," Cactus said.

"Look who's talking," Preacher tossed back at him. "And we don't keep secrets. No one cares what we do." He sucked in a breath, because he hadn't meant to open that door.

And saying such a thing to Cactus was the worst person of all. Sure enough, his eyes sharpened, and he narrowed them as he studied Preacher. "You think no one cares what you do?"

Preacher shrugged. "No one pays attention to us. If you didn't live here, you'd have never known about this date." He turned back to the mirror. "No one asks us anything. We're completely overlooked." He straightened his collar in the mirror, refusing to meet Cactus's eyes though his brother drew closer to him.

"Preacher," he said, his voice low and kind. "I'm sorry. I didn't know I did that."

"No one does." Preacher sighed and let his hands drop back to his sides. "Look, just forget about it. No one else needs to know."

"I think they do."

"No." Preacher turned around and came nearly chest-to-chest with Cactus. "They don't. It won't change anything anyway, and it's not worth bringing up. We certainly don't want pity texts or attention."

Cactus tilted his head, clearly thinking hard about what Preacher had said. He wished he'd kept his mouth shut.

"Give thanks to the Lord, for He is good," he said, stepping past Cactus to the bed. He sat down and started pulling on his socks and cowboy boots.

"You're going to quote scripture at me?" Cactus asked.

"I'm grateful for what I have," Preacher said, standing.

"Maybe it would be different coming from you. I don't know. I just think…you see everything that goes on around here. I know you do."

Cactus didn't deny it, because he didn't need to. He was the most observant of them all, because he didn't try to be in the spotlight, ever.

"Just think about why Judge has already started planning for the Christmas light show. Or why he snips at Mister literally all the time. Or why he's just getting louder and louder the older he gets. He's desperate for attention and approval. Mostly from Bear, but it wouldn't hurt coming from you, or Ward, or Ranger, or even Bishop." Preacher took a deep breath, his throat so dry. He normally didn't talk this much. "Everyone *loooves* Bishop."

Cactus's eyes widened, because Preacher had spoken with a level of sarcasm and bitterness that had truly revealed how he felt. No, he didn't pick fights with Mister just so he could be right. He didn't push in line or yell during family meetings just to get people to look at him. He didn't design elaborate light shows that took months to plan, cost thousands of dollars, and then hours and hours to set up and take down.

But he was starving for attention just as much as Judge. His way of dealing with it was to retreat. Pull back. Say less. Show up as little as possible. If anyone had noticed at all, they'd said nothing to him, which only reinforced his belief that he was not important in this family, and he was not needed on this ranch.

"I'm sorry," he said, dropping his eyes to the floor and caging all of his raging feelings. They throbbed because they hurt so much. "I apologize I let myself get out of control,

Cactus. *Please*, you don't need to say anything to anyone." He looked up, pleading with his older brother now. "Especially Bishop. I do love Bishop."

Cactus pulled him into a hug, and Preacher dang near lost the battle with his emotions. He pressed his eyes closed and clutched his brother as tightly as he could. If he didn't, Cactus might step back and see how very near to crying Preacher was.

"I had no idea you were hurting so much," Cactus whispered. "I'm so sorry." He tried to pull away, and Preacher couldn't let him. Not yet. Thankfully, he stood still and hugged Preacher for as long as it took for him to gain control of himself.

When he was sure his eyes wouldn't be glassy and his voice would work, he stepped away.

"You know I look up to you, right?" Cactus asked.

Preacher met his gaze, shaking his head. "What in the world for?"

"Because you're so steady," Cactus said. "You're reliable and responsible. If something needs to be done, you know who Bear suggests? Who *I* go immediately to? Who Ranger brings up? You. It's always you, Preacher, because you're resourceful, and smart, and loyal. We know you'll get the job done according to the family values, and then we don't have to think about it."

Preacher could only stare at Cactus, the words not quite making sense.

"Hasn't Bear spoken with you about being foreman?"

Preacher shook his head, somewhat flabbergasted. "No. Not once." His next thought moved to Judge. If Preacher—

who was younger than Judge—got made foreman, Judge would only spiral further into his self-loathing. He could never do that to Judge.

Cactus sighed and pushed his hand up the back of his neck. "Well, I may have just messed up. We've been talking about it for months." He sighed as he dropped his arm. "I thought he'd have said something by now, even in passing."

"He hasn't." A chime sounded on his phone, and Preacher stepped over to his dresser, where he'd laid it. "I need to go, or I'm going to be late."

"Go," Cactus said. "Have fun with your mystery woman." He smiled at Preacher, and while it didn't hold its normal weight and luster, it still told Preacher that his brother loved him. "I really am sorry."

"I am too," Preacher said. "I didn't mean to bring it up at all."

"I'm glad you did." Cactus put one hand on Preacher's shoulder. "You should get to tell us—all of us—things like this."

Should and *could* were two different things, but Preacher only nodded. He dang near blinded himself walking past the reflective refrigerator, and the urge to go change his shirt one more time built within him.

He didn't though, because Cactus barred the way back to his bedroom. Instead, he got in his truck and went on down to town. He texted Ellison that he'd be there soon, and he ran inside Cowboy House to find another shirt.

Fifteen minutes later, Preacher pulled up to the downtown park right on time, quickly getting out of his truck and texting Elli that he'd arrived and was walking toward the meeting spot for the tour.

He'd never seen a picture of her. He hadn't sent her one of him. She'd told him that she'd be wearing a white dress with red and blue stars on it, and he slowed as he reached the entrance. He quickly pushed the button up on his phone to make his notifications vibrate, and he looked out into the park, trying to find her.

The tour group loitered a dozen paces away, the docent carrying a bright orange flag. Humiliation heated his face, and they hadn't even started the tour yet. He'd grown up here in Three Rivers, and he felt somewhat silly taking a tour at all.

Families filled the park today, as part of it had been sectioned off and filled with water to make a fishing pond. Everywhere he looked, he found red, white, and blue, and he glanced down at his navy and white striped polo.

He didn't see a woman in a white dress anywhere. The seconds ticked by, and he estimated he could look for another thirty before he'd better go check in or risk getting left behind.

"Looking for someone?"

He turned toward the woman standing there, and she wore a white dress with the splashy stars on it. "Yes," he said, his heartbeat turning into a motorboat engine. Elli was pretty, in a cute kind of way. She had a young face, and Preacher panicked over her age for a moment.

"Me too," she said, tucking her dark hair behind her ear. Preacher preferred a blonde, but he wasn't going to close doors just because of hair color. "Some guy I've never met." She gave him a quick smile. "Who does that?"

"I think a lot of people do that," he said.

"Yeah," she said. "Losers. At least that's what my sister says."

"That you're a loser for meeting a man you haven't met?"

"She says he could be a serial killer or something."

"It's the middle of the day," Preacher said. "With literally hundreds of people around." He gestured to the park, which buzzed with activity. A couple of cops even strolled by. "Blessed is the man who trusts in the Lord."

Elli peered at him, and Preacher cleared his throat. "Sorry. I, uh, didn't mean to lecture." He really needed to take the Bible quotes down a notch.

She smiled though, and Preacher relaxed a little. "I'm going to tell my sister that," she said. "She's a little overprotective of me."

Preacher only nodded. Elli took out her phone and tapped. "I need to find my date, though, because our tour looks like it's leaving."

Before Preacher could say he was her date, his phone rang. Elli lifted hers to her ear and took a step away.

Oh my word, he thought. *What do I do here? Idiot. You should've told her you were looking for her the moment you saw her dress!*

He held up his phone, which had her name on the screen, and said, "Elli."

She turned back to him, a few seconds passing while she connected all the dots. Then she laughed, hung up her phone, and threw her arms around him. "Preacher Glover."

He stepped back, nervous now but trying not to show it. "Ellison Garfield."

She nodded toward the tour group. "We really should go."

"Yep." He indicated she should go through the gate first, which she did, and Preacher followed her. "I'm not a serial killer, by the way. You can tell your sister that too."

Elli laughed again, shaking her head. "How embarrassing. You should've told me what you were wearing." She swatted at him playfully, and Preacher could only grin.

She was definitely a little younger than he'd like, but he told himself he couldn't make for-sure judgments in the first ten minutes.

They joined the tour, and Preacher actually enjoyed learning about the town where he'd grown up. "I had no idea that statue represented a real person," he said once the docent had explained about the pioneer woman who stood in the center of Main Street, a fountain pouring from her outstretched hand.

"If I get stood up at the altar," Elli said. "I don't want it to be memorialized in stone and bronze forever." She shook her head and glanced back toward the fountain. "What a sad story."

"Did you grow up here?" he asked as they followed the group down the street. He'd been asking little questions like that for the past hour or so.

"No," she said. "I moved here with my sister about three years ago."

"Is your sister married?"

"Yes."

"But you're not."

Elli gave him a playful smile, her eyes halfway between blue and green. "No. Would I be on this date with you if I was?"

"You never know," he said with a smile. "How old are you?"

"Twenty-five."

Definitely too young for him. In another month, he'd be thirty-eight, and that was practically forty. He also noted she did not ask him any of the same questions in return. He wasn't a big talker, and he definitely couldn't be the one to carry the conversation in a relationship.

"Up here we have the oldest ice cream shop in five hundred miles," the docent said. "Triple Cream." She turned and walked backward. "The owners have lived in Three Rivers for five generations, and they pride themselves on homemade ice cream daily, as well as serving the largest ice cream cones in the whole state of Texas."

"What's with Texas and how big everything is?" Elli asked.

"You're not from Texas, are you?" he asked.

"No, I am," she said. "I just have never understood why everything has to be so big here." She smiled at him. "What's your favorite ice cream?"

"Vanilla," he said, though it wasn't.

"Oh, come on," she said, twittering with a laugh. "Boring."

Preacher smiled, but it pinched along the edges.

"Here," the docent said, pausing and pointing behind the group. "You can see the evidence of the construction I've been talking about. Three Rivers is the second-fastest growing city in the state of Texas right now. It's in a huge construction boom, with several companies deciding to come here. That brings more people, and that brings more of everything."

Preacher frowned as the two tall buildings he could see past the tops of the trees. He didn't want Three Rivers to change. It had already seen a massive population increase, and it didn't feel as small and quaint as it once had.

"One of those buildings is going to be a new regional drug testing facility," she said, her voice somewhat boastful. "The other is going to be a privately-owned company called HealNow, which tests a variety of substances to speed the healing time for surgery patients."

She continued down the street, but Preacher kept his eyes on the tall buildings until Elli said his name.

"Yeah, coming." He caught up to her and asked, "What do you think about those big buildings?"

"Think about them?" She tucked her hair for at least the bajillionth time and looked at him. "I don't think anything about them."

Preacher nodded, kept his opinions to himself, and prayed the tour guide would talk faster. Then this date could end, and he could retreat to the ranch, lick his wounds, and find a different way to meet women.

Chapter Twenty

W illa collected the papers from the tray in the copier and turned back to the customer. "Let me get the confirmation sheet." She'd made it through the first week at Wilde & Organic on a wing and a prayer.

She and the fax machine had been mortal enemies from minute one, but Willa had been stroking it and promising she'd close the lid oh-so-gently if it would just send the blasted faxes. Then she wouldn't have to deal with a super-heated face and try to come up with excuses for why she couldn't do her job.

"Here you go," she said, smiling at the woman in her twenties who'd needed to send in some proof of insurance.

"Thanks." She left with her toddler in tow, and Willa watched them walk out of the gourmet grocery store. The job at Ackermans Bakery hadn't worked out, because Willa would've had to go into work very early in the morning—

three a.m. early—and there was no way to make that work with Mitch.

The position for the gift baskets had been hired out already, and Heidi hadn't known her manager had done that. So Willa had called Whitney Walker, and three days later, she'd started behind the customer service desk at Wilde & Organic.

July was slipping away like water over a cliff, and Willa could admit that she'd never been as happy as she was right now. Mitch came home from Shiloh Ridge day after day, his fingers flying for half an hour as he told her everything that had happened that day.

Cactus brought him all the way back to Willa, as the car she'd managed to buy didn't have air conditioning. He insisted that he didn't mind, but Willa's guilt weighed her down a little further with each passing day.

She blinked as someone approached the desk. "Can I help you?" she asked.

"Yes, I wanted to get some of the roses out here."

"Sure." Willa pulled out the drawer and retrieved the key ring. She walked around the counter and met the customer at the refrigerated floral case. "Let me just get this open." Her fingers shook as she fitted the small key into the tiny lock, and then she slid the glass back.

She got out of the way as the man selected the blooms he wanted. She relocked it, and then met him back at the register. After he'd paid and walked away, Willa turned and started filing the receipts from the vendors the store bought from.

She was good at keeping track of small details and organizing things, and this job allowed her to use those skills, pay all of her bills, and talk to people. She liked all of those things, and she enjoyed the sense of self-reliance that infused her with confidence.

Her shift ended, and she left a note for Jojo, who'd be in for the evening shift in a couple of hours. Out in the parking lot, she got behind the wheel of her car and started it. Or tried to start it.

The engine chugged and chugged, and it would not start. Sighing, she got out of the car and looked at it, wishing there were little sticky notes to tell her how to get it to run. She didn't even know how to open the hood.

She bent over and looked inside the car, searching for a button or lever to pop the hood.

"Willa?"

She jumped and straightened at the same time, the voice so familiar. She turned toward it and found Bear there. "Oh, Bear, hello."

"Everything okay?" He looked from her to the car.

Willa didn't see Sammy anywhere, or anyone else from his family. "The car won't start."

He frowned but made no move to try to help her. "I'm pretty useless with machines," he said. "It's Bishop and Ace who can get anything fixed. Or Sammy, but she's only coming down to the shop once a week now." His voice trailed off, and Willa really just needed a ride home.

She didn't have to work tomorrow, and she could figure out how to get to work on Monday.

"Listen," Bear said, and she'd heard Cactus say that so many times. "Why don't you let me get you a more reliable source of transportation? You can pay me whatever you can afford, and Cactus doesn't have to know."

Willa opened her mouth to say something, but nothing came out.

"I know you didn't want to take his money," Bear said. "I totally get that, because he's your boyfriend, and it feels weird. I could just be your bank."

Willa regained her senses and studied the tall cowboy. A bead of sweat ran down her back, and she had no idea how Bear could stand there in heavy jeans and a long-sleeved shirt, even if it was a light color. Cactus had explained that they wore long-sleeved shirts on the ranch to protect their skin from the sun, injuries, and insects.

"I don't know, Bear." She looked at the faded red car she'd gotten from a neighbor down the street for only six hundred dollars. "I could just have Sammy look at this one."

"See if it'll start again," Bear said. "Let me hear what it's doing."

Willa got behind the wheel again and twisted the key. The car's engine sputtered and tried to catch, but it couldn't.

"Willa," Bear said. "Come get in my truck. This thing isn't going anywhere."

"What's the problem with it?" she asked, getting out and then reaching back in to get her purse.

"It sounds like it's thirsty," he said. "That thing is bone-dry, and I wouldn't be surprised if the pieces have melted together." He indicated for her to walk further into the lot, and she had to wait for him to point out which giant pickup truck in the row belonged to him.

"There is...." Willa's embarrassment knew no bounds. "You're going to have to help me get in that."

"I can do that," Bear said kindly. He did too, standing right behind her and practically lifting her all the way to the bucket seat.

"Thank you," she muttered, her face burning like the surface of the sun.

He started down the road, the blessed air conditioning sweeter than Willa had anticipated. She didn't know what to say to Bear, and Willa finally turned toward him with, "How's your mother?"

"Real good," Bear said. "Mitch is doing fantastic on the ranch."

"I'm glad," Willa said. "He talks nonstop about it. About you. About Ward. About Benny, and The General, and I'm not sure if you knew, but he has a real crush on a horse named Hammy."

Bear laughed, and the sound carried joy. "That's Cactus's palomino. You should see the two of them ride that horse."

Willa could picture it, but she knew it wasn't even close to what she'd find in real life. She knew Cactus cared about Mitch a whole lot, and she knew he took good care of him at Shiloh Ridge. Cactus loved all children, and Willa had been teasing him that humans under the age of eighteen were his kryptonite. He hadn't denied it, and Willa could see the sparkling light in his eyes when she teased him.

"Oh, you missed my turn," Willa said, pointing to the left.

Bear gripped the wheel with one hand and kept driving.

Willa swallowed, not sure what to do or say now. "Bear?"

"I already texted Oakley," he said. "She's pulling her five best used cars, and you're going to pick one."

"Bear."

"When's your birthday, Willa?" he asked.

She folded her arms and refused to answer.

"I'll ask Cactus."

"Don't you dare," she hissed.

"I'm fairly sure you haven't had one yet this year. Cactus would've moved the whole state to make sure it was the best day of your life." He cut a look at her out of the corner of his eye. "So whenever it is, this is going to be my gift to you. Free and clear."

"I'll pay you."

"Are you going to refuse a birthday gift?" Bear asked. "Because, if so, I should let Cactus know...."

Willa looked out the passenger window, hating the inadequacy streaming through her. She felt trapped, the same way she had in Temple. "There's no way for me to win here," she murmured.

"It's not about winning or losing," Bear said. "You don't need to feel guilty." He cleared his throat. "Maybe...maybe the Lord put me in the parking lot at Wilde & Organic at exactly the right time. Maybe He wants me to help you like this. You can refuse it, sure. Or you can take it and thank the Lord for His care."

Willa pulled back her tears. "Thank you, Bear. I'm going to take it, and I'm going to get down on my knees tonight and thank the Lord for you and your family."

He shook his head. "That's not necessary."

Willa thought it was. She also thought she'd really like to

be part of Bear's family, and she thought of his younger brother, the man who had everything a shade darker than all the other Glovers, even in his attitude and demeanor.

Bear pulled into Mack's Motor Sports and went around to the side of the huge building. Oakley stood there with six cars lined up, and Willa's gratitude overflowed. "Bear, these are far too nice."

"Nonsense," he said, coming to a stop. He didn't get out of the truck, and Willa turned as her door opened and Oakley stood there. "She'll take good care of you from here," Bear said. "I have a conference call I have to get to."

"Oh, okay." Willa inched forward, and Oakley got up on the running board to help Willa down.

"Thank you," Willa said, wishing the ground would open up and swallow her whole. She stood a couple of inches taller than Oakley, and she felt like a giant next to the thin, petite woman.

"Don't worry," Oakley whispered, sliding her hand into Willa's. "Now, all of these will be good for you. No climbing in and out, as these are all small crossovers. Sedans you have to sink so far down, and these aren't like that. You sit up higher, and it's like getting in and out of a minivan. It's very easy."

Willa nodded, touched by Oakley's kindness.

"None of these are older than three years. The highest miles is on the blue one, and it has forty thousand."

Willa didn't even know where to start, and she simply turned into Oakley and hugged her.

"Okay, Willa," Oakley said. "You cry if you want to,

okay?" She held her tight and rubbed her back. "Sometimes life is so hard, and it's okay to cry."

Willa did, letting go of all of the things she couldn't hold back anymore. Oakley wept with her, and Willa finally realized it. "Oakley," she said, pulling back. "What's wrong? Are *you* okay?"

Oakley smiled through her tears and tried to laugh. It came out as mostly air, and she swiped quickly at her eyes. "I'm fine," she said. "I'm just...life can be overwhelming sometimes, you know?"

"Oh, I know."

Oakley faced the cars. "Do you like any of these?"

"I like all of them," Willa said.

"Let's get you in them," Oakley said, back to her calm and collected self. "I'm sure one will speak to you."

"THAT'S IT," CACTUS SAID, TAKING THE PAPER BAG OF groceries from her as she met him at the hood of her car. She still couldn't believe the sporty white SUV belonged to her. She'd written a letter of thanks to Bear—being clear to tell him she'd pay him back over time—and now that August had arrived, things on the ranch were accelerating.

Cactus would keep taking Mitch during the day until school started, and then Willa would work while he attended fifth grade.

"Look at this place," she said, gazing at the house. "You said this was a cabin. The Edge Cabin."

"It used to be," he said, smiling at the house and then her.

"We really can't stand out here. The air's too hot to breathe." He started toward the back steps, adding, "Thank you for bringing up these groceries."

"Of course," she said, following him. She held onto the handrail as she took the six steps to the back deck.

"This is all new," Cactus said. "I used to just have a cement block here, but Montana designed this deck, because she knows I like to eat outside."

"I didn't know that about you," she said, reaching up and then pausing before she touched him. He kissed her every time he saw her—every single time. Willa loved kissing Cactus, and today, she smiled at him, ran her hand down the front of his chest, and kissed him first.

The groceries in his hand fell to the deck, and he wrapped her up and kissed her back. The man knew how to go slow and experience every moment of a kiss. Willa always wanted to go faster than him, but he'd taught her to slow down and savor things. Once she'd done that, he turned her loose, and she got to kiss him with a little more passion.

"Willa, your son is in the house," he murmured.

"He can't hear us," Willa whispered back, putting her hands on either side of his face and guiding his mouth back to hers. She broke the kiss earlier than normal and said, "Cactus, I am grateful for you."

He pulled in a breath through his nose, almost making a gasping sound, and kept his eyes closed. "Why?" he whispered.

"Because you've taken such good care of me," she said, her stomach quaking. "And Mitch. I love how you love my son, and I love how animals of all types love you. I love your good heart, and I love how you just say what's on your mind."

"I don't say everything," he said.

"No?" she teased. "You're holding back sometimes?"

"I hold back all the time," he said.

"Interesting."

"Come on," he said. "I want to give you the tour, and then we'll have dinner."

"All right."

He bent and got the sack of groceries, then led her inside. "This is the kitchen," he said. "As you can see."

A beautiful kitchen spread before her, with the newest, nicest of everything. The gray floors showed the natural wood grain and flowed through the whole space, from front to back. Rugs in orange, yellow, and blue sat on the floor in the living room, and matching curtains in gray and orange hung over the windows.

"Wow," she said.

"This is three times as big as it was before," he said, setting the groceries on the counter. "All the furniture is new. New couches, and that rocking chair is for me and Link so he can read to me and I can pretend to listen while I take a little catnap." He grinned and indicated the table to her left. "Eating here or right outside. Montana is still building the picnic table that will be out there, and she has to do the roof extension too."

"Your family has a lot of money," Willa said, watching him.

Cactus's eyes flew to hers. "Uh, yeah. The ranch has a lot

of money, and I personally have a lot of money." He searched her face. "Is that a problem for you?"

"I don't see how," she said.

"I wish you would've let me buy you that car," he said, frowning. "I would have."

"It's fine," Willa said. "Show me the rest of the house." She laced her fingers through his.

Cactus called the dogs, and that brought Mitch up over the back of the couch too.

Mom, he said, and he came over to give her a hug.

"Hey, my son." She grinned at him. "Cactus is giving me a tour."

"Why don't you take the dogs out?" Cactus suggested.

Okay. Mitch clapped a couple of times, and Galaxy and Tank came trotting over to him. They went out the back door, and Cactus nudged her toward the doorway that led out of the dining room. "Half bath up there," he said. "Right off the living room. And I have three bedrooms back here now. I used to just have the one."

"Same flooring throughout," Willa said. "It's seamless, Cactus. Just like you."

He chuckled. "I have no idea what that means, but I'll take it." He tugged her back into the kitchen and released her hand to preheat the oven.

That done, he said, "Okay." His chest lifted as he breathed in, and Willa picked up on his nerves. He opened the back door and reached for her hand again.

"I thought it was too hot to breathe back here," she said, enjoying the feel of his skin against hers.

"It is," he said, but he walked outside anyway.

Mitch and the dogs played in the yard, Mitch throwing a ball for Galaxy and Tank. Both dogs chased after the orange orb, and Willa felt like she'd entered a fairytale, this one with a western theme, and the disabled princess and her deaf son would get to ride on horseback into the sunset to have a happily-ever-after with the handsome, good-hearted cowboy prince.

"They didn't take out too many trees," she said.

"We're goin' back to that one," Cactus said, his voice lower than she'd ever heard it. Every step he took got slower and slower, and Willa choked on his nerves.

"Cactus," she said.

"Remember I told you I was married before?" he asked quietly.

"Yes."

He took a few more steps, and the air cooled as they entered the shade of the tree. He continued until he stood almost immediately next to the trunk. His eyes were down, and Willa followed his lead.

A headstone stood there, and Willa sucked in a sharp breath.

"My wife's name was Allison," Cactus said. "We had a son." He crouched down and brushed his fingers across the top of the stone, and then over the letters. Willa didn't have to get closer to read them.

"His name was Bryce Charles Glover," Cactus said. "He only lived four days."

Willa put her hand on his back, because Cactus had pain streaming from him and filling the air around the two of them.

He didn't say anything else, and after a few minutes, he straightened. She slipped her arm through his and leaned into his back. "I'm so sorry, Cactus."

He tucked his hands in his pockets and finally looked up. He gazed into the distance and drew in a deep breath. Blowing it out and then breathing in again, he took a few more minutes before he said anything.

"I am in a good place with all of this now." He ducked his head, his chin pointed toward her. "I really am."

"Thank you for sharing him with me."

Cactus turned into her then, his eyes burning holes into hers. "I want to share everything with you." He kissed her then, and this time he was the one moving fast and pouring his feelings into the touch.

Willa had never been this close to a man before, not even the one she'd had a child with or the one she'd married. Before Cactus, she hadn't even been sure she knew true romantic love.

Now, with him, she did.

As he slowed down, Willa could see her whole future with Cactus Glover, right here at Shiloh Ridge Ranch.

Fear blipped through her, and she sincerely hoped she wouldn't make a mistake that would ruin this relationship like she'd ruined all of her previous ones.

Chapter Twenty-One

Cactus had fallen in deep with Willa Knowlton. Before, he might have been terrified. Now, he simply felt like the Lord had finally answered his decade-long prayer.

He took control of himself and broke the kiss, feeling freer than ever before. He slipped his hand into Willa's as she leaned into his side. "I loved being a father," he said. "I wanted a lot of kids."

He hoped he wasn't ruining anything, and that she'd want more kids too. What about you?" he asked quietly. "Do you want more children?"

"I do," she said. "I love Mitch with my whole heart, and I'd love for him to have some siblings."

Relief flowed through Cactus with a powerful rush. "Great," he said, releasing some of the air trapped in his lungs. He blinked, bright, white, sparkling diamonds flashing before his eyes.

Behind them, Tank barked, and Cactus turned that way.

Mitch's cry filled the air a moment later, but Cactus was already moving toward him. He reached the boy in a few seconds, meeting his tear-filled eyes.

"It's okay," he said, looking from Mitch to the blood on his knee. "Just a skinned knee." He picked the child up and relished the way he wrapped his skinny arms around his neck.

Willa arrived, and she signed a few things to her son. "He said he just slipped." Her phone rang as Cactus turned toward her.

"It's Holly Ann," she said, looking up. "Could be about the holiday choir."

"I bet it is," he said. "I'll take him inside. Come in when you're done."

Her eyes lit from within as she nodded, and she answered as he walked away. Inside, he set Mitch on the brand-new kitchen counter and told him to stay. He pulled a clean washcloth from the cupboard above the microwave and got it wet.

He wiped the blood away, revealing a series of tiny scratches. "No big deal," he signed. "I'll get a Band-Aid." He turned to get it, nearly tripping over Tank. "Dog, back up." He flung his arm out to catch himself, glaring at the dog.

Tank followed him down the hall, but Galaxy stayed with Mitch while Cactus got the bandage. With that taped securely in place, Cactus wiped Mitch's tears and smiled at him. "Good as new."

Thank you, Cactus. Mitch brought his infectious smile back, and Cactus picked him up and put him on the floor.

"Yep. You can help me start dinner. Get out the garlic and rosemary."

Mitch started to do that while Cactus retrieved his chef knife and cutting board. He put a pan on the stove and when Mitch stepped away from the fridge and put the garlic on the counter, Cactus moved into the fridge.

I don't know what rosemary is, Mitch said, and Cactus showed him the woody sprigs.

"It's an herb," he said, having to spell out the last word because he didn't know the sign. "It'll flavor the steak."

He pulled out the steak and a stick of butter and turned back to the new peninsula Montana had installed. The whole house was drastically different, and Cactus couldn't say he hated it.

In reality, it matched his new life perfectly, and he wouldn't have been happy in the dumpy cabin as whole as he felt now.

"Turn on the burner, Mitch." He indicated how to do it, and the boy did. "We'll put oil and butter in there and get the pan really hot." He turned back to the island and smashed some garlic and chopped a shallot. He spun and put those in the pan while the butter started to melt.

I like the fire, Mitch said. *Our stove doesn't do that.*

Cactus smiled at him and said, "It's a gas range, not electric." Tank started to edge into the kitchen, and Cactus gave him a glare. "Out."

The dog hung his head and backed up a step or two. Galaxy lay by the back door, her head turned away from Cactus as if she had no interest in the steak whatsoever.

"Get out some potatoes," he said to Mitch. "Get them peeled."

Mitch got to work while Cactus tended to the stovetop. When the oil and butter was nearly smoking, he put the two ribeyes in the pan. It spat and hissed, and he pulled Mitch over to watch. "See?" Cactus signed. "You stand back and you lay them in gently. It's hot, like, *really* hot."

I can feel it, Mitch said.

"We'll put the herbs in with the garlic in a minute." He ran hot water into a pot and set it on another burner, Mitch making painstakingly slow progress with the potatoes.

The back door burst open, and Willa entered. "I'm doing the community choir for the Christmas Festival," she said, pure joy in her voice. She giggled and danced into the kitchen, right into Cactus's arms.

"That's great news, my love," he said, grinning at her.

She stilled and looked up into his eyes. Cactus realized what he'd said, and he cleared his throat. "What are you going to do? Tryouts? Or take everyone like last year?" He released her and moved back to the pan on the stove. He wanted a nice sear on this meat, and he simply let it sit in the hot fat.

"I'm going to have everyone in the Festival choir," she said. "They're paying me again, which is amazing. And the Arts Council wants me to do a special Messiah Sing-in." Her voice pitched up, and Cactus drank in her enthusiasm. It had been so long since he'd really felt like that about anything, and it was intoxicating.

"Wow," he said. "A Messiah Sing-in."

"Yeah, so that's going to be a separate choir. I'm going to do auditions for that one."

"Two choirs?" Cactus raised his eyebrows. "When are you going to have time to rehearse with two choirs—and the church choir?"

"I'll figure it out," she said. "I need to get the auditions going right away for the Sing-in. *The Messiah* is really hard to sing."

"Yes, it is," he said, turning to get his aromatics to flavor the butter. He moved the cutting board next to the stove, something he'd never have been able to do in his old kitchen. He flipped the steaks, admiring the deep brown crust on the first side.

"Look," he said to Mitch, tapping him on the shoulder. After the boy turned, he repeated himself. "Look. That's called a sear, and it's what you want on a steak. You let it sit and cook. Don't move it."

Don't move it, Mitch repeated. *I'm almost done with the potatoes.*

"Go on and finish then." Cactus probably should've started the potatoes first, but steak excited him way more than mashed potatoes.

"You're teaching him to cook," Willa said

"A man has to be able to make his own way in the world," Cactus said, smiling at her. He diced the potatoes really small and dumped them in the boiling, salted water. He spooned more butter with the herbs, garlic, and shallots over his steak, and then slid the pan right into the preheated oven.

"Did I tell you Ward is working on getting a road built out here?"

"No," Willa said. "That's probably a good thing."

"It's time," Cactus said. "I used to ride in on horseback if I needed to, but…it's time." He didn't want to say he couldn't expect her and Mitch to do that, but that was exactly what was on his mind. "It might be a few more months, because we're re-graveling the whole ranch. We've got to do the road to Ace's new house too, and the one out here will take more work. They have to grade and prep the land, put in rebar, all of that."

"You put rebar in a gravel road?"

"Yes, ma'am."

"Who knew?" She grinned at him, and Cactus experienced true happiness.

"Well, you do now." He leaned over and kissed her, pulling back when Mitch yelped.

The hiss of water on fire filled his ears, and Cactus spun to find the potatoes had boiled over. "It's fine," he signed quickly, reaching to re-light the burner and take the lid off the pot at the same time. With it under control, he said, "Happens all the time when you boil stuff. You have to keep an eye on it."

So no kissing, Mitch said, his left eyebrow arching up.

Cactus blinked at the boy, not quite sure what to say. He wasn't an infant, but he wasn't a teenager either. He was stuck in this weird in-between place where Cactus wasn't sure how much he knew or understood and how much he didn't.

He looked at Willa, who's face had turned bright red. She burst out laughing in the next moment, and she rushed at Mitch and hugged him tight and close.

"No, I guess not," Cactus said with a chuckle. "Definitely no kissing while you're boiling potatoes."

A COUPLE OF WEEKS LATER, CACTUS STOOD IN A REHEARSAL with Willa and the rest of the people who'd made the cut for *the Messiah* Sing-in. Willa had assigned everyone parts instead of letting them choose, and Cactus could see her professionalism from a mile away.

"Okay," she said after they'd been practicing for an hour. "That's it for today. Next Saturday, one p.m. Be here with your part for *Comfort Ye My People* memorized. I know it's only the end of August, but the Arts Council wants the program the first week of December, and that only gives us a few months."

The crowd started to break up, and Cactus tucked his music into the backpack he'd brought. The people Willa had selected were incredible, and he couldn't believe he'd made it into the choir. Yes, he knew he had a good voice, but he definitely wasn't the best one there. He'd said he'd sing for the Festival choir or the church choir, but not both, and Willa said she wanted him in the church's Christmas program. They met on Thursday nights, and Cactus hadn't had any problem making those rehearsals.

"Ready?" he asked Mitch while Willa continued to clean up. "Let's get your stuff put away and use the bathroom before we go." They had an appointment out at Courage Reins that afternoon—their first all together.

Cactus could admit he'd experienced some nerves over today's session, but he was trying to stay positive.

Mitch did what he asked, and ten minutes later, Cactus aimed his car north toward Three Rivers Ranch. Willa talked easily about her plans for the Sing-in, her joy over being asked to do it obvious and her nerves about providing a good enough show equally as apparent.

"I'm thinking just twenty numbers," she said. "But how do you cut anything from *the Messiah?*"

She wasn't really asking him, as she'd told him that before. He just said, "I don't know," and kept listening to her talk.

They arrived at the facility, and Reese Sanders himself met them in the lobby. "Good to see you again, Cactus."

"You too," Cactus said, grinning at him and shaking his hand. Reese had sustained some pretty bad injuries during his time in the military, and he stood a full foot shorter than Cactus. Maybe more.

"This is my girlfriend, Willa Knowlton," Cactus said, the words rolling out of his mouth easily. He'd never said them aloud, and wow, he liked it. "And her son, Mitch." He signed all of that, adding, "Mitch, this is Reese."

"Nice to meet you," Reese said, and he signed it too.

"Impressive," Cactus said, smiling at him.

"I learned like, three things." Reese chuckled. "Come on, let's get you guys with your horses." He started to limp away, using both crutches today as he stutter-stepped. "You've all ridden a horse before, yes?"

"I haven't," Willa said before Cactus could. "I didn't know we'd ride today." She looked at Cactus with fear and accusation in her eyes. "You said I could just walk it or roll it a ball."

"You can," Cactus said at the same time as Reese.

"We want you to ride if you can," Reese said. "It does bond you with the animal, but a lot of people start out on the ground." He glanced over his shoulder, his smile warm and affectionate. "Whatever you're comfortable with, Willa."

She pursed her lips and nodded. Cactus squeezed her hand, silently begging her to forgive him.

Reese gave him to Dreamland, the same horse he'd been working with before, and he took Mitch and Willa down the aisle to two other horses. An attendant came to stay with Mitch, and she could sign. He caught Willa's eye and lifted his eyebrows as if to say, *See? I did a good job with this.*

She nodded, and that was all the acknowledgement Cactus needed. He lost track of her after that, and he thoroughly enjoyed riding Dreamland, brushing her down, and just taking an hour to be with himself, the sky, and the Lord.

Once they were all back in the car, he asked, "So? How was it?"

Mitch started signing like the wind, and Willa translated his excitement for his horse—a nearly black one named Puddles—for Cactus as he drove.

"And you?" he asked once Mitch had calmed down. He cut a look at her out of the corner of his eye.

"It was fun," she said vaguely.

"Did you ride?"

"Not today." She gave him a closed-mouth smile and looked back out the windshield. "But I did enjoy it. You were right about telling the horses secrets. Very therapeutic."

His nerves danced, and he gripped the wheel for a moment. "Secrets."

"No, not really." She grinned at him. "Just nice to say whatever I want and not have anyone to judge me."

"Oh, come on," he said. "You live with a deaf boy. You can say whatever you want all the time."

She burst out laughing, and he did too. "I suppose you're right," she said. "It was...different though. I really liked it."

"So we'll go again in a couple of weeks?"

"Sure."

He dropped them off at her house, and he had to get back up to the ranch to help Ward with the gravel for Ace's driveway, so he wasn't planning to stay. He walked her to her door and leaned in for a kiss.

"Oh, will you wait for a second?" Willa asked, her fingers releasing his collar. "I've got a check for Bear." She hurried away from him while Cactus tried to figure out why she'd have a check for Bear.

She grabbed something from the fridge and sure enough, it was a check. She handed it to Cactus, who frowned at it. "What's this?"

"For my car," she said.

He looked up at her, shock moving through him. "What?"

Trouble entered Willa's expression. "For my...car. Bear bought my car. Well, I mean, he said.... I make payments to him."

Disbelief tore at Cactus's insides now. "What? Why? When...why didn't you let *me* do that?"

"He said he was going to talk to you about it," Willa said with a frown. "He didn't?"

"No, he did not." Stupid Bear. Foolishness filled Cactus from top to bottom, and he didn't know what to say. Why would his older brother finance a car for Willa? Why couldn't he *ever* just let other people take care of their own business? Why did he have to encroach on Cactus's space?

"It's not a big deal, Cactus," she said quietly, as if she could sense the storm inside him.

It was a big deal to him, but he didn't want to argue with her. His history with Bear ran deep, and she didn't know all of it yet. He lifted the check. "Okay. See you at church tomorrow?"

She nodded, and he spun away before he said or did something he'd regret.

By the time he made it back to Shiloh Ridge, he was downright fuming. He pulled to a spitting stop in front of the homestead and swiped the idiotic check from the passenger seat. He marched toward the house just as Bear came outside.

"What's with you?" he called as Cactus took the last few steps on the sidewalk and then leapt the stairs two at a time to get to the porch—and his nosy, meddling older brother.

"You financed my girlfriend's car?" He threw the check at Bear, wanting to throw a punch. He caught movement behind Bear, noting Sammy had followed him. "How dare you?" He hadn't meant to yell, but the rage inside him definitely warranted it.

"Why can't you just leave things alone? Why does the mighty Bear Glover have to come to everyone's rescue?"

"Whoa, whoa," Bear said, holding up both hands. "What is—why is this a big deal?'

"Why is this a big deal?" Cactus repeated, his chest heaving. "She's mine, Bear. I don't need you to take care of her. *I* want to take care of her. You made it so I *can't* take care of her. I'm second to you now, and you've got this bond with her that *I* want. I'm always freaking second to you!"

He lunged at Bear, swinging for all he was worth. He caught Bear on the side of the face, because even his brother wasn't superhuman.

Before he knew it, Bishop was in his face, both hands on his chest, pressing him back and saying, "Stop it, Cactus. Cool down." Ace joined him, one arm flung out as if Cactus could get by Bishop.

With the fury still swirling inside him, he thought he might.

Ward had joined the fray, and he stood beside Bear, one hand on his chest as if Bear would roar and bare his grizzly teeth before ripping Cactus's throat out.

Let him try, Cactus thought, glowering past his siblings and cousins to stupid Bear. *I'm ready for him.*

Chapter Twenty-Two

B ear wiped his lip, blood coming away on his hand. He glared at Cactus, his own anger rearing and pulsing against the back of his throat. "I just wanted to help."

"I didn't ask you to help," Cactus yelled. "You're an idiot if you thought this was okay."

"What's going on?" Ward demanded.

Cactus raised his eyebrows in challenge, and Bear knew he wouldn't answer. Nerves radiated through Bear, and he threw a somewhat nervous look to his wife, who stood just outside the doorway, their baby on her hip. She wasn't happy with him over this situation, and in fact, had said Cactus would be "livid" when he found out.

Bear had told her Cactus wouldn't find out. *So you're going to keep secrets from him?* Sammy had asked him. *And expect Willa to? No, Bear. This had bad news written all over it.*

But Bear hadn't known how to fix the situation. Maybe

he did like wearing the red cape and flying in to save the day. He'd never considered himself a man with a hero complex, but maybe he was.

"He bought Willa's car," Cactus finally said, the words more of a growl really. "After I offered to buy her a car, and she said no."

"I just found her broken down in the supermarket parking lot one day," Bear said, tasting the metallic, sharp taste of blood in his mouth. "That's all."

"Why wouldn't she let you buy her one?" Bishop asked Cactus, his back still fully turned to Bear. He hadn't removed his hands from Cactus's chest either, and Bear should thank the Lord above that Bishop and Ace had been walking by the homestead. Ward had been inside, and Sammy had yelled for him the moment Cactus had lunged at Bear.

He wiped his lip again, which stung, as Cactus remained silent.

"She said she couldn't take your money," Bear said. "I was there. I bought her the car as a birthday gift." He knew the moment the words left his mouth that he'd made a mistake.

Sammy actually gasped, and Cactus said, "Get off me, Bishop. I'm going to kill him." He struggled against Bishop and Ace, and Ward whistled through his teeth and yelled for Ranger.

"I mean it, Bear. I'm going to *kill* you!" Cactus growled and shoved Bishop away, but the younger man just hurled himself right back at Cactus, saying, "Stop it, Charles. You're going to regret this."

"He's going to regret buying *my* girlfriend a blasted car

for her birthday." His chest heaved, and he swatted Ace's arm away from his chest. "Leave me alone. Let me *go*."

Ranger came jogging out of the homestead a few seconds later and took in the scene. Ward had moved a few feet closer to Cactus, who had quieted but still didn't like Bishop's hands on him. Finally, Bishop said, "Okay, Cactus. I'll stop if you'll stay. Okay?" He dropped his hands but kept his body between Cactus and Bear.

"Bartholomew," Sammy said in a very dangerous tone. "You apologize to him right now."

Bear looked at her helplessly. "I thought I was trying to help."

"I know that." But his wife's stance didn't change.

"I don't want your help!" Cactus yelled from across the porch. "You should've called me. You should've let *me* do this."

Bear could see that now. He'd just wanted to help Willa. He liked her too. *It's not the same, and you know it.*

He did know it. He'd known Cactus would react like this, and deep down, he knew he had every right to. It was exactly why he hadn't told his brother what he'd done.

"I'm sorry," Bear said, his voice barely audible. Ranger came closer to him, but Bear couldn't look at anyone right now. Humiliation and shame pulled through him. Yanked, really, and it hurt.

"What am I supposed to do now?" Cactus asked. "I can't top a car for the woman's birthday, and I look like a complete idiot. Outshined by my older brother all over again. My blasted *married* older brother." He shoved past Bishop, who darted in front of him again. "Leave me alone, Bishop."

He started down the front steps. "That goes for *every* one of you! All y'all can just leave me alone. I don't want to talk to any of you for a long time." He flew toward the sidewalk. "Dear Lord," he bellowed into the sky as he strode away from the house. "Why am I part of this idiotic family? Why can't they mind their own goldarn business?"

Bear heard the pure pain and anguish and fury in his brother's petition to the Lord, and he hated himself keenly in that moment. Every eye landed on him, and Bear couldn't shoulder the weight. He couldn't look up.

"Bear," Bishop said with plenty of frustration and disdain in his voice. "Come *on*, man." He left too, running down the steps with Ace hot on his heels. They both called after Cactus, who hadn't gone to his car, but was marching down the road toward the cemetery and True Blue.

Ward, Ranger, and Sammy looked at him, the only sound baby Stetson, who let out a burp and then a babble. Normally, Bear would've laughed and marveled at his son. But he couldn't think straight right now. When the sounds of boots on gravel finally faded to silence, Bear looked up.

"Did you really buy Willa Knowlton a car?" Ranger asked, extending the check Cactus had thrown toward Bear.

He couldn't take it. He hadn't cashed the first one either. He couldn't nod or shake his head. He looked at Sammy, who glared at him with bright eyes. "I told you that would end badly," she said. "Everything he said is true. What *is* he supposed to do now?"

"I hate to say it, but I agree with her," Ward said. "Surely you can see it from his side, Bear."

"I can," Bear barked, glaring at him now. "I get it."

"How are you going to fix this?" Ranger asked, his gaze moving past Bear. "He was *livid*, Bear. And we'd just gotten him back."

"I don't know," Bear said, pushing away from the pillar where he'd been standing. He walked toward Sammy and the entrance to the house. "I guess I'm going to have to pray and hope the Lord helps me."

"Better start now," she said dryly. "And not stop for a few weeks."

He went by her and straight upstairs to their apartment. Sammy had once been upset with him because he always had a solution for everything. He did like to run to the rescue, because it was easy for him.

He pressed his back into the door and looked up. "Help me," he said. "Why do I do this? How do I stop doing it?"

He'd bought food for hundreds of people after the tornadoes. He'd paid for the room at the rec center for the Walkers, though they had plenty of money. He'd arranged for countless repairs on Sammy's parents' home. And hers. Anything he had to do, he could do. He knew people, and he had money.

Why couldn't he help?

But he knew he shouldn't have done this particular thing. He had marginalized Cactus, and he had made it impossible for him to provide Willa with the most amazing birthday gift. He'd taken the spotlight from Cactus, and he had made it very hard for him to be the one to be Willa's saving grace.

He sighed. "I don't know what to do. Just tell me what to do, and I'll do it."

Wait, came to mind, and Bear hated that. He didn't want to wait. He wanted to get the problem fixed.

Even as he pressed against the thought, it came again.

Wait, and then apologize.

Chapter Twenty-Three

"When's her birthday?" Bishop asked, keeping his gaze on the ground. It was uneven, but that wasn't the only reason. Cactus would talk if Bishop didn't look at him. He hated that he was back to that tactic, as it was one he and Ace hadn't had to use for a while now. Probably a year.

"The beginning of October," Cactus said. "We were going to take Mitch to a movie, then drop him off at Patrick's. I booked the Downtown Dinner Cruise, and I was going to...." His voice stopped, and Bishop exchanged a glance with Ace.

"You bought her a diamond ring," Ace said. "Didn't you?"

Cactus didn't answer, which was as good as a yes.

Bishop could still hear his brother yelling, *I don't need you to take care of her. I want to take care of her. You made it so I can't take care of her.*

He hadn't hesitated, because he was familiar with the anger in Cactus's voice. He and Ace had changed direction instantly, both of them running toward the front porch as Cactus hurled himself at Bear.

"I've messed everything up again," Cactus said, his voice filled with anguish now. "Why is this so hard? I was doing so good too. *So* good. I'd told her about Bryce, and she wants more kids, and I'm all the way in love with her, and now what? I feel like I've taken two hundred steps backward, and I didn't even know it." He shook his head. "Can you guys just leave me alone, please?"

Bishop finally looked at Cactus when his voice broke on the last word.

"Please," he said again, his voice barely audible and his eyes shiny with tears.

"I don't know if I dare," Bishop said honestly. "I'm worried about you."

"I'm worried about me too." Cactus kept walking, and they made it past the trees blocking the meadow from the view of the road. Ace's plot of land expanded before their eyes, and Bishop wished he'd chosen it.

The house's foundation had been poured, and Montana had started framing it that day.

"This looks great, Ace," Cactus said, coming to a stop.

"It's the first time I've seen it," Ace said. "It does look great."

The three of them stood there, and Bishop wasn't sure what the others were thinking. He was at a complete loss about where to go now, or what to do next. Bear and Cactus hadn't always gotten along, but they'd never come to blows. Cactus would get irritated and retreat to the Edge Cabin, or

Bear would growl and roar. In the end, they came back together. They apologized, and they moved on.

Bishop honestly wasn't sure if there could be any moving on from this.

"Are you ready for the wedding?" Cactus asked next, his voice deathly haunted.

Ace glanced at Bishop again, his anxiety plain. He didn't want to talk about his happily-ever-after when Cactus didn't have his. Bishop shrugged, because he didn't know what to do either.

"Yes," Ace said simply.

Cactus nodded. He looked at Bishop, and this time, Bishop didn't look away. "I'm sorry, Cactus. I just didn't want you to hit him. I think you would've regretted it later, and that would've just given you one more thing to beat yourself up about."

His brother nodded, resignation in the dark, deep blue depths of his eyes. "I wanted to so badly, though." He pressed his eyes closed. "I think it would've felt so good."

"For about ten seconds," Ace said. "Then it wouldn't anymore."

"You're probably right." Cactus exhaled and opened his eyes. "Can I just go sit over there alone? I'm not going to break anything." He walked away, and Bishop let him go.

He went across the whole lot to the edge of the meadow, then sat down on a boulder there that overlooked the land down the slope.

Bishop stepped next to Ace and said, "What are we going to do?"

"Keep them apart so one of them doesn't kill the other," Ace murmured.

"I've never seen Cactus so mad."

"Me either."

Bishop sighed. "Bear's an idiot."

"Sometimes." Ace sighed too. "Sometimes we all are."

"But this bad?" Bishop shook his head. "Honestly, what was he thinking?"

"I don't know," Ace said. "He does tend to want to save the world. Make sure everyone is taken care of. He probably thought it would be helping Willa, which it did, and Cactus, because he could do what Cactus couldn't—buy her the car."

"Exactly," Bishop said. "He did what Cactus couldn't. What I don't get is why he can't stop and think—hey, maybe I shouldn't do this to my brother. What will he do if I buy his girlfriend a car?"

Bishop's own anger started to grow, and he tamped it down. This wasn't his situation, and he didn't need to get involved any more than he already had. "It's not like Cactus has had a whole bunch of girlfriends. It's obvious to anyone how much he loves Willa, and Bear should've known."

"I agree," Ace said. "I'm not arguing with you. I just don't think he did it maliciously."

"No, probably not."

"He's stupid, not mean."

Bishop started to chuckle, and Ace did too. After a few seconds of cleansing laughter, Bishop sighed again. "The thing is, Bear's *not* stupid. That's what makes this so hard."

"He did a stupid thing," Ace amended. "We all do stupid

things. This one is just really big." He gestured toward Cactus, who bowed his head. "Looks like he's praying."

Bishop could only nod, because Cactus had always been such a good example of his faith. Sure, he might not have gone to church every week, but going to church didn't make one a saint.

The way they treated others did that. The way they quietly lived their convictions did that. The way Cactus had never deviated from praying to God to know what to do and how to do it told Bishop what kind of man his brother was.

He quickly closed his eyes and said, "Dear Lord, whatever Cactus is praying for, please grant it unto him. Help all of us to know what to say and do for both Cactus and Bear, and guide us back together as a family."

"Amen," Ace said, and when Bishop opened his eyes, Ace slung his arm around his shoulders. "You're a good man, Bishop."

"So are you." Bishop smiled at his cousin. "I'm glad we're in this together. Will you *please* tell me if I ever do something stupid like that?"

Ace chuckled. "Absolutely, brother. Absolutely."

Chapter Twenty-Four

Preacher frowned around the groom's room, wishing Ace and Ida had chosen to get married in a double ceremony like Ranger and Bear had.

But no. Ida was getting married today, and Brady had asked all of the Glover men to be in his wedding party. That meant a skin-tight bowtie around Preacher's neck, choking him. It meant another day in a tuxedo. It meant another haircut and hundreds more people at Shiloh Ridge.

Then, they'd do it all again in three weeks, when Ace and Holly Ann tied the knot.

Preacher was already dreading that day, and this wedding hadn't even started yet.

Well, it had. He had the monkey suit on, after all.

He reached up and tugged at his collar, but it didn't go anywhere. At least he'd brought a date to this wedding. In fact, he pulled his phone out of his pocket to check the time.

He'd told Cameron Sudsbury to come right when the wedding started. Then she wouldn't have to sit alone for very long.

He'd met her at one of the summer dances the town did in the downtown park. He was going to take that information to his grave, though, because men his age didn't normally attend the summer dances. They were for teens and twenty-somethings, and Preacher hadn't been either of those for over a decade.

Cameron went by Cami, and she'd been on the volunteer squad for the dances. He'd met her as she'd started breaking down the dancefloor they laid over the grass. "Are you on the night cleanup crew?" she'd asked.

Preacher hadn't had the guts to tell her that he'd actually attended the dance. So he'd fibbed and said yes, let her put him to work, and flirted the best he could to try to get her number. To his great surprise, it had worked, and they'd gone to dinner once.

It hadn't been terrible, and he'd felt the first inklings of a spark. Since the harvest was upon them, Preacher didn't get off the ranch much, and the only way to see Cami was to get her to this wedding.

She'd readily agreed to come, and he swallowed back another round of nerves. He'd mentioned to exactly one person that he was bringing a date, and Mister had seemed pretty surprised.

When Preacher had asked him why, he'd said, *No one brings dates to family weddings, that's all.*

Well, Preacher was going to. He couldn't stand the

thought of loitering about while everyone else danced, drinking disgustingly sweet punch, and wishing he could go home and change his clothes. It felt too much like high school, and Preacher wasn't going to suffer like that as a thirty-eight-year-old.

His birthday had passed without much fanfare, as usual. The Glovers weren't huge gift-givers anyway, but Preacher had been hoping for more than a gift from Mother, one from Judge, and a cake he'd only gotten one piece of by the time he'd come in from the ranch.

He'd only gotten that because Oakley had saved it for him, and her kindness did touch him when he thought about it.

Just another way you were overlooked, he thought as Brady Burton's father said, "Time to line up, everyone."

Preacher stayed where he was, because his spot was only halfway back. Existing right in the middle of the family had its perks, but also its drawbacks. He watched Bear and Cactus perform a delicate dance, something they'd been doing for weeks now.

Everyone from here to Oklahoma had heard about the near fistfight on the front porch at the homestead, and Preacher and Mister had texted about it until three a.m. one day. Mister was just glad he wasn't the only one with problems in the family.

Preacher had told him over and over that the problems between him and Judge weren't actually his. Mister didn't believe him, and Preacher had given up trying to convince him otherwise.

He glanced at Judge, the brother just older than him as he finally wedged himself into the line in front of Ward. They were only separated by four months, and Ward would be thirty-eight come December.

"How's Mister?" Preacher whispered, as he did worry about his brother living at Bull House.

"He's real good," Ward said with a smile. "And Judge?"

"Driving me crazy," Preacher muttered. "All we talk about is Christmas lights or work."

"At least you're not hearing about his wedding plans twenty-four-seven," Ward said darkly, shooting a look over his shoulder, back toward where Ace stood.

"True," Preacher said with a smile. "Roads are lookin' good."

"Thanks. You boys are gettin' the fields in fast this year."

"That's because King Bear bought another tractor."

They grinned at one another, and while the things Preacher and Ward said could be construed to be mean or imply that they didn't love their family, the opposite was true. Maybe Ward didn't want to talk about Ace's wedding plans all the time. Didn't mean he didn't love his brother. Preacher still loved Judge even though the Christmas light show took over both of their lives for literally six months out of the year.

He faced the front when the music started to play, and he walked down the aisle toward the altar like a good, obedient Glover. He caught Cami's eye as he passed, a smile forming on his face. She lifted her hand in a little wave, and he nodded to her. She had dark hair and dark eyes, and she wore a little too much makeup for his liking. Still, he wasn't going to slam a door because she painted black around her eyes when he wished she wouldn't.

Today, she wore a bright pink party dress that stuck out like a neon yellow road sign, and once he'd taken his place behind the altar, he noticed several people looking at her. Including Mother and Aunt Dawna.

Brady came down the aisle with his parents, and then he turned to face the huge barn door in the back. Ida came through it with Ward, both of them beaming at one another. Ida had sewn her own dress, and Preacher had never seen anything like it. The white lace swirled in spots, the white turning colored—pale yellow, blue, green, and pink—as it swooped and created flowers. He could smile at his cousin and the radiance pouring from her. She obviously loved Brady Burton, and he loved her.

Ward passed Ida to him, clapping him on the shoulder, and the pair turned toward Pastor Corning. Brady wore his dress uniform, which was deep and dark, with stripes on the shoulder and colored squares on the front. He wore a stiff, policeman's hat, and he stuck out without a cowboy hat on his head, that was for sure.

The pastor said beautiful things about love and family, reminding Preacher why he wanted to find someone he could love as much as Brady loved Ida. His eyes wandered to Cami, but she was looking down at her phone.

He frowned, though he wondered how he'd act at someone else's wedding where he didn't know anyone. *You wouldn't get your phone out*, he thought, and he knew he was right.

"You may kiss your bride."

That was the cue to whoop and holler, but Preacher did neither. He left that to Ace, Bishop, Judge, and Mister, instead just clapping and smiling at the happy couple as they kissed.

When he could, he stepped over to Cami. "You made it."

"This place is *incredible*," she said. "I want to take pictures of everything." She wore a light in her eyes he liked, but when she touched his chest, there was nothing there.

Preacher kept his smile on his face and danced with her. He laughed with her. He talked with her, and pretended to care about her parakeets—birds were a big no for him—and her job driving a school bus.

He knew he wouldn't be calling her again though.

"Ice cream?" he asked right after the first dance had happened. The bouquet tossing was next, and then Preacher hoped he and Cami could make a graceful exit, and he could get on home and get out of his tuxedo.

"Oh my gosh," Cami said for probably the tenth time that evening. "She got Below Zero to come?" She looked at Preacher with delight. "Yes, I want some."

"All right." Preacher wasn't sure what the big deal was, but he could go for a sweet treat any day, any time. He stepped over to the booth in the corner by the kitchen, which looked like the owner had taken a huge cattle trough, turned it on its side, and stuck some flags in it.

A menu hung on the front in blocky letters. "Looks like they have chocolate, vanilla, wedding cake, or Nutella," he said. "Then you get to mix in some toppings."

They waited while a few other people got their scoops, and then Preacher stepped up to the metal tub.

The woman there had gorgeous blonde hair that looked like she'd skipped using a comb and instead had gathered her hair into its chunky bun with her fingers. She had beautiful blue eyes, and a golden glow in her skin that made Preacher want to ask her if she spent time outside or just possessed the feminine glow naturally.

Her mouth moved, but he didn't hear her. She started to work, her muscles lifting the heavy bottle of chocolate ice cream base and pouring it into a regular-sized mixing bowl. He could see the machine behind her, though, and his interest shifted from the woman to the process.

Sound came rushing back at him, and he heard her ask him what he wanted. Thankfully. "I'll take vanilla with the peanut butter cups," he said.

She nodded, no smile in sight, and turned to set the bowl on the machine. She locked it all in place, turned it on, and stepped back.

At first the mixer just spun, then a big, billowy white cloud came out of the bowl. Cami bounced on her feet and clapped, squealing as she did. Preacher looked at her, sure she hadn't just made such a sound over liquid nitrogen freezing the ice cream. The clouds continued to foam while the mixer kept spinning, and he could admit it was a pretty cool thing.

But not squeal-worthy. The woman hadn't gotten a new horse or anything. It was ice cream.

The woman behind the metal tub smiled as she filled a new bowl with his choices. She stepped over to the machine and swapped out bowls. While his ice cream got the puffy cloud and then "steamed," she scooped Cami's into a cup.

"How does it do that?" he asked her.

The woman lifted her blue eyes to Preacher's, and everything caught inside him. Absolutely everything.

Chapter Twenty-Five

Charlie Perkins stared at the cowboy in front of her. She'd met a million of them if she'd met one, that was for dang sure. This one, though...there was something different about him.

What, she didn't know.

"You do know how it works, right?" he asked, a half-smile now riding his mouth.

Charlie blinked, because she'd gone mute for a moment. "Yes," she said, glancing at the woman in the neon dress at his side. If he liked women like that, he most certainly would not like her.

Ida Glover had assured her she could wear her tank top and jeans to the wedding, but standing in front of this man, she felt like she should've at least tried by putting on mascara. A shirt with sleeves. Something.

"Liquid nitrogen takes the temperature down to negative three hundred and twenty-one degrees in a matter of seconds," she said, turning to get his bowl off the machine. As she stirred and scooped it out, she continued. "Since it freezes so fast, there's no time for large ice crystals to form, which is why this is the smoothest and creamiest ice cream you'll ever have."

She put a fake smile on her face as she handed over his peanut butter cup ice cream.

"Thank you, ma'am." He tipped his cowboy hat and dropped a bill into the tip cup she'd painted like a black-and-white dairy cow. It was a hundred-dollar bill.

Charlie's mouth turned dry, and she wanted to call the cowboy back over and tell him she didn't need his charity.

Maybe he thought it was a one-dollar bill, she thought. Someone else stepped up to the station, and she blinked to focus on their face instead of staring at the handsome cowboy as he walked away.

Another cowboy stood there, this one as handsome as the last, just in a different way. They had to be brothers, because the man in front of her had a similar jawline, and those blue eyes that didn't quite match the dark hair curling out from beneath his hat.

"You know what just happened, right?" he asked just as she said, "What flavor would you like for your base?"

They looked at one another, and Charlie's pulse picked up again, this time for a different reason than with the last cowboy.

"Vanilla," he said as she asked, "What just happened?"

She glanced around the hall, where several couples danced, people loitered at tables with cake and ice cream— her ice cream—and still others stood in groups talking.

She'd catered a few events now, and Below Zero had tons of room to grow. Her goal was to get a permanent stand somewhere, as she'd been setting up in the two grocery stores in town, or at the summer dances, or outside the bakery since she'd opened the doors two months ago.

"Mix in?" she asked.

"Can I have more than one?"

"Yes, sir."

He grinned at her. "I'll take the chocolate chips and the brownie bites."

Charlie dutifully poured in the base, then added a scoop of each topping. She turned and locked the bowl onto the base, her right arm smarting with the effort it took to do that. She'd done it so many times tonight already, and she reminded herself this was a good gig.

She'd given away almost all of her business cards already, and she estimated she'd served three-quarters of the guests here tonight. *All good for business*, she told herself.

She turned to get the cup for his treat and found him lifting the hundred-dollar bill from her tip cup. "Hey," she said, instantly reaching for the money.

He grinned at her and let her take it. "Look at that."

"Look at it?" Behind her, the machine stopped whirring, which meant the ice cream had churned. She stuffed the bill in her pocket and turned to get this customer out of her hair. She could take a five-minute break after him.

She used the metal scraper to get the ice cream off the sides of the very cold bowl, then scooped it all up nice and neat and round and dropped it in the cup. "There you go."

"Thank you, ma'am." He too tipped his hat, and Charlie

stepped out of the booth before anyone else could approach her stand.

She headed for the restroom at the back of the hall, spying a whole group of cops—good-looking cops—as she went. Several of them watched her, but she didn't smile at them. She was interested in dating, but she'd only been in town for a couple of months. She wanted to get her footing stronger before she introduced a man into her new life in Three Rivers.

She wanted her business to have time to grow.

She needed more time to pass so the traditional towns-people here would have the opportunity to come to terms with the growth of Three Rivers.

See, Charlie worked for HealNow, the new testing and chemical lab in town, and not everyone was super happy about the company—or the twelve-story building—being here.

She still wasn't sure she was happy being here. She'd worked for HealNow for long enough to request a transfer and get it, so she hadn't started making connections yet. In fact, she hadn't even finished unpacking.

In the ladies' room, she shut herself in a stall and pulled out the hundred-dollar bill. On the back side, she found some writing in black pen.

Preacher Glover.

And his phone number.

She looked up, alarmed. How in the world had he written that on this bill while standing in front of her? It took fifteen seconds for the ice cream base to freeze once the liquid nitrogen hit it. Her mixers were calibrated for another ten seconds of mixing to introduce the precise quantity of air to make the ice cream light and almost fluffy.

The whole process took maybe forty-five seconds. Then she scraped, balled, and served.

There was no way this Preacher Glover had time to write anything on a hundred-dollar bill. Not only that, he'd been with a date. And his last name suggested a relation to Ida, the woman who'd hired her for tonight.

Charlie had met Ida the first week she'd been in town. They'd both been reaching for the same box of stuffing at the grocery store, and something had just clicked between them. "Maybe if you'd known she had a hot brother or cousin or something...."

But Charlie could've said that for any of the cowboys there that night. Preacher wasn't special.

As she looked back at the money, she actually wondered if he carried pre-marked bills around with him, dropping them in front of the women he deemed worthy. Disgusted, she considered throwing the money in the trashcan.

"Don't be ridiculous," she told herself. "It's a hundred bucks. Cash it in for smaller bills and move on." With a plan in mind, she tucked the bill in her back pocket and started to return to her booth. She wasn't going to call the arrogant cowboy, that was for dang sure.

A man didn't fit into her plans right now, and certainly not one who thought he could put his name and phone number on a hundred-dollar bill and find the woman of his dreams.

Chapter Twenty-Six

Lois Glover hugged her sister-in-law and pressed against her own tears. "How are you holding up? Two kids getting married within three weeks of one another."

Lois was the one who'd planned Ida's and Holly Ann's weddings, so she knew the level of exhaustion it took for a seventy-nine-year-old woman to plan two weddings happening in the space of three weeks.

She loved it with every fiber of her being though. She'd always wanted to plan events, and there was nothing better than a wedding. The flowers, the decorations in the hall, the dresses, the ties, the suspenders, the cake, the food, the actual ceremony itself.

Lois loved it all. She loved that every little detail could be different, but the result was the same—a happy couple starting their life together.

"I'm good," Dawna said with a smile. "You've done all the work."

"Oh, please. I saw Ida's dress, and someone did something with Holly Ann's hair." She smiled fondly at Dawna, this woman she'd known for about fifty years now. She'd married Stone first, and when she'd learned that they'd be sharing the ranch with his brother and whoever he married, she'd started praying that it would be someone she could get along with.

She needn't have worried, because Dawna was the sweetest woman in the world. Powerful too, in both spirit and tongue, and she'd raised a family of five with care, precision, and strictness.

Lois had done the same. One had to when they were outnumbered seven to two. She'd waited for years for her six sons to realize they could band together and easily overpower her. If they'd ever noticed it, they'd never done it.

She'd only gotten the one girl, and Arizona had challenged Lois far more than any of her other children. She also loved her fiercely, and if pressed, she'd have to admit she was the closest to Arizona.

Bishop was a close second and Bear right behind him.

That was how Lois knew about what had happened with Cactus, Willa, and Bear. Bishop had told her about the argument, and Bear had confessed what he'd done a few days later. Lois had been praying for all of them ever since, but she wasn't sure the situation had been resolved yet.

Cactus had been answering her texts with one or two words, and all of the reports from the other children confirmed that she wasn't the only one he didn't want to talk to.

She needed to sit him down and talk to him. Tell him not

to disappear, not to cut himself out of the family where he belonged. Not again.

Her mother heart wept for all of them. She just wanted them all to be happy. She had lived on Earth long enough to know she couldn't force them to get along. Preacher and Arizona had been like oil and water from the moment Lois and Stone had brought the baby girl home from the hospital.

Judge had been ruthlessly teasing Mister from the moment they could both talk. Cactus and Bear butted heads occasionally.

But they've never thrown punches, she thought.

She turned as the music started, and she linked her arm through Dawna's and led her to the front row, where they'd witness Ace and Holly Ann's wedding. The two older women stayed standing as Ace entered the hall.

"He looks so happy," she whispered to Dawna, who sniffled in response.

Lois loved Ace as if he were her own son, and she beamed at him as he took his spot in front of the altar.

Holly Ann entered the hall on the arm of her father, a retired detective from the Three Rivers Police Department. Her dress hugged her curves and fell in billowy layers once it reached her hips. Her underskirts peeked out in shades of purple, and when Lois caught a glimpse of her heels, she saw black.

Holly Ann sure was different but refined too. Sophisticated. Gorgeous. Perfect for Ace.

Once she reached Ace, the music changed, and her father barely got out of the way before Ace and Holly Ann started dancing. Lois burst out laughing, as did many others, and just as abruptly as the tune had started, it stopped.

They faced the pastor, and Lois eased herself into the chair next to Donald. He reached over and took her hand in his, and Lois turned toward him with a smile. He stoked the fire inside her, as much as she'd fought against it. He'd asked her out four times before she'd said yes, and she'd kept their relationship a secret for months after that.

They'd been dating for over a year now, and Lois wondered what the endgame was. She'd been living on the main floor of the homestead, in a one-bedroom suite that was plenty big for just her. Bishop made her breakfast almost every morning, and Ranger, Sammy, or Bear manned dinner in the evenings.

She got to see Stetson every single day, and Lois could not imagine not being at Shiloh Ridge Ranch.

At the same time, if Donald wanted to marry her, there was nowhere for them here.

There's the Top Cottage, she thought. Ace and Holly Ann would only be there for a few months, at most, and she couldn't get married that fast anyway.

Why couldn't you? she asked herself, and there wasn't an answer. Of course she could. All she needed was a dress and a preacher. She didn't need the elaborate weddings her children and nieces and nephews had been putting on.

This year alone, the barn where they sat for this wedding had already seen three weddings. Today's was number four. Could hers be number five?

Donald's hand on hers tightened, and she looked at him again. He leaned toward her, and she inched her head back and to the side. "What do you think?" he asked. "Of us doin' this?"

They hadn't spoken much of marriage, maybe a word here or one there, so surprise filled her. "Is that a proposal?"

"No," he whispered, chuckling. "I'm just wondering where your head is."

Lois would like to know that too. She looked at Ace and Holly Ann, holding hands in front of the altar, pledging themselves to each other. It was a beautiful thing to behold, and a wonderful thing to sacrifice for someone else.

She blinked, and she could see herself marrying Donald Parker. "I'm interested in talking about it some more," she murmured.

He nodded, squeezed her hand again, and settled back into his chair.

Willa Knowlton was once again officiating the wedding here, and Lois automatically looked around to find Cactus. As far as she knew, he and Willa were still getting along just fine.

She didn't find him on the first two rows with everyone else, and a frown pulled through her very soul. He sat back a couple more rows, right on the end, with Mitch beside him. He signed to the boy, and Lois's heart filled with love for the both of them.

She'd bought a baseball bat and glove for Mitch a month or so ago, and Willa had been the one to tell her how much the child loved them. Lois enjoyed figuring out what each person liked and providing them with something to bring them joy.

She'd been buying sketch books for Lincoln for a while

now, and she'd sent Aurora a couple of gift cards to her favorite store in the mall. She knew how very important it was for teenage girls to have cute clothes.

Mitch loved baseball, because he didn't have to hear to play it. He could run fast, and he'd been playing on a community team since school started. He could see the ball exceptionally well, and all the signals for when to run, steal, or stay on base happened with hands.

It was the perfect sport for him, and Willa had told Lois that Mitch used his glove and bat every single day.

The ceremony concluded, and Lois stood to help Dawna up. They both clapped for a minute, and then Dawna stepped over to her boy. Lois stayed at Donald's side, perfectly happy there.

With a jolt, she realized she had work to do. "Let's get the tables set up," she said. Donald went with her to help, and only ten minutes later, Ranger stood in front of a microphone.

"Thanks for bein' here, everyone," he said. "They're going to serve dinner now, and then we'll cut the cake, and that's it. A bit different this time, so hang tight while they bring out the food."

He never was one for big speeches, and Lois wondered why Ace had asked him to do it. The food came out of the kitchen quickly, and Lois relaxed once she saw everyone had been served.

Whitney Walker buzzed around the room, snapping pictures, and when she came to Lois's table, she leaned into Donald and put a smile on her face. Whitney grinned at her, and said, "Just the cake, right?"

"Yes, please," Lois said, glancing around to see if Etta had brought it in yet. She'd wanted to make the cake for Ida's wedding, but Ida had her heart set on a custom cake from Sophia May. She'd gotten it too, and it had been truly spectacular, with eleven tiers, right up to the top one that had only been two inches in diameter.

Etta placed another flower on the cake, and somehow her gaze went right to Lois's. She nodded, and Lois stood up. Both Holly Ann and Ace saw her, and they rose to their feet too.

"Time to cut the cake," Lois said. "Everyone gather 'round."

The family did, and Ace cut a slice of cake and acted like he'd feed it to Holly Ann delicately. But he'd always been one of the rowdier Glover boys, and sure enough, he ended up smashing it into her face.

"Oh, you're dead," she said, not even bothering with the knife. She grabbed a fistful of cake and shoved it in Ace's mouth. Lois simply did not understand this part of the wedding, but it was one of the only things Ace and Holly Ann had wanted.

She clapped while most others laughed and laughed, especially Bishop. Then, just like that, the wedding ended. Ace and Holly Ann walked out of the barn with their family and friends lining both sides of the foyer, cheering and applauding.

He held the door of the tiny red sportscar he'd rented, and as he peeled away from the barn, Holly Ann sat up and faced the crowd. She tossed her bouquet from the car as the tires finally got purchase on the new gravel here, and they flew down the lane in a cloud of smoke and a roar of dust.

Lois took a deep breath, and said, "All right then," before turning back to the barn. Everyone helped to clean up, but she noticed Bear and Cactus on opposite sides of the room. Likewise, Judge and Mister barely acknowledged one another.

She looked up when she heard Judge say, "You have *no idea* what it takes to do the light show."

Lois found him facing off with Mister near the back wall. She instinctively took a step that way but stopped herself from committing. They were adults, and they had to learn how to get along.

In times like these, though, she wished Stone were still here. She felt like some of the precarious relationships in the family had definitely crumbled more since he'd passed.

"I know you're driving everyone, including me, crazy with it, and it's barely October," Mister said.

Preacher stepped over to them and diffused the situation. Lois exchanged a glance with Don. "You want all this?"

"I have four grown children," he said. "Your kids aren't unique in their relationships." He gave her a smile and folded another chair. Little by little and person by person, the barn emptied until it was just her and Don.

She retrieved her purse from the brides' room and linked her arm through his. "Do you want a big, traditional wedding?"

"No, ma'am," he said. "You?"

"Not really."

He paused right in the middle of the now-empty hall and

gently took her purse from her. He set it on the ground and took her into his arms. They started to sway to a silent slow song, and Lois calmed completely. Being held felt wonderful, and she smiled as her eyes drifted closed.

Don cared about her, and he'd take good care of her. She wanted to care for him too.

Peace filled her, and she pressed her cheek to Don's and inhaled the woodsy, almost citrusy scent of his cologne.

"Lois," he whispered as they swayed back and forth, back and forth. "I love you. I love spending time with you, and I'd love to call you my wife."

Lois inched back so she could see his face. Hope as bright as stars shone in his eyes. "Will you marry me?"

She didn't need to ask if he'd just proposed this time. "Yes," she said, her grin genuine and filling her whole face. "Yes, I love you too, and yes, I want to be your wife."

He ducked his head and chuckled, never one to use too many words. Stone had been similar, though he'd definitely voiced more opinions than Don usually did.

"What do you think about a Christmas wedding?" he whispered, leaned closer and closer to her.

"I think that sounds perfect," she murmured, her eyes already closed. He kissed her, and Lois allowed herself to float away in the loving embrace of such a good man.

She'd have to tell the children, and soon, but for right now, she just wanted to be Donald Parker's fiancée without anyone else knowing—and to keep dancing in the still, silent barn her first husband had built with his own hands.

Chapter Twenty-Seven

T ripp Walker gave up trying to talk to Oliver before they'd even reached the northern edge of town. The boy was not happy, and he didn't want to talk about Aurora Martin.

"Uncle Wyatt says he has a surprise for you," Tripp tried, and Ollie looked up from his phone.

"Yeah?"

"Yeah."

"I think I already know what it is," the sixteen-year-old said. "It's something for my truck."

"Did he tell you that?"

"He implied he'd gotten something that would make driving better." Ollie shrugged. "It doesn't matter now. I'm not driving out here anymore." He looked out the windshield. "Is Grandpa coming today?"

"Yes, Jeremiah is bringing him." Tripp looked at Oliver again, his heart filled with worry for the boy. He wasn't a little boy anymore, but that didn't mean Tripp didn't need to be concerned about him. "Why?"

"I'm almost done with that app he's been helping me with," Ollie said. "My teacher said it was, and I quote, incredible." That got a smile to appear on his face, and Tripp's spirits lifted to see it.

"Yeah? You didn't tell me that." Oliver had enrolled in an elective computer science class at the high school, and the teacher was a former employee of Google and Dell. He had the kids doing real computer science, not just coding a sequence of commands to put in a number and get out a letter.

Ollie really liked the class, and it was barely October, and Tripp had liked listening to him talk about what they learned.

"I guess I forgot," Ollie said, and the conversation stalled again.

Tripp tried to stay relaxed, but he couldn't stop praying for Oliver. His girlfriend of the last year had broken up with him a week or two ago, and he'd been in a funk since. He barely spoke around the house, and while he usually wanted to go to Seven Sons and work, he'd been calling Jeremiah after school and saying he couldn't come.

Not only that, but as the oldest cousin, all the little boys and girls in the Walker family loved Ollie with the heat of the sun. He was incredible with them, but he'd snapped at Isaac, his half-brother, that morning, and he'd told his mother he didn't want to babysit all the kids while the adults talked, something he'd always done happily.

Things change, Ivory had told Tripp, but he suspected it was something more than that.

He considered other topics he could bring up, but in the end, he stayed quiet. He made the turn off the highway and onto dirt road, and a couple of miles later, he rounded a curve and watched the enormity of Three Rivers Ranch expand before him.

He'd never wanted a ranch, though he had lived at Seven Sons and helped there in a pinch. But he loved visiting the ranch that Jeremiah and Skyler tended to, and he always felt loose pieces get stitched back together when he came to Three Rivers.

He went past Bowman's Breeds on his left and the commercial front of Courage Reins on the right, pulling past both homesteads and around to a parking lot behind the indoor arena. He and his brothers had come out to this ranch a couple of years ago, after a trio of twisters had touched down and caused a lot of damage.

Courage Reins and the buildings it comprised had suffered the most damage, and as part of the rebuild, Pete Marshall had put in this lot.

"Look, they're already here," Tripp said, pulling in next to Wyatt's enormous truck. He needed a vehicle that big to house his body and personality. Or the new hat he'd just come out with in time for the holidays—the True Texan—which was thirty percent bigger than his regular line of cowboy hats.

Ollie got out of the truck, and Tripp watched him for half a second before turning off the ignition. "Please, send him the help he needs today," he whispered before following his son.

Oliver wasn't really his son, but Tripp considered him as such. His father wasn't anywhere in the picture, or even the same art gallery, and Tripp had been raising Oliver as his for almost eight years now.

Ollie called him Dad, and Tripp lifted his hand to say a non-verbal hello to Jeremiah as Wyatt presented Oliver with a steering wheel cover and a huge grin. Ollie remembered his manners, saying, "Thanks, Uncle Wyatt. This is great," and hugging the taller, broader cowboy.

"I'll put it in the truck," Tripp said, and Ollie handed it to him before turning to Daddy. He started talking about the app as Tripp walked away, and when he returned, all four of them were huddled around Oliver's phone.

Tripp stayed out of the circle, because he could ask to see it later. He listened to the teenager talk, and his voice did carry some of its normal excitement.

"Walkers," someone called, and they all lifted their heads toward the blonde-haired woman. "You're with me today. Let's go." She carried a clipboard and wore a smile, gesturing for them to come over to the gate that led into the pathway between the indoor and outdoor arenas.

"Anyway," Oliver said, tucking his phone into his back pocket. "It's not done yet, but I think it's coming along."

"It's comin' along real nice," Daddy said, beaming at Oliver as if he'd just cured cancer. Tripp's heart warmed at the love his father had for the boy, and he stepped to Jeremiah's side and touched his arm to get him to slow.

His older brother did, and he looked at Tripp with questions in his eyes. Tripp let Daddy, Wyatt, and Ollie take a few more steps, glad when Wyatt asked Oliver another question that kept the kid talking.

"He's struggling," he said. "I know you've been letting him stay home in the afternoons, but I don't think it's helping him."

Jeremiah looked up to the group ahead of them and back to Tripp. "He said he was sick."

"I know." Tripp shook his head. "He's fine. Aurora broke up with him."

"Ah, I see." Jeremiah nodded. "Okay, I'll make sure he knows I need him."

"Thank you," Tripp said. Everyone wanted to feel needed and necessary, and he'd noticed over the years that Oliver thrived when he felt that way.

They caught up to the others and got assigned horses. Tripp stayed close to Oliver, though he'd ridden a horse plenty of times. He could saddle a horse easily, and he knew where to stand and what to do.

"Can we add one to your group?" Helena asked. "I forgot to call and let you know."

"It's fine," Tripp said. "You guys do group sessions in sixes." He glanced behind her, and it wasn't hard to see the tall cowboy standing there. "Oh, hey, Cactus."

He knew the Glovers, at least by name. Bear came to Seven Sons more than any of the others, but they'd all come to Momma's parties last year, and he knew they were good cowboys, and good men.

"Hey." Cactus put a smile on his face that didn't stay long, and Tripp quickly said a prayer for him too.

"Okay," Helena said. "We're doing a ride out to Standing Rock today. You can walk your horse at any time. You can spread out or stay close. You need to be able to see me all the time, or you're out of bounds." She smiled around at everyone. "You get twenty minutes with your horse here at the beginning, and we'll leave at three-fifty, okay?"

Tripp nodded, and only Wyatt said, "Okay, Helena. Thanks."

Daddy had already wandered off with his paint horse, and Jeremiah had his hand on the nose of a Tennessee walking horse. Tripp looked at his bay, glad to be standing a foot or two from the quiet, strong beast in front of him.

His heartbeat slowed, and Tripp took a long, deep breath. He'd never considered himself someone who needed to see a counselor or do any type of therapy. But he sure did love coming out here and working with the horses.

A few paces from him, Ollie said, "Hey, Bountiful. You missed me, didn't you?"

Tripp smiled and kept his head angled away from his son, hoping he'd hear more.

"Oh, this is the perfect group to talk to."

Tripp looked up at the sound of Pete Marshall's voice. The man had founded Courage Reins about twelve or thirteen years ago, and he put one foot up on the bottom rung of the fence separating him and an auburn-haired woman from Tripp, the others, and all the horses.

"How's it going, Ollie?" Pete asked, his voice ever so cheerful.

"Fine." Ollie walked over and shook Pete's hand.

"Doesn't seem like it."

"That's why we're here, I guess," Ollie said, glancing over to Tripp. Caught eavesdropping, Tripp went on over and shook Pete's hand too, looking pointedly at the woman.

"This is Molly Benson," he said, grinning at her. "She and her husband—"

"Fiancé," she corrected quickly.

"Fiancé," Pete said. "Are lookin' to start an equine therapy unit in Colorado. She came to observe and ask questions."

"Oh, that's great," Tripp said, smiling at her.

She smiled back, and she had lovely green eyes and a smattering of freckles across her face. "So you guys just come out to ride?"

"Sort of," Tripp said.

Interest entered her eyes. "Do you mind if I tag along with you?"

"I don't," Tripp said, glancing at Ollie. "On the group sessions, they let you sort of do your own thing, as long as you stay somewhat close to the group."

"Okay," she said, climbing the fence and jumping down next to him. "I won't ask you anything too hard." She glanced at Oliver. "What about you...I'm sorry. I don't know any of your names."

"Oh," Tripp said with a chuckle. "I'm Tripp Walker. My son, Oliver."

"How old are you, Oliver?"

"Sixteen, ma'am," he said, migrating back to Bountiful.

Molly stayed closer to Tripp while he saddled his horse, and he told her what he was doing. "This is part of the therapy," he said. "I think I was told it helps people to have to take care of their animal, because the horse relies on them. It gives them a sense of accomplishment and power they often feel like they don't have."

Molly nodded and typed a few notes in her phone. Pete returned with two horses before the twenty minutes expired, and Molly swung onto the back of a horse easily enough. It was clear she didn't ride all the time, but she was competent enough.

"We're specializing in children," she said, guiding her horse closer to Oliver. "Can I ask you what you like about coming out for a group lesson?"

Tripp's chest tightened, but Oliver gave Molly a friendly smile. "I like coming with my family," he said.

Tripp edged his horse a bit away from Oliver but stayed close enough to hear.

"So you don't really have a need," Molly said.

"Sure I do," Ollie said. "I like talking to the horses. I like saddling them, and teaching them to push the ball."

"I just saw that," she said. "We've got our kids walking the horses in rings, but we haven't moved on to balls yet."

"All of that is fun," Ollie said. "It helps me remember that my whole life doesn't happen at my own house, or at school."

"Interesting," Molly said. "What do you mean by that?"

If Tripp had asked the question, he'd have gotten a huff and an eyeroll. But for her, Oliver said, "You know, like how everything feels like such a big deal. My mom is always nagging me about my room or putting my boots away."

She was, but that was what moms did.

"And at school, you're always so worried about being smart, or cool, or wearing the right clothes or whatever." He let out a long breath. "But then I come out here, and none of it matters. The horses don't care if I failed my chemistry test or said something stupid to a girl or whatever."

Tripp looked at Ollie, who looked back at him. "Did you fail your chemistry test?"

Oliver smiled and shook his head. "No, Dad. I'm just saying."

"I'm sure it was the comment to the girl," Molly teased, and Ollie looked back at her. Her demeanor changed quickly, and she said, "Oh, there *is* a girl. I'm sorry."

Ollie cleared his throat and faced the horizon in front of him again. Tripp hadn't seen the look on his face, but Molly had obviously noticed something.

"Yeah," Oliver said. "And I was hoping the sky and the wind and the horses would remind me that there's other girls. And that it's okay that she broke up with me." He sighed and shook his head. "But I still feel the same. I still want to be with her."

"You'll never believe this," Molly said. "But I swear it's true. I had this boyfriend in high school. We started dating —I mean, not really dating, but you know how kids are— when we were in sixth grade. We stayed together for a long time, and then I broke up with him when I was fifteen."

"What happened?" Oliver asked.

"Oh, my parents weren't happy with how serious we were, because we were so young. His weren't either."

Tripp purposely didn't look at Oliver, but he felt the glare the teen sent him anyway. He and Ivory hadn't told him he had to break up with Aurora. They'd been advising him to be careful. To really be sure of his feelings.

"Sounds familiar," Oliver said.

"Hey," Tripp said. "We never said you needed to break up with her."

Ollie looked like he might argue, but he didn't. "So what won't I believe?" he asked Molly.

"He's my fiancé now," she said with a smile. "We broke up when we were fifteen, but the Lord brought us back together last year." She looked at Oliver with pure delight in her eyes. "So it's not over, Oliver. You might just be on hold for a while. Maybe God has something for you to learn from this. Maybe there's something *she* has to learn. Maybe there's something different for you in your future, and maybe He'll bring you back together when the time is right."

She let several seconds go by, and then she added, "And maybe He won't. I'm just saying, this break-up feels like the end of the world, but it's not."

"You know what?" Oliver asked. "You're right. I don't believe you."

Molly laughed and said, "I'll call him right now. Do you want me to call him?"

"Kinda," Oliver said, chuckling.

"Your mom and I had to try a couple of times," Tripp said, and Oliver dang near fell off his horse he whipped around so fast.

"You did?"

"Yep." Tripp grinned at him. "I'll have to tell you about it sometime."

"Now is sometime," Oliver said. "Start talking, Dad."

Chapter Twenty-Eight

W illa stood in the shower and breathed in the scent of eucalyptus. In for four counts. Out for four. The tiny, four-ounce bottle set her back thirty dollars, but she got anxiety if it started to run low. She'd learned to buy two bottles at the same time, so she never ran out of the mist that calmed her like nothing else could.

Technically, she should be behind the mic during church today, but Patrick had switched with her so she didn't have to preach on her birthday. She wanted to sit next to Cactus and hold his hand, snuggle into his side, and feel the peace and spirit of the Lord. She never experienced those things on her days to preach, and she'd needed a relaxing birthday.

"Thirty-seven today," she muttered to herself. Before school had started for Mitch, Willa had been dreaming of having a new last name—Glover—by the New Year. She and Cactus's relationship had accelerated to the point where they were kissing all the time, and spending almost every evening together.

Everything had changed when he'd taken that check to Bear. Apparently, they'd gotten into a pretty massive argument, and to Willa's knowledge, Cactus had not spoken to his brother unless absolutely necessary since.

Things had been tense between them at Ida's wedding, as well as Ace's, and Willa hated that she'd been caught in the middle of it. She hadn't even known how she'd managed to mess things up so spectacularly, but she had.

She always did.

She got out of the shower and got dressed, making sure to put in her copper hoops to go with her new burnt orange sweater with a single green stem stitched across the chest. She loved the subtle nod to pumpkins, and Willa adored autumn, everything about it.

Fine, maybe not raking the leaves. She did all the yard work here at the rental house, and that saved her a few hundred dollars each month.

She found Mitch in the kitchen, buttering a piece of toast. She signed "Good morning, baby," to him and drew him into a hug. He still wore his pajamas, and she added, "You finish up and go get dressed. Uncle Patrick is talking today."

Wait, wait, Mitch said sliding his toast back onto the countertop. *It's your birthday, Mama!* He seemed made of glitter and sparkles and sunshine, and she couldn't help the warm smile that came from her.

Happy birthday to you, he started sign-singing, and Willa

led him as if he was the greatest choir in the world. They laughed together, his slightly warped voice twining with hers. She hugged him tight, and though Mitch was a little boy, he sure did have some strength in his arms to hug her back.

I got you something. Just a second. He dashed off down the hall, and Willa set about making coffee for herself. She might have time for it to brew before they had to leave, and she quickly switched the maker on before she'd measured out the grounds.

Mitch returned to the kitchen with a professionally wrapped present in bright purples. Surprise dove through Willa as she finished with the coffee grounds. "Where did you get this?"

Cactus took me shopping before the horseback riding yesterday, he said. *The lady at the store wrapped it.*

"I can see that." Willa took the present, her mind lingering on the man who'd bought it. Sure, Mitch had given it to her, but Cactus had bought it. He'd told her he had some plans for her birthday, but he hadn't detailed them.

Now, though, they were going to church together, and then he'd invited her, Mitch, Patrick, Mariah, and Gigi up to Shiloh Ridge for a family lunch with all the Glovers. Willa had been around them before, but in a bigger venue, at a bigger event.

Cactus said the Sabbath Day dinners could be more intense, because the space was smaller, but the men and voices just as big.

Open it, Mitch said, and Willa pulled herself out of her thoughts. She gave her son a smile and peeled back the paper. A new coffee machine peeked up at her, and her eyes widened. "Mitch," she said. "This is amazing." She ripped off the paper fully to reveal the best hot drink machine on the market.

It made coffee, of course, but also heated water for hot chocolate, soups, or broth. This one came with an assortment of coffee cups and hot chocolate cups, and Willa set it on the counter to thank her son.

"Now, go get dressed," she said after she'd knelt and hugged him, as the scent of coffee filled the air. "We have to leave in five minutes."

She picked up her phone to text Cactus about the coffee maker and saw he'd already messaged her. She silenced her phone at night, and she flipped the switch down to turn the sound back on. His text read, *We don't have to come to dinner up here today. I could take you guys for pizza or barbecue. In fact, let's drive to Oklahoma. I know a great place there that serves the best brisket in the whole world.*

Willa smiled at the tension in his words. Her thumbs hovered over the screen, and she finally tapped out, *We can't go to Oklahoma. Patrick has too much work for that. I'd love to go with you sometime, though. Just me and you.*

She sent that, and then said, *I just opened the coffee machine. Thank you so much. I've wanted one of those for years.*

I'm glad you like it, he said. *Happy birthday, my love.*

Since he'd said that out at his cabin—which was really now a beautiful home—he'd been using that term of endearment instead of *beautiful*.

He hadn't hidden how he felt about her, which had only added to her belief that they'd be married by the end of the year. She didn't want a long engagement, and if he wanted a lot of children, they needed to get married and get started on the family she wanted too.

Cactus had said nothing about marriage or diamonds or engagements. He'd retreated in the past six weeks, and the only time Willa felt like she saw the man she'd started to fall for was at choir practice. When the man opened his mouth to sing, it was like an angel took over his body and shone through his eyes.

At yesterday's Messiah Sing-in practice, he'd shown her the certificate he'd gotten in the mail from The Children's Heart Foundation. He'd made a donation to them, and he'd told her more about the congenital heart disease his son had been born with.

Many babies were able to have the life-saving surgeries they needed to survive, but his son hadn't. His case had been one of the worst, and instead of trying to perform the surgery on his day-old body, Cactus and his wife had decided to simply allow the child to live as long as he could.

Four days.

Willa couldn't even imagine the heartache losing a baby would cause within her, and Cactus had described it as a deep wound on his soul. *It takes a long time to heal*, he'd said. *You look fine on the outside, but the soul itself is mortally wounded.*

Willa had some idea of how he felt, because she'd lost her son due to her own negligence. A split-second decision, doing something she'd done many times before. Now, though, she never looked at her phone while driving. She knew the consequences now, and she knew she'd gotten out of her situation with relative ease.

She poured her coffee and took a few sips, then stepped over to the light switch on the wall and flipped it on and off. She called, "Mitch," and waited for him to come out into the hall. "Time to go," she signed.

He didn't have shoes on, and she went down the hall to help him. A few minutes passed while she tied his tie right and waited for him to put on his shiny church shoes. Then she took a comb and a spray bottle and got his hair to cooperate.

One more swig of coffee later, they hurried out to the car and over to the church. The wind blew quite aggressively today, but Cactus waited outside under the tree near the entrance to the parking lot. Mitch waved to him, and the moment Willa put the SUV in park and the locks disengaged, her son bolted from the car.

Cactus had started walking toward them, and his smile filled the gray day with new light. Willa waited while he scooped Mitch into his arms and the two of them talked about her gift and how surprised she was.

Cactus's gaze strayed to her a couple of times, until he finally put Mitch down and came toward her. "Happy birthday," he said, gathering her into his arms right there in the parking lot. He kissed her, the touch warm and beautiful.

Someone catcalled, and Cactus backed up. He grinned at Bishop and Ace, then took Willa's hand in his. "Can we sit in the back-ish?"

"It's my birthday," she said. "Don't you think I should get what I want?" She grinned up at him, and he smiled back. She could tell it didn't quite have the luster it usually did, though, and she hated that he existed behind this film of waxed paper now.

"Are you okay?" she asked.

"Yes," he said. "I'm fine."

"Have you spoken to Bear?"

Darkness filled his face, and Willa had her answer. "I really think you should," she said.

"Yes, well, I don't trust myself not to start swinging again."

He'd told her everything that had happened at the homestead, including why, and Willa had assured him and reassured him that the car was nothing. That she'd pay him if that was what he wanted.

He hadn't wanted that. He hadn't been able to articulate what he wanted, other than he didn't want Bear stepping in and saving the day.

Willa understood—or she thought she did. Cactus wanted to be the one to help her, and instead, his brother had done it. She wished she'd been able to see her mistake as it was happening. At the time, she'd needed a car, and just as God had dropped manna from heaven for the Israelites, he'd dropped Bear into the parking lot at Wilde & Organic.

She could see Cactus's side, and when he'd asked her why she hadn't refused Bear's offer the way she had his, she hadn't had a suitable answer for him. He hadn't been happy about that either, but he didn't blame her.

He didn't need to; Willa blamed herself plenty.

She stepped into the church, glad to be out of the wind. "We can sit in the back-ish," she said.

He gave her a grin and said, "I think there will be a row

for us." He wore a devilish glint in his eye, and Willa's pulse skyrocketed.

"Cactus."

"What?" He led her across the foyer and opened the door. "You pick the row."

She stepped inside the chapel and froze. The very back row on her right had balloons tied to the end of the pews. Yellow, pink, purple, and blue. They all had white printing on them that read *Happy Birthday!* and they waved lazily in the currents from the air conditioning.

"Cactus," she said.

"I think that row has been saved for us," he whispered.

Willa's face heated as the weight of many eyes landed on her, but she moved down the row and sat right in the middle.

"Happy birthday, pastor," the father in the row in front of her whispered.

"Thank you."

Several others smiled at her, some waved, and everyone that passed from that moment on wished her a happy birthday.

Cactus sat next to her, and the fact that he'd called attention to himself wasn't lost on Willa. He hated people looking at him, and yet he'd made sure they would, simply so she'd have a fun birthday surprise.

"Is this my gift?" she asked, one eye up at the pulpit and most of her attention on her boyfriend.

"Part of it," he said.

"Cactus, I told you I didn't need anything."

"Yeah, and my brother bought you a car." He glared at her,

but it only lasted a moment. "I thought I'd just do nothing and let the day pass as if nothing were different about it." He shook his head, his sarcasm coming through loud and clear.

"I'm taking that car back," she whispered just as Patrick got up to stand behind the mic.

"What?"

"It's causing too many problems," she whispered, sudden tears behind her eyes.

"Willa." Cactus slipped his fingers through hers, and Willa couldn't stay mad at him when he touched her so delicately and said her name with so much emotion. "I'm sorry." He put his mouth right at her ear, so while Patrick spoke into a microphone, all Willa could see and hear and experience was Cactus Glover.

"I don't mean to be so prickly about this," he continued. "It's just...I don't know. I'm still trying to get past it."

"Yeah, and if I didn't have that stupid car, you wouldn't have to be reminded of it every time you saw it."

"Then what are you going to do for a vehicle?"

"I have a bunch of jobs right now," she said. "I'll figure something out."

Mitch leaned forward and looked at her and held his finger to his lips, and Willa could only blink at him. He was deaf. There was no way he'd heard her and Cactus whispering.

"Did he just shush you?" Cactus asked.

"He shushed *us*," Willa said. She looked at Cactus, and the two of them started laughing at the same time. She held hers in silently, everything about Mitch telling her to be quiet as if she'd distracted him from his uncle's speech absolutely hilarious.

A COUPLE OF HOURS LATER, WILLA STOOD ON THE NEWLY graveled parking area in front of the homestead at Shiloh Ridge Ranch. Patrick and his girls had only been a couple of minutes behind her, Mitch, and Cactus, and she wanted them to go inside together.

Well, Mitch had run inside to find Lincoln the moment they'd arrived, but she and Cactus waited outside. The windows had all been thrown open, and the noise coming from the house made Willa turn her head.

"I told you," Cactus muttered.

"I've been here before," Willa said. "I love your family, Cactus." Patrick's car crested the hill. "I'm not so sure about Pastor Corning, though. He's going to be blown away." She actually giggled at the thought.

Her brother got out of the car, his two girls climbing out of the back seat. "Aunt Willa," Gigi said, skipping over to her. "Look at the bracelet Missus Angie made for me." She held up her wrist so Willa could examine the cross-stitched bracelet there.

"Pretty," she said, smiling at her niece.

"Uncle Cactus, can you put me on your shoulders?" Gigi looked up at the tall, Texan cowboy with pure hope in her eyes.

"I sure can, little miss." He beamed at her and swung her right up into the air, causing her to squeal. He handed his cowboy hat to Willa and lifted Gigi up and into position. "What can you see up there?"

"There's dogs comin'," she said.

"A black one and a gray one?"

"Yep. And some gray and black spotted ones."

"Those are the cattle dogs," Cactus said. "And Galaxy and Tank." He walked away from the cars, and Willa went with him, the sight of the little girl on his shoulders more than she could take. He was seriously so good with kids, and she wondered why that didn't translate to adults.

"Can you see a little cemetery over there?" he asked, lifting one of his hands off her leg to point.

"Oh...uh...yeah! Yeah, I see it."

"My daddy is buried there," Cactus said.

"How'd he die?"

"Gigi," Willa said, admonishing her.

"It's fine," Cactus said. "He was real sick, little miss. Have you heard of cancer?"

"Yeah, my grandma had cancer. She died too."

Cactus looked at Willa, plenty of questions in his eyes. "Her mother's mother," Willa said. "Not my mother."

He nodded and gazed over the land. "We better go inside. Sammy likes to stick to a schedule, and she puts the baby down for a nap right after lunch."

"Can I hold the baby?" Mariah asked, looking up at Cactus as if he held the answer to all of life's hard questions.

"I'm sure you can hold the baby," Cactus said, smiling down at her. "Let's go inside." He led the way, and Patrick fell into step beside Willa while Cactus took two dogs and the two girls with him.

"He sure has a way with kids," her brother said. "And animals."

"Yes," Willa said, smiling at Cactus's back. It still bothered her that he hadn't spoken to his brother, especially because he claimed they were close. But what was she to do? Force him to talk to Bear?

She couldn't do that any more than she could direct the wind. It kicked up again just as she started up the steps, and Patrick put his hand on her arm to steady her. She smiled as she trained her eyes on the ground. "Patrick," she said when they reached the top of the steps. "You're such an amazing brother, and I love you."

He looked at her with surprise in his eyes. "I love you too, Willa." He embraced her and said, "Happy birthday, sissy."

She giggled and swatted at him when he chuckled too. "Don't call me that."

"Whatever you say." He grinned his way into the homestead, and the noise of everyone greeting him nearly knocked Willa back onto the porch. She closed the door behind her, which seemed crazy, and followed everyone into the kitchen.

No less than four cakes sat on the counter, and Willa could only blink at them. Somewhere, someone said, "One, two three!" and then room burst into song as everyone in the Glover family and her family sang *Happy Birthday* to her.

She could hear delicate soprano voices and tenors, but really, the loudest voice, the one that struck a chord down deep in her soul came in the form of a bass.

She met Cactus's eyes, and his shone with love for her.

Willa could see it. She could feel it. She wanted to experience it every day for the rest of her life.

How? she wondered, glancing away from him, her eyes easily landing on Bear, who stood about as far from Cactus as possible, way back in the corner of the room, with Brady Burton, the cop who'd married Ida.

She needed to get rid of the car, and she started looking around for Oakley before the song even ended.

Chapter Twenty-Nine

Cactus knew happiness when he saw it. He spent so much time analyzing others, and he found happiness on Willa's face. He hoped it would stay throughout the party, and then the rest of the day, and his stomach flipped when he thought about the rest of the birthday gift he'd gotten for her.

"Okay, okay," Bishop said, actually getting up on a chair and waving his arms. The room quieted, and Cactus stepped over to Willa, peering down into her face.

"Okay?" he asked, and she nodded, her hazel eyes soft and kind. He turned toward Bishop as he outlined the four birthday cakes there—strawberry pistachio, vanilla with chocolate frosting, German chocolate, and carrot with cream cheese frosting.

"Holly Ann made one," Bishop said. "Etta made one. Sammy made one, and I made one. We're having a little contest." He beamed rainbows from his eyes and the width of his smile. "So, anyone who samples all four cakes can vote for their favorite."

Etta reached up and handed Bishop a decorated shoe box, and Cactus just shook his head. It looked like a fourth grader had decorated a box to collect their Valentines.

"You just put your vote in here," he said.

"What do you win?" someone called.

"Bragging rights," Bishop said. "And there might be a little money riding on it. Oh, and whoever wins gets to enter in the bake-off for the Christmas Festival."

"There it is," Cactus said. Bishop wanted to enter the bake-off, but he didn't want to go up against Holly Ann. Or Etta, who really was a whiz with flour and sugar.

"Let's eat," Bishop said. "Bear?"

"Ward's gonna pray," he said from the back of the room, and Cactus's chest tightened. He did need to talk to Bear. The man had come out to the Edge Cabin every week since their argument, and thankfully Cactus had only been home once.

He'd ignored his brother, choosing to send him a text that said he was just getting in the shower and he'd talk to him later.

Of course, he never had. Guilt moved through him for the lie, white as it might be.

Ward started praying, and Cactus whipped his hat off his head, thoughts of the diamond he'd bought for Willa dancing through his head. He couldn't ask her today. It was too cliché. But with Bear buying her a blasted car, Cactus's bar was really, really high.

"All right," Ranger said the moment Ward said, "Amen."

He got up on the chair Bishop had been on. "First, happy birthday to Willa." He smiled at her. "We're glad she and Mitch are here, as well as Pastor Corning and his girls." He looked down at Oakley, who'd come to his side.

Ranger took a big breath and looked out over the sea of people in the spacious kitchen, dining room, and living room. "Oakley and I are going to have a baby."

The room paused for a moment, then the whooping started. They all started stomping their cowboy boots on the hard floor, and Cactus whistled through his teeth, his emotions riding a high crest for a moment.

They swooped down, down, down into jealousy, and he swallowed against the swell of it. He hated that smiling was suddenly hard, and he hated that his immediate thought was of himself at all.

Ranger and Oakley had struggled to get to this point, suffering some losses and going through some rough patches. They had every right to make an announcement like this, and Cactus wanted to be nothing but happy for them.

He *was* happy for them. He simply wanted a child too.

Ranger and Oakley accepted their congratulations, and Cactus took them both into his arms at the same time. "I'm so happy for you both," he said.

Ranger patted him on the back, but Oakley clung to him as if she needed him to stand. He wasn't sure what to make of it, and Ranger stepped over to Ace to hug him.

"Oakley?" Cactus asked, because while he knew the woman, and they were friends, they'd never really spent a lot of time together. He was fairly certain he'd scared her the first time she'd met him. He'd had that affect on people, especially with his long hair.

She gripped him tight, and for such a petite woman, she sure possessed some strength. "I'm so sorry I sold that stupid car to Bear," she said, her voice high and tinny. "He called me, and I'd literally just found out I was pregnant and hadn't lost the baby yet, and I wasn't thinking straight. I should've called you."

"Oh, come on now," Cactus said. "It's not your faut at all." He pulled away and looked into her tear-filled eyes. "Tell me you haven't been worried about this all these weeks."

Her chin trembled, and Cactus felt like a bigger jerk than he already did. He pulled her back to his chest and said, "It's not your fault, Oakley. Not even a little bit."

"Etta Mae Glover, what is on your hand?"

Oakley jumped away from Cactus as if he'd caught fire, and she strode the three steps to where Etta and Montana stood. Montana gripped Etta's left hand, though Etta was trying to pull it away.

"That's an engagement ring," Montana said.

Oakley looked at Etta, and the pleading on her face said it all.

The doorbell rang, but no one moved. Everyone stared at Etta, who finally got her hand away from Montana.

"I'll get it," Willa said, and Cactus felt like he was moving in slow motion as his head turned to watch her leave the kitchen. She returned a few seconds later, Noah Johnson right behind her. The man was easily as old as Cactus, and he had half a head of gray hair.

He carried himself well, and he should, as he owned a lot

of land up in the hills that had recently been sold to make new subdivisions.

No one moved. No one spoke. Cactus looked from Noah to Etta and back, playing ping-pong between them. Everyone else seemed to be doing the same.

"I was going to talk to Mother first," Etta said, rolling her eyes. She walked across the kitchen to Noah and looked up into his face. She said something Cactus doubted even Willa could hear, though she only stood a few paces away.

Noah nodded, and then Etta stepped to his side and linked her arm through his as she surveyed the group. "Noah and I are engaged."

The women shrieked together, and Cactus's eyes rounded. Had they practiced that to make sure it happened in tandem?

Either way, Ida, Sammy, Holly Ann, Oakley, Arizona, Montana, and Aurora converged on Etta. Even Mother and Aunt Dawna made their way across the room to the happy couple.

"We've prayed," someone yelled, and it sounded dangerously like Judge. "I'm eating."

Cactus watched the line form, but he stayed out of the way, where he liked to be. Someone tugged on his shirt, and he looked down at Mitch.

What happened? he asked.

"My cousin got engaged," he said. "They're going to get married." He smiled at Etta and Noah, because they looked good together. He wondered if people said that about him and Willa.

Another wave of jealousy threatened to drag him under

and cut him up on the rocks. He wanted to get married again desperately. He thought of the diamond ring, and as he overheard Etta telling the story of how Noah had proposed, he knew he couldn't just hand it to Willa for her birthday and make her open it herself.

There had to be a story, and he frowned as he picked up a plate and put a couple of bites of all the different cakes on it. He handed it to Mitch, and said, "You taste them all, boy. Vote for the best one." He tapped the box, and Mitch's expression radiated joy and surprise.

I can eat cake before my meal?

"Yep," Cactus said. With the announcements of other people getting their dreams of marriage and family, today was definitely an eat-dessert-first type of day. He took extra-large servings of all four cakes and joined the child at the table, along with Lincoln and Aurora.

"No Ollie today?" he asked, forking up his first bite of carrot cake. This had Holly Ann written all over it, and Cactus expected greatness as he put it in his mouth.

Aurora looked up at him, her eyes bright with tears. "We broke up."

"Oh, shoot," Cactus said, his chest pinching. "I'm sorry, Aurora. I didn't know."

She shook her head and sniffled, ducking away to wipe her face. "It's fine. Don't tell my mom I cried." She pulled in a deep breath and blinked, quickly erasing the evidence of her distress.

His heart squeezed extra-hard for her. "You come out to my cabin any time," he said. "You can cry out there all you want."

She nodded and smiled through another round of watery eyes. "Can I play with Galaxy and Tank?"

Mitch started signing, and Cactus translated for him, saying, "He says Tank is real good with a ball now, and yes, he wants you to come out to the cabin to play with the dogs." He grinned at the boy and then the teenage girl, wishing he could protect them all from the hard, disappointing, or hurtful things in the world.

A WEEK LATER, CACTUS HAD JUST RETURNED TO HIS CABIN for a solitary, silent lunch when his phone rang. The number bore an area code that made his pulse quicken. He hurried to pull off his gloves and swipe on the call. "Hello?"

"Charles Glover, please," a woman said.

"This is him." He continued into the kitchen to get a bottle of water from the fridge.

"Mister Glover, my name is Rosalee Larkin. I work with Paws With a Cause."

"Oh, my goodness," Cactus said.

Rosalee laughed lightly. "I get that a lot. It's my great pleasure to let you know we have a hearing dog for Mitchell Knowlton. My records say he's ten, so he's likely in school. We come to you, and the dog we have for him has been raised and trained in Georgia. So we just need to set up a time to introduce Mitch and Frost, and then we'll go over paperwork, payment, and the things you'll need to plan on having so you can keep the dog after the initial meeting."

Cactus's mind blanked, the water now forgotten. He

didn't have Mitch's schedule memorized, though he knew the boy had baseball practice on Mondays and Wednesdays. Games were usually on Friday or Saturday, or both, but the season was almost over.

Willa had choir practices three days a week—Wednesday, Thursday, and Saturday. He was moving into birthing season, but was actually experiencing a brief lull in his veterinary work on the ranch.

"Honestly, ma'am," he finally said, looking around his cabin as if he'd never seen it before. "You tell us when you'll be here, and we'll be available."

"Oh, I like you, Mister Glover." She typed so loudly he could hear it on his end of the line. "Let's see…I've got availability with his trainer to come next Thursday. Would that work?"

"Yes," Cactus said, searching frantically for something to write with now. He didn't see anything in the vicinity, and he cursed himself for not being prepared.

"With the time difference, the travel…I think they'll be there in the late afternoon. I'll send you the full itinerary once it's final."

"Will it just be that afternoon?" he asked. "Or Friday too?"

"If Frost and Mitch get along, our trainer will stay for four or five days to help everyone learn what the dog knows. We have a very high success rate for matches between dogs and kids, and we think Frost will be the perfect hearing dog for a boy like Mitch."

Cactus nodded, and said, "Okay." He'd need to clear the whole weekend, and he needed to call Willa the moment this call ended. His patience ran thin as Rosalee talked about the paperwork she'd send him, how he could send the rest of the payment, and a packing list she'd also email.

The call finally ended, and Cactus dialed Willa with shaking fingers.

"You got lucky," she said. "I just went on break."

"Paws With a Cause just called," he blurted. "Mitch got a dog, and they're coming next Thursday."

"Wow," Willa said, pure shock and awe in her voice. "What a blessing." Her voice broke, and Cactus wished he could take her into his arms and assure her he'd do anything for her. Anything for Mitch too, because he loved them both.

He'd danced with her in the Edge Cabin on her birthday, giving her a personal peanut butter pie and a diamond pendant she could wear every week at church. She'd gaped at it, and he'd appreciated Holly Ann's help with the gift.

The diamond ring still sat in the junk drawer between the fridge and the stove, and he found himself stepping over to it now. He took out the black box and flipped open the lid while Willa talked about getting the days off at work and how they'd tell Mitch.

"Let's go to dinner tonight," he said. "His favorite place."

"Good idea," she said. "He loves Pizza Pipeline."

"Pizza Pipeline it is then."

"Cactus," Willa said, her voice holding onto the final consonant sound in his name. "I...I don't know what to say."

"There's nothing to say, Willa."

"A hearing dog costs twenty thousand dollars."

"I have over five billion dollars in the bank," he said. "And that's after my seven-figure donation to The Children's Heart Foundation."

Willa made a choking noise, and Cactus knew he'd never put his wealth in numbers for her before.

"Listen," he said. "Will you come to my family's angel tree celebration?"

"Yes," she said, and he knew she'd started crying. She'd once said that people could cry because they were happy, but he always felt foolish when he brought her to tears.

"You don't even know what it is."

"I don't need to know," she said. "You're going to be there, and that means I want to be there."

"It's the last Sunday of the month," he said, gazing out the window above his kitchen sink. "Big dinner. Big annual family meeting. Then we decorate a special tree for all of our angel loved ones. People who've passed. People we're missing. That kind of thing."

"Sounds lovely."

"Please don't cry."

"My son is getting an amazing gift from a beautiful man," she said. "I'm allowed to cry."

Cactus smiled to himself. "Willa...." He wasn't sure if he could tell her he loved her over the phone. Shouldn't that be said in person for the first time?

His phone bleeped and buzzed at him, and Bishop's name came up on the screen. "My brother is calling," he said. "I'll pick you two up at five-thirty?"

"Yes," Willa said, and Cactus switched the call, needing to ask Bishop a very personal question.

"What's up?" he asked to start with.

"First, Bear's headed your way."

Cactus's jaw tightened, though his usual anger didn't immediately roar into flames. It did burn through his chest though, the embers still plenty hot. "Second?"

"Second, I have three more cakes to taste-test. What are you doing tonight?" Bishop had won the taste test last week with his strawberry pistachio cake, and Cactus really wanted to sample his concoctions.

"We just found out Mitch is getting his hearing dog next week," Cactus said. "Willa and I are telling him tonight."

"So I'll leave them in your fridge, and you'll eat them for breakfast."

"I like the way you think." Cactus chuckled with his brother.

"Cactus, when are you going to propose to Willa?"

Cactus sucked in a breath, which somehow prompted Bishop to keep talking instead of shutting up.

"I mean, you're so integrated into her life. Getting a hearing dog for her son, taking him to dinner tonight to tell him. I mean, you literally sounded like you were *already* married and *already* that boy's father."

Cactus didn't know what to say, and his mind raced with how much time he had for this conversation before Bear showed up at the cabin. He needed to make a sandwich and get out of there.

He pulled out the bread as Bishop said, "I just don't know what you're waiting for."

"I'm trying to figure out a good proposal," he said. "You've heard those women. They twitter about it with each other, almost like they're comparing notes."

"Can't be worse that how I flubbed everything up," Bishop said.

Cactus slathered mayo and mustard on both pieces of bread and grabbed out the turkey. He layered it on, tossed a bite to each dog, and shoved everything back in the fridge. "Soon, I hope," Cactus said. "Maybe at the angel tree thing."

"Ohhh," Bishop said, exhaling as he spoke. "You should hang the engagement ring on the tree and make sure she sees it."

Cactus's brain fired. "You know, that's not a bad idea."

Tank stood up, his eyes trained on the front door. Cactus grabbed two bottles of water, and said, "I have to go, Bish. Talk to you later." He hung up, shoved his phone in his back pocket, and picked up his sandwich. "Come on, guys," he said, opening the back door. "Let's go."

He slipped out the back door just as someone knocked on the front one. Embarrassment and guilt started a tug-of-war inside him, but he still didn't know how to look at Bear without wanting to rearrange his face.

Jogging into the barn, he slid the door closed and kept the dogs quiet with bites of meat and bread until he was sure his brother had left.

"Help me," he prayed as he dusted breadcrumbs from his fingers. "Help me to forgive him and help me to heal faster than I am." Everything took so dang long, and Cactus was tired of warring with himself and trying to justify his feelings.

His phone chimed, and Cactus pulled it out. Sammy had texted, and boy, that was a low blow. *We miss you, Charles,* she'd said. *I know you need time, and I want to give it to you, but please know both Bear and I love you, and we're here any time you want to come back. Any old time at all.*

He'd just finished reading when an emoji of a cactus came in, and then a heart, and his guilt tripled.

"Super low blow," he muttered, projecting his displeasure with the guilt trip onto Bear. He'd probably called Sammy and told her Cactus wouldn't answer the door.

Cactus had never wanted to disappoint Sammy, and he valued their friendship greatly.

Bear didn't ask me to text you, by the way. I know you, Charles, and I can see you've read these messages.

He's just worried he'll never be able to apologize, and he's dying a little bit more inside each day.

Cactus sighed and looked up, refusing to look down right away though another text came in. Eventually, though, as the phone kept buzzing, he did continue to read.

You take the time you need. I told him he was an idiot for doing what he did, but he really is trying to make it right. If you could even take one step toward him, he'd cover the rest of the distance. You are terribly important to him.

And to me and Lincoln.

The texts stopped there, and Cactus honestly didn't know how to respond. He decided to go with emojis, and he sent a wrench, a teddy bear, a baby rattle, and a lizard. One item which represented each person in the Bear Glover family.

Then he sent a heart—four of them—because he did love Bear, Sammy, Lincoln, and Stetson.

He just needed more time to erase the wound on his

heart Bear had inflicted, and sooth his wounded pride from the actions he'd taken against his brother.

He'd yelled horrible things, and he'd actually hit Bear in the face.

Cactus shook his head, his guilt nearly gutting him. "I'm sorry," he whispered to the dirt at his feet. Galaxy looked up at him, her eyes wide and loving. He reached down and patted her. "I'm sorry, Gal. I acted like a fool, and it's humiliating."

He realized then that it wasn't about him facing Bear and maintaining control of his anger. Cactus didn't want to face Bear and have to admit that he'd done something wrong. He had to apologize too.

And digging oneself out from underneath sin and shame was hard work and took a long time.

"Soon," he told the dogs and the barn. He'd apologize to Bear soon. He'd propose to Willa soon. Mitch would have his hearing dog soon.

Funny how so much could hinge on such a simple, four-letter word.

Another one entered his mind, and Cactus seized onto it. *Love.*

Could love really conquer all? Could it conquer embarrassment? Stupidity? Inappropriate actions and words?

Cactus wanted to believe it could, and he told himself one more time that he'd finish digging himself out of this hole and then he'd go find his brother and make things right between them.

Soon.

Chapter Thirty

Willa sat at the piano and played through the hymns she'd selected for the church's program. She had more time to prep for this one, as Patrick had asked her to perform it on Christmas Eve, which fell on a Sunday this year.

She paused in her playing and reached up to make notes for the second verse of Silent Night. She knew who she'd be working with in the church choir, and she actually had enough men to do something with a few arrangements this year.

The door at the back of the chapel opened, and Felicia Meyer entered. She usually arrived first, and she unwound her scarf from around her neck. "Phew," she said as she arrived at the choir seats. "The wind out there is insane."

Willa stood from the bench, because her back began to twinge if she sat on something so hard for so long. "I heard the wind was going to be stiff this weekend."

"It's started already," Felicia said, pushing her hands through her streaked blonde hair. She looked at Willa, and then around the chapel. "Where's Mitch?"

"Patrick has him tonight." Willa flashed her a smile and went to put her notes for Silent Night in her binder. "How are things at the nursery?"

"Surprisingly busy," Felicia said as she moved up to the row where sopranos sat. "We've got a big sale on autumnal bulbs, and people are going crazy."

"I should put some of those in my yard," Willa said, as she did love it when the spring blooms poked through the dirt at the first sign of the earth growing warm again.

"Come on by." Felicia smiled and looked at her phone.

Others began to arrive, including Cactus, and she met him halfway down the aisle, stretched up to kiss him, and smiled at him. "I got the harness ordered," she said. "And all the food. It should all be here before next Thursday."

"Great," he said with a smile, his large hand on her waist and holding her close in a subtle way. He gazed down at her, and it wasn't until someone else started to pass that Willa remembered they weren't alone.

This was choir practice, and she had a job to do. She ducked her head, her face so hot, and turned back to the choir seats. She and Cactus walked the rest of the way down the aisle, and she said, "Okay, everyone, we're going to be working on Silent Night tonight. Come get your music."

"Mave, will you play the introduction?" The pianist started to play, and Willa moved closer to the seats. "We're going to sing the traditional arrangement, split in our parts, for the first verse. This hymn is in A-major, so we'll start with a scale there to warm up." She glanced at Mave, who switched seamlessly into a scale, moving up and back down.

Willa lifted her hand, and she led everyone up the scale, where they held—held—then moved back down. She nodded to Mave, who went right back up. At the top, she sang three notes, hitting each one with her hand so everyone would stay with her, and they went back down again.

They'd all sung scales as warmups before, and Willa actually enjoyed the routine. She settled into her teaching mode, and they started the hymn.

The first verse actually sounded quite nice, and Willa beamed at her choir. "Beautiful," she said. "I just need my tenors not to slur the words on the second line. Now, my men, you're going to sing the second verse yourself. Ladies, you're going to hum beneath them." She turned to Mave. "Gentlemen first, please."

She took her upper hand off the keyboard, and Willa led the men through the words. "Much better, tenors. Basses, listen to Cactus, if you would. He's got the pitch right on all the notes, and some of you are a bit flat on those highest notes."

She turned to the ladies. "Okay, you guys are going to hum in your parts. I want it below the actual words, so we don't need anything too loud." That would be hard for a couple of the ladies in the group, which was almost why Willa had chosen to do it.

She backed up a few steps and said, "The third verse will be hummed by everyone, so let's see how it goes with the second and third verses, one right after the other."

Mave played a few notes of introduction, Willa raised both her hands, and the men came in right on time.

Willa yelled out reminders as needed, and with the notes of the hummed third verse hanging in the air, a stillness existed in the chapel that could only suggest that God Himself approved of their singing.

She held very still and basked in the spirit and warmth, hoping everyone in the company could feel it too. The minister inside her wanted to point it out, but she also knew that most of the time, it didn't need to be pointed out.

"Very good," she finally said. "That's all for tonight." She tucked all her music away and made sure the chapel was clean and the lights out before she stepped outside with Cactus.

The wind stole her binder from her, eliciting a yelp from her throat. "No!" she cried, as she had dozens of papers and sheet music meticulously organized in that binder. Cactus chased after it, only taking a couple of steps before he stomped on it to keep it from spinning further away from them.

"Got it," he yelled, but Willa could barely see him through all the dust. He stepped back over to her, and Willa curled into his chest. "I don't think I can get up the canyon."

"Can we even get to my place?" Willa wasn't sure she could. She could barely see two feet in front of her.

"I'll drive," he said, looping his arm through hers and clutching her binder to his chest. He hurried her to his car, where she sank into the seat and sighed in relief. He could barely open his door against the wind, and when he finally sat behind the wheel, he exhaled in a slightly angry hiss.

"This is crazy," he said.

"The weatherman did say there'd be wind."

"This is almost like a tornado," he said, starting the car. The temperature had dropped quite a bit too, and Willa held her hands up to the warm air once it started blowing from the vents. Cactus drove very slow, pausing for a long time at every corner, and a ten-minute drive took thirty.

Along the way, Willa called Patrick and told him about the wind. He said he'd keep Mitch, and the moment she hung up, the school district sent a text that school had been canceled the next day.

"Insane," she said once Cactus had pulled into her driveway.

"Let's get inside," he said. "I know you can't run, so is the door locked? I can run up and open it and come back for you."

She nodded, her nerves frayed along the ends. Rain started to pelt the windshield, and Willa fished her keys from her bag. "Maybe stay here altogether," he said, peering up and out of the windshield. "Maybe we should wait for a minute. The rain doesn't normally last too long."

Willa didn't want to wait in the car. It felt eerie in there, with the noisy rain, the darkness, and all the shaking from the wind. "I'll do my best," she said. "I'm going to leave my bag and everything here." She gripped her phone, and she hadn't worn a jacket to work that day. This morning had been a completely different weather pattern, and she hadn't come home before going to the church for practice.

"All right," he drawled. "Let's go." He opened his door and took off like a shot. Willa hadn't even closed her door when he disappeared into the darkness, and she kept her head down to protect her eyes and to be able to see the sidewalk.

As she walked as quickly as she could, the wind threatened to push her right over, especially on her weak side. A siren began to wail, and Willa raised her head sharply. "Cactus?" she called.

If he answered, she couldn't hear him past the wild rushing sound of the wind, nor the siren that continued to blare. Was this a tornado? She didn't even know where to shelter, as the house didn't have a basement.

She took another step, and then another. She heard her name, and she tried to find Cactus. "Over here," she yelled. "Cactus."

He appeared a moment later, panting. "I lost you," he said. "Come on." He guided her the rest of the way to the steps and held her steady as she moved up them. They made it inside the house, where he closed and locked the door.

Relief streamed through her, but not for long. "Is that a tornado siren?"

"Yes," he said, tapping on his phone. "I'm letting everyone know where I am, and then we need to check to see if there's really a tornado."

"Would they sound the siren if there wasn't?"

"Yes," he said. "Sometimes they do it just to indicate a severe storm." He moved away from the windows. "We should still shelter in the center of the house." He met her eyes, and everywhere Willa looked she saw glass. "I'm guessing that's the bathroom."

"Probably." She led the way in that direction and indicated it. "I'm going to get out of this wet shirt. I'll be back in a minute." In the safety of her own bedroom, she stripped off her blouse and found a comfortable sweatshirt. She couldn't help thinking about the size of that bathroom in the hall, and she wasn't sure she'd even fit in the room with a man the size of Cactus.

She took off her shoes and socks and slipped on her fuzzy slippers, then padded the few steps to the bathroom. Cactus leaned against the counter, his attention on his phone. "It's not a tornado," he said. "It's supposed to blow by before ten o'clock tonight."

"Why'd they cancel school then?"

"Could be some damage." He tucked his phone away and drew her into his chest. The lights flickered and went out, and Willa started to giggle.

Cactus chuckled too, the deep sound of his voice rumbling through her ears and her face as she pressed herself against his breastbone. "I think we're going to be eating ice cream for dinner," he said. "Before it melts."

"So this is definitely a win," she said.

"I'll get it," he said. "You sit on down, and I'll be right back."

Willa followed him out into the hall and with the aid of the flashlight on her phone, she gathered an armful of clean towels. She laid them on the floor as a type of pad, and then she sat with her back against the wall. She groaned, because she'd never get up from the floor without help.

Cactus returned with a couple containers of ice cream, as well as the sliced meat and cheese from her fridge and a flashlight he'd found somewhere. He sat next to her, also groaning, and said, "Wow, that's a long way down." He chuckled and handed her a spoon. "Chocolate chip or triple chocolate?"

"Chocolate, of course. That chocolate chip is for Mitch."

He handed her the chocolate container and opened the other one. "What's your dream wedding like?" he asked. With her phone shining light toward the ceiling from the counter, and the flashlight balanced on the edge of the tub, his face danced in shadows.

"I don't really have a dream wedding," she said, her pulse doing a bit of pounding. "I think it would be fun to be married at Christmastime, with a lot of wreaths and the scent of pine." She shrugged. "I honestly haven't thought about it much."

"Wreaths and pine is more than I have," he said.

Willa wanted to say something else, but fear froze her vocal cords. She ate another bite of ice cream, and it somehow thawed her throat. "Honestly, Cactus, if you're standing at the altar as I limp toward it, that's the dream wedding." She whispered the last couple of words, stunned she'd been brave enough to say such a thing.

And she meant it.

Cactus picked up the lid for his ice cream and snapped it back into place. "You done?" he asked kindly.

She handed it over, her lungs rioting against her for holding her breath for so long. She pulled in a long, deep breath. "That's all? That's all you're going to say?"

He twisted and put the ice cream on the floor on his other side. He faced her again, leaning his head back against the wall. "I've been in love with you for months," he whispered. "My dream wedding is the one where you walk toward me, with Mitch on your arm, and Galaxy and Tank as the wedding party." He smiled softly and blinked. "Because I just want you. I love you, Willa Knowlton."

Joy burst through her, and she reached up and trailed her fingers down the side of his face. "I love you too, Charles."

His smile widened, and he kissed her. His lips touched coldly to hers, and she kissed him back, this moment beautiful and special and perfect, even if it was happening in her dark bathroom while the house shook around them.

A WEEK LATER, WILLA WOKE AFTER ONLY A COUPLE OF hours of sleep. She went into Mitch's room, which flashed a light on the wall across from his bed when the door opened.

He started to stir, and by the time Willa reached his bedside and touched his shoulder, he'd actually opened his eyes. "Time to get up," she signed. "We're going to breakfast with Cactus's mother, and then we have to go pick up the dog food before Frost and Nancy get here."

She had the itinerary, and she'd studied it until she'd memorized it. Nancy Cranbury was Frost's trainer, and though Willa had been praying for a solid week that Frost would bond with Mitch instantly and Nancy would stay to teach them all how to work with the hearing dog, she started again.

"Can we pray?" she asked Mitch, and he looked up at her with all the innocence of an angel child.

Can I? he asked as she sat on the edge of his bed.

Willa nodded, her throat already so tight. Mitch began to sign, his eyes squeezed closed in a way that almost looked painful. *Dear Lord*, he signed. *Thank you for this day. Thank you for Cactus and Galaxy and Tank. Thank you for our house and our car. Thank you for the earth. Thank you that I don't have to go to school today. Bless Frost and Nancy as they fly from Georgia that they will be safe and happy. Help Frost not to be scared in the car, and help me and him to get along really fast. I already love him, and I just know he'll love me if he's not scared and tired from the flying and everything.*

Mitch opened his eyes and met Willa's. Everything pinched inside her as she tried to hold her emotions back, and then she decided to just let it all out. Tears leaked out of her right eye, and she reached out and cradled her son's face in her hands. "I love you, Mitch."

Bless Mama to be so happy, and help her to get all her work done so we can be home at night together. Amen.

"Amen," she added.

Hours later, she sat on the front steps with Cactus's hand in hers while Mitch rode his bike in the street. A car turned into the driveway, and she and Cactus stood as a single unit.

"I'll get him," he said, already striding away from Willa. She went to the bottom of the steps and hugged the pillar there, hoping and praying with everything she had. It wasn't much more than *please, please, please*, but she knew the Lord heard all types of prayers.

A woman emerged from the minivan, and she wore a pair of black pants and a polo with Paws With a Cause splashed across the front. "You must be Willa," she said.

"Yes." Willa put a smile on her face and went down the sidewalk to meet Nancy. "And you're Nancy."

"Yes." She had light-colored hair that actually held a purple hue, and fell in curly waves to her shoulders. "Was Mitch that boy I passed on his bike?"

"Yes, ma'am," she said. "My boyfriend went to get him. Sometimes it takes a minute, because he obviously can't hear you." She painted a smile on her face, because her nerves made her talk too much.

"Here he is." Nancy had turned, and she approached Mitch now. She couldn't be older than thirty, and she greeted Mitch with a hug. "Are you ready?" she asked and signed, and Mitch slid his hand into Willa's, looking up at her.

I'm ready, he signed, and Nancy moved over to the side of the van. She opened the door, but a dog didn't come bounding out.

"Frost should wait for you to invite him out," she said. "Unless you tell him to get out and check the surroundings. I'll have him do that." She signed to the dog, and said, "Check around."

A beautiful, light beige cocker spaniel emerged from the van, his head swinging left and right, looking all around. His tail wagged, and he sniffed the ground in a wide arc, going back and forth.

A few seconds later, he returned to Nancy and put his paw up on her calf.

"That's how he tells you it's safe," she said. "We know Mitch isn't blind, but it's still a good skill for him to practice." Nancy bent down and scratched Frost's head. The dog had white on his tail, ears, chest, and the ridge of his back, as if he'd been frosted with the color.

Willa loved him, and she felt Mitch's excitement at her side.

"Meet Mitch," Nancy said, and Frost trotted toward them. Mitch released her hand and skipped toward the dog. They met, him throwing his arms around the twenty-pound dog as he fell to his knees, and the animal sniffing him and sniffing him.

He licked his face, his tail rotating like a helicopter blade. He came over to Cactus and then Willa too, and they both gave him a pat and let him sniff them.

"Oh, this is great," Nancy said with a smile. "Should we see what he can do?"

"Definitely," Cactus said.

"Let's start with the doorbell," Nancy said. "Since Frost is one of our smaller dogs, he's been trained to alert his human with a bark and a touch. A lot of deaf people, especially children, are attuned to vibrations, so the bark helps even if they can't hear it auditorily."

Willa nodded along, and she passed Nancy on the porch and closed the door behind her. Frost moved around, sniffing everything in the near vicinity. When the doorbell rang, he gave one sharp bark and trotted over to Mitch, lifting his right paw and putting it against Mitch's shin. He looked up at the boy, who looked down at him.

Frost barked again and returned to the door, where he barked one more time.

Nancy opened the door and said, "See how he alerts the

deaf person, then takes them where they need to go? Do you have a deaf doorbell?"

"Yes."

"Can we disable it? Then Mitch won't know where the sound is coming from. I understand he has a phone?"

"Yes." Willa felt overwhelmed, and she could only speak in single-word sentences. Cactus wasn't speaking at all, so she didn't feel too badly.

She disconnected the doorbell and put Mitch's phone face-down while Nancy explained that Willa or Cactus could tell Frost to get Mitch. "So when he's out on his bike, he'll be with him, obviously. But you can call him, and say, 'Bring Mitch,' and he'll bring him."

"Wow," Cactus said. "Can we try that?"

"Sure." Nancy smiled. "Tell him to bring him right now. Go stand in the kitchen or somewhere you'd call him."

Cactus went into the kitchen and opened the fridge. "Frost," he said. "Bring Mitch."

The dog barked and went to Mitch, who stood next to the dining room table. He touched him, then trotted over to Cactus and sat down. Mitch followed.

Nancy beamed at the two of them. "So Mitch, when he comes to get you, he's taking you somewhere because he's heard something you haven't. So you have to go with him."

"This is so amazing," Willa said, her voice breaking. "So we can have his teacher do that, or his friends, or whatever."

"Our dogs are trained for school bells," she said. "So when the recess bell rings, he'll get Mitch, and they'll go in together. I think you said you got the harnesses?"

"Yes," Cactus said, his voice gruff. "We got everything on the list."

Willa continued to watch the demonstration, and Nancy eventually left, saying she'd be back in the morning, and they'd go to school, the store, a park, and many other situations and places where Frost could assist Mitch.

As Cactus walked her out, Willa signed furiously to her son, telling him to be sure to thank the cowboy who'd made this hearing dog possible.

The moment Cactus walked back into the house, Mitch ran at him. He hugged Cactus tightly around the waist, and he signed up to Cactus. *Thank you for the dog, Cactus. I love him so much.*

Cactus crouched down and smiled at Mitch, signing, "I'm glad, Mitch. He's great, isn't he?"

I love you, Cactus. Thank you, thank you.

Surprise filled his face, and then Cactus relaxed again. *I love you too, boy.* He hugged Mitch again, and Willa had to turn away when he looked at her so she didn't burst into tears. She'd never dreamed someone would be able to love her, let alone her disabled son.

Chapter Thirty-One

Cactus watched as an unfamiliar station wagon sedan pulled into the lot in front of the homestead. Surprise filled him at the sight of Willa behind the wheel. That wasn't the little SUV Bear had bought for her.

He went down the steps and sidewalk as she and Mitch got out of the car. The boy ran past him with Frost hot on his heels, yelling at the top of his lungs. The word made no sense, because Mitch couldn't hear himself saying it, and Cactus assumed he was yelling for Lincoln to come see Frost.

"You got a new car," he said to Willa.

"Yes," she said, barely glancing at him. "Can you get the rolls out of the back for me?"

"Sure thing." He stepped past her and collected the six dozen rolls she'd picked up at the bakery for Bishop. "Why'd you get a new car?"

She turned back to him, her normal beauty striking him

in the chest. "Because I don't want anything between you and Bear. Now there's nothing." She held up the envelope. "All of his money is right here, *and* I got my own car." She grinned at him. "It felt really good too," she added. "To be able to buy my own car. Like this rush I haven't had in a while."

Cactus couldn't be mad about that, and he smiled too. The only thing still stabbing at him was the fact that Willa had to deal with selling a car and buying a new one in the first place. If he could be more forgiving, if he could get past his issues faster, she wouldn't have had to do that.

He slipped one arm around her—quite the feat with seventy-two rolls in his hands—and kissed her. A couple of weeks had passed since they'd eaten ice cream in her dim bathroom, the power out and a storm raging around them

Eighteen days since he'd said "I love you, Willa."

And she'd said it back.

He'd been planning with Bishop and Ace, Preacher and Judge, for all eighteen of those days, and he felt like he had the perfect proposal ready for tonight. Willa had mentioned a Chrismas wedding, and this would give them sixty days. Eight weeks.

He'd thanked the Lord for True Blue, because securing a venue seemed like the hardest part of getting married. He'd thanked the Lord for Patrick Corning, because the man had cleared his schedule so he could officiate at Willa's wedding. He'd called her parents and invited them for Christmas.

Everything was ready.

An eerie sense of calmness came over Cactus as he

walked with Willa toward the homestead. Mitch hadn't bothered to close the door, and they went inside, where warmth filled the space, as did cheery yellow lights, and plenty of laughter.

Cactus could admit he loved the family gatherings now. He adored Christmas and their angel tree tradition.

"I'll check," someone said, and Cactus froze, because he knew that voice.

Sure enough, Bear came striding out of the kitchen, adjusting his cowboy hat on his head. He stuttered to a stop when his eyes caught on Cactus's, and the tension in the house expanded and bled through every wall, every crack, every windowpane.

"Afternoon, Bear," Willa said pleasantly as she left Cactus behind. "Here's your money for the SUV. I appreciate the gesture and you actually buying the car, but I managed to get one of my own."

She glanced over her shoulder at Cactus, her eyes telling him he better talk to his brother and make things right. Like, today. Now.

"Thanks," Bear murmured as she continued into the kitchen.

Cactus switched his eyes from her back to Bear's face. Neither of them said anything, and Cactus's heart pounded so hard. Why did healing take so much time? Over two months had passed since he'd nearly broken Bear's nose with his fist. Why hadn't he been able to come to terms with what had happened, say the apologies he needed to say, and move on?

"Cactus," Bear said. "I'm really sorry for this." He raised the envelope. "It was not my intention to rescue her so you couldn't. I did not—I *would* not—do anything to hurt you intentionally."

Cactus nodded, because he knew all of that. Sammy had texted it all to him weeks ago, and he knew Bear was a good man. Maybe had a bit of a hero complex, but still a good man.

Bear sighed when Cactus said nothing. "I understand you're proposing to Willa tonight."

Cactus moved his gaze to the woman who'd rejoined them in the foyer. Her hand fluttered up to her throat, her eyes widening by the nanosecond. "What?"

"Oh, holy stars in all the heavens," Bear muttered. "I am never speaking again." With that, he stomped toward the stairs, where Cactus stood. "I have to get the baby. Excuse me."

Cactus stepped to the side, still numb, and watched Bear take the steps two at a time.

"Is that true?" Willa asked, bringing his attention back to her.

"It was supposed to be a surprise," he mumbled.

She came toward him, her hazel eyes blazing with a strength he really admired. She paused just out of his reach, and Cactus actually swallowed at the fierceness he felt coming from her. "What?" he finally asked.

"I love you," she said. "I want to be with a man who knows how to take care of me and Mitch. One who learned sign language the moment he found out my son was deaf.

One who knows my favorite food, and I know his, and one who will dance with me though I'm stilted and slow." She swallowed too, her eyes so bright.

"I want a man whose faith exceeds my own, who loves God, and loves his family. A man who knows what pain is, and how to overcome it. A man who has strength because of the things he's learned in the past, and a man who knows how to forgive, forget, and forge forward."

She took the remaining steps to him and put her palm against his chest, as if holding him back. "Cactus, I thought that man was you. I know it is, but your refusal to forgive Bear and make things right is giving me some serious doubts." She shook her head as her eyes filled with tears. "I've been with a man who didn't know how to forgive. Heck, I've been that woman before. I won't go back to that. Without forgiveness, there is no love."

He had no idea what she was saying, but he understood what "doubts" meant. It meant if he asked her to marry him, she'd say no. In front of his whole family. At the event every single person attended, every year, without fail.

This is a bad idea anyway, he realized. The angel tree celebration shouldn't be tied up with his engagement.

"I'm trying," he said.

"Not hard enough," she shot back. "It's been two months, Cactus. Over a *car*. What are you going to do when I mess up? Refuse to speak to me for a year?"

"You won't mess up like he did."

"You don't know that."

"Healing takes a long time," he said. "It's okay for it to

take time." His therapist had taught him that. "I'm slow, Willa. I know that. Remember how I barricaded myself out on the edge for a decade?" He shook his head, because he knew he was slow, and he knew he was messed up. "I'm embarrassed of how I acted with Bear. I need…I don't know. I need someone to think I'm a decent human being, even though I made a huge mistake. I need someone to love me even though I'm not perfect. I need someone to be on *my* side."

"Sweetheart," she whispered, lifting her hand to his face. "*I'm* on your side. I think you're a decent human being. I love you."

"You want me to do what I'm not ready to do."

She ducked her head and said, "Perhaps. I apologize."

Cactus took a deep breath. "I was going to propose tonight, but I think I'll wait." He put one tentative hand on her hip and slid it up her back. "I just want to give you the Christmas wedding you want," he whispered. "I want to give you *everything* you want. Everything Mitch wants. I want to take care of you and love you and get the same in return."

"And I want the man you were before you started hiding behind your shame again."

Cactus's throat tightened, and he nodded. She stepped away and took the rolls from him. "Bishop wanted these. I didn't mean to interrupt and overhear Bear."

"It's fine." He watched her go, and Cactus felt torn between two worlds. One in the kitchen, with all the happy, smiling Glovers, and one out at the Edge Cabin, where he could be as surly as he wanted, eat what he wanted, and do what he wanted. No smiling necessary.

He turned toward the steps as Bear came down them, a sleepy Stetson in his arms. The boy had clearly been crying, as big, fat tears still stuck to his dark lashes.

"Listen," Cactus said as Bear slowed. He stopped a couple of steps up.

Cactus took them, and then took his nephew from his brother. Stetson looked up at him, brightening when he recognized Cactus. He babbled and reached for the brim of his cowboy hat, but Cactus dodged out of the way of the eight-month-old's chubby fingers.

"You and I need to talk," Cactus said.

"Anytime," Bear said. "I didn't mean to let the cat out of the bag about the proposal."

"It's nothing." Cactus shook his head. "I shouldn't do it tonight anyway." Tonight was about Daddy and Uncle Bull. It was about Grandmother and Bryce. It wasn't about *him*.

"Charles," Sammy said, and both he and Bear turned toward the woman. She hurried toward them, panic on her face.

"Relax, Sammy," Cactus said dryly. "I'm not going to punch your husband."

"Did you two make up then?" She looked hopefully between them and took the baby from Cactus.

"Not yet," Bear said.

"Working on it," Cactus said as more of a growl.

"Well, your mother just said she had an announcement to make, so can you guys put this on hold for a minute?" She looked between them, nodding as if she'd spoken and it would be so.

"An announcement?" Bear asked, going down the steps

with Sammy. Cactus let them go, because he already knew what Mother was going to say. She and Donald Parker were engaged. Cactus had gone to breakfast with them when Mitch had gotten his hearing dog, and she'd told him then.

Even she knew he needed more time than everyone else to process things and come to terms with them.

Willa knows too, he told himself as he continued into the kitchen. He just needed to go see Bear, get things right between them, and then he could propose to the woman he loved.

The moment he stepped under the arch, Mother raised both of her hands. "Okay, we're all here." She smiled around at the group, and Cactus took in the enormity of the crowd. They had dogs and a grumpy cat, fiancées and wives, new husbands and teenagers. All of the men—even Brady Burton—wore cowboy hats, and Cactus finally felt like he belonged right where he was.

"Don and I are engaged!" she said. Before the squeals and congratulations could start, she added, "We're going to get married right after the New Year, so mark January eleventh on your calendars. The barn here at the ranch is already booked." She exchanged a glance with Cactus, who touched his first two fingers to his lips.

His mother had moved her wedding plans from Christmas to January so Cactus could have the holidays for him and Willa. Foolishness hit him, and as others swarmed Mother, he quickly pulled out his phone and texted Bishop, Ace, Judge, and Preacher.

Need to call an audible, he said. *I can't ask Willa to marry me tonight. Need a new plan. Can we meet for breakfast tomorrow at the Ranch House?*

He sent the message and tucked his phone away. Bishop had just finished hugging Mother, and he checked his phone. His eyes flew to Cactus, and then he started searching for Ace.

But the man appeared in front of Cactus. "Why can't you ask her tonight?" he asked.

"Yeah," Bishop said, and he must've shoved people to the ground to get to Cactus so fast. "Why not?"

"It's just not right," Cactus said. "She basically told me she'd say no if I didn't make things right with Bear first." He kept his voice low, hating that Judge was now heading his way. "Plus, it's the angel tree, and I don't know. This was a bad idea."

"It was a *great* idea," Judge said, arriving at Bishop's side. "We have the Christmas tree, and it's all planned out for who would put the ring on just before Willa steps over. Come on, Cactus. You can't chicken out."

"He's not chickening out," Preacher said. "This is happening tonight."

"No," Cactus said firmly. "It's not." He shook his head. "She'll say no, and then I'll be horribly embarrassed, and I might never come back in from the edge." He looked at the four men who'd helped him plan this. "I still want to do it. I'm not getting cold feet." He glanced past Ace as Etta got up on the chair. "Dinner's about to start. I can't explain it all right now. I have one more thing to do before I can propose. We'll just meet in the morning and make a Plan B."

"Fine," Bishop said. "Ranch House?" He looked at Preacher, who nodded.

"I have a meeting with Bear at nine," he said.

"We'll be done way before then," Cactus said, trying to think of another Chrsitmas tree he could use.

"What are you boys talking about?" Aunt Dawna said, stepping right into the midst of them. "Cactus Glover, you did not tell me your lovely girlfriend plays bridge."

Cactus blinked at his aunt. "I didn't know she played bridge."

"Well, she just said she did—that she's actually won a contest or two—and I sure would love it if you'd bring her over to my apartment so I can play with her." She beamed at Cactus like this would be the best thing that ever happened to any of them. "I need some help setting up my tree too. Ranger got it out of storage, but one of the lights was out, so I ordered a new one, and I can't get it out of the box."

A smile formed on Cactus's face, and he took Aunt Dawna into a hug. He met Bishop's eyes, and Ace's, and Judge's, and Preacher's, and he knew the Lord answered prayers.

"I'd love to bring her by tomorrow," Cactus said, a bit of panic blipping through him. "Maybe Tuesday...and we'll help you with the tree, and you can beat the pants off of her in bridge."

Aunt Dawna trilled out a laugh, but she didn't deny she'd destroy Willa at the card game. She walked away, and Cactus looked around at his brothers and cousin. "Tuesday night," he said. "Who can come help Aunt Dawna decorate her tree?"

A COUPLE OF HOURS LATER, DINNER HAD ENDED. THE family meeting had gone off without a hitch. Arizona stood in the arched doorway and yelled, "Everyone gather into the foyer, please. To the foyer!"

"You know what we need?" Mother asked as she moved with the crowd toward the doorway that led into the foyer. "An intercom system."

"No," Bear growled. "I live here with my family, Mother. Besides, I hated it when you'd call us on Saturday morning to do chores over the blasted intercom."

"Seriously," Judge said. "Just because you sang didn't make it less annoying."

"Yeah," Preacher said. "We never got even one day a week to sleep in." They all gave Mother a dark look, but she just laughed.

Cactus was in complete agreement with them. He might never set foot in the homestead again if it was equipped with an intercom. That would just make loud people louder. He'd also hated the Saturday-morning wake-up calls over the intercom, his mother singing some stupid song from *The Sound of Music* to get them all up and working around the house. As if they didn't have enough work to do around the ranch every other day of the week—and on Saturday too.

He simply stayed out of the conversation and followed the group into the foyer at the back of the crowd, just the way he liked it. Dinner had been casual and easy, with Bear way down at the other end of the table, and he found Willa standing near Oakley in the foyer. He stepped to her side and slipped his hand into hers, glancing down at her. He squeezed, asking permission to hold her hand.

She squeezed back and looked up at him with bright eyes and said, "This is so exciting."

He smiled at her as Bishop and Bear paired up to talk about the tree. They did this every year, but surprisingly, Cactus didn't mind. He loved the reminder of what this tree meant and why they put it up so early.

"Welcome to our angel tree decorating," Bear said. "Most of us know about this Glover family tradition, but we seem to have someone new with us every year." He nodded at Willa, and she acknowledged him back.

"This tree is for anyone and everyone who's not with us tonight," Bishop said. "Loved ones who've gone back to heaven, or loved ones far from us for one reason or another." He indicated the box beside him. "We'll get this tree set up first, and Zona will get the ornaments open. Then, you come get the ornaments you'd like and hang them on the tree. Every time we see it, we're reminded of the angels watching over us, that we're working to get back to."

"We hang garlands on the white tree to remind us of the rebirth available to all of us," Bear said. "That's what the holly vines mean, and the angel tree reminds us that spring will always come, and rest can always be found in Christ."

Pure harmony flowed through Cactus as Bishop said something about the angel they'd asked Ward to put on the top this year, his mind lingering on the meaning of the holly vines. It was a winter green among acres of brown, gray, and white. Something that grew when nothing else did.

It did remind him that he could repent and do better, and

he seized onto that thought, willing and ready to use it to make things right between him and Bear.

Then him and Willa.

"This year," Bear said. "I thought it might be fun to have a few people—anyone who would like to—say what the angel tree means to them. I didn't ask anyone in advance, so don't be shy."

He looked around, and for once, no one in the Glover family said a single word.

Cactus looked at Mother as the seconds stretched, and when she met his eye, his heart started thumping strangely behind his ribs. He knew what that meant, and he fought against the prompting to say something. What would he even say?

Mother raised her hand slightly. "I love the angel tree, because it reminds me of Grandmother and Grandfather. It reminds me of holidays on this ranch with my parents, as well as my dear Stone." She smiled around at the group. "His mother made all of the ornaments, and I remember meeting her for the first time. Dad had brought me here to meet his family, and she sat in a rocking chair in the living room, something boiling on the stove while her needles moved as she crocheted."

She paused for a moment, the atmosphere tender and quiet. "She was working on a tiny pine tree, and she barely looked up at me as she asked, 'You think you can live on this ranch, Lois?' I had no idea what to say." She laughed. "I was meeting her for the very first time. Stone and I had been dating for maybe two or three months, but we were married in only two or three more." She looked up at her fiancé, her eyes bright. "I've lived on this ranch ever since, and it'll be very hard for me to leave it. Knowing I can always come here and see this angel tree will comfort me and allow me to remember the past while moving forward into the future."

Don smiled down at her and brushed his lips along her cheek.

"Thank you, Mother," Bear said. As he drew in another breath, assumedly to move on, Cactus blurted out, "I love the angel tree, because it reminds me of where I come from."

Every eye swung to him, and he sure did hate that. He swallowed and squeezed Willa's hand. She clung to him too, and perhaps she did love him, cheer for him, and stand on his side.

"The ornaments remind me of Grandmother and of a simpler time, and sometimes I need that. I always hang a baby rattle for Bryce, and it took me five years to get to the point where I could do that without completely breaking down. Remembering allows me to see how far I've come, and encourages me to take the next step on my own journey."

He hung ornaments for his father too, and Allison, strange as that may seem. But he'd said enough, and he looked at Bear. He made a fist and touched it to his heart, at which point, Bear did the same, though his eyes held a hint of shock.

"Thank you, Cactus," he said. "Zona?"

"The ornaments are all here," she said. "There are plenty for everyone, so you don't need to shove." She looked to her right. "Judge."

"I want the sleigh, and someone always takes it," he said.

"Come get it right now then," she said crossly. "I don't want to get trampled this year."

Judge did what she said, and once he had the sleigh in his hand, others moved forward to get the ornaments they wanted too.

Cactus hung back, because he didn't much care which ornaments he put on the tree for Dad or Allison, and no one would take the rattle from him.

"I want to hold that baby," Willa said, sliding her hand away from Cactus. "Be right back." She entered the fray, found Sammy, and took Stetson from her. Her whole countenance lit up, and Cactus sighed.

"She's amazing," Oakley said.

"She sure is," he agreed. "Listen, I'm wondering if you can come to a meeting with me and Bear tomorrow," he said. "Say around ten?"

Oakley looked at him with plenty of inquisition. "A meeting with you and Bear?"

"You can bring Ranger," Cactus said. "It'll be fast, I swear."

"All right," she said.

He nodded and went to get his baby rattle. With it in his hand, he stepped over to the tree and found an empty bough. "I sure do love you, my son," he whispered. He'd just hung the ornament when Mitch tugged on his shirtsleeve. "What, boy?"

Lift me up so I can put this one up high? Mitch asked. *It's for my dad.* He held up a star—one of many—and Cactus lifted the boy up as high as he could so Mitch could hang the star near the top of the tree.

He stayed in his own zone, hanging a few more ornaments. He watched Willa put on two and then disappear into the kitchen again, taking the baby with her. A new distance definitely existed between them, but Cactus only needed a day to erase it.

Hopefully.

Chapter Thirty-Two

Preacher went into the kitchen, where he found Bear pouring himself a cup of coffee. "Is there enough for me?"

"Yep." Bear slid the glass pot back on the burner and smiled at Preacher as he stirred sugar into his brew.

Preacher got a mug out of the cupboard and poured himself a cup too. He didn't mix anything into it and took it over to the huge kitchen table under the windows. "Why am I here, Bear?" He didn't mince words, and he had two herds to move that morning.

"This is why." He tossed a rolled-up poster on the table and sat down across from him. "Bishop and Montana have been working on that for the better part of six months."

"What is it?" Preacher abandoned his coffee and peeled the rubber band off the paper. He rolled it out and laid it flat. It didn't take long for him to see the map, with houses and barns roughed in and labeled.

"You started without me?" Montana asked, her work boots clomping on the floor.

"Just barely," Bear said. Preacher glanced up as Montana joined them at the table.

"This is the Kinder Ranch," Preacher said.

"In theory," Montana said. "The actual ranch is full of broken-down buildings and fields we're not utilizing well because of them."

Preacher looked up at her in surprise.

"We're going to clean it all up," Montana said. "Renovate or rebuild the homestead. Put in a line of eight cowboy cabins. Put in fences for new grass pastures and get the land solid for farming."

"Great," Preacher said, looking away from the homestead in the heart of the plantation. "What does this have to do with me?" He didn't mean to sound grumpy or stand-offish. He just hated having his time wasted.

He hated how silent his phone had been for the past month. Fine, six weeks. He told himself at least dozen times before breakfast that it was entirely possible Charlie hadn't even seen his name and number on the hundred-dollar tip he'd given her at Ida's wedding.

"I think you'd like to live in that newly renovated house," Bear said. "Manage the cowboys in those cabins, as well as lots of other things here at Shiloh Ridge. We need another foreman, Preacher, and I think you're the man for the job."

Cactus had mentioned the possibility of this, but Preacher honestly hadn't thought it would happen. Months had passed since then, and Bear had said nothing.

He was saying something now.

He thought of Judge, as well as the charred bridge between him and Mister. They got along decently well, but Mister didn't tell Preacher anything, and he hated that. He understood why—he didn't trust Preacher not to tell Judge— but he didn't like it. He also didn't tell Judge anything, so Mister really had no reason to be worried.

"Why me?" He looked a Bear. "Why not Judge? He's older than I am."

"Judge is not a natural leader," Bear said simply. "You are. It comes with a raise in salary, and a whole new set of responsibilities. Ward's been working out kinks in his role for months, and his input will be invaluable for helping you to know what you'd be over."

"Will Judge feel bad?" Montana asked.

"I'm not sure," Preacher said. "I don't want to be the reason he feels bad. I have very few—" He swallowed back the words, because he didn't need to divulge so much right now. Or ever.

"I can talk to him," Bear said. "I doubt he'll even want to be foreman, Preach. He knows who he is."

"Does he?" Preacher asked. He wished he did.

Bear looked at him quizzically. "Of course." He glanced at Montana. "Montana and Bishop will work with you on the design of the house, and it's likely the project will take at least a year. There's a lot of clean-up to be done down there, and then the complete rebuild."

Preacher nodded. "Can I think about it?"

"Of course."

Preacher stood up and picked up is undrunk coffee. "Okay. That's it?"

"That's it." Bear stayed in his seat, watching Preacher.

"Okay, thanks, Bear. I'll let you know real soon." With that, he left the homestead, his thoughts knotting around Judge and how he might take the news.

"I JUST DON'T THINK YOU SHOULD MAKE A DECISION LIKE this based on how Judge will take it." Mister looked at Preacher, who didn't look back as they waited for Duke to come out of the farmhouse where he lived with their sister.

The big red front door opened, and both Zona and Duke walked onto the porch. She tipped up and kissed him, and he grinned as he came down the steps and got in the back of Preacher's truck.

"Sorry, guys."

"It's fine," Preacher said. "How's married life?"

"Pretty darn good," Duke said, meeting Preacher's eyes in the rearview mirror. "Can't complain."

"I'm texting Beau," Ace said.

Preacher set the truck down the dirt road from the Rhinehart's ranch, and if Beau Peterson left now, they'd probably arrive at the mall in downtown Three Rivers at the same time.

"Does he know his machine is done?" Duke asked.

"He said they called him," Ace said. The conversation rotated around the video games the five of them liked to play, and Preacher let the talk happen without him. He hadn't even had a whole day to consider being the foreman at

Shiloh Ridge, but he'd had plenty of time to think about why Charlie Perkins hadn't called him.

Over a month, in fact.

He could use the Internet, and he'd looked up Below Zero. It was her company, and they didn't have a storefront in Three Rivers. She was a mobile operation, and she'd done a few fairs and festivals this summer. That was it.

She had to be new to town, and he wondered how she paid her bills by serving ice cream a handful of times in months.

She'd come and gone from his mind since Ida's wedding, and he'd done nothing to try to get in touch with her again. His job at Shiloh Ridge kept him plenty busy, and he didn't normally go to town for festivals.

Your life will only get busier if you take the foreman job.

"Vote," he said when a lull entered the conversation. "Bear asked me to be the second foreman on the ranch. Should I take it?"

"Yes," Mister said.

"Yes," Ace said.

"Why wouldn't you?" Duke asked.

"That's not how a vote works," Mister said. "It's yes or no."

"But there has to be a reason why he wouldn't," Duke said. "Otherwise why would he need a vote at all?"

"He's worried about Judge," Mister said. "I don't know why. That guy doesn't worry about how anyone else will feel when he does stuff."

Preacher glanced at Mister, the darkness in his voice

incredibly easy to hear. "You haven't even spoken to him in months."

"I have too," Mister said. "We talk about the ranch just fine."

"I mean a meaningful conversation. Like about real life and stuff."

"Why would I?" Mister asked indignantly. "So he can tell me how stupid I am because I like video games or how I'm going to get fat if I only eat peanut butter sandwiches?" He shook his head. "No, thank you."

"He's just trying...."

"Trying to what?" Mister demanded.

"I don't know," Preacher said, glancing at Ace in the rearview mirror. "Fit in. Find a place, at least."

Ace nodded, his eyes a bit wide and worried. "He just wants to feel important."

"By making me feel *un*important," Mister said. "Sorry, but I'm old enough now that I don't have to put up with that. I don't have to be treated like garbage just because he's family."

"I agree with Mister," Duke said quietly, his eyes trained out the window.

"But wouldn't you want to be forgiven?" Ace asked, peering at Duke. "I mean...you left for years, Duke. Your family forgave you. Maybe Judge just needs that, and he and Mister can start over."

"I think our situations are different," Duke said. "But yes, I'm eternally glad my father forgave me and welcomed me back. But I wasn't making fun of him every other second to make myself feel better. I was just...." He sighed and a pained look crossed his face. Preacher looked out the windshield again to give him some measure of privacy since Ace could stare with the best of them.

"I was just very angry at the world for a very long time," Duke finally said.

"Maybe Judge is too," Preacher said, because that statement fit his brother pretty well, in his opinion. Sometimes it fit Preacher too.

"I had to apologize for what I'd done," Duke said. "I made it right."

"Judge just thinks he's right," Mister said. "You don't see him apologizing."

"Maybe he doesn't know how," Ace said.

Mister blew out his breath in a frustrated sigh, and Preacher actually pressed on the gas to get them to the mall faster. "So I should take the foreman job," he said, bringing the conversation back to its original topic.

"I would," Duke said. "With a ranch as big as yours, with all the moving pieces, you guys need a few foremen, and you're super organized, Preach."

He nodded. "Should I talk to Judge about it first?"

"Only if you feel like you should," Duke said.

Preacher wasn't sure how he felt, and that was the real problem. Ace moved the conversation back to gaming, and they arrived at the mall a few minutes later. Beau waited in his pickup near the restaurant they'd agreed on.

After lunch—where they talked about video games, ranching, and more video games—they went into the mall to pick up Beau's rebuilt computer.

"Why didn't we drive around to the other side?" he

complained, but Preacher didn't mind walking through the mall.

They turned a corner, and the crowd thinned a little bit. He caught sight of a familiar blonde up ahead, and he started to slow a bit. Who was that?

All at once, he knew her.

The woman striding toward him was Charlie Perkins. His heart somersaulted, and his stomach squeezed at him until he blurted, "Charlie," almost as she went by his group. She paused and looked toward him, finally latching onto his face.

She looked him up and down, and wow, Preacher was so lacking under her scrutiny. "Preacher Glover," she said.

Hey, she knew his name. He looked back the way she'd been coming, because it looked like she'd been running from something. Or someone. "What are you doing here?"

"I had a meeting here earlier," she said evasively. Her eyes darted around to the four cowboys he stood with. "What are you guys doing at the mall? Bro shopping trip?"

"These are not all my brothers," he said.

"Brothers and cousins," she amended, no smile in sight. "Isn't that who you live with and everything?"

Technically, no. He wondered why she was being so salty. He'd given her a hundred bucks for thirty seconds of work. On a bill with his name and number on it. She hadn't used it, and he told himself she probably hadn't even seen it. Or maybe his handwriting had been too illegible. He had scrawled it quickly, with his date three feet away.

"This here's Mister," he said. "He is my youngest brother."

"Ma'am." Mister touched his cowboy hat and grinned at

Charlie. Preacher should've told him about the hundred he'd put in her tip jar, because it looked like Mister liked what he saw.

"Duke Rhinehart," Preacher said, indicating the next man. "Not my brother."

"Brother-in-law," Duke said, selling him out with a grin as wide as the Mississippi. "I married Arizona earlier this year."

Charlie smiled and shook his hand, then turned her raised eyebrows on Preacher. "Brother-in-law has 'brother' in it."

Preacher couldn't help smiling too. "That is does." He indicated Ace. "My cousin Ace."

"Ah, a cousin," she said, her voice clearly saying *I included cousins with brothers, Preacher.*

"And Beau Peterson," he said. "No relation whatsoever."

"Nice to meet you," Beau said, but it was clear he wanted to keep moving.

Preacher wanted to stay with Charlie and ask her all kinds of things about herself. Maybe he could buy her coffee, or they'd waste the whole afternoon together and he could then take her to dinner.

"Anyway," he said when the silence had gone on long enough to turn awkward. "We're just headed over to Gaming Guru to pick up Beau's computer."

"You play video games?"

Preacher almost didn't want to admit it. "In the few moments of downtime I have," he said. "You?"

"What do you boys play?" she asked, ignoring his question. She reached up and tucked her blonde curl behind her ear, and that caused her to release the cinched arms across her chest. She relaxed visibly, and Preacher sure did like this new softness in Charlie Perkins.

"I like Solitary Ops," Duke said. "Or Warfare Frontier."

Preacher could play the army games too, but they weren't his favorite. Mister agreed, as did Beau and Ace.

"And what about you?" Charlie asked, and Preacher wasn't well-versed in women, but it sure did sound like she was flirting with him. "You play first-person shooter games?"

The fact that she knew Solitary Ops and Warfare Frontier were first-person shooter games impressed him.

"Oh, no, ma'am," he said real serious. He even shook his head and everything. "I'm all-in on Farm Frenzy."

A beat of silence passed, and then the five cowboys burst out laughing, Preacher included. To his great surprise, Charlie joined them, her blue eyes sparkling with delight. Something moved through Preacher he hadn't felt in a very long time, and he wasn't even sure what it was now.

All he knew was that he liked Charlie Perkins and wanted to get to know her a lot better. She had his number—maybe—and he desperately wanted hers.

People and noise moved around them in the busy mall. Beau insisted they keep moving so he could get his machine. Preacher waved his hand as Duke said, "We'll see you down there, okay, Preach?"

"Yeah," he even said. But he couldn't look away from Charlie. The moment they were alone, Preacher knew it keenly. Her eyes came back to his, and the moment was awkward again. "Sorry," he said. "I didn't mean to tease you like that."

"It's fine." She smiled at him again and shifted her feet. He noticed she didn't carry a purse or bag at all.

"What did you say you were doing here?" he asked.

"I met with the mall office about having an ice cream kiosk here on the weekends," she said. "And I met some girlfriends for lunch."

"Ah." He nodded. "Are they who you were running from?"

Charlie's smile disappeared, and Preacher cursed himself for thinking he could have a conversation with a woman. Honestly, he needed an earpiece and Ace telling him exactly what to say.

"Your brothers and cousins seem fun," she said. "It was good to see you."

He knew what that meant: *I'm leaving, and I hope I never run into you again.*

"Hey, Charlie," he said as she took the first step away. She paused and turned back, and Preacher told himself that meant something. "Could I get your number? Maybe you'd like to come hang out with us when we play."

Surprise flitted across her face, and she opened her mouth, but nothing came out.

"We usually just text to set up times to get on the server together," he said. "Since no, we don't all live together up at Shiloh Ridge." He grinned at her, hoping she understood he was teasing her. "And we just finished lunch too, but I'm sure you'd be welcome to hang out with us if you wanted."

She'd recovered from his bold question, and she cocked her hip now, the hand she put there also holding her phone. "You think I want to hang out with you and your brothers?"

The joy vanished from his soul. "No, probably not." He

touched the brim of his hat. "Good to see you, ma'am. Good luck with your kiosk." He turned and walked away, telling himself to *go, go, go!*

Do not look back.

He didn't need to embarrass himself any more than he already had.

"Preacher," she called, and he stopped, pressed his eyes closed, and took a deep breath.

When he turned back to her, she was walking toward him. He waited as she got real close to him, right inside his personal space.

"I have your number from that hundred-dollar bill," she said, her voice almost a whisper and her face maybe six inches from his. "I can text you about hanging out and playing games?" She made it sound like a question, like she needed his permission to use the number he'd given her.

"You have the money still?"

"Don't tell me you don't carry around bills like that, all with your personal contact info on them," she said, scoffing.

"You're kidding," he said, leaning away so he could see her face better. "Who would do that?"

A flush worked its way across her face, and embarrassment ran through her eyes.

"Oh, I see," he said, connecting all the dots lightning fast. "You think I carry around a stack of hundreds with my name and number on them, tossing them out to every pretty woman I meet. Is that it?"

"You were at a wedding with a date," she said. Code for *yes, that's what I thought.*

"One of the worst dates of my life," he said, stepping

back. His chest felt so tight, and he had no idea what to do in this situation. He fell further away from her. Two steps, four, six. "Text me if you want," he said. "We tend to play in the early evenings and on weekends. I'll have to ask the boys if you're welcome, but I think it'll be fine. They're pretty chill."

He lifted his hand in farewell, turned, and walked away.

Every step felt like it took all of his energy, and he told himself to simply make it out of her sight and then he could collapse.

He didn't, though. He made it down to the gaming store, where Beau stood with a salesman, getting a demo on his new machine. Everyone else had gathered around to watch, and Preacher fell into place beside Mister.

"Did you get her number?" Mister asked real quiet.

Preacher just shook his head, and to Mister's eternal credit, he didn't ask anything else.

Chapter Thirty-Three

Cactus loitered in the kitchen, waiting for Bishop and Ranger to come inside. Preacher and Montana had left about ten minutes ago, and Cactus knew Bear waited upstairs in the conference room where they held ranch meetings.

Ward peanut buttered a piece of toast and faced him. "You sure you want me there?"

Cactus nodded. He needed to apologize to everyone, otherwise the journey wouldn't be complete.

"What happened with you and Willa yesterday?" he asked. "I thought you were going to propose."

Cactus regretted involving Ace and Bishop, for he knew the secret had been spilled by those two. Everyone in the family liked them, and they couldn't keep secrets for very long. Not that his feelings for Willa were secret, and he didn't care if the whole world knew he loved Willa Knowlton.

"I...wasn't...It wasn't the right time," he said. "I'm hoping to do it this week."

Ward nodded, something dark riding in his eyes as he bit into his toast.

"What about you?" Cactus asked. "Seeing anyone?"

"Only if livestock counts," he said.

"Hey, sometimes I've counted them." Cactus grinned at him. "Sometimes my only meaningful conversations for the day happened with the pigs or Hammy."

Ward smiled back and finished his toast. "They delayed me on the gravel again," he said. "By the way. From the Ground Up can't even get the gravel we ordered."

"It's fine," Cactus said. "She's gotten out to the Edge Cabin just fine on the rutted road."

"She's got a new car now."

Cactus opened his mouth but paused. "Oh, right."

"I'm going to get it done," he said. "If I have to call someone else, it'll be done by the time you and Willa get married."

"She wants a Christmas wedding."

Ward's eyes widened. "I'll get on the phone this afternoon."

Cactus waved him away. "I can make a few calls too."

"Don't worry about it. I'll do it."

The back door opened, and Bishop walked in with Ranger. They kept their conversation going while Ranger poured himself a cup of coffee, ending with, "Talk to Ward about it."

Bishop looked at Ward, who simply raised his eyebrows. "Another time," Bishop said, glancing at Cactus. "This is going to be quick, right? I have a conference call in twenty minutes."

"Super quick," Cactus said, his stomach falling to his boots. "Let's go upstairs. Oakley's up there, right?"

"Should be," Ranger said, heading that way. "I'll go get her."

Cactus led the way upstairs, and everyone followed him into the conference room. Bear rose from his chair, looking at the others as they filed in behind him. "What's going on?"

"I asked them to come," Cactus said. Ranger and Oakley arrived only a few seconds later, and she looked around nervously. Cactus didn't sit down at all. He put his hands on the back of the chair he normally sat in. "Thank you all for coming. I figured I'd talk to you all at the same time. I asked Ace to come, but he had plans with Preacher, I guess."

Cactus had spoken to him privately, and he didn't want to do it over and over. Maybe he was taking the easy way out by asking them all to come to this meeting. He didn't know. It had felt right at the time.

"I wanted to apologize to each of you. Bear, obviously, for letting my temper rule me, and for hitting you." He sucked in a breath and looked at the table, then forced his gaze back to his brother's. "I'm horribly embarrassed by my behavior, and I had no right to put my hands on you."

He drew in a breath and looked at Bishop. "I wanted to apologize to you, Bish, because I know you're close with Bear, and I probably caused some rift there. Also, I put you and Ace right in the middle of an uncomfortable situation, and I shouldn't have."

"You do not need to apologize to me," Bishop said.

"But I do," Cactus said. "And to Ranger and Oakley, I wanted to apologize. You got caught up in the middle of things too, and my behavior made you doubt your decisions and put you in a situation you probably didn't want to be in. I apologize for that."

"That's as much my fault as yours," Bear said. "I called Oakley to pull cars for Willa."

Cactus nodded, acknowledging what Bear had said. "And Ward, I wanted to apologize to you for the same reason as Bishop. You had to pick between me and Bear, and I know you don't like doing that. No one should have to feel like they need to protect anyone from me."

Cactus hung his head. "I made a huge mistake—probably several—in those few minutes, and I am sincerely sorry. I hope you'll all forgive me."

"Nothing to forgive," Ward said. "On my end." He looked around the table.

Ranger and Oakey nodded, and she said, "You're a good man, Cactus. It was a very difficult situation, and no one blames you."

He did. He blamed himself. First for letting his temper control him, and second for not forgiving Bear as easily as he wanted to be forgiven.

"That's it," he said. "Everything else I have to say, only Bear needs to hear. You can stay if you want, but...yeah." Cactus pulled the chair out and sat down.

"I've got to go," Bishop said. "Thanks, Cactus. You're awesome." He left with Ward, Ranger, and Oakley, and Cactus looked across the table to Bear.

"You're my brother, and I love you," Cactus said. "I'm sorry I withheld that forgiveness from you for so long."

"I know why you did."

"Still." Cactus shook his head and looked at a piece of framed art on the wall. "I talked to Doctor Thompson about it, and you know, he says to give myself time to heal. Time to think through things. Time to examine what I really want. I like that about him, because I'm slow, and I like feeling like I have the time I want to figure things out."

Bear nodded as if he understood, but Cactus wasn't sure he did.

"But after a while, I was just using that as a shield. I ran from you when I knew you were coming, and I shouldn't have. You were trying to make things right, and I should've let you."

"You're fine, Cactus," he murmured.

Cactus shook his head and removed his cowboy hat. He ran both hands through his hair and looked at Bear again. "Willa expects me to forgive faster."

"I doubt that," Bear said. "I think she expects you to be the man you profess to be. A man of God, and men like that, Charles, forgive."

"I always knew I'd forgive you," he said.

"I knew that too."

"Maybe I was just holding onto my hurt feelings, because they fed something in me I needed."

"Who knows why?" Bear said. "Who knows why I thought it would be okay to buy your girlfriend a car? I mean, what idiot does *that*?"

"I know your heart, Bear. You didn't do it on purpose."

"I know *your* heart, Cactus, and I should've known how you'd react."

Cactus gave him a small smile. "We could go around and around. Bottom line is, I hate not talking to you. Do you know I've resorted to Bishop and Ace to help me plan this proposal?"

Bear started to chuckle, and Cactus joined in. "I heard Preacher and Judge were in on it too," Bear said.

"Now you know how far I've fallen." They laughed together, and Cactus got up at the same time Bear did. They met in the middle of the table and embraced. Cactus held Bear tight, the cleansing spirit of forgiveness moving through him.

"Thank you, Bear."

"Thank you, Cactus." He clapped Cactus on the back and stepped back. "Now, let's go over this proposal to make sure you're not going to embarrass yourself again."

THE FOLLOWING EVENING, CACTUS PULLED UP TO NESTLED Oaks, the assisted living facility where Aunt Dawna lived. Willa, Mitch, and Frost rode in the car with him, and he eased into the circle drive to let them out. "I'll go park and meet you inside."

"Tell me why we're here again," Willa said.

Cactus looked at her, surprised he had to go over it again. "To help her with her tree. She asked me to come help." His brothers and Ace should be here already, and they were planning to pretend as though they'd just popped in, and they were all there by coincidence. "Plus, you said you played bridge, and my aunt is a champion bridge player. She loves anyone who plays."

The blank look on Willa's face didn't settle his nerves. "Bridge?"

"Yes," Cactus said. "Didn't you tell her on Sunday that you played bridge?"

"No," Willa said. "I don't even know what bridge is."

Cactus turned toward her to give his neck some relief. "What?"

"I was talking to her," Willa said. "I'm not sure what she heard—oh."

"Oh what?"

"I said my *parents* played bridge." She grinned and giggled. "But I didn't like it and preferred *cribbage*."

"I see," Cactus said, smiling too. "Maybe she thought you said you preferred bridge. Cribbage and bridge sort of sound the same."

She turned toward the entrance. "I can't play bridge, Cactus. Is she going to want to play a game tonight?"

"I have no idea," he said. "She asked me to come help her with the tree and said I should bring you because you played bridge."

"Well." She shrugged. "We can at least help with the tree." She twisted and added, "Come on, Frost. Let's go, Mitch." The three of them piled out of the car, and Cactus went to park. He hurried through the wind and chill that had arrived with November and found Willa in the foyer. She chatted with the receptionist, of course, because Willa could talk to anyone.

Mitch and Frost had migrated further into the center, where several of the residents had crowded around them. "What's he doing?" he asked Willa.

"Showing off," Willa said with a smile. She finished her conversation with the receptionist and Cactus whistled at Frost. The dog barked and put his paw on Mitch, then started toward Willa and Cactus.

Mitch signed a few more things, then followed the dog. *There's a guy here who can sign*, he told Cactus. *Isn't that cool?*

"Sure thing." Cactus looked into the main room of the center, but everyone had gone back to their activities. They opted for the elevator, and several minutes later, Cactus knocked on his aunt's apartment door.

Ace opened it, and a whole conversation happened. "Hey," he said smoothly, just the right amount of surprise in his voice. "What are you doin' here?"

"What am *I* doin' here?" Cactus asked. "What are *you* doing here?"

"Mother wanted help with her tree." He stepped back and opened the door further. "I brought Preacher and Judge with me."

"She asked me the same thing."

Ace shook his head and grinned at Willa. "I think my mother is losing her marbles."

Willa smiled back at him. "Good. Maybe she'll forget she thinks I play bridge."

"Mother doesn't forget anything about bridge." Ace gestured for them to come in. "Come on. We just barely got it out of the box."

Cactus gripped Willa's hand and crossed into the apartment. Judge and Preacher labored with the tree, bickering over where the cords needed to go so they could be plugged into each other.

"Cactus," Aunt Dawna said, delight on her face. "There you are. Look at these boys. They showed up to help me with the tree too."

"You asked me to, Mother," Ace said, shooting her a look. Wow, he was good. Cactus loved his cousin in that moment, and he released Willa's hand to help put on the top section of the tree.

"Let's get it all fluffed out," he said, and he signed the instructions to Mitch. Frost went to sit beside Aunt Dawna, who cooed at him as if he were a puppy. Frost had spent the past two years training to be a hearing dog, but he certainly wasn't saying no to getting a scratch from the elderly woman.

"Ornaments," Preacher said, indicating several boxes on the coffee table. "Everyone all in. Let's get this done."

Cactus started putting on a box of silver balls, and Willa interacted with Aunt Dawna for a few minutes. He very nearly dropped every single ornament he picked up, and the way Preacher, Judge, and Ace kept tossing him knowing looks only annoyed him. Involving them in his proposal had definitely been a huge mistake.

Mitch got his mother's attention and wanted her to come help. She smiled at Aunt Dawna and came to help. She hooked a red ball with plenty of ridges, and Cactus nodded to Ace. He detoured into the kitchen without a sound and as Willa hung her ornament and returned to the box for another one, Ace hung the diamond ring Cactus had bought for Willa on the tree.

He looked at Mitch, and they didn't need to speak or sign for the boy to know what he needed to do. When Willa turned back to the tree, Mitch got her attention and signed for her to come put her ornament over by his. She grinned at him and did what he said.

Cactus couldn't move, but he wasn't sure how obvious the diamond would be. He hadn't hung it, and he didn't know where Ace had put it.

The seconds felt like years, and then Willa froze. She sucked in a breath, and Cactus knew she'd seen the ring.

"Go," Ace hissed at him, but it wasn't until Preacher actually gave him a little push that Cactus stepped toward Willa. He distinctly remembered getting down on one knee when he'd asked Allison to marry him, and this time, he needed to do better.

Willa reached toward the tree, and Cactus rounded it just as she removed the engagement ring from the bough. Cactus dropped to both knees and said, "I love you, Willa Knowlton. You'd make me the happiest man in the world if you'd marry me this Christmas."

She faced him, her eyes wide and moving from the ring to Cactus. "This thing is huge," she whispered.

"Is that a yes or a no?" He reached for the ring, and she handed it to him. He studied it for a moment, then looked up at her again.

"Yes," she said, and Mitch leapt into the air, one of his strange yelps coming from his mouth. Cactus laughed, and Willa did too, though tears streamed down her face.

"Oh, come on," he said gently. "I'm always making you cry."

"Good tears," she reminded him, and Cactus slid the ring on her finger. She gazed at it, and then him, taking his face in her hands and leaning down to kiss him.

Applause and cheers filed the apartment, and Cactus reminded himself that he wasn't alone with his fiancée, and he better mind his manners.

Chapter Thirty-Four

❧❧❧

"Will you please send that to me?" Willa asked Preacher. He'd gotten the whole proposal on video, and she could admit the whole thing had been beautiful. Well-planned. Absolutely perfect. Cactus had used Mitch in the event, and she didn't even care that three other men had witnessed it.

She felt like she'd been waiting her whole life to be engaged to a man like him, and she couldn't stop smiling.

"Of course," he said, glancing up. "I can do a little editing on it so the lighting is a bit better. Run it through a sound equalizer, so the sound is perfect."

"If you'd like," she said, looking at him. "You don't need to go to too much trouble."

"He likes it," Cactus said. "Preach loves computers and stuff." He grinned at his brother, and Willa would not let go of his hand.

"I do like it," he admitted, smiling. "I won't take long. I'll get it done tonight and email it to you."

"Okay." She gave him her email address and tugged on Cactus's hand. "Can I talk to you for a second alone?"

"Sure," he said, a hint of surprise on his face. "Mitch," he signed, and the boy looked up at him. "We'll be outside for just a sec. You stay here with my brothers, okay?"

Okay, he said, and he grabbed onto Cactus and hugged him. Then he hugged Willa, and then he picked up another ornament and found an empty spot on the tree for it.

"I love him to bits," Cactus said once they'd stepped into the hallway.

"I know you do," Willa said softly. She only took three steps and then moved quickly in front of him and stopped. "I love *you* to bits," she said. "Thank you for making that special and amazing."

He simply gazed down at her. "Thank you for inspiring me to be a better man, someone who deserves an amazing woman like you."

She kissed him, and while she'd always wanted to go fast and let him know how much he stoked her fire, tonight, she kissed him slowly, which heated things up just as easily and just as quickly as a more frantic kiss.

"Do you really think we can get married by Christmas?" she whispered against his lips.

"No," he said. "It's going to be the twenty-sixth."

She giggled and pressed her forehead against his breast-bone. "You've got this all worked out, don't you?"

"Some things," he said, his voice husky and warm. "Patrick is booked, and he's already invited your parents for the holidays. I've scheduled the barn at the ranch with everyone in the family. Holly Ann is going to make dinner, and I told her family only, but that includes her dad and sister's family. Montana's aunt and uncle. Sammy's parents. I think Duke's parents might come too."

He kept his arms securely around her, and she breathed in the spicy warmth of him. "Something small then."

"You know, thirty or forty people. The ceremony. Food. Done."

"No dancing?" she teased, looking up at him.

He looked at her with a glint in his eyes. "I'll do what you want, my love, but last time we danced, you said I needed lessons."

"I'll teach you," she said, giggling. The man didn't really need lessons, but she couldn't have him being perfect at everything. "The ceremony. Food. Dancing. Done."

"Yes, ma'am," he said. "I'd love to see Mitch escort you down the aisle to me," he said. "And I'm going to be wearing this real nice navy blue tuxedo I've already ordered."

"You can order clothes?" She swept something invisible from his broad shoulders. "With shoulders like these?"

He grinned at her. "I've got an appointment with the tailor when the suit comes in."

"So I need a dress and flowers."

"My mother would literally be over the moon if she could help you plan your wedding. She'll take over the decorations for the barn and everything."

"I'll talk to her." Willa gazed up at him. "Do you really want me, Cactus?"

"More than anything," he whispered, dipping his head to

kiss her again, and Willa fell into his touch, thanking the Lord for every moment she'd experienced with Charles Glover.

"OKAY, PEOPLE," WILLA CALLED OVER THE NERVOUS chatter in the room they'd been given in the tabernacle. "We're five minutes out. They just flashed the lights. Settle down. Save those voices."

Willa had no idea if she could pull off this Sing-in. She pressed her eyes together and prayed, suddenly getting the idea that she should do that with the whole group. Her eyes snapped open again, and she said, "I'd like to say a prayer. Would that be all right with everyone?" This wasn't the church choir, but they all knew she was a pastor.

No one objected, and she gave everyone a few more moments to settle down. She bowed her head and let the Lord settle her. "Dear Lord," she said. "We ask for Thy blessing tonight. We have been working on the music and songs for this Messiah Sing-in, and we want to give Thee honor and accolades. Please bless all those here with clarity of mind and open ears to hear the pitches they need to hit. Bless them with calmness and joy, and bless those in the audience to feel of Thy love for them this holiday season."

Willa took a deep breath, nothing more to say. Her heart had been poured out in prayer, and she said, "Amen," and got several in response.

She clapped her hands together a few times. "Okay, let's line up."

They'd only practiced in the tabernacle once, and it had happened earlier that morning. She'd barely left the building, and Cactus had gone out to get lunch for the two of them. She didn't want to eat dinner until after the Sing-in, because she hated feeling full in front of a crowd.

Once she finished this concert, she'd focus on the Christmas Festival choir fully, as they had ten performances over the next two weeks.

Then she'd have a week to focus on the church choir for their Christmas Eve performance.

In the past month, she'd managed to find a wedding dress, and Lois Glover had taken over the rest of the plans—the flowers and the décor. Cactus had taken care of everything else.

Willa loved him, and his family, so completely, and they'd taken things from her plate so she could focus on her three choirs. That endeared them to her, and the next thing she knew, the coordinator for the program tonight opened the door and said, "We're ready."

Willa stepped out into the hall, her thick binder clutched in her hand. She paused just outside the doorway and smiled at the first alto who came out. "You've got this," she said.

"This is going to be great," she said to the next woman.

Every single person got an encouraging word and a smile, and when Cactus stepped into the hall, she said, "You are the best singer here. You're going to kill it." She kissed him quickly, and he moved on.

Once everyone had exited, she followed her choir, the prayer running through her mind again. *Bless them. Bless them all to be happy and satisfied with their performance, especially Cactus.*

He'd been increasingly nervous about the performance as it drew nearer, and Willa had told him ten times that of course he was the man for the bass solo in *The People That Walked in Darkness.*

The choir was announced, and Willa took her spot at the music stand. She took her time to get her binder open and the music where she wanted it. They had a full orchestra they'd practiced with four times, and she felt the weight of dozens and dozens of eyes on her.

She lifted one hand. She drew a deep breath.

She started, and the music filled the air. It filled her soul. It filled her life with love, and joy, and peace. She adored the harmonies in *The Messiah*, and she found comfort in the greenery hanging behind the choir, reminding her that while winter had come to the Earth for now, spring would always follow. The Lord would always deliver His people.

As *Comfort Ye My People* started, Willa held back her emotion so her eyes wouldn't fill with tears. She needed to see the music so she could have a performance she could be happy and satisfied with too.

As she led her choir, and then the congregation through the songs in *The Messiah*, Willa felt as though everything in her life had finally aligned. Her heart had finally healed from the trauma she'd inflicted upon it.

She was finally ready to be the person the Lord wanted her to be. The person He'd been guiding her to become. The person she'd always wanted to be.

Chapter Thirty-Five

❧

Cactus looked at himself in the full-length mirror in the groom's room, the navy blue his absolute favorite. His shirt shone with the brightest of whites, and while he'd originally told Willa he'd be wearing a tuxedo, he'd hated it.

He'd switched out the coat with the horrendous tails and the shirt with the choking collar for something as elegant but not as formal. She said she didn't care, and as he slid his hands down the front of his jacket, he knew he'd made the right choice.

The trim on the jacket shone with the silk edging, and it beamed out from his pockets too. He wore a white and silver flower in his breast pocket, and he adjusted the collar on his shirt as Bear slipped into the room.

"Got it," he said, hurrying toward Cactus. "Mother had it polished." He handed the string tie to Cactus, who looked at it against his palm.

"Daddy wore it," he said. "I've seen it in their wedding pictures."

"Mother's been trying to get one of us to wear it," Bear said. "No wonder you're her favorite."

Cactus laughed, because that so wasn't true. Bear was her favorite. Or Bishop. Honestly, it was probably a tie between the two of them.

He did love his mother, and she loved him, and Cactus felt loveable for the first time in many, many years. He flipped up his collar and threaded the tie around his neck. The silver piece in the front was almost shaped like the Superman logo, but it had a G in it for Glover.

That gleamed with a dark onyx color, and the strings fell down over his shirt with the black buttons.

Bear helped him with the collar in the back, and he smoothed his hand along Cactus's shoulder. "You're ready."

"I hope so," he said.

He adjusted the top button on his vest and fastened the buttons on his jacket. "Buttoned or open?" he asked, undoing them again.

"I'd leave it open," Bear said. "You guys are going a little less formal, and that makes the most sense to me."

He and Willa had adjusted their plans a little bit. He wasn't going to walk out alone and wait at the altar. He, Willa, and Mitch were going to march down the aisle together, the family they wanted to be. Mitch was going to stand at the altar with them during the ceremony. Willa was going to change out of her wedding gown immediately following dinner for the dancing she wanted so much.

Cactus honestly didn't care. Whatever she or Mother told him to do, he'd done and would continue to do.

He reached for the custom cowboy hat he'd had made to go with the suit, and he settled the bright white hat on his head. It too had blue trim around the brim, and when he looked in the mirror this time, he looked like he was ready to get married.

"Let's go," Bear said, and Cactus followed his brother out of the room. The groom's room sat at the end of the hall, with the brides' room right next door. The bathrooms sat on the other side of the doorway that was currently covered with the large barn door.

Once that opened, the ceremony would begin.

The pretty piano music Willa had recorded for the wedding played over the speakers, even back here, and Cactus shifted his feet while he waited for Willa to come out.

"He's right there."

Cactus looked up to find Patrick standing down at the corner. Mitch faced Cactus, and a smile filled his whole soul. "Come on, boy," he said, and Mitch ran toward him.

Cactus chuckled as he picked up the child, groaning too. "You've gotten too big to pick up," he said.

Mitch beamed down at him. *Do you like my hat?* He reached up and put his palm flat against his white hat.

"I sure do." Cactus set the boy down and took his hand. "Your suit looks nice too." Mitch wore a navy blue suit too, not quite as formal as Cactus's. He didn't wear a vest, for example, and his tie was of the regular variety, a blue, silver, and white striped article that seemed a little too big for the kid.

His shirt was white and crisp, and the cowboy hat matched that. He wore dark cowboy boots too, just like Cactus, and the only thing they needed now was the bride.

Cactus glanced to the door of the brides' room, wondering if Willa had chickened out.

She hasn't chickened out, he told himself. *Don't be ridiculous.*

Mitch shook his hand out of Cactus's, causing him to look left again as the boy ran off. He skidded on the floor to hug Frost, and Cactus shook his head. "Mitch," he said, and he then told Frost to bring the boy back.

Frost barked and led him back over to Cactus. The dog wore a navy bowtie around his neck, and he seemed to know he was about to participate in something regal and majestic. He certainly trotted like he did.

"You can't slide on the ground, bud," Cactus said, crouching down and brushing the dirt and dust and who knew what else from the boy's dark pants. "These pants show everything."

He got him all fixed up and said, "Get his leash on him."

Frost doesn't need a leash, Mitch said, looking somewhat perturbed Cactus had suggested such a thing at all.

"Then tell him to stay right by you," Cactus said. "There's not much room out there."

Mitch signed something to the dog, and Frost moved right next to him. He looked up at Cactus again. *Did you see he's wearing a tie too?* Mitch beamed like this was the greatest day of his life.

"I saw," Cactus said, smiling at Mitch.

Finally, the door opened, and women started spilling out of the room. Sammy wiped her eyes and beelined for Cactus right across the hall. "I'm so happy for you, Charles."

"Thank you, Sammy," he murmured. She stepped out of his arms, nodded at him, and went down the hall. The sound of the barn door being slid open met Cactus's ears as Zona exited the room. Then Montana, Holly Ann, and Oakley.

They all smiled at him, and he kept nodding at the lot of them.

Mother emerged, and she too had tears in her eyes. She embraced Cactus, who held her tight and said, "Thank you, Mother." Willa's own mother was quite a bit older than Mother—almost ninety—and she hadn't been able to do much.

"She is so lucky to have you," Mother said, but Cactus was pretty sure she'd gotten that backward. She pulled away, smiled through her tears, and hurried down the hall too. Don waited for her there, and she slipped her hand into his before they walked into the hall beyond that gaping doorway.

The door opened one more time, and this time, Willa appeared. Cactus sucked in a breath, his pulse suddenly firing left and right through his body. She wore a dress that swelled over her chest to thick straps that went over her shoulders. The fabric shone in the lights, without a stitch of lace in sight. She held a magnificent splay of flowers in her hands that seemed to have feathery blooms and oversized roses in a variety of breeds and colors. Ivory, blush, blue, burgundy, and some that had been sprayed silver. It was Christmassy and yet not at the same time.

The dress flared around her hips and hugged her legs to

her knees, then flared again. She'd warned him that she'd need his help to walk very far, and that he couldn't go very fast down the aisle.

He stepped over to her now, offering his arm and the words, "You are stunning."

"Thank you, cowboy," she said. "You don't look so bad yourself."

He grinned at her, and she laced her arm through his. "Slowly, remember."

"I remember, my love." He led her toward the end of the hall, extending his hand to Mitch too. With Willa on his right, and Mitch on his left, he rounded the corner and faced the hall.

Everyone had already stood and was waiting for them. He smiled, because it was a small affair, and these were all the people who loved him most. The chairs had been dressed in ivory fabric, with burgundy bows to go with the yards and yards of greenery that had been draped along the railing lining the loft, the serving window that led into the kitchen, the windows at the front of the hall.

Barrels held massive pots of poinsettias, pine boughs, and plenty of ivory and blush roses. Mother had done a marvelous job of making this wedding full of holiday charm but also distinguishing it from Christmas.

"It's your Christmas wedding," he murmured.

"It's gorgeous," Willa agreed.

"Here we go," he said, stepping out of the doorway. The journey down the aisle took thirty seconds, though it certainly felt longer than that with all the eyes on him.

His face felt like someone had lit it on fire by the time he reached the bed of a wagon that had been filled with flowers —roses, poinsettias in both white and red, and plenty of that winter greenery that reminded him of rebirth—jars of flickering lights, jewels that sparkled, and even wild grasses.

Patrick stood on the other side of it, and Willa stepped quickly over to her mother and father and gave them both a hug and a kiss before rejoining Cactus at the western altar. The pastor smiled at the two of them, and said, "I have the great pleasure of standing with two of my favorite people today." He looked fondly at Willa. "My baby sister and an amazing man and friend." He switched his gaze to Cactus, who certainly didn't think he deserved that introduction.

"I've had the great pleasure of watching Willa and Cactus as they fell in love this year. I've seen him bring her food when she needed it, and I've seen him learn sign language so he could communicate with her son. I've seen her accommodate her activities to include him, and I've watched her open doors in her life that she thought were welded closed."

Cactus hung on every word, because he held great respect for Patrick, and it was interesting to hear an outside perspective of the relationship he'd been inside of.

"I knew in the summertime that Willa and Cactus would end up right here, at an altar, with each other. When he joined her choir, I knew that was a great sacrifice for him, but he did it for her. See, Willa tried to get him to sing with her last year, and he was fairly, well, prickly about it."

Twitters came from the crowd, with one of his relatives laughing outright. Cactus couldn't deny it, so he simply shrugged.

"Willa started staying in more, or going up to this mysterious ranch where she seemed to find the answers she'd been searching for. When I came up to Shiloh Ridge for the first time, I suddenly understood the magic of this place. No, it's not magic," he said. "It's spirit. The spirit here is incredible, and it comes from all of you, but none more than Cactus himself."

Again, not entirely true—or even true at all.

"I'll stop prattling on," Patrick said. "I understand the bride and groom have written their own vows." He grinned at Willa. "My sister will go first."

Willa shook her gorgeous hair over her shoulders and faced Cactus, both of her hands clasped in his. "My dearest Cactus, the first time we met, I assumed you were an employee at the tack and feed store. You were kind and helpful, and one of the handsomest men I'd ever laid eyes on. I'd only been in town for a couple of weeks, and I was seriously considering leaving Three Rivers."

Her smile wobbled and her hands in his tightened. "But every day I stayed, I felt different. I healed, and I kept reflecting on you time and time again. The first time I heard you sing, it was as if God had peeled back a layer of heaven and let me in, and though I went about it all wrong, I wanted to have you in my life."

Cactus's love for her expanded and grew, and he smiled at her encouragingly.

"I started falling for you last Christmas Eve, when I showed up here without speaking to you for almost three weeks, a deaf ten-year-old in tow. You didn't ask me a ton of questions—or any at all—and I appreciated that so much. You let me be who I was, and you accepted me for who that woman was. You learned sign language, and you exhibited patience. You're kind, hard-working, forgiving, and everything else I want in a partner. We work together harmoniously, and I love that about us the most. I love *you*, and I hope we can build a beautiful life together."

Cactus ducked his head, her love for him almost too much to handle.

"Your turn," she said in a stage whisper that caused some more light laughter.

"Well, I'm not as eloquent as all that," he said. "When we met in the tack and feed store, I'd literally just wrestled a pig to the floor for someone else. I'd gone to town with my cousin, because the woman he liked actually did work at the tack and feed store. I hadn't been off the ranch much, and there you were. Such an open, accepting face. Gorgeous eyes. Beautiful hair. And something in your spirit that touched me."

He glanced at Mother, because he'd gone terribly off-script. "I started attending church only on the weeks you preached. Everyone in the family realized it. I started dating more, though everyone I went out with turned into a disaster. Well, that was me. *I'm* the disaster."

He smiled at her, his heart beating so hard now. "I'm way off what I had prepared."

"It's fine," she said.

"I very nearly messed things up between us," he said, trying to find the beginning of his speech. "But I love you with everything in me. I know the Lord put you in my life when He did so I could have the experiences I needed to get to the point where I could tell you everything in my past, and you'd accept me just how I am. I started to think of our relationship—of you and Mitch—as the holly vines we have here today—this bright spot in the winter of my life. The reminder that spring will always come, and the Lord Jesus Christ will not and had not abandoned me."

He cleared his throat, about to go off-script again. "You said we work together harmoniously, and I feel the same. The harmony between us, for me, is in the holly. When either of us isn't sure if we'll overcome, the other one is there to remind us that we will. You'll help me when I'm deep in my winter, and I'll help you when you're deep in yours."

He needed to wrap this up, and fast. Time to get back on track. "I want to be a better man for you, and I pledge myself to you from today until forever."

He nodded like that was that, his throat so dry and scratchy. He hated public speaking, but just like the solos he'd done in the two choirs of Willa's he'd joined, he'd survived. Maybe even done a good job.

"Wonderful," Patrick said, and Cactus and Willa faced him again. "Do you, Willa Jean Knowlton, take Charles Cactus Bryce Glover to be your lawfully wedded husband, to have and to hold, for this life and the next, with all of his faults, skills, and strengths?"

"I do," she said.

"And do you, Charles Cactus Bryce Glover, take Willa Jean Knowlton to be your lawfully wedded wife, to have and to hold, for this life and the next, with all of her faults, skills, and strengths?"

"I do," he said.

"I now pronounce you husband and wife." He'd barely

finished speaking when all the men in Cactus's family raised the roof with their voices. For the first time in twelve years, Cactus didn't hate the noise. He didn't hate that they were all constantly trying to be the loudest. He didn't hate being in the room with forty other people.

He laughed with Willa, wrapped her in his arms, and kissed her, this beautiful wife of his.

"I love you," he murmured against her lips before kissing her again. And while she couldn't say it back because of his kiss, he felt it in the touch of her mouth against his.

Read on for the first couple of chapters of the next book in the Shiloh Ridge Ranch in Three Rivers series, **THE CHEMISTRY OF CHRISTMAS**.

I hope you enjoyed Cactus and Willa's romance! I love them so much. And Mitch. And Frost, Tank, and Galaxy. And all the Glovers. And Ollie and Aurora...

Sneak Peek! The Chemistry of Christmas
Chapter One:

❦

Preacher Glover yawned, but he kept his horse moving. Sidewinder plodded along, keeping the cattle going where they needed to go. He'd spent hours moving herds today, as he did most other days.

Today felt a little different, sure, because Cactus had just tied the knot mere hours ago. Preacher still wore his suit, in fact, but the work around the ranch didn't stop because two people said I do.

He'd gotten out of cleaning up in True Blue in favor of getting outside to move the last of the herd, and he signaled to Mister, who rode a couple hundred yards to his right. The two of them had plans to get online later, but Ace wouldn't be joining them. He and Holly Ann would be down in town, eating with her family. Duke and Zona had agreed to a game night at the Rhinehart Ranch, and Beau had said something about a date with a new woman who he wouldn't name.

Preacher had texted Charlie about the gaming, but she

hadn't answered yet. His mind caught on the blonde woman, and he could picture her easily though they hadn't spent a lot of in-person time together. She came on their Chatty feed all the time, and he had yet to beat her at a game of Solitary Ops.

The woman had amazing gaming skills, and Preacher would like her just for that. She sometimes texted only him, in a private Chatty room, and sometimes the messages simply came on his phone. He hadn't asked her out, because she didn't seem too keen on dating, and he'd rather have her in his life as a friend than not at all.

He couldn't help thinking about her in a romantic way though. She was smart and funny, absolutely gorgeous, and Preacher had liked her from the moment he'd seen her making ice cream with liquid nitrogen at his cousin's wedding.

He didn't have hundreds with his name and number written on them, despite what she'd originally believed. He'd barely dated at all, thank you very much. He hadn't told anyone about his feelings for Charlie, but the men he spent time with had to know. Duke had said something a few weeks ago, and Preacher hadn't denied anything.

He hadn't confirmed anything either, and Mister had answered for Preacher, saying he didn't want to ruin things with Charlie because she was the best gamer they'd met in years.

Preacher had laughed, as if that was the reason why.

"Ho there," he called, and the cow trying to go left when he should stay right got back in line. Moving the herd didn't take many brain cells, so Preacher had plenty of time to obsess over Charlie.

He'd considered asking her to be his date to Mother's wedding, and he said the words out loud. "Maybe you'd like to come up to the ranch for my mom's wedding. I'm not a bad dancer."

Charlie would say, "Like as your date?" with plenty of bite in her voice, as if dating him was incomprehensible.

"As friends," he said, contributing his half of the conversation out loud. Only cows could judge him—and Sidewinder, though the horse was used to listening to Preacher talk to himself. "I just don't want to go to another wedding alone, especially my mother's."

Having Mother get remarried was weird enough, and Preacher just wanted the day to come and go. Sixteen more days, and it would be done. The year of weddings, where literally six Glovers had tied the knot, would be over.

Etta still had a wedding coming up, but not for another four or five months, and Preacher wouldn't have to be so central to that one. "Still have to wear a tie," he muttered. It wasn't the white shirt and tie he didn't like, because he wore one of those every week when he went to church. It was the ceremony of things. The way he showed up and no one looked at him or even noticed if he was there or not.

His phone chimed, and he reached back and pulled it from his pocket. His pulse picked up when he saw Charlie's name, and not in the Chatty where he'd invited her to play later.

Are you done with the wedding? she'd asked. *I just got something I want to show you.*

He could ride a horse hands-free, so he used both hands to tap out, *Done with the wedding, but I'm out moving cattle. Last herd. Should be finished in about twenty minutes.*

I can video call, she said before he could send the message. *It'll be fast.*

He sent his first message, and then added, *Sure, call.*

His phone rang in a strange up and down tone, indicating the video chat. He swiped up to answer it, and a couple of seconds later, she came up on his screen. "There you are," she said, smiling at him. "I wasn't sure you'd have service out there."

"We're fairly close to the epicenter of the ranch," he said, grinning back at her. She wore her sandy, streaked blonde hair in two braids, one falling over each shoulder. "Just moving a herd from one pasture to another."

"Sounds exciting."

"I can do it while on a video chat," he said dryly. "So no, it's not exciting." He didn't even have to watch the cattle. Sidewinder would keep them in line if they started to stray. He did look out over the land, and the sun had started to set, bringing with it gold and purple—and a newfound cold.

"I can game later," she said. "You'll shower and stuff first, right?"

"Yep."

"That'll give me time to eat," she said. "But I wanted to show you this new flight simulator I got."

"Oh, sweet," he said.

"I'm going to switch you around," she said. "Don't get dizzy." She moved the phone before he could look away, and it was disorienting.

He groaned, and she giggled, and Preacher definitely had to ask her to come to Mother's wedding with him. The screen settled, showing her massive monitor, which had the best video card and sound system installed.

"Look how I can take off from that airport in Greece," she said, and of course, she did it flawlessly. The excitement in her voice infected him, and he laughed at her.

"That's great, Charlie," he said. "But can you land?"

"I've blown up twice," she admitted. "But the third time's the charm, right?"

"Sure," he said. "Let's see it."

"I can't just turn around and land," she said. "My flight plan is taking me to Paris."

"Of course," he said dryly. He didn't hate flight simulators, but they weren't his favorite. Charlie loved them though, and she'd told him in one of their private chats that if she hadn't become a chemist, she'd like to be a pilot. Her father was a pilot, and Charlie loved planes.

"I won't bore you with the flight," she said. "Hit me when you get on tonight."

"Okay," he said, and he knew she was about to end the call. "Charlie," he practically yelled.

She swung the phone back around, leaning it against the monitor so it angled up at her face. She didn't look at it, but kept her attention on the flight simulator as she said, "Yeah?"

"My mother's wedding is coming up, and I'm not a bad dancer, and I...." He trailed off, because all the words were in the wrong order. "She loves dancing."

"Okay," Charlie said, glancing down at the phone.

"Would you come to the wedding with me?"

"As a date?"

At least he'd pegged her response with near one hundred percent accuracy. She picked up the phone and held it at eye level.

"No," Preacher said. "Just as my friend. I just don't want to stand there like a loser against the wall during the dancing. Mother's hinted she wants us all to dance." He'd spent plenty of time in junior high against the wall at dances. In high school, he'd stopped going to save himself the humiliation, but he couldn't skip out on his mother's wedding.

"I don't own a dress," she said.

"Sure you do," he said. "I've seen you on Sundays in church clothes."

"Those are skirts," she said. "Not dresses." She gave him a wide smile. "I've never owned or worn anything like the last woman you went to a wedding with. That things was...bright."

They laughed together, and Preacher actually found the action cleansing. He loved the bell-like sound of Charlie's laugh, and he shook his head. "We all make mistakes, and if you'd ever tell me about the last guy you went out with, I'm sure I could find something to tease you about."

She shook her head and mimed zipping her lips.

"It's not like I chose that dress for her, you know," he said.

"But you chose her, and a woman like her chooses dresses like that."

He'd seen Charlie in black skirts and white blouses, and he didn't mind those at all. She wore makeup to church, as far as he could tell, and her hair had always looked curled and cute on the Sabbath. "We all make mistakes," he said. "If that's my biggest one, I'll take it."

She grinned at him. "I don't know how to dance."

"You don't need to," he said. "It's the man's job to lead the woman in a dance. You just follow me, and we'll be fine."

She looked dubious, though the playful glint in her eye hadn't gone out yet. She could go from hot to cold in less time than it took to blink, and Preacher had seen her do it several times. Then she'd sign off the Chatty, and he'd pretend like he didn't care.

"I think I'm going to have to see your dancing skills before I agree. You're talking a shopping trip, Preach. And I don't do that unless absolutely necessary."

He chuckled, but Charlie was dead serious. She hadn't set up a kiosk in the mall, but she had told him she worked at HealNow, the new company in town that had gone into one of the tall buildings Preacher hated.

She seemed available for gaming almost all the time, and she'd only mentioned one friend in their couple of months of playing and talking. A woman named Shoshana, and Preacher assumed she worked with Charlie.

"Tell me when you can get together," he said, every cell in his body rejoicing at the very idea. And if they danced, he'd get to touch her, and breathe in the scent of her skin. He imagined her to smell like peaches and cotton, but he didn't actually know, because they'd spent very little time together.

"No, you tell me," she said. "You're the busy one."

"We're operating on a holiday schedule until the New Year," he said. "So we're doing essentials only."

"You're moving cattle on your brother's wedding day," she said, cocking her head. "You'll still work eight hours a day."

He grinned and conceded the point with, "But it's not twelve hours."

"So...tomorrow?"

"Tomorrow's fine," he said, thrilled with the possibility of seeing her tomorrow. Touching her tomorrow. Being with her tomorrow. "Tell me what you like to eat, and I'll pick it up on my way in. Unless you want to go out to dance? We only need like five square feet."

She looked away from the camera and then quickly back. "My place is fine. I'll have to clean it up a little, but I should have time."

"I don't care if it's clean or not."

She only smiled and said, "I'll text you a place to get food, okay? I have to go."

"Oh, all right," he said. "Talk to you later."

"Yep. Bye." She was gone just like that, and Preacher frowned at his phone. Looking away from the device left him night-blind for a few seconds, and he nearly dropped his phone when Mister yelled at him.

"Yep," he yelled back, though he wasn't sure what his brother had even said.

It didn't matter. Preacher had a date with Charlie Perkins.

PREACHER PEERED THROUGH THE WINDSHIELD ON THE right, sure Charlie had missed a number or something in her address. The houses out here were massive and all brand-new. No one lived behind a coded gate in Three Rivers except for those who'd bought the luxury homes out in the subdivision northeast of town.

He'd been driving for what felt like hours, and the food he'd picked up twenty-five minutes ago would surely be cold. He'd texted her when he'd left Down Under, the barbecue place in town that Preacher actually liked.

Ranger had told him about it, and they'd gone together a couple of times in the past couple of years. Charlie apparently liked Texas barbecue, and she'd ordered a lot of meat and a lot of bread to go with it.

Preacher turned another corner, and only three homes sat on this street. They all hulked in the night, with huge dark shapes against the moonlight, as well as the lights coming from the buildings themselves.

The one with the numbers she'd sent him had lights under every window, all illuminated. Not only that, but bright, colorful Christmas lights hung along every perfectly straight eave, indicating the lines of the roof.

There were a ton of those on the two-story house with the three-car garage.

"This is incredible," he said to himself, wondering what in the world Charlie did to be able to afford a place like this. He knew people like Wyatt Walker lived out here, and the dude was a billionaire rodeo champion.

Could Charlie be one too?

He hardly knew her, and Preacher's heartbeat boomed again and then again as he put his somewhat rickety pick-up in park. He hadn't bought a new vehicle for something like eight or nine years, because he didn't need one. He could use this one until the day it decided to stop, his family's frugalness embedded inside him.

He reminded himself that he had plenty of money too as he picked up the box with all the food in it and headed for the front door.

Charlie opened it as he put his boot on the top step, and she stole his breath straight from his lungs, causing him to gasp.

"Hey," she said, everything about her feminine and soft. She had one hand curled around the back of the door, and she wore an oversized gray sweatshirt with a sports brand on the front of it, a pair of baggy jeans, and slippers. Legit slippers the color of sheep's wool.

"Look at you," he said, drawing his eyes down the length of her body and back up. "The wedding will be a little more formal than this." He was surprised he'd gotten so many words out, and he hoped he wouldn't say something tonight to drive Charlie away.

He'd considered talking to Ace and Bishop before the date, but had vetoed the idea every time it had come up. He'd told exactly one person where he'd be tonight—Judge—and his brother had only looked at him with arched brows and said, "Okay, drive safe."

That was it.

Preacher could actually do with a bit more meddling.

Charlie smiled at him and tucked her loose curls behind her ears. "I didn't go to work today."

"No?"

"Didn't feel like it."

"Wow, I wish I could stay home when I felt like it." He looked up at the ceiling that stretched above him. "This place is incredible."

"Thanks," she said, closing the door behind him. "I've only been here about six months or so, so it's still pretty sterile."

Art hung on the walls in silver and gold frames, and Preacher was no expert, but they looked like professional paintings. She'd put a rug down in front of the door that led back into the house, but he waited for her to go first. She went behind the staircase that led up and into a living room filled with dark gray couches that looked like he could sink into them and never get out.

No TV in the room, but a crackling fireplace, plenty of potted plants, and wide open blinds on the windows. He did not like that, and he looked away from the darkness beyond the glass.

She passed a dining room table that could seat at least ten and led him into the kitchen. He could only stand and gape. Holly Ann would die here, and then she'd bustle around, making desserts and meals happily until the day she died.

Dark gray granite countertops sat atop lighter gray cabinets, and all of the appliances were black. The bar seated eight along its length, and he couldn't find a dish or a glass or a single thing out of place.

He looked at Charlie and scoffed, the only sound he could come up with. He felt like he barely knew her, and he told himself that was what he was doing there. Getting to know her.

"You're surprised by the house."

He put the box of food on the counter, almost feeling bad for dirtying it. "Yes," he said, kicking himself for being so blunt. He should've said, "A little," or "Not at all. I live in a huge mansion myself."

Bishop had remodeled the Ranch House a couple of years ago, and it was much more spacious, with an updated layout that made sense. They had new appliances and furniture too, but nothing like this. He couldn't even fathom why someone would ever need a house this nice, especially on a ranch.

The stuff he tracked in on his boots would ruin the stark white floor in her kitchen in a single day.

"Do you live here alone?" he asked.

"Of course not," she said, and he relaxed a little. She had roommates. Of course. That was how she could afford somewhere like this. "David Archuleta and Paul McCartney live here with me."

She flashed him a grin and started unpacking the food.

Preacher frowned, his mind racing at the names of the two celebrities. "What?"

"Archie and Paulie," she said. As if on cue, two cats entered the kitchen. They jumped up onto the counter, one right after the other, and padded toward the food. "No," Charlie said, holding out her hand. "No. Get down."

The cats ignored her, but they did stop just shy of the box of food. Charlie took it and the bag of sauces she'd already taken from it around the counter, the cats—and Preacher—tracking her every move.

Preacher finally decided to act like he came to houses like this all the time. He shed his jacket and draped it over the back of one of the chairs at the dining room table, turning back to Charlie. She'd watched him, and she quickly looked away when his eyes met hers for a brief moment.

"I'll get out plates," she said, clearing her throat.

Preacher joined her in the kitchen as she did, and they scooped food onto their plates. She took hers to the huge table, and he followed, not sure what to say or do next. They ate for a few moments, and then Charlie sighed.

"I suppose you want to know a few things."

"I suppose I have a few questions."

"Lay 'em on me, cowboy."

"So you own this company called Below Zero, but as far as I can tell, you don't—aren't in business. You don't make money from that."

"Only for special occasions," she said. "Weddings and summer fairs."

"Okay," he said, glad that he'd worked that out correctly. "And you work at HealNow regularly."

"Yes," she said.

"Full time?"

Charlie shot him a glance. "Not full time, actually."

Preacher looked at her, his fork full of brisket only halfway to his mouth. "So you work part-time at HealNow, make ice cream for a wedding here and there, and live in a house like this?" He took the bite of food, his mind whirring. He swallowed quickly, so she wouldn't answer.

"I'm sorry," he said. "This is none of my business. I'm basically asking you how much you make, and that's rude." He gave her a smile. "I don't care." He had way more money than most cowboys, and he'd hate all the questions and gaping stares if he chose to buy a place like this one—which he could easily do.

Charlie blinked at him, clear surprise in her expression.

"What?" he finally asked when she kept quiet.

"You just—most people needle at me until they get the answers they want."

"I don't want to be rude," he said. "It doesn't matter to me what you do or how you got your money. It's not my business." He focused on his plate, wishing he'd ordered the spicy barbecue sauce. It hadn't been on her list, and he'd just forgotten.

He seemed to forget his own name when it came to Charlie Perkins, that was for dang sure.

"Okay, come with me," she said, standing up.

He hadn't finished eating yet, and he looked from his plate to hers. She hadn't either. "Where are we going?"

"Just into my office," she said. "It'll be two minutes." She picked up one cat and told the other to come with her. She walked away, and Preacher scrambled to his feet to follow her.

The office sat on the other side of the living room, through a doorway that branched left and right. On the left sat a bathroom, and she paused at the right-side door, her hand on the doorknob.

She looked over her shoulder at him, and then pushed into the room.

Preacher drew a deep breath and followed her.

The front window sat straight in front of him, with a couch to his right and an armchair nearly in front of the windows. The wall to his left held a long, built-in desk with no less than four monitors, three of which were on and showing various things. Email, a video, and some forum or something. Chat room, maybe.

The room continued to the left after a fireplace broke up the desk, and Charlie had put another desk over there that fit into the corner. Two more monitors sat there, and then on the other L-side of the desk sat a huge, flat-screen television. All of those were dark.

"Wow," he said.

"I work for HealNow a few days a week," she said. "Because I like what they stand for and what they're working to achieve. Plus, I'm the only one authorized to work in the veterinary department in this branch, so they need me to come in. I do the Below Zero ice cream, because it's fun for me, and I like seeing people's reaction to the liquid nitrogen."

She gestured to the screens, the desks, the whole set up. "But this is what I really do."

Preacher looked back and forth, his eyes finally coming back to the pretty woman who'd bitten him with her high ponytail and that cloud of liquid nitrogen. "What is this, exactly?"

"Have you heard of Nexus?" she asked.

"Yeah, of course, everyone's heard of...." He trailed off, his eyes widening. He saw the cameras on each monitor now. He saw the different controllers, each of them sitting benignly on a shelf, as if someone had put them there for display.

"I'm the top female gamer on Nexus," she said. "I have almost forty thousand subscribers, and I just signed a new sponsorship with SlimDown, because I drink one every morning during my breakfast broadcast."

Preacher looked back at her, new appreciation filling him. If he hadn't been smitten by her before, he certainly would've been with this new information.

"Forty thousand subs?" he asked. To subscribe to a gamer's feed on Nexus, it cost five dollars per month. Five time forty thousand was two hundred thousand dollars per month, and that money was Charlie's.

"How much are the fees on Nexus?" he asked. "Never mind. That was rude."

She grinned at him and stepped toward him. She hesitated, the physical barrier between them rigidly intact.

She broke it, putting her hand on his chest, which allowed him to slide his hand along her waist. "I get about six million views each day, cowboy. I'm very, very wealthy, and I earn all that money playing video games."

He swayed with her, thinking this was pretty easy dancing. He took a long breath, leaning down and getting that soft cotton he expected, along with barbecue sauce and… cherry. Not peach.

Still amazing, he thought.

"No wonder I can't beat you at Solitary Ops," he whispered.

She giggled, the sound burrowing right into his cowboy heart and implanting itself, and whether that was a good thing or not, Preacher wasn't sure.

Sneak Peek! The Chemistry of Christmas
Chapter Two:

Charlie Perkins couldn't believe what she'd revealed to the handsome cowboy. She couldn't believe he stood in her office. Of course, she wasn't aiming to keep her identity a secret. Most of her friends at HealNow knew she gamed, and the information about her was readily available online.

She had bought this house behind the gate for a bit of privacy and security, and she'd moved to Three Rivers for a slower pace of life—and her job had relocated her without costing her a dime. She did love working for HealNow, and she wanted to stay current in the world of chemistry, because she consulted with Sanderton Games on the science they used in several of their titles.

Everything she'd told Preacher about herself and her jobs was absolutely true, as the man had a way of making her want to be pure and clean and wholesome for him.

"Brands and saddles," he said suddenly, stepping back.

"You must think we're the biggest bunch of idiots on the planet." He wore horror in those blue eyes that had captured her from the very beginning.

"Of course not," she said. "Playing with you and your friends is...refreshing. It's fun."

"Have we been on the live-stream?"

"Of course not," she said. "You think I'd record without telling you?" She shook her head. "No. Of course not."

Nexus was a second home for Charlie, and she felt like she knew some of her online fans as personal friends. It made having in-person friends a bit hard, if she were being honest, because she never fought with the guys online.

She could get on and watch others play video games, or she could live-stream when she played, get donations and more subscribers, and enjoy chatting for an hour or two. She hadn't joined Nexus eight years ago with the intent to build the account to the level where it currently sat, but she wasn't complaining either.

In fact, every morning and every night when she knelt in prayer, she thanked the Lord for His goodness in blessing her with the success she'd had on Nexus. She happened to be very good at puzzles and games, and her natural ability to play video games had turned into a full-time career, almost by accident.

She wanted Preacher's arm around her again, and this time, she wished he'd use both of them when he held her to dance. She did miss the physical touch of another human being, especially a strong, sexy man.

"I did tell everyone this morning that I was having

someone over tonight," she said, smiling up at him. "A fellow gamer, but also this guy I'd met a while back...."

Preacher's eyes only got wider.

"Have you been on Nexus?" she asked.

He nodded, his mouth pressing into a thin line. He rubbed his lips together and settled his face into a normal look, and Charlie's head seemed to heat by ten degrees. The man was pure deliciousness, and he didn't even know it.

Maybe she liked him more because he wasn't a gamer. Maybe she liked him more now than when they'd first met, because she knew her assumptions about him had been completely false. He would never carry around bills with his name and number on them. They'd been friends for two months now, and he hadn't even asked her out, despite some of her best flirting attempts.

She was still searching for the game he liked best, and she'd thought she'd had him with flight simulators. But no, he'd listened to her talk about them, but in the end, he hadn't been too keen to play all the time.

She'd find his kryptonite one day, she was sure. Every gamer had one.

"So you know that sometimes my fans and I...we chat. They can type things in, and I read them out while I'm playing. That kind of thing."

"Yes," he said.

"Well, they suggested we play together tonight while you were here. I said I'd feel you out and see what you thought."

Preacher did not look happy about that. "I thought we were dancing tonight. And eating. I think I took three bites."

"Let's go eat and dance," she said, gesturing for him to go first.

He did, spinning right on that cowboy booted heel and striding out of the room. Charlie sighed, because this was about how all of her relationships went. Men liked her because she was cute. Being on Nexus, she was well-aware of this. She had men commenting on her feed all the time about how she was the only one they subbed to, and it was because she was blonde and "cute."

Charlie didn't want to be *cute*. She wanted to feel beautiful and cherished—and not because of some move she could do on a first-person shooting game. Not because of anything to do with video games at all.

You also don't have a relationship with Preacher, she told herself. *It's a friendship, and those are two totally different things.*

By the time she arrived at the table, he'd already retaken his seat. She did too, and the distance between them felt eternal. She sighed. "You're mad."

"I'm not," he said, because Preacher never said more than absolutely necessary. It was "I'm not," not "I'm not mad." That would require an extra word.

"You seem mad."

"I'm processing." He put a very large bite of baked beans in his mouth. "I'm trying to decide if I want to be on the live-stream with you."

"It would be easy," she said. "Casual. I showed everyone the new simulator this morning, and the joystick. I talked about you, and how I'd have to learn to dance, and I got a ton of men offering to teach me." She kicked a smile in his direction, but he only looked even more disgusted. "I told them all no, of course." Charlie wished she could stop talking, but she'd started this ball rolling, and it had to go all the way down the hill.

Her mama had taught her that. *Don't push the boulder if you don't want to get to the bottom of things, Charlie.*

"I laugh them off, Preach. I said there was guy who'd asked me to go to his mother's wedding, and that he'd teach me to dance, and that you were coming over tonight. That's it."

"And they suggested you have me on the feed."

"Yes."

He nodded and finished his beans. He then swiped up a bite of mashed potatoes and brisket, dunked it all in barbecue sauce, and ate it. As soon as he swallowed, he said, "There's a couple of things in my head. One, I'm thirty-eight years old. I'm not a guy. I'm a cowboy, or I'm a man."

Yes, he definitely was both of those.

She nodded, willing to correct her terminology if it would make him happy. "Okay."

"Second, if you're calling me a guy, I'm worried you're way too young for me." He shook his head. "Which is stupid, because we're just friends, and it doesn't matter how old you are. But see, in my head, I'm thinking I'd like to take you out dancing again, and to dinner, and to a movie, and all kinds of other things, and get to know you better. And that sounds like dating, in which case, it definitely *does* matter how old you are."

He took a giant breath and ducked his head. "It's a circular second thought."

Charlie giggled, unable to hold back the sound. "I can see that."

He wouldn't look at her, and Charlie finished her pulled pork and slathered cinnamon butter on her roll. "I won't call you a guy again," she said. "I'm thirty-seven, Preach. It's just video game talk. Most of my followers are in their early twenties, and I look young, so I don't disclose my age online."

He nodded, and she knew there were more thoughts swirling behind those beautiful eyes. "That addresses your two thoughts."

"Kind of," he said.

"Kind of?" she teased, knowing full-well what she didn't address.

"There's the middle of that second thought," he mumbled. "The part about us goin' out."

"That," she said, hitting the T hard. "Depends on how the dancing lesson goes tonight."

Preacher looked at her, the moment playful and fun, and his stoic face finally broke into a grin. "I'm a good dancer."

"But are you a good *teacher* of dance?" she asked, pushing her smoked turkey around her plate. "That's the real question."

"Let's find out," he said, pushing away from the table. "You ready?"

"I've taken maybe three bites," she teased, and Preacher laughed. She took one more bite of turkey and stood up. "Okay, I'm ready."

"Praise the heavens," he said dryly, and she'd come to know his mannerisms of speech over the past couple of months. *Brands and saddles* was how he swore, and he was always praising the heavens. He did it when he did a great move during a game, or when his sarcasm came out.

"Right here?" she asked, looking down at her stocking feet. "I guess you did say we only need five feet."

"Right." He cleared his throat. "So at the wedding, there will be some slow dances. Those are pretty easy." He took a small step toward her, and then back. Then he sort of lunged at her, and put his left hand on her waist, and his right took hers.

Pops and zings shot through Charlie, and she couldn't stop the smile that spread across her face. He smelled like cedar and oranges, barbecue sauce, and something even spicier and pinier and more male under that. No matter what it was, it tickled her nose and made her want to lean in even farther.

She stepped a bit closer, and his hand tightened on her waist. "It's my mother's wedding," he said. "So we won't be super intimate. One hand out at all times. It's how my father taught us boys to dance when we started junior high." He smiled down at her, and with that cowboy hat tipped down, a little pocket of very intimate space was born.

They wouldn't be super intimate, her left eye. This was the most intimate she'd been with a man in five years. Her pulse seemed to know it as it raced from all the extra adrenaline.

"You put your hand on my shoulder. Yep, like that." He stepped in again, as she wasn't nearly as tall as he was, and the closer he got, the less she had to reach for him. "And we move back and forth like so." He started to sway with her, but it was more than that. He moved his feet, like, actually moved them.

"You move your feet," he said, his voice a near whisper. "It's not a sway. And you go with me, Charlie. I'll take us forward and back, left and right, all with little steps."

Charlie could barely hear him over the pounding of her heartbeat in her ears. "Like, we could go into the kitchen?"

"Mm hm." He moved a step right, taking her with him. She expected his feet to come down on hers, or hers on his, but it never happened. "My right foot it always on the outside," he said. "Yours is too. See?"

She could not see, because she could not look down. She could curl into his chest and press her cheek to his heartbeat, or she could look past his shoulder to the right. She supposed she could lean into him and press her left cheek to his chest and look away from him too, but she didn't know why she'd ever do that.

She wanted to be enclosed in the safety of his arms and feel the warmth of his breath as it wafted across her face. Thoughts of kissing him danced through her mind, which was absolutely ridiculous, as she didn't even know the man's real name.

"What's your Nexus handle?" he asked, his voice low and oh-so-sexy.

"The Chemist," she said. "I'm not hard to find. I use my real picture and everything."

"Hm. I noticed you didn't eat any barbecue sauce. Is that because you don't like it?"

"I like the spicy stuff, and I forgot to mention it to you."

"I love the spicy kind too," he said, and he wore a smile

in his voice. Charlie didn't dare look at his face for fear of breaking this moment, and it was one of the better ones of her life. "How long have you worked at HealNow?"

"Thirteen years."

"And when did you found Below Zero?"

"Four years ago."

She could honestly answer his questions all day and all night, as long as he'd keep dancing with her.

"Here we are," he said, and Charlie pulled away slightly and looked around.

"Holy brands and saddles," she said, somewhat stunned. "You danced us into the kitchen." She met his eye then, and oh, that was a mistake. The man had complete power over her with those eyes, and he had to know that.

He grinned at her, and she grinned back up at him. "What do you think? Decent dancer? Good enough teacher to earn myself another date?"

Another date, yes. She should start there instead of grabbing onto the man's lapels and pulling him in for a kiss. "Yeah," she said. "I think I can stand to see you again."

"Inside this house or outside?" he said. "I'd invite you up to the ranch, but I live with my brother." Something shuttered over his expression too, and Charlie had the feeling he wouldn't be telling anyone in his family about tonight—or any future dates—for a long time.

"Here or wherever," she said. "There's a new place that went in the building next door to HealNow. It's a Tepanyaki restaurant. Have you been to one of those before?"

"I...no," he said, even more of his face closing off. He stepped back, breaking the dance. "I try to support the local restaurants that have been in Three Rivers for generations. You know, the mom-and-pop type of things."

"Oh," Charlie said, taken aback by his statement. "I'm sure that's fine too."

"Do you normally stream in the evenings?" he asked.

"Yes," she said. "Here and there. I publish a schedule every week, so people know when to tune in. I didn't specifically put anything on the schedule for tonight, though."

"I'll get on with you, if you want," he said. "I'd kind of like to see how you do it."

Relief streamed through Charlie, because she hadn't driven Preacher away with her talk of subscribers, younger men hitting on her, or her poor dancing skills. She'd flirted with him successfully, and he'd rewarded her with a slow, close dance that still had her skin buzzing.

"All right," she said. "We'll play Journeyman, how 'bout that?"

"My favorite," he quipped, and Charlie laughed.

"I'm going to figure out which game is your favorite," she said. "I really am."

He chuckled too, gently lacing his fingers through hers. "This is okay?"

More than okay, but Charlie only nodded.

"Okay," he said, starting toward the living room and then the office. "I'm at least decent at Journeyman."

"We'll be on the same team," Charlie said, thinking that would take some of the pressure off him. "It'll be super fun."

"Oh, okay," he said with that classic Preacher sarcasm. "Super fun. Can't wait for that."

Charlie sat in front of the ultra-wide monitor and tapped

to get everything awake and ready. "You have to get in close here, Preach, or you won't be on the screen. See where the camera is?" She reached up and pressed a button. "You know what? I think I can make the zoom wider...yep. There we go."

She and Preacher fit in the frame easily, and she clicked to get Journeyman up and going. "I talk during the livestreams," she said. "You can too, or just say hello. Whatever."

"I've seen a few feeds on Nexus," he said, but his nerves poured from him in waves. Charlie's stomach clenched around her dinner, because she'd never had anyone on her livestream with her before.

She looked at him, again fighting the intense urge to kiss him, and asked, "Are you ready for this?"

"Hit play, sugar," he drawled, and Charlie thought she should totally get him to be as cowboy country as possible on the feed. She could get female gamers to come over then, and she'd get every man who'd ever heard of Nexus subscribing if they felt like one of their own would be on-screen.

Instead of responding, she clicked on the screen where Nexus sat, tapped GO LIVE, and said, "Hey, hey, everyone out there in the Nexus. It's ya'girl Charlie here tonight, and I have that friend I talked about this morning with me." She looked at Preacher then, wondering what he thought of her ridiculous intro.

He beamed with the brightness of two suns, that was what.

She giggled at him and swatted at his bicep. Chats started

popping up on the side of her forum before she'd even faced the screen again. The ones with the bright orange slugs next to them were paying subscribers, and her face heated at the comments flying by.

Holy hotness went by, as did *He's a cowboy?! Wow, Char, you've been holding out on us!* among other things.

"Let's give people a minute to get over here," she said, working incredibly hard not to clear her throat. "And then I'll do the formal introduction of this fine man sitting next to me, and we'll be playing a two-player game of Journeyman." She clicked to start the timer, which would literally count down from sixty, and she muted her mic.

Turning to Preacher, she said, "Sometimes the comments aren't G-rated."

"I'm thirty-eight, baby," he said. "I can handle some comments."

"I can mute everyone who's not a subscriber, and I can tell them to behave when the sixty seconds are up." She wiped her hands nervously on her jeans. Preacher saw the movement and brought his eyes back to hers.

"I'm fine, Charlie."

"Sometimes I have to act a little fake," she said.

"Then I'll know who you really are." He smiled at her, reached out, and tucked her hair behind her ear. "Don't worry so much."

"I think this is a bad idea." What planet had she been on when she'd thought having him join her live on Nexus would be a *good* idea? Obviously not this one.

"We're live already," he said.

Before she could decide if she should cause a system-wide

failure, or "accidentally" trip the Internet, the timer started to chime at her.

She turned back to the screen. Nine, eight, seven....

She unmuted herself and put a smile on her face. *Nothing for it now*, she thought.

"All right, everyone. Wow, look how many of you there are tonight." She grinned at the camera in front of her. I told you I might have a friend on with me tonight, and it happened! My first friend livestream, and you're all here for it. Now, this handsome man's name is Preacher, and that right there should tell you what kind of comments I'm expecting to see tonight."

Preacher lifted his hand in a wave, his smile wide and stunning.

"That's right, Dollface," she said, reading the comment at the top of the stream. "He is gorgeous, isn't he?" She turned and smiled at Preacher. "Yes, we're just friends right now. I've been playing with him and his friends for a couple of months."

She scanned a few more comments. "We've got Tiny-Twinkle, NinjaMonkey, Thimble, Fireball, and about fifty more of you who want to know if he's my boyfriend." She grinned at Preacher again, noticing that his smile had definitely slipped.

She leaned closer to the screen and lowered her voice to a mock whisper. "Not yet, you guys, and you're making this awkward for me, okay? He's the first man I've liked even a little bit in years, so can you just stop?" She grinned at the screen, because this was how she made her money, after all.

She hadn't lied though. Not even a little bit.

The comments flew, positively flew, and Charlie could barely see them before they were gone.

"Y'all are lively tonight," she said. "I see Unicorns-and-Sunshine, Hailey's Comet, and Talksalot saying they won't ask any more questions about the boyfriend-status of Preacher and I. Thank you, guys. All right, I'm going to switch us over to in-window mode, and we'll get started with Journeyman. You ready, Preach?"

"So ready," he said, and he gripped the controller like he might need to strangle it to stay sane.

That voice—I'm fanning myself, someone commented, and one of her subscribers—Winnie the Pooh—made a similar comment.

What have I done? Charlie thought, but she acted like she was thrilled to be online with Preacher, playing Journeyman, and she hoped she could give him a proper apology and any explanations he needed once the stream finished.

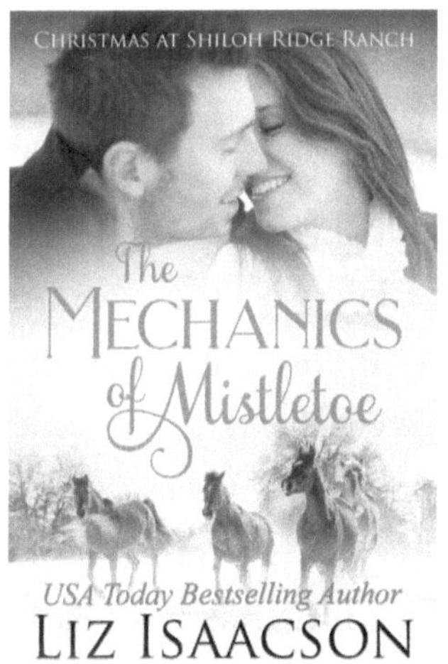

The Mechanics of Mistletoe (Book 1): Bear Glover can be a grizzly or a teddy, and he's always thought he'd be just fine working his generational family ranch and going back to the ancient homestead alone. But his crush on Samantha Benton won't go away. She's a genius with a wrench on Bear's tractors...and his heart. Can he tame his wild side and get the girl, or will he be left broken-hearted this Christmas season?

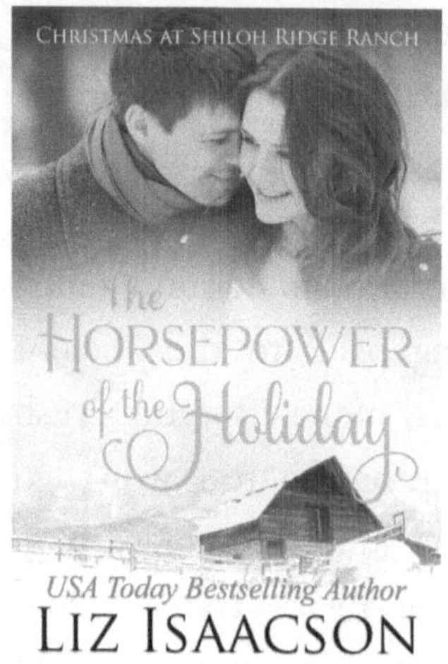

The Horsepower of the Holiday (Book 2): Ranger Glover has worked at Shiloh Ridge Ranch his entire life. The cowboys do everything from horseback there, but when he goes to town to trade in some trucks, somehow Oakley Hatch persuades him to take some ATVs back to the ranch. (Bear is NOT happy.)

She's a former race car driver who's got Ranger all revved up... Can he remember who he is and get Oakley to slow down enough to fall in love, or will there simply be too much horsepower in the holiday this year for a real relationship?

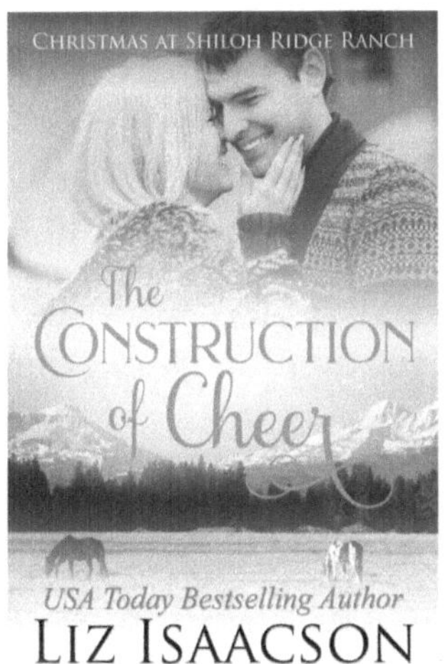

The Construction of Cheer (Book 3): Bishop Glover is the youngest brother, and he usually keeps his head down and gets the job done. When Montana Martin shows up at Shiloh Ridge Ranch looking for work, he finds himself inventing construction projects that need doing just to keep her coming around. (Again, Bear is NOT happy.) She wants to build her own construction firm, but she ends up carving a place for herself inside Bishop's heart. Can he convince her *he's* all she needs this Christmas season, or will her cheer rest solely on the success of her business?

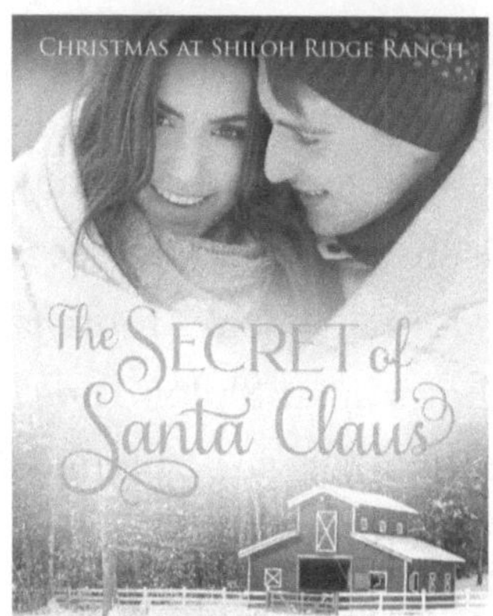

The Secret of Santa (Book 4): He's a fun-loving cowboy with a heart of gold. She's the woman who keeps putting him on hold. Can Ace and Holly Ann make a relationship work this Christmas?

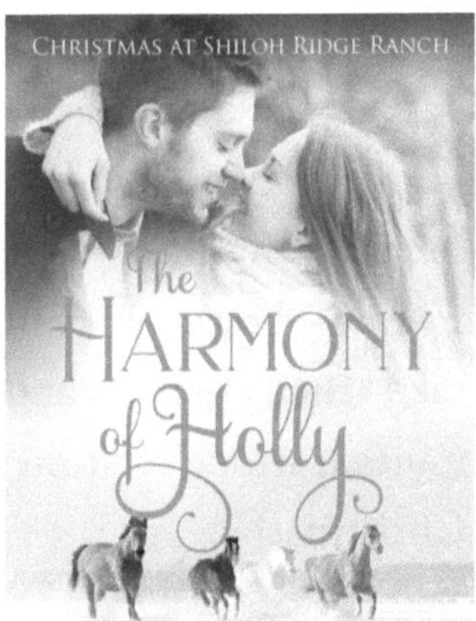

The Harmony of Holly (Book 5): He's as prickly as his name, but the new woman in town has caught his eye. Can Cactus shelve his temper and shed his cowboy hermit skin fast enough to make a relationship with Willa work?

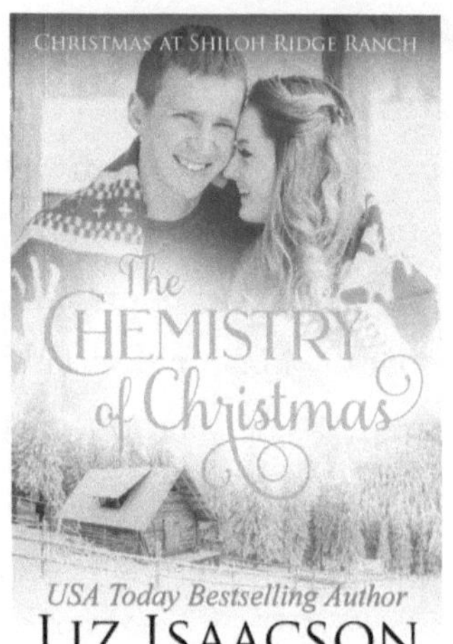

The Chemistry of Christmas (Book 6): He's the black sheep of the family, and she's a chemist who understands formulas, not emotions. Can Preacher and Charlie take their quirks and turn them into a strong relationship this Christmas?

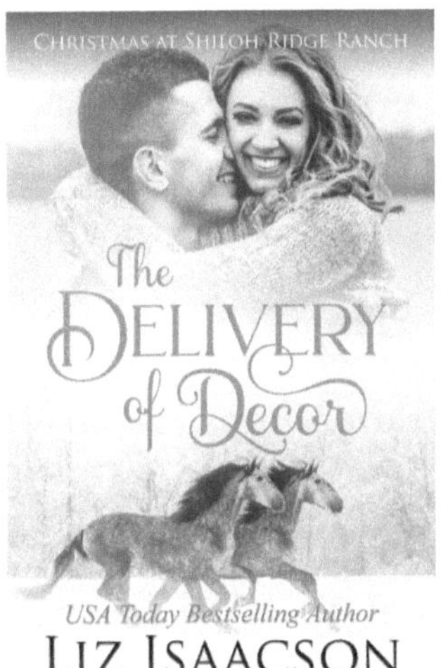

The Delivery of Decor (Book 7): When he falls, he falls hard and deep. She literally drives away from every relationship she's ever had. Can Ward somehow get Dot to stay this Christmas?

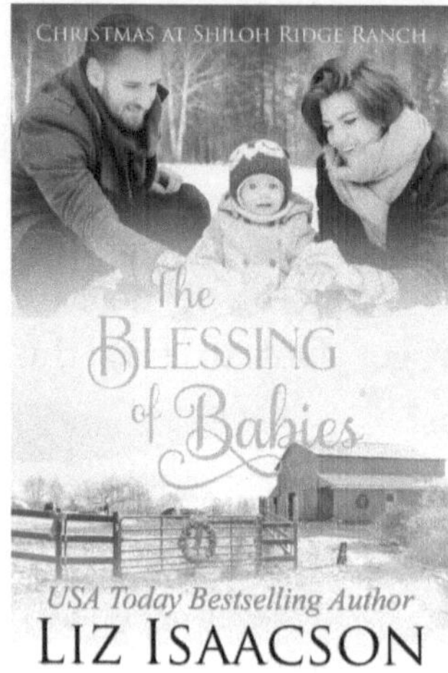

The Blessing of Babies (Book 8): Don't miss out on a single moment of the Glover family saga in this bridge story linking Ward and Judge's love stories!

The Glovers love God, country, dogs, horses, and family. Not necessarily in that order. ;)

Many of them are married now, with babies on the way, and there are lessons to be learned, forgiveness to be had and given, and new names coming to the family tree in southern Three Rivers!

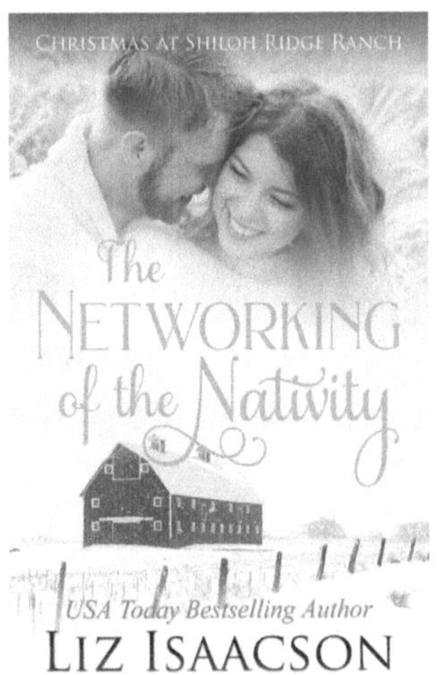

The Networking of the Nativity (Book 9): He's had a crush on her for years. She doesn't want to date until her daughter is out of the house. Will June take a change on Judge when the success of his Christmas light display depends on her networking abilities?

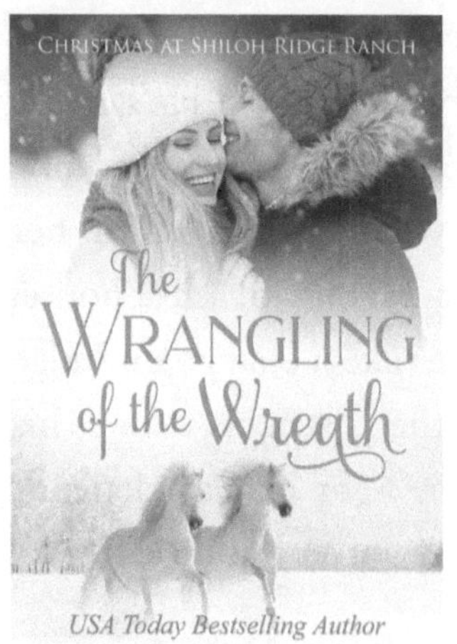

The Wrangling of the Wreath (Book 10): He's been so busy trying to find Miss Right. She's been right in front of him the whole time. This Christmas, can Mister and Libby take their relationship out of the best friend zone?

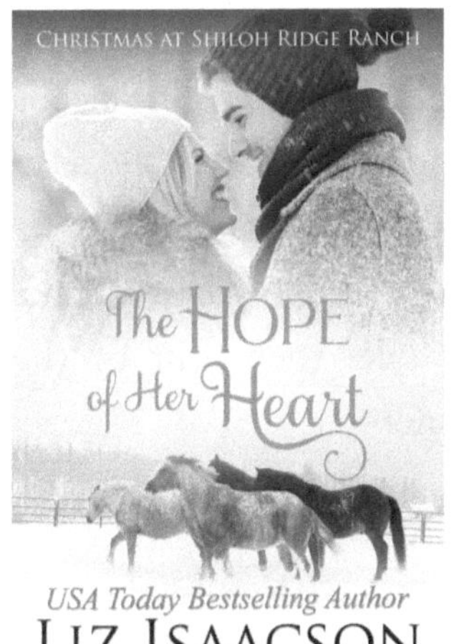

The Hope of Her Heart (Book 11): She's the only Glover without a significant other. He's been searching for someone who can love him *and* his daughter. Can Etta and August make a meaningful connection this Christmas?

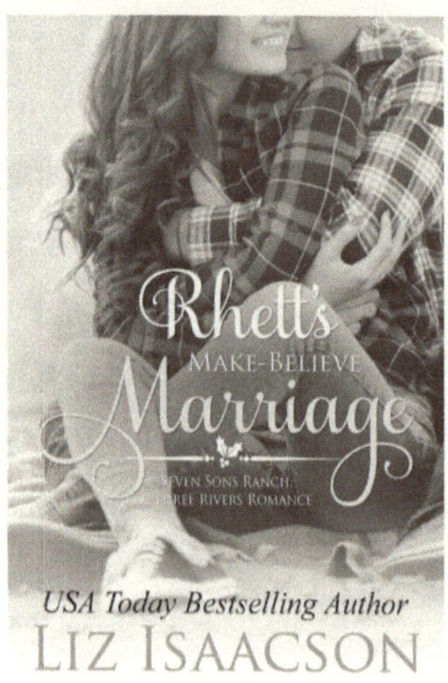

Rhett's Make-Believe Marriage (Book 1): She needs a husband to be credible as a matchmaker. He wants to help a neighbor. Will their fake marriage take them out of the friend zone?

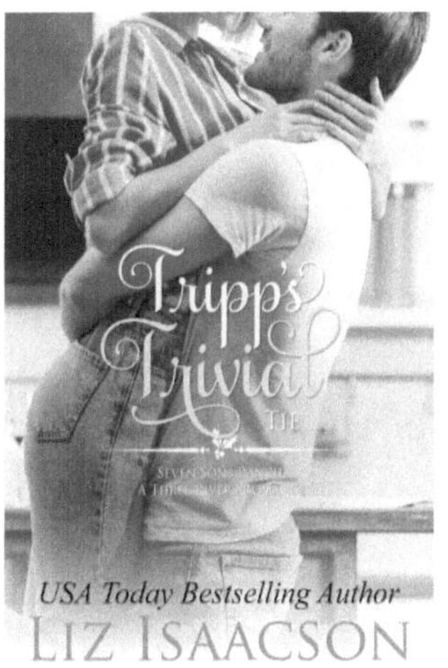

Tripp's Trivial Tie (Book 2): She needs a husband to keep her son. He's wanted to take their relationship to the next level, but she's always pushing him away. Will their trivial tie take them all the way to happily-ever-after?

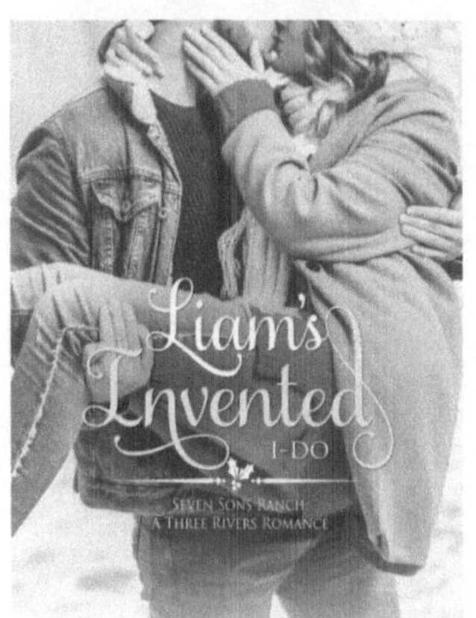

Liam's Invented I-Do (Book 3): She's desperate to save her ranch. He wants to help her any way he can. Will their invented I-Do open doors that have previously been closed and lead to a happily-ever-after for both of them?

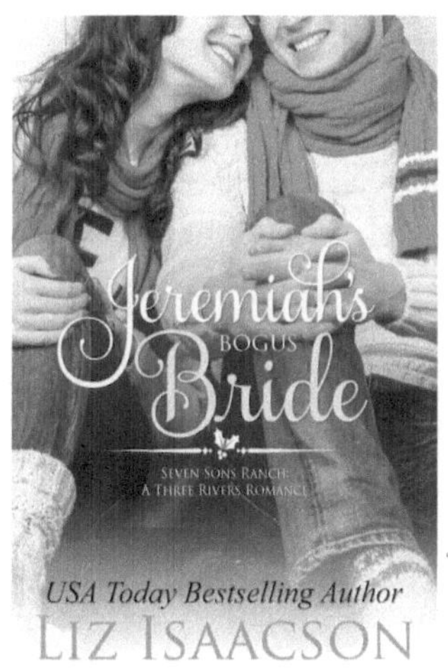

Jeremiah's Bogus Bride (Book 4): He wants to prove to his brothers that he's not broken. She just wants him. Will a fake marriage heal him or push her further away?

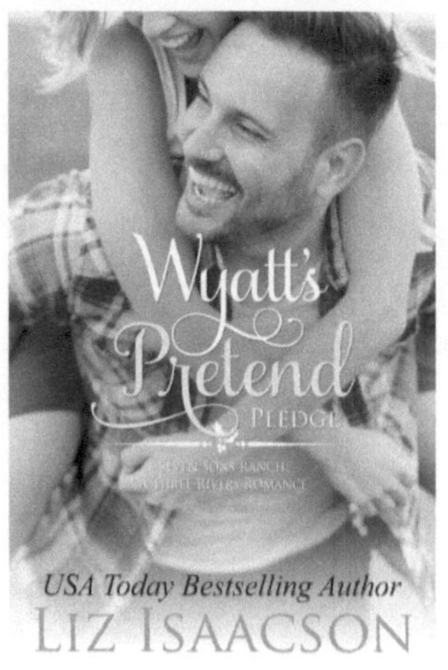

Wyatt's Pretend Pledge (Book 5): To get her inheritance, she needs a husband. He's wanted to fly with her for ages. Can their pretend pledge turn into something real?

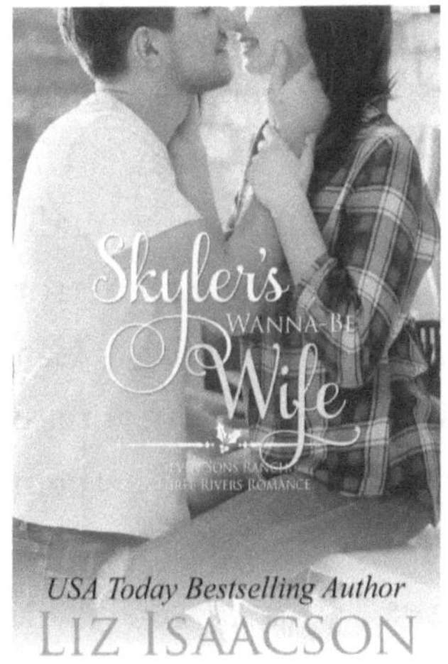

Skyler's Wanna-Be Wife (Book 6): She needs a new last name to stay in school. He's willing to help a fellow student. Can this wanna-be wife show the playboy that some things should be taken seriously?

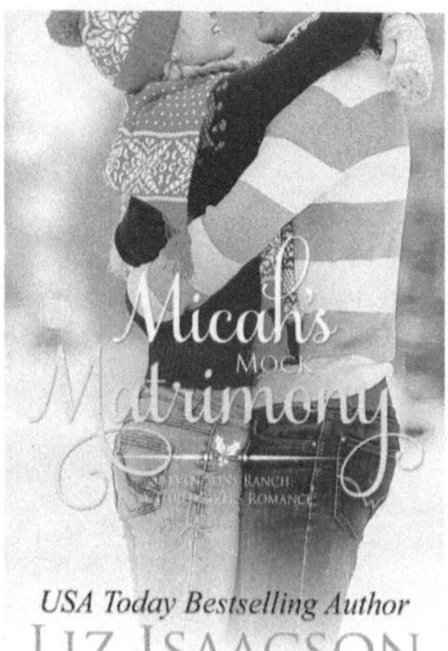

Micah's Mock Matrimony (Book 7): They were just actors auditioning for a play. The marriage was just for the audition – until a clerical error results in a legal marriage. Can these two ex-lovers negotiate this new ground between them and achieve new roles in each other's lives?

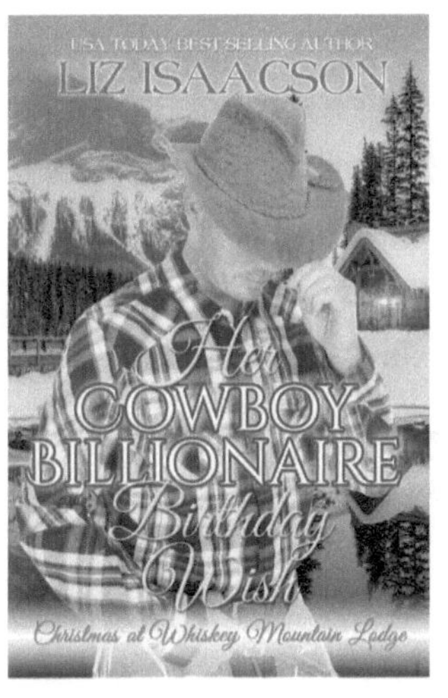

Her Cowboy Billionaire Birthday Wish (Book 1): All the maid at Whiskey Mountain Lodge wants for her birthday is a handsome cowboy billionaire. And Colton can make that wish come true—if only he hadn't escaped to Coral Canyon after being left at the altar...

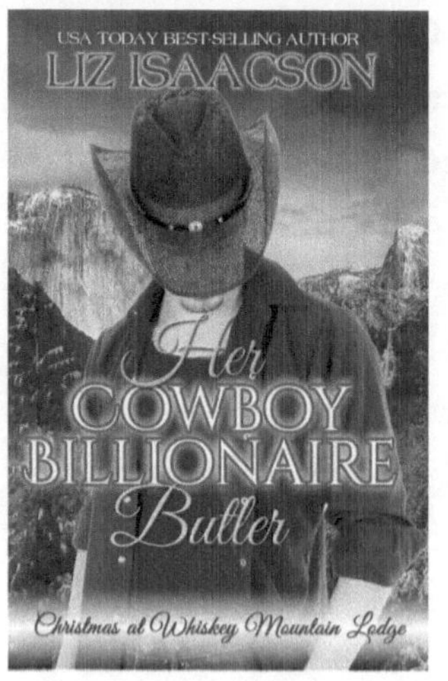

Her Cowboy Billionaire Butler (Book 2): She broke up with him to date another man...who broke her heart. He's a former CEO with nothing to do who can't get her out of his head. Can Wes and Bree find a way toward happily-ever-after at Whiskey Mountain Lodge?

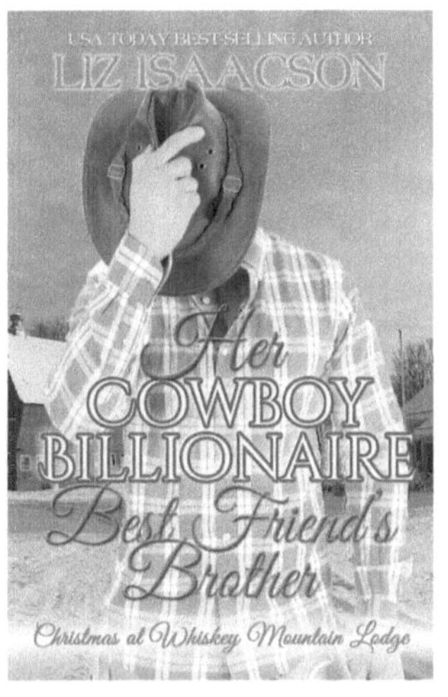

Her Cowboy Billionaire Best Friend's Brother (Book 3): She's best friends with the single dad cowboy's brother and has watched two friends find love with the sexy new cowboys in town. When Gray Hammond comes to Whiskey Mountain Lodge with his son, will Elise finally get her own happily-ever-after with one of the Hammond brothers?

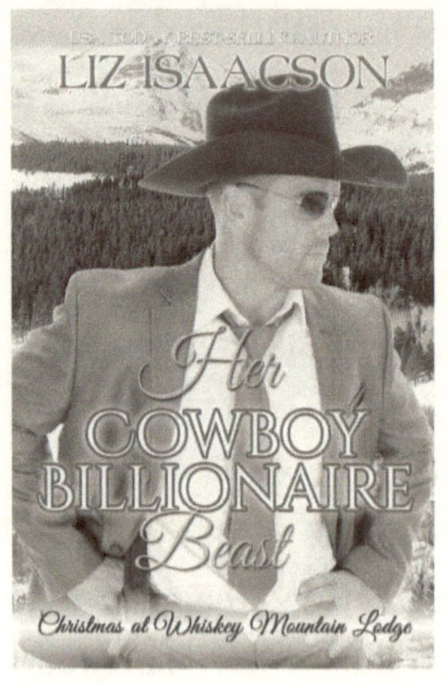

Her Cowboy Billionaire Beast (Book 4): A cowboy billionaire beast, his new manager, and the Christmas traditions that soften his heart and bring them together.

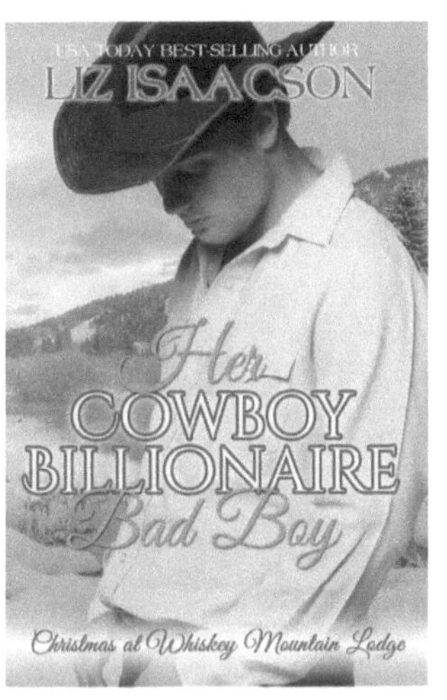

Her Cowboy Billionaire Bad Boy (Book 5): A cowboy billionaire cop who's a stickler for rules, the woman he pulls over when he's not even on duty, and the personal mandates he has to break to keep her in his life...

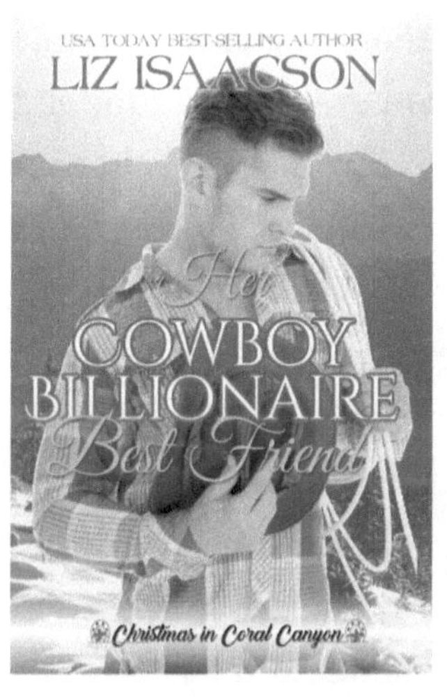

Her Cowboy Billionaire Best Friend (Book 1): Graham Whittaker returns to Coral Canyon a few days after Christmas—after the death of his father. He takes over the energy company his dad built from the ground up and buys a high-end lodge to live in—only a mile from the home of his once-best friend, Laney McAllister. They were best friends once, but Laney's always entertained feelings for him, and spending so much time with him while they make Christmas memories puts her heart in danger of getting broken again...

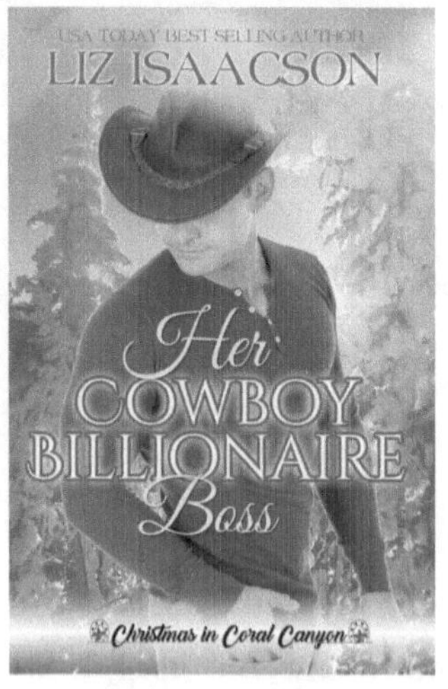

Her Cowboy Billionaire Boss (Book 2): Since the death of his wife a few years ago, Eli Whittaker has been running from one job to another, unable to find somewhere for him and his son to settle. Meg Palmer is Stockton's nanny, and she comes with her boss, Eli, to the lodge, her long-time crush on the man no different in Wyoming than it was on the beach. When she confesses her feelings for him and gets nothing in return, she's crushed, embarrassed, and unsure if she can stay in Coral Canyon for Christmas. Then Eli starts to show some feelings for her too...

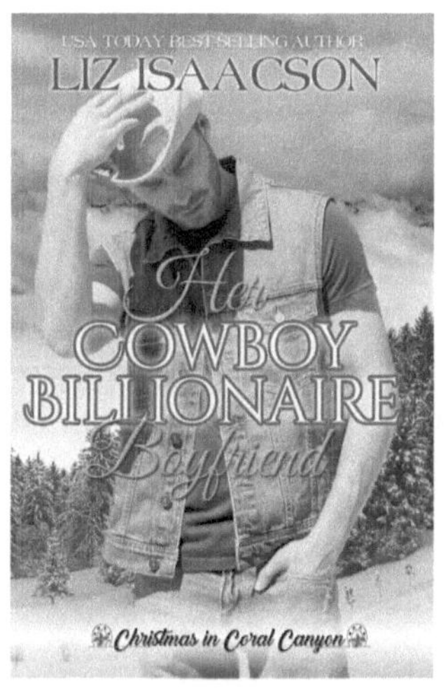

Her Cowboy Billionaire Boyfriend (Book 3): Andrew Whittaker is the public face for the Whittaker Brothers' family energy company, and with his older brother's robot about to be announced, he needs a press secretary to help him get everything ready and tour the state to make the announcements. When he's hit by a protest sign being carried by the company's biggest opponent, Rebecca Collings, he learns with a few clicks that she has the background they need. He offers her the job of press secretary when she thought she was going to be arrested, and not only because the spark between them in so hot Andrew can't see straight.

Can Becca and Andrew work together and keep their relationship a secret? Or will hearts break in this classic romance retelling reminiscent of *Two Weeks Notice*?

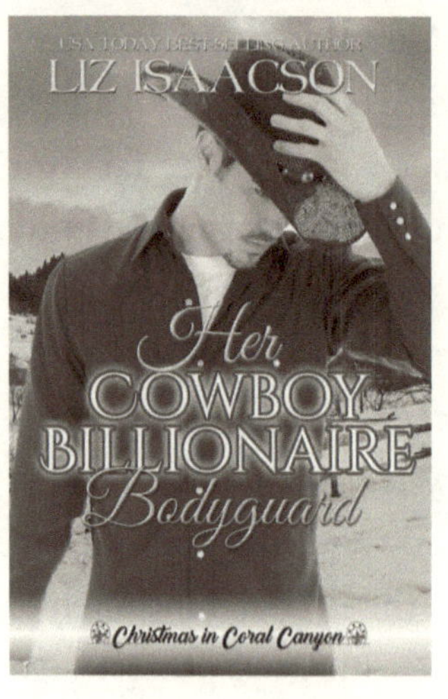

Her Cowboy Billionaire Bodyguard (Book 4): Beau Whittaker has watched his brothers find love one by one, but every attempt he's made has ended in disaster. Lily Everett has been in the spotlight since childhood and has half a dozen platinum records with her two sisters. She's taking a break from the brutal music industry and hiding out in Wyoming while her ex-husband continues to cause trouble for her. When she hears of Beau Whittaker and what he offers his clients, she wants to meet him. Beau is instantly attracted to Lily, but he tried a relationship with his last client that left a scar that still hasn't healed...

Can Lily use the spirit of Christmas to discover what matters most? Will Beau open his heart to the possibility of love with someone so different from him?

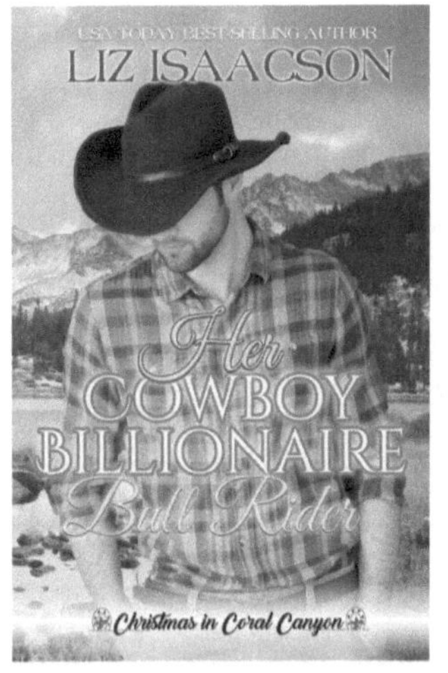

Her Cowboy Billionaire Bull Rider (Book 5): Todd Christopherson has just retired from the professional rodeo circuit and returned to his hometown of Coral Canyon. Problem is, he's got no family there anymore, no land, and no job. Not that he needs a job--he's got plenty of money from his illustrious career riding bulls.

Then Todd gets thrown during a routine horseback ride up the canyon, and his only support as he recovers physically is the beautiful Violet Everett. She's no nurse, but she does the best she can for the handsome cowboy. **Will she lose her heart to the billionaire bull rider? Can Todd trust that God led him to Coral Canyon...and Vi?**

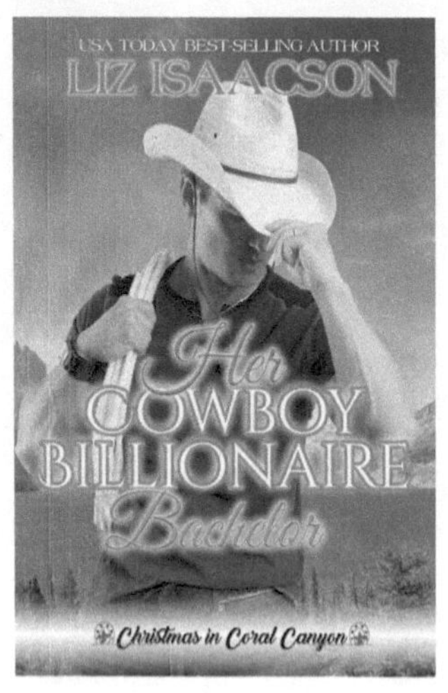

Her Cowboy Billionaire Bachelor (Book 6): Rose Everett isn't sure what to do with her life now that her country music career is on hold. After all, with both of her sisters in Coral Canyon, and one about to have a baby, they're not making albums anymore.

Liam Murphy has been working for Doctors Without Borders, but he's back in the US now, and looking to start a new clinic in Coral Canyon, where he spent his summers.

When Rose wins a date with Liam in a bachelor auction, their relationship blooms and grows quickly. **Can Liam and Rose find a solution to their problems that doesn't involve one of them leaving Coral Canyon with a broken heart?**

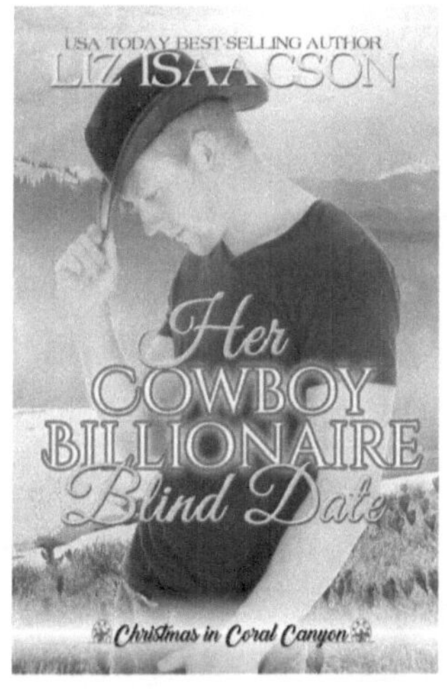

Her Cowboy Billionaire Blind Date (Book 7): Her sons want her to be happy, but she's too old to be set up on a blind date...isn't she?

Amanda Whittaker has been looking for a second chance at love since the death of her husband several years ago. Finley Barber is a cowboy in every sense of the word. Born and raised on a racehorse farm in Kentucky, he's since moved to Dog Valley and started his own breeding stable for champion horses. He hasn't dated in years, and everything about Amanda makes him nervous.

Will Amanda take the leap of faith required to be with Finn? Or will he become just another boyfriend who doesn't make the cut?

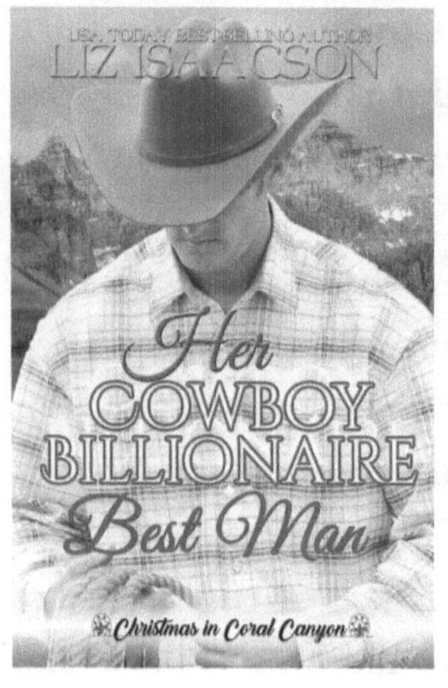

Her Cowboy Billionaire Best Man (Book 8): When Celia Abbott-Armstrong runs into a gorgeous cowboy at her best friend's wedding, she decides she's ready to start dating again.

But the cowboy is Zach Zuckerman, and the Zuckermans and Abbotts have been at war for generations.

Can Zach and Celia find a way to reconcile their family's differences so they can have a future together?

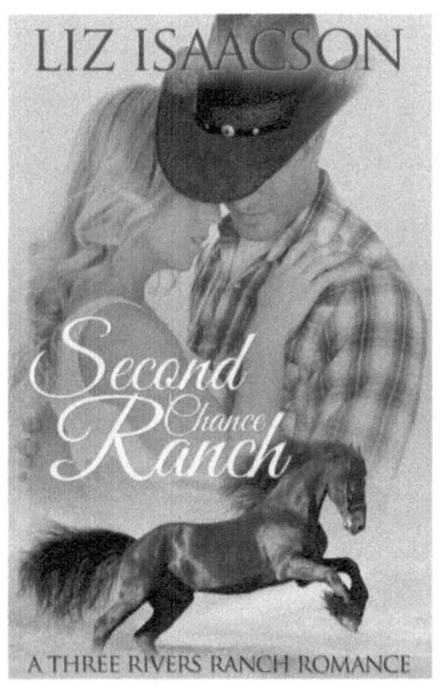

Second Chance Ranch: A Three Rivers Ranch Romance (Book 1): After his deployment, injured and discharged Major Squire Ackerman returns to Three Rivers Ranch, wanting to forgive Kelly for ignoring him a decade ago. He'd like to provide the stable life she needs, but with old wounds opening and a ranch on the brink of financial collapse, it will take patience and faith to make their second chance possible.

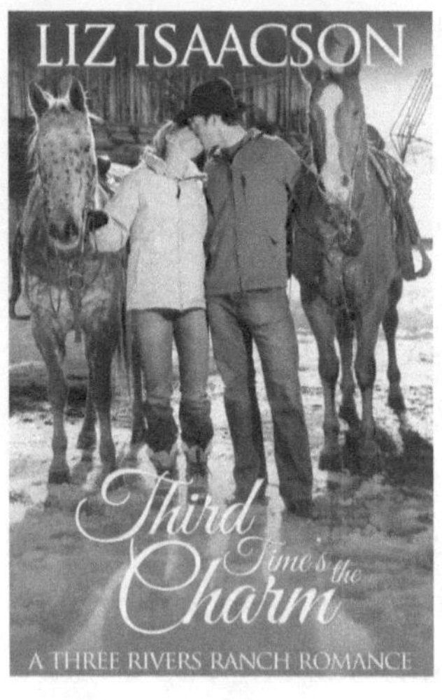

Third Time's the Charm: A Three Rivers Ranch Romance (Book 2): First Lieutenant Peter Marshall has a truckload of debt and no way to provide for a family, but Chelsea helps him see past all the obstacles, all the scars. With so many unknowns, can Pete and Chelsea develop the love, acceptance, and faith needed to find their happily ever after?

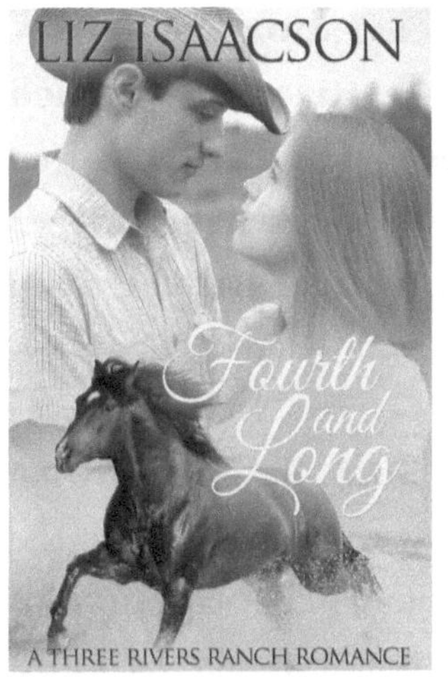

Fourth and Long: A Three Rivers Ranch Romance (Book 3): Commander Brett Murphy goes to Three Rivers Ranch to find some rest and relaxation with his Army buddies. Having his ex-wife show up with a seven-year-old she claims is his son is anything but the R&R he craves. Kate needs to make amends, and Brett needs to find forgiveness, but are they too late to find their happily ever after?

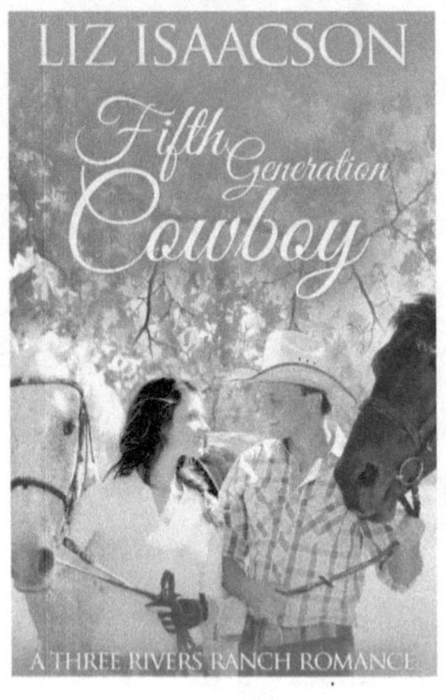

Fifth Generation Cowboy: A Three Rivers Ranch Romance (Book 4): Tom Lovell has watched his friends find their true happiness on Three Rivers Ranch, but everywhere he looks, he only sees friends. Rose Reyes has been bringing her daughter out to the ranch for equine therapy for months, but it doesn't seem to be working. Her challenges with Mari are just as frustrating as ever. Could Tom be exactly what Rose needs? Can he remove his friendship blinders and find love with someone who's been right in front of him all this time?

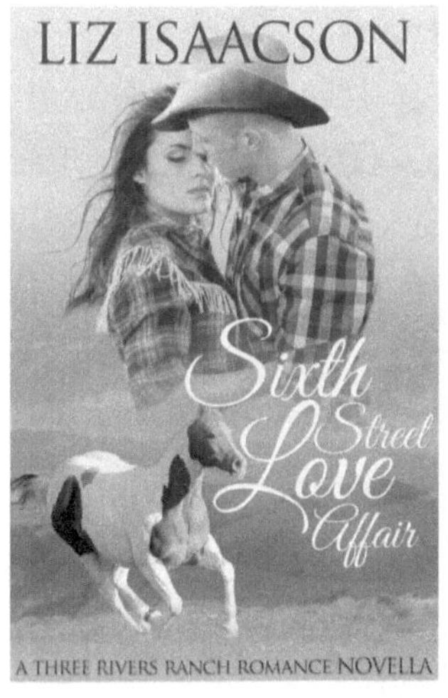

Sixth Street Love Affair: A Three Rivers Ranch Romance (Book 5): After losing his wife a few years back, Garth Ahlstrom thinks he's ready for a second chance at love. But Juliette Thompson has a secret that could destroy their budding relationship. Can they find the strength, patience, and faith to make things work?

The Seventh Sergeant: A Three Rivers Ranch Romance (Book 6): Life has finally started to settle down for Sergeant Reese Sanders after his devastating injury overseas. Discharged from the Army and now with a good job at Courage Reins, he's finally found happiness—until a horrific fall puts him right back where he was years ago: Injured and depressed.

Carly Watters, Reese's new veteran care coordinator, dislikes small towns almost as much as she loathes cowboys. But she finds herself faced with both when she gets assigned to Reese's case. Do they have the humility and faith to make their relationship more than professional?

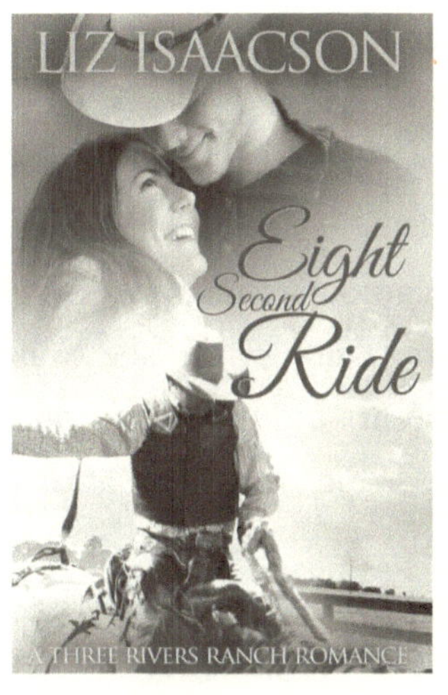

Eight Second Ride: A Three Rivers Ranch Romance (Book 7): Ethan Greene loves his work at Three Rivers Ranch, but he can't seem to find the right woman to settle down with. When sassy yet vulnerable Brynn Bowman shows up at the ranch to recruit him back to the rodeo circuit, he takes a different approach with the barrel racing champion. His patience and newfound faith pay off when a friendship--and more--starts with Brynn. But she wants out of the rodeo circuit right when Ethan wants to rejoin. Can they find the path God wants them to take and still stay together?

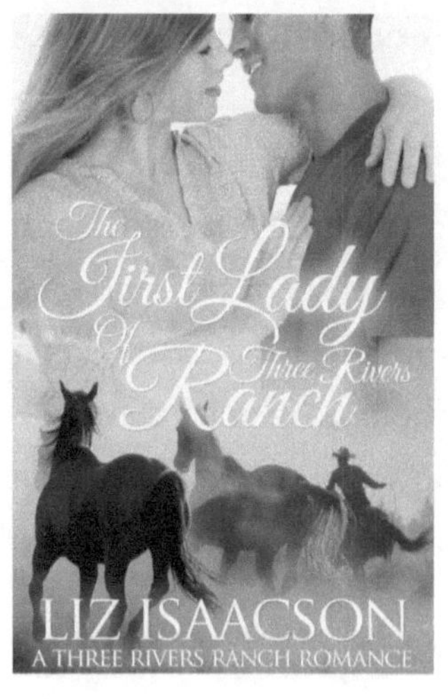

The First Lady of Three Rivers Ranch: A Three Rivers Ranch Romance (Book 8): Heidi Duffin has been dreaming about opening her own bakery since she was thirteen years old. She scrimped and saved for years to afford baking and pastry school in San Francisco. And now she only has one year left before she's a certified pastry chef. Frank Ackerman's father has recently retired, and he's taken over the largest cattle ranch in the Texas Panhandle. A horseman through and through, he's also nearing thirty-one and looking for someone to bring love and joy to a homestead that's been dominated by men for a decade. But when he convinces Heidi to come clean the cowboy cabins, she changes all that. But the siren's call of a bakery is still loud in Heidi's ears, even if she's also seeing a future with Frank. Can she rely on her faith in ways she's never had to before or will their relationship end when summer does?

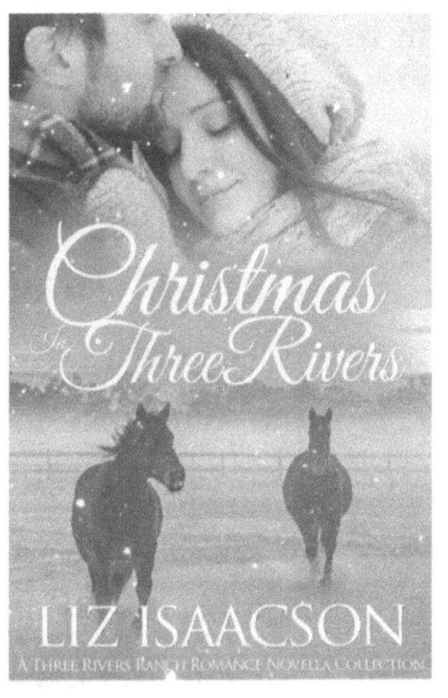

Christmas in Three Rivers: A Three Rivers Ranch Romance (Book 9): Isn't Christmas the best time to fall in love? The cowboys of Three Rivers Ranch think so. Join four of them as they journey toward their path to happily ever after in four, all-new novellas in the Amazon #1 Bestselling Three Rivers Ranch Romance series.

THE NINTH INNING: The Christmas season has never felt like such a burden to boutique owner Andrea Larsen. But with Mama gone and the holidays upon her, Andy finds herself wishing she hadn't been so quick to judge her former boyfriend, cowboy Lawrence Collins. Well, Lawrence hasn't forgotten about Andy either, and he devises a plan to get her out to the ranch so they can reconnect. Do they have the faith and humility to patch things up and start a new relationship?

TEN DAYS IN TOWN: Sandy Keller is tired of the dating scene in Three Rivers. Though she owns the pancake house, she's looking for a fresh start, which means an escape from the town where she grew up. When her older brother's best friend, Tad Jorgensen, comes to town for the holidays, it is a balm to his weary soul. A helicopter tour guide who experienced a near-death experience, he's looking to start over too- -but in Three Rivers. Can Sandy and Tad navigate their troubles to find the path God wants them to take--and discover true love--in only ten days?

ELEVEN YEAR REUNION: Pastry chef extraordinaire, Grace Lewis has moved to Three Rivers to help Heidi Ackerman open a bakery in Three Rivers. Grace relishes the idea of starting over in a town where no one knows about her failed cupcakery. She doesn't expect to run into her old high school boyfriend, Jonathan Carver. A carpenter working at Three Rivers Ranch, Jon's in town against his will. But with Grace now on the scene, Jon's thinking life in Three Rivers is suddenly looking up. But with her focus on baking and his disdain for small towns, can they make their eleven year reunion stick?

THE TWELFTH TOWN: Newscaster Taryn Tucker has had enough of life on-screen. She's bounced from town to town before arriving in Three Rivers, completely alone and completely anonymous--just the way she now likes it. She takes a job cleaning at Three Rivers Ranch, hoping for a chance to figure out who she is and where God wants her. When she meets happy-go-lucky cowhand Kenny Stockton, she doesn't expect sparks to fly. Kenny's always been "the best friend" for his female friends, but the pull between him and Taryn can't be denied. Will they have the courage and faith necessary to make their opposite worlds mesh?

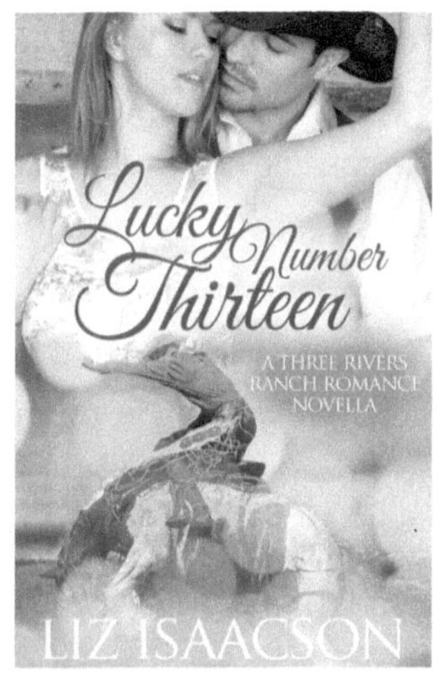

Lucky Number Thirteen: A Three Rivers Ranch Romance (Book 10): Tanner Wolf, a rodeo champion ten times over, is excited to be riding in Three Rivers for the first time since he left his philandering ways and found religion. Seeing his old friends Ethan and Brynn is therapuetic--until a terrible accident lands him in the hospital. With his rodeo career over, Tanner thinks maybe he'll stay in town--and it's not just because his nurse, Summer Hamblin, is the prettiest woman he's ever met. But Summer's the queen of first dates, and as she looks for a way to make a relationship with the transient rodeo star work Summer's not sure she has the fortitude to go on a second date. Can they find love among the tragedy?

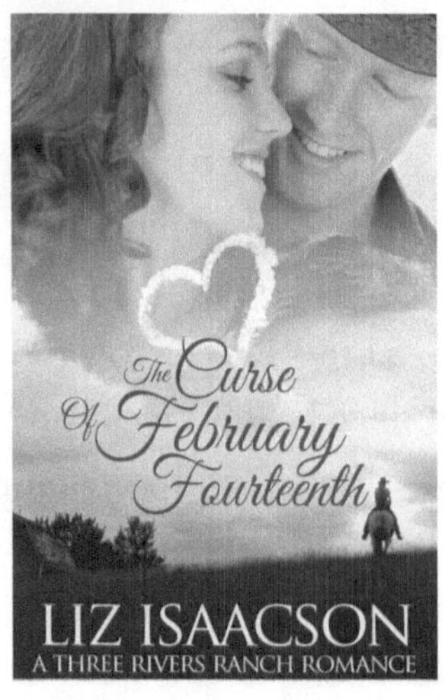

The Curse of February Fourteenth: A Three Rivers Ranch Romance (Book 11): Cal Hodgkins, cowboy veterinarian at Bowman's Breeds, isn't planning to meet anyone at the masked dance in small-town Three Rivers. He just wants to get his bachelor friends off his back and sit on the sidelines to drink his punch. But when he sees a woman dressed in gorgeous butterfly wings and cowgirl boots with blue stitching, he's smitten. Too bad she runs away from the dance before he can get her name, leaving only her boot behind...

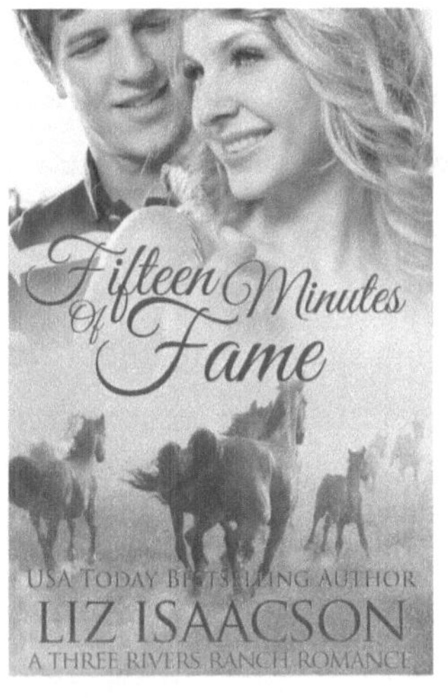

Fifteen Minutes of Fame: A Three Rivers Ranch Romance (Book 12): Navy Richards is thirty-five years of tired—tired of dating the same men, working a demanding job, and getting her heart broken over and over again. Her aunt has always spoken highly of the matchmaker in Three Rivers, Texas, so she takes a six-month sabbatical from her high-stress job as a pediatric nurse, hops on a bus, and meets with the matchmaker. Then she meets Gavin Redd. He's handsome, he's hardworking, and he's a cowboy. But is he an Aquarius too? Navy's not making a move until she knows for sure...

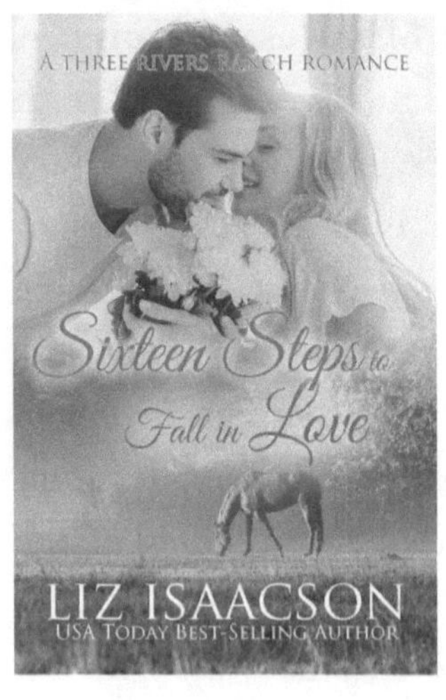

Sixteen Steps to Fall in Love: A Three Rivers Ranch Romance (Book 13): A chance encounter at a dog park sheds new light on the tall, talented Boone that Nicole can't ignore. As they get to know each other better and start to dig into each other's past, Nicole is the one who wants to run. This time from her growing admiration and attachment to Boone. From her aging parents. From herself.

But Boone feels the attraction between them too, and he decides he's tired of running and ready to make Three Rivers his permanent home. **Can Boone and Nicole use their faith to overcome their differences and find a happily-ever-after together?**

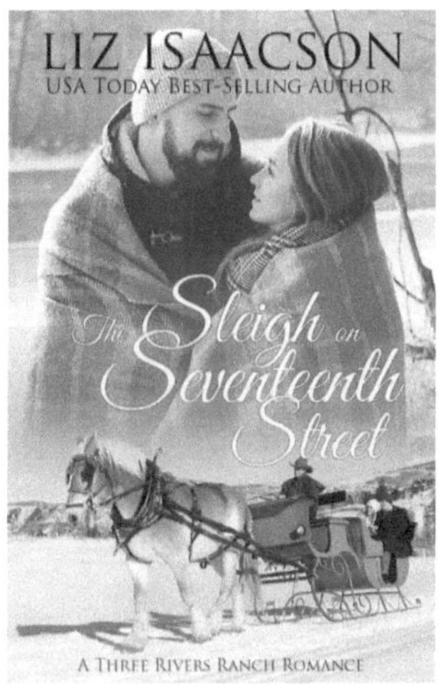

The Sleigh on Seventeenth Street: A Three Rivers Ranch Romance (Book 14): A cowboy with skills as an electrician tries a relationship with a down-on-her luck plumber. Can Dylan and Camila make water and electricity play nicely together this Christmas season? Or will they get shocked as they try to make their relationship work?

Books in the Last Chance Ranch Romance
series

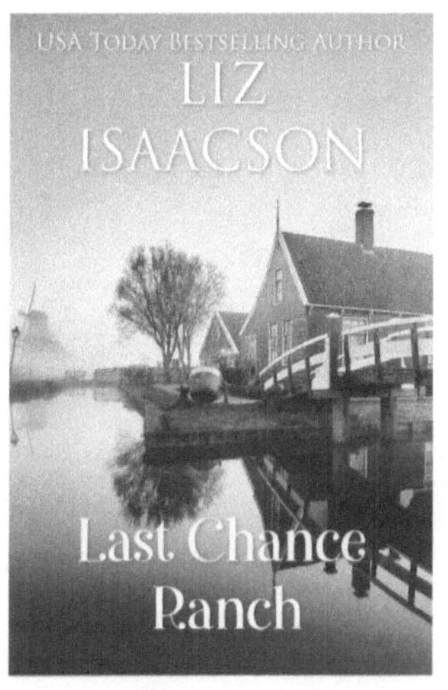

Last Chance Ranch (Book 1): A cowgirl down on her luck hires a man who's good with horses and under the hood of a car. Can Hudson fine tune Scarlett's heart as they work together? Or will things backfire and make everything worse at Last Chance Ranch?

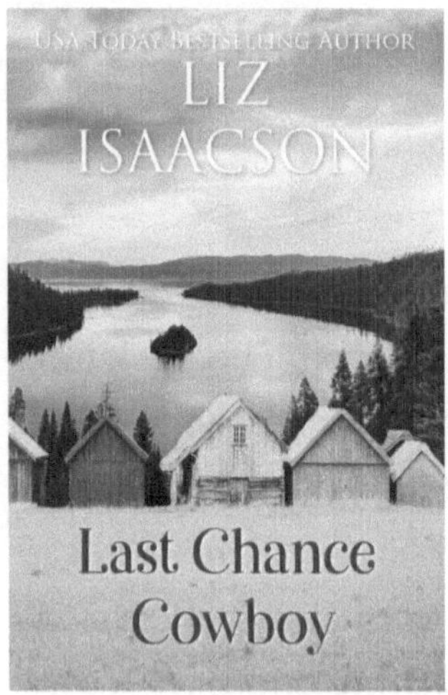

Last Chance Cowboy (Book 2): A billionaire cowboy without a home meets a woman who secretly makes food videos to pay her debts...Can Carson and Adele do more than fight in the kitchens at Last Chance Ranch?

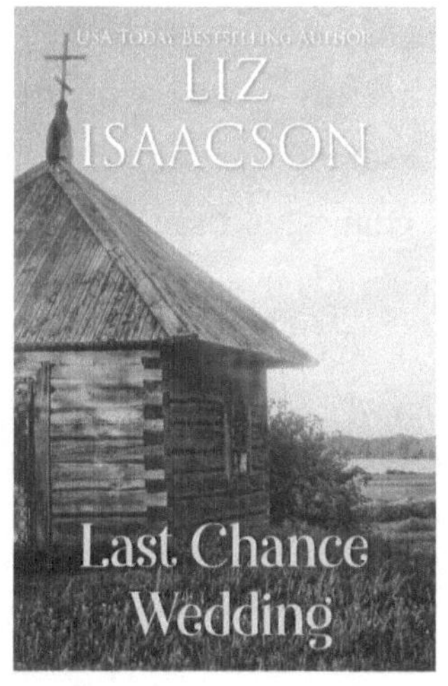

Last Chance Wedding (Book 3): A female carpenter needs a husband just for a few days... Can Jeri and Sawyer navigate the minefield of a pretend marriage before their feelings become real?

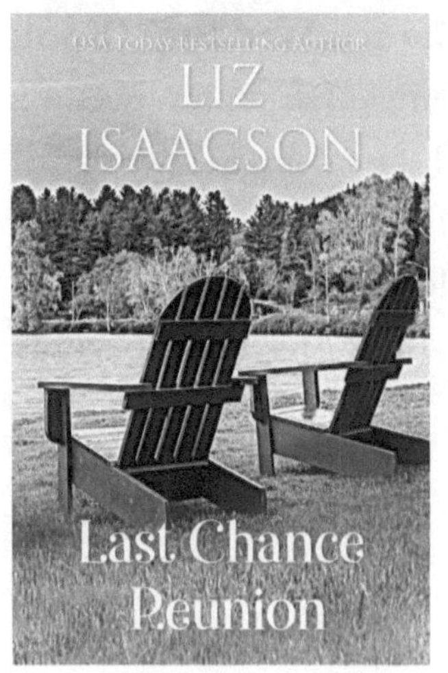

Last Chance Reunion (Book 4): An Army cowboy, the woman he dated years ago, and their last chance at Last Chance Ranch... Can Dave and Sissy put aside hurt feelings and make their second chance romance work?

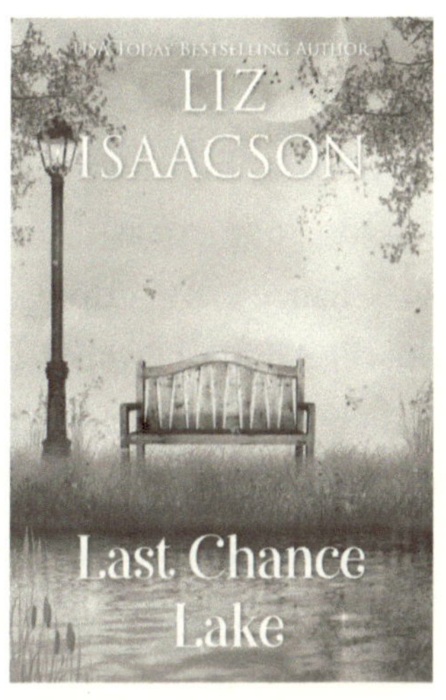 **Last Chance Lake (Book 5):** A former dairy farmer and the marketing director on the ranch have to work together to make the cow cuddling program a success. But can Karla let Cache into her life? Or will she keep all her secrets from him – and keep *him* a secret too?

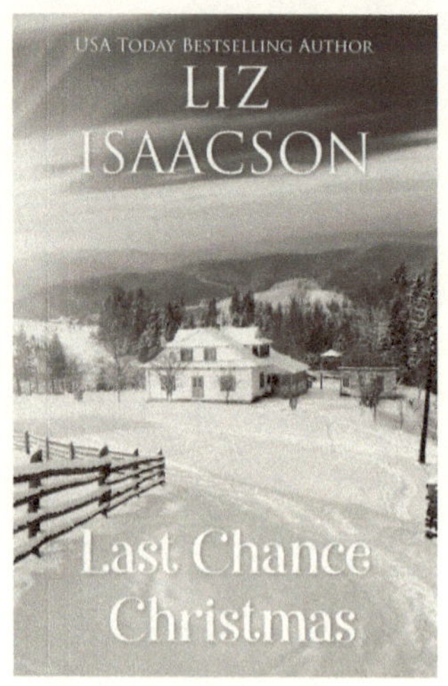

Last Chance Christmas (Book 6): She's tired of having her heart broken by cowboys. He waited too long to ask her out. Can Lance fix things quickly, or will Amber leave Last Chance Ranch before he can tell her how he feels?

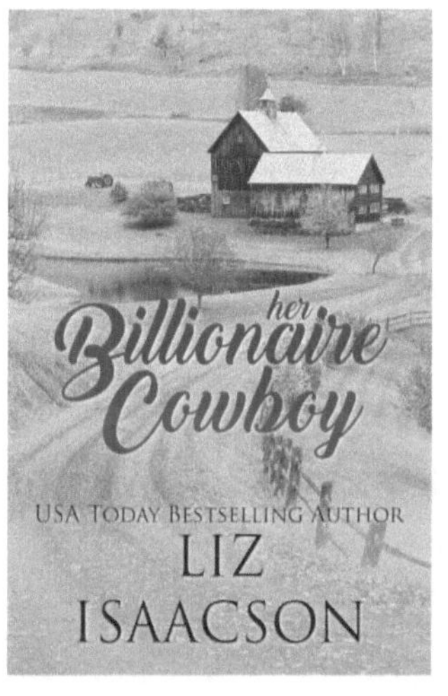

Her Billionaire Cowboy (Book 1): Tucker Jenkins has had enough of tall buildings, traffic, and has traded in his technology firm in New York City for Steeple Ridge Horse Farm in rural Vermont. Missy Marino has worked at the farm since she was a teen, and she's always dreamed of owning it. But her ex-husband left her with a truckload of debt, making her fantasies of owning the farm unfulfilled. Tucker didn't come to the country to find a new wife, but he supposes a woman could help him start over in Steeple Ridge. Will Tucker and Missy be able to navigate the shaky ground between them to find a new beginning?

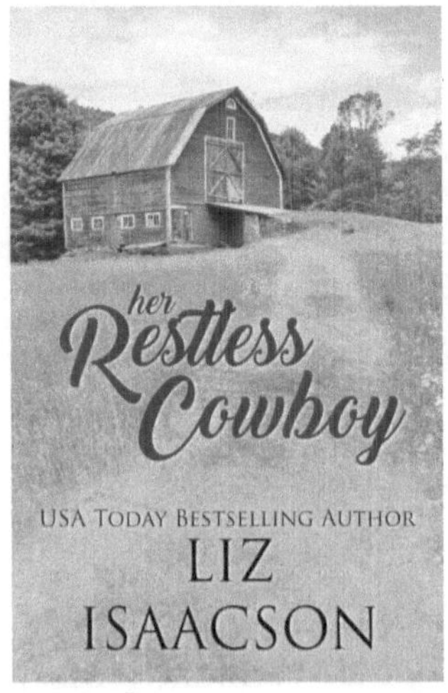

Her Restless Cowboy: A Butters Brothers Novel, Steeple Ridge Romance (Book 2): Ben Buttars is the youngest of the four Buttars brothers who come to Steeple Ridge Farm, and he finally feels like he's landed somewhere he can make a life for himself. Reagan Cantwell is a decade older than Ben and the recreational direction for the town of Island Park. Though Ben is young, he knows what he wants—and that's Rae. Can she figure out how to put what matters most in her life—family and faith—above her job before she loses Ben?

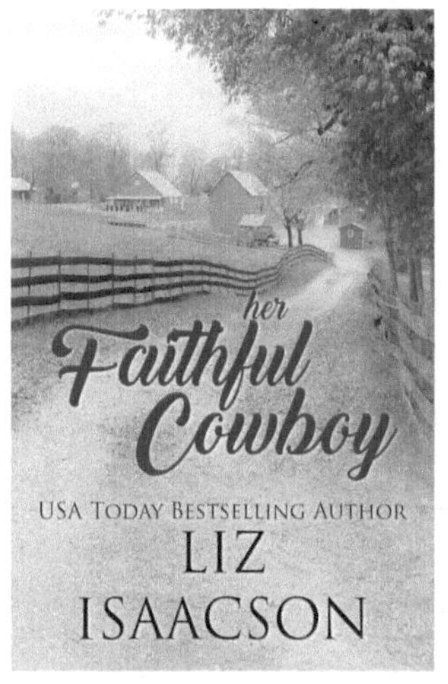

Her Faithful Cowboy: A Butters Brothers Novel, Steeple Ridge Romance (Book 3): Sam Buttars has spent the last decade making sure he and his brothers stay together. They've been at Steeple Ridge for a while now, but with the youngest married and happy, the siren's call to return to his parents' farm in Wyoming is loud in Sam's ears. He'd just go if it weren't for beautiful Bonnie Sherman, who roped his heart the first time he saw her. Do Sam and Bonnie have the faith to find comfort in each other instead of in the people who've already passed?

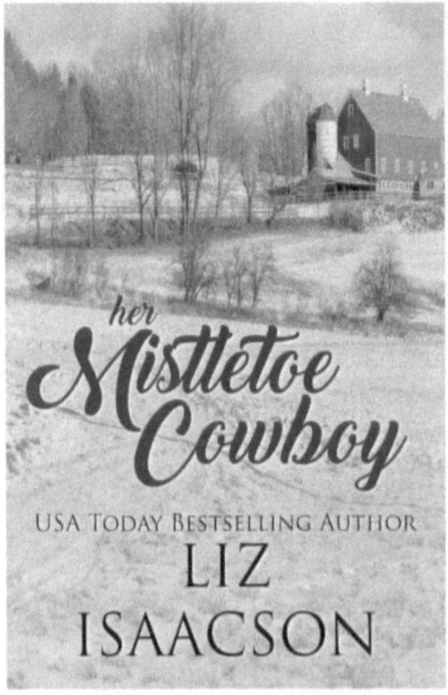

Her Mistletoe Cowboy: A Butters Brothers Novel, Steeple Ridge Romance (Book 4): Logan Buttars has always been good-natured and happy-go-lucky. After watching two of his brothers settle down, he recognizes a void in his life he didn't know about. Veterinarian Layla Guyman has appreciated Logan's friendship and easy way with animals when he comes into the clinic to get the service dogs. But with his future at Steeple Ridge in the balance, she's not sure a relationship with him is worth the risk. Can she rely on her faith and employ patience to tame Logan's wild heart?

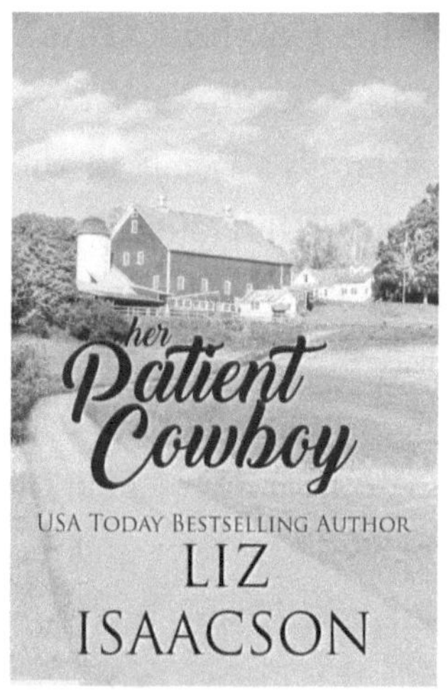

Her Patient Cowboy: A Butters Brothers Novel, Steeple Ridge Romance (Book 5): Darren Buttars is cool, collected, and quiet—and utterly devastated when his girlfriend of nine months, Farrah Irvine, breaks up with him because he wanted her to ride her horse in a parade. But Farrah doesn't ride anymore, a fact she made very clear to Darren. She returned to her childhood home with so much baggage, she doesn't know where to start with the unpacking. Darren's the only Buttars brother who isn't married, and he wants to make Island Park his permanent home—with Farrah. Can they find their way through the heartache to achieve a happily-ever-after together?

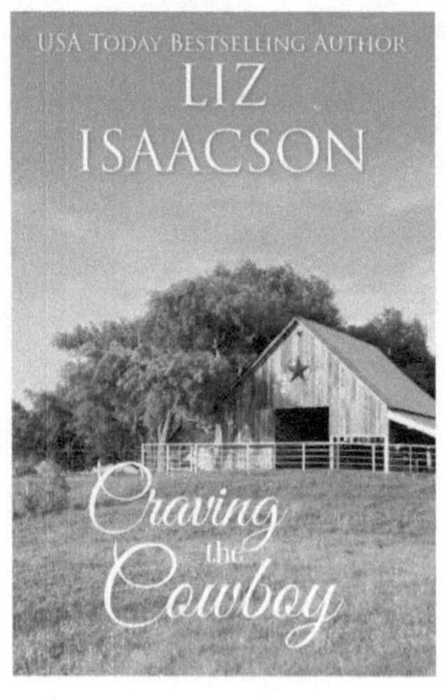

Craving the Cowboy (Book 1): Dwayne Carver is set to inherit his family's ranch in the heart of Texas Hill Country, and in order to keep up with his ranch duties and fulfill his dreams of owning a horse farm, he hires top trainer Felicity Lightburne. They get along great, and she can envision herself on this new farm—at least until her mother falls ill and she has to return to help her. Can Dwayne and Felicity work through their differences to find their happily-ever-after?

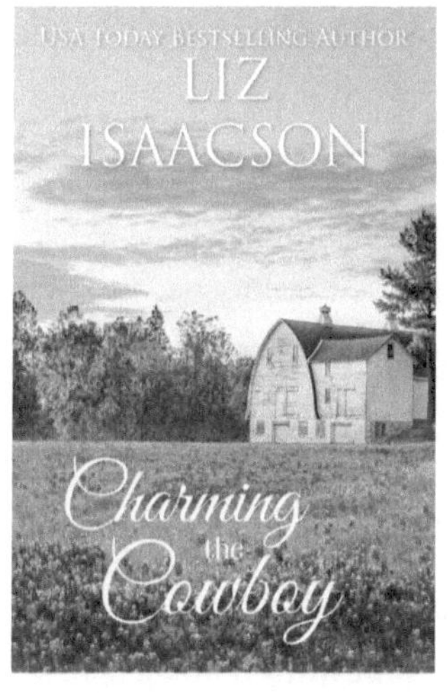

Charming the Cowboy (Book 2): Third grade teacher Heather Carver has had her eye on Levi Rhodes for a couple of years now, but he seems to be blind to her attempts to charm him. When she breaks her arm while on his horse ranch, Heather infiltrates Levi's life in ways he's never thought of, and his strict anti-female stance slips. Will Heather heal his emotional scars and he care for her physical ones so they can have a real relationship?

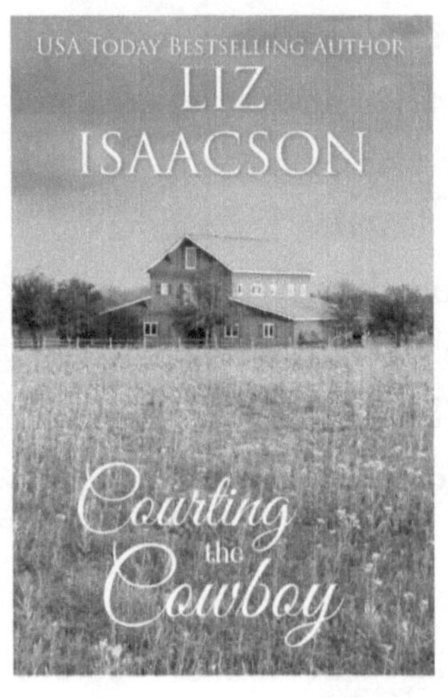

Courting the Cowboy (Book 3): Frustrated with the cowboy-only dating scene in Grape Seed Falls, May Sotheby joins Texas-Faithful.com, hoping to find her soul mate without having to relocate--or deal with cowboy hats and boots. She has no idea that Kurt Pemberton, foreman at Grape Seed Ranch, is the man she starts communicating with... Will May be able to follow her heart and get Kurt to forgive her so they can be together?

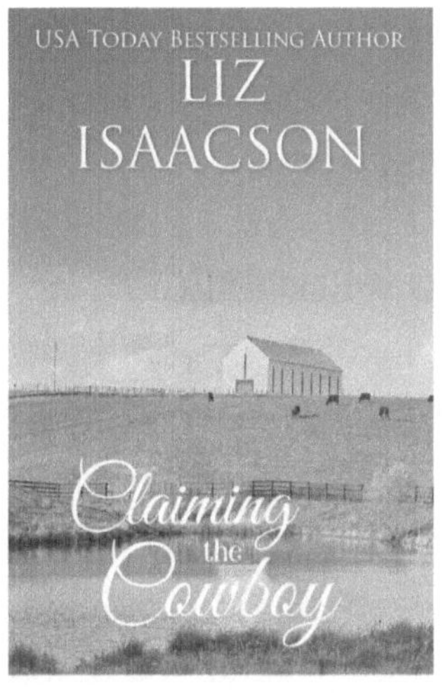

Claiming the Cowboy, Royal Brothers Book 1 (Grape Seed Falls Romance Book 4): Unwilling to be tied down, farrier Robin Cook has managed to pack her entire life into a two-hundred-and-eighty square-foot house, and that includes her Yorkie. Cowboy and co-foreman, Shane Royal has had his heart set on Robin for three years, even though she flat-out turned him down the last time he asked her to dinner. But she's back at Grape Seed Ranch for five weeks as she works her horseshoeing magic, and he's still interested, despite a bitter life lesson that left a bad taste for marriage in his mouth.

Robin's interested in him too. But can she find room for Shane in her tiny house--and can he take a chance on her with his tired heart?

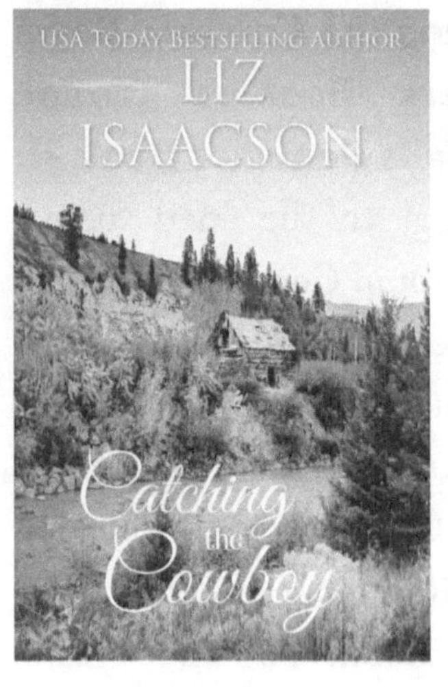

Catching the Cowboy, Royal Brothers Book 2 (Grape Seed Falls Romance Book 5): Dylan Royal is good at two things: whistling and caring for cattle. When his cows are being attacked by an unknown wild animal, he calls Texas Parks & Wildlife for help. He wasn't expecting a beautiful mammologist to show up, all flirty and fun and everything Dylan didn't know he wanted in his life.

Hazel Brewster has gone on more first dates than anyone in Grape Seed Falls, and she thinks maybe Dylan deserves a second... Can they find their way through wild animals, huge life changes, and their emotional pasts to find their forever future?

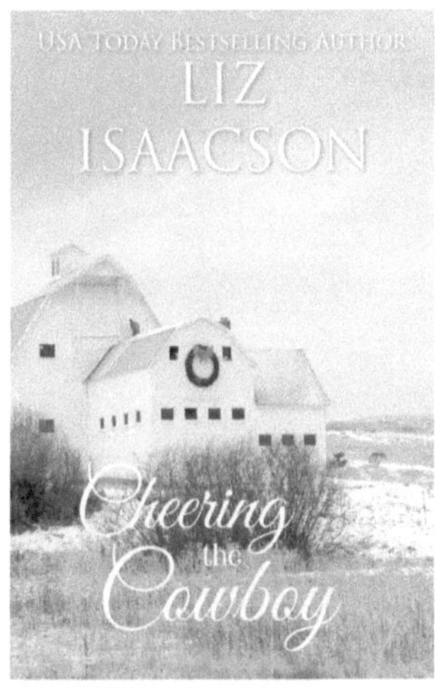

Cheering the Cowboy, Royal Brothers Book 3 (Grape Seed Falls Romance Book 6): Austin Royal loves his life on his new ranch with his brothers. But he doesn't love that Shayleigh Hatch came with the property, nor that he has to take the blame for the fact that he now owns her childhood ranch. They rarely have a conversation that doesn't leave him furious and frustrated--and yet he's still attracted to Shay in a strange, new way.

Shay inexplicably likes him too, which utterly confuses and angers her. As they work to make this Christmas the best the Triple Towers Ranch has ever seen, can they also navigate through their rocky relationship to smoother waters?

Praise for Liz Isaacson

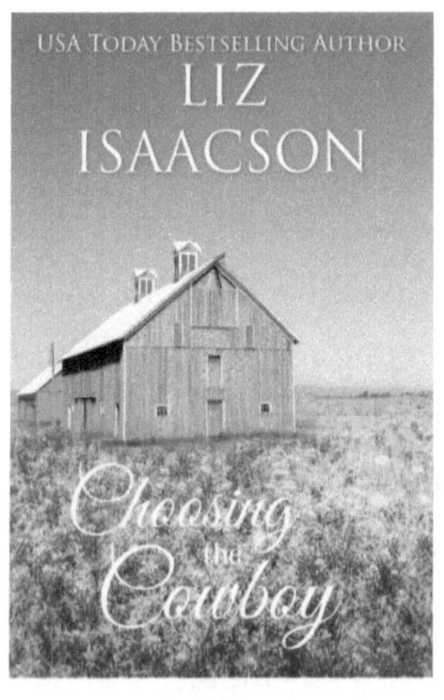

Choosing the Cowboy (Book 7): With financial trouble and personal issues around every corner, can Maggie Duffin and Chase Carver rely on their faith to find their happily-ever-after?

A spinoff from the #1 bestselling Three Rivers Ranch Romance novels, also by USA Today bestselling author Liz Isaacson.

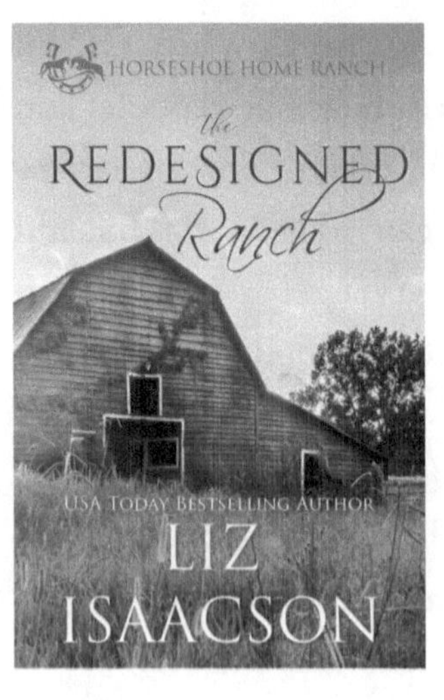

The Redesigned Ranch (Book 1): Jace Lovell only has one thing left after his fiancé abandons him at the altar: his job at Horseshoe Home Ranch. Belle Edmunds is back in Gold Valley and she's desperate to build a portfolio that she can use to start her own firm in Montana. Jace isn't anywhere near forgiving his fiancé, and he's not sure he's ready for a new relationship with someone as fiery and beautiful as Belle. Can she employ her patience while he figures out how to forgive so they can find their own brand of happily-ever-after?

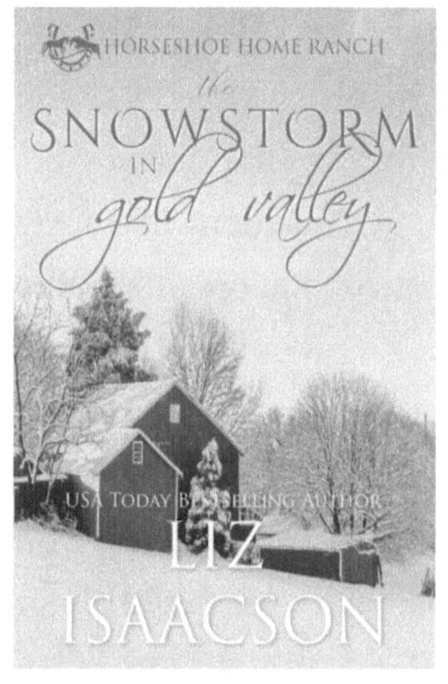

The Snowstorm in Gold Valley (Book 2): Professional snowboarder Sterling Maughan has sequestered himself in his family's cabin in the exclusive mountain community above Gold Valley, Montana after a devastating fall that ended his career. Norah Watson cleans Sterling's cabin and the more time they spend together, the more Sterling is interested in all things Norah. As his body heals, so does his faith. Will Norah be able to trust Sterling so they can have a chance at true love?

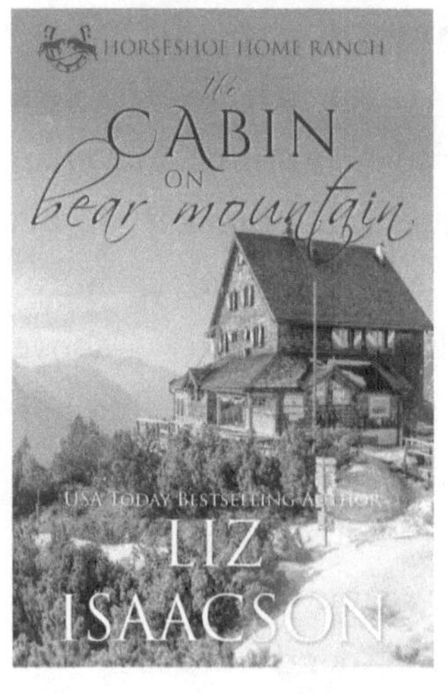

The Cabin on Bear Mountain (Book 3): Landon Edmunds has been a cowboy his whole life. An accident five years ago ended his successful rodeo career, and now he's looking to start a horse ranch--and he's looking outside of Montana. Which would be great if God hadn't brought Megan Palmer back to Gold Valley right when Landon is looking to leave. Megan and Landon work together well, and as sparks fly, she's sure God brought her back to Gold Valley so she could find her happily ever after. Through serious discussion and prayer, can Landon and Megan find their future together?

Be sure to check out the spinoff series, the Brush Creek Brides romances after you read FALLING FOR HIS BEST FRIEND. Start with A WEDDING FOR THE WIDOWER.

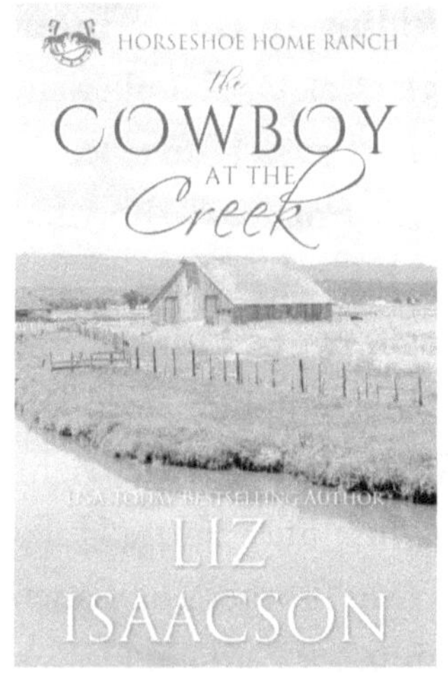

The Cowboy at the Creek (Book 4): Twelve years ago, Owen Carr left Gold Valley—and his long-time girlfriend—in favor of a country music career in Nashville. Married and divorced, Natalie teaches ballet at the dance studio in Gold Valley, but she never auditioned for the professional company the way she dreamed of doing. With Owen back, she realizes all the opportunities she missed out on when he left all those years ago—including a future with him. Can they mend broken bridges in order to have a second chance at love?

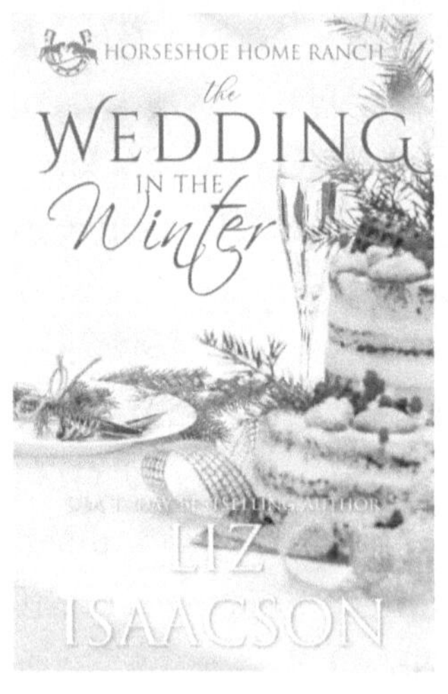

The Wedding in the Winter (Book 5): Caleb Chamberlain has spent the last five years recovering from a horrible breakup, his alcoholism that stemmed from it, and the car accident that left him hospitalized. He's finally on the right track in his life—until Holly Gray, his twin brother's ex-fiance mistakes him for Nathan. Holly's back in Gold Valley to get the required veterinarian hours to apply for her graduate program. When the herd at Horseshoe Home comes down with pneumonia, Caleb and Holly are forced to work together in close quarters. Holly's over Nathan, but she hasn't forgiven him—or the woman she believes broke up their relationship. Can Caleb and Holly navigate such a rough past to find their happily-ever-after?

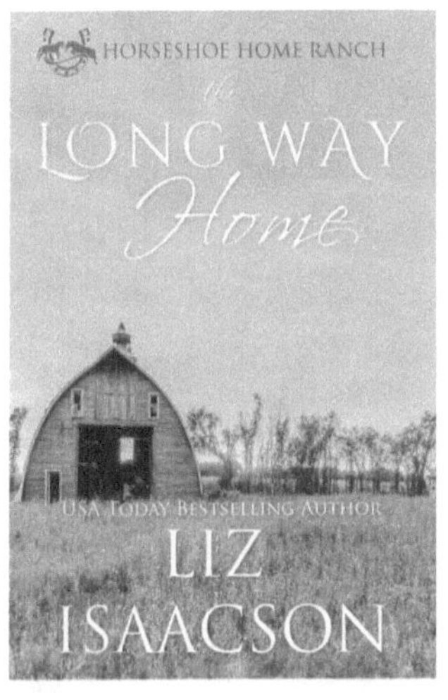

The Long Way Home (Book 6): Ty Barker has been dancing through the last thirty years of his life--and he's suddenly realized he's alone. River Lee Whitely is back in Gold Valley with her two little girls after a divorce that's left deep scars. She has a job at Silver Creek that requires her to be able to ride a horse, and she nearly tramples Ty at her first lesson. That's just fine by him, because River Lee is the girl Ty has never gotten over. Ty realizes River Lee needs time to settle into her new job, her new home, her new life as a single parent, but going slow has never been his style. But for River Lee, can Ty take the necessary steps to keep her in his life?

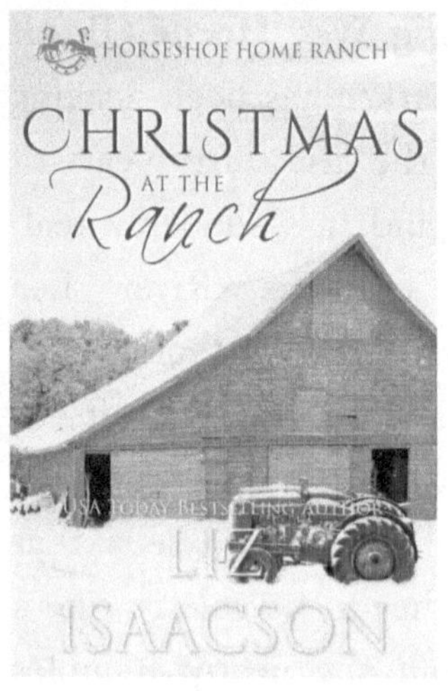

Christmas at the Ranch (Book 7): Archer Bailey has already lost one job to Emersyn Enders, so he deliberately doesn't tell her about the cowhand job up at Horseshoe Home Ranch. Emery's temporary job is ending, but her obligations to her physically disabled sister aren't. As Archer and Emery work together, its clear that the sparks flying between them aren't all from their friendly competition over a job. Will Emery and Archer be able to navigate the ranch, their close quarters, and their individual circumstances to find love this holiday season?

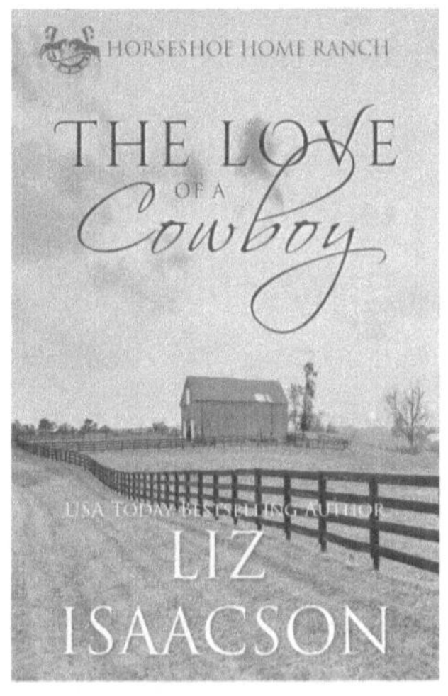

The Love of a Cowboy (Book 8): Cowboy Elliott Hawthorne has just lost his best friend and cabin mate to the worst thing imaginable—marriage. When his brother calls about an accident with their father, Elliott rushes down to Gold Valley from the ranch only to be met with the most beautiful woman he's ever seen. His father's new physical therapist, London Marsh, likes the handsome face and gentle spirit she sees in Elliott too. Can Elliott and London navigate difficult family situations to find a happily-ever-after?

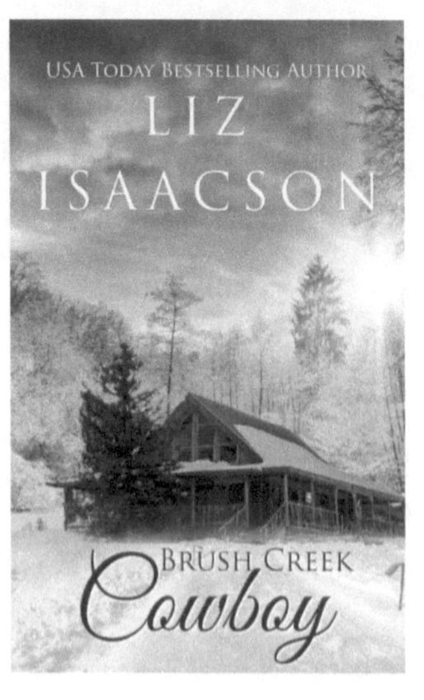

Brush Creek Cowboy: Brush Creek Cowboys Romance (Book 1): Former rodeo champion and cowboy Walker Thompson trains horses at Brush Creek Horse Ranch, where he lives a simple life in his cabin with his ten-year-old son. A widower of six years, he's worked with Tess Wagner, a widow who came to Brush Creek to escape the turmoil of her life to give her seven-year-old son a slower pace of life. But Tess's breast cancer is back...

Walker will have to decide if he'd rather spend even a short time with Tess than not have her in his life at all. Tess wants to feel God's love and power, but can she discover and accept God's will in order to find her happy ending?

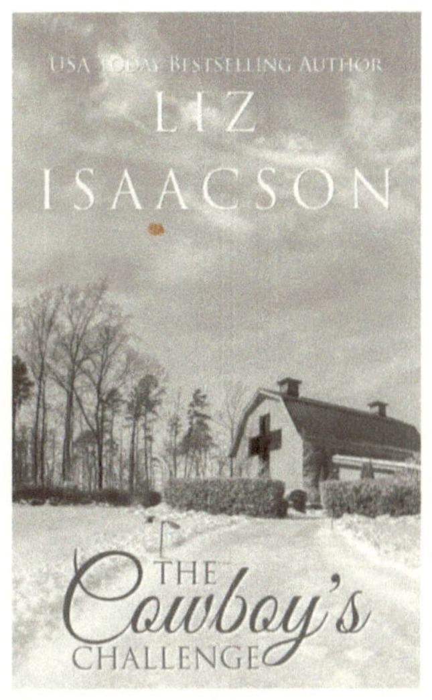

The Cowboy's Challenge: Brush Creek Brides Romance (Book 2): Cowboy and professional roper Justin Jackman has found solitude at Brush Creek Horse Ranch, preferring his time with the animals he trains over dating. With two failed engagements in his past, he's not really interested in getting his heart stomped on again. But when flirty and fun Renee Martin picks him up at a church ice cream bar--on a bet, no less--he finds himself more than just a little interested. His Gen-X attitudes are attractive to her; her Millennial behaviors drive him nuts. Can Justin look past their differences and take a chance on another engagement?

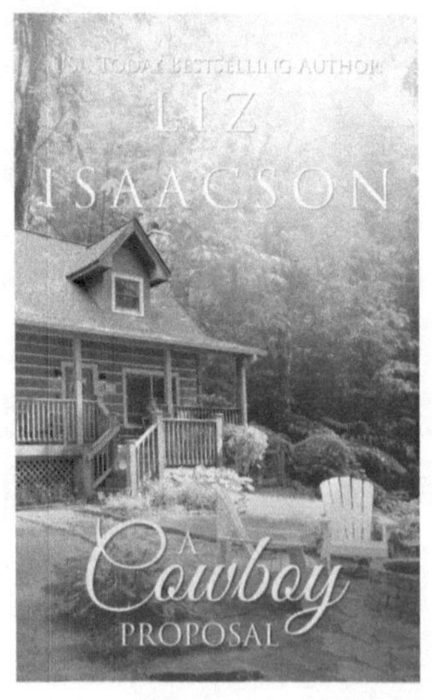

A Cowboy Proposal: Brush Creek Brides Romance (Book 3): Ted Caldwell has been a retired bronc rider for years, and he thought he was perfectly happy training horses to buck at Brush Creek Ranch. He was wrong. When he meets April Nox, who comes to the ranch to hide her pregnancy from all her friends back in Jackson Hole, Ted realizes he has a huge family-shaped hole in his life. April is embarrassed, heartbroken, and trying to find her extinguished faith. She's never ridden a horse and wants nothing to do with a cowboy ever again. Can Ted and April create a family of happiness and love from a tragedy?

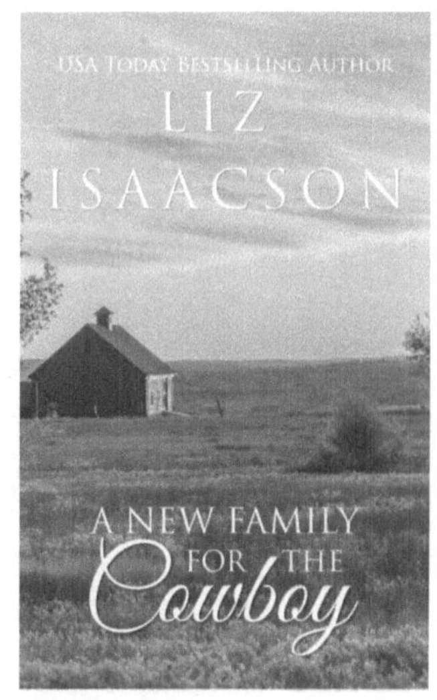

A New Family for the Cowboy: Brush Creek Brides Romance (Book 4): Blake Gibbons oversees all the agriculture at Brush Creek Horse Ranch, sometimes moonlighting as a general contractor. When he meets Erin Shields, new in town, at her aunt's bakery, he's instantly smitten. Erin moved to Brush Creek after a divorce that left her penniless, homeless, and a single mother of three children under age eight. She's nowhere near ready to start dating again, but the longer Blake hangs around the bakery, the more she starts to like him. Can Blake and Erin find a way to blend their lifestyles and become a family?

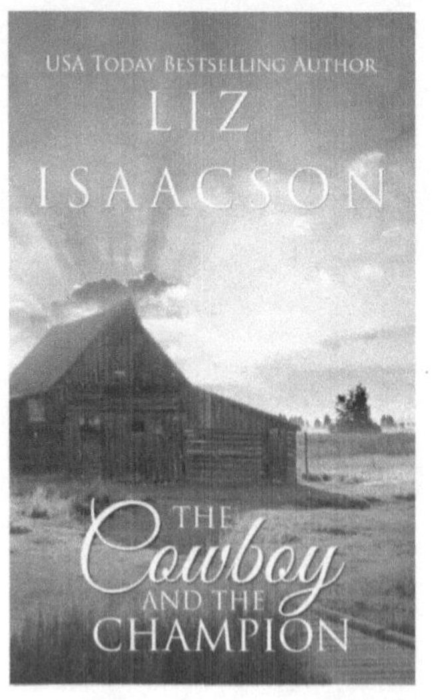

The Cowboy and the Champion: Brush Creek Brides Romance (Book 5): Emmett Graves has always had a positive outlook on life. He adores training horses to become barrel racing champions during the day and cuddling with his cat at night. Fresh off her professional rodeo retirement, Molly Brady comes to Brush Creek Horse Ranch as Emmett's protege. He's not thrilled, and she's allergic to cats. Oh, and she'd like to stay cowboy-free, thank you very much. But Emmett's about as cowboy as they come.... Can Emmett and Molly work together without falling in love?

Schooled by the Cowboy: Brush Creek Brides Romance (Book 6): Grant Ford spends his days training cattle—when he's not camped out at the elementary school hoping to catch a glimpse of his ex-girlfriend. When principal Shannon Sharpe confronts him and asks him to stay away from the school, the spark between them is instant and hot. Shan-

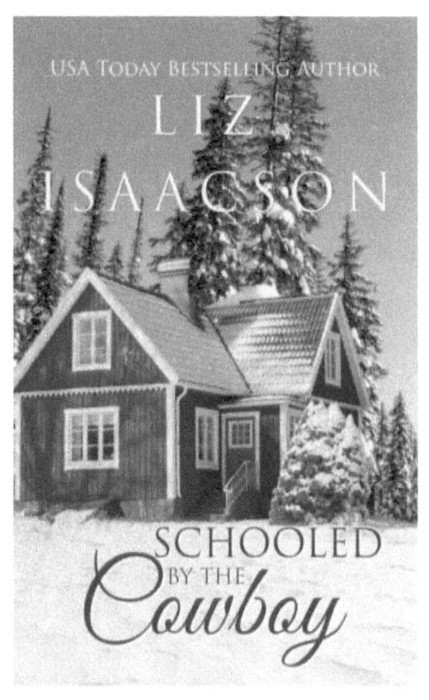

non's expecting a transfer very soon, but she also needs a summer outdoor coordinator—and Grant fits the bill. Just because he's handsome and everything Shannon's ever wanted in a cowboy husband means nothing. Will Grant and Shannon be able to survive the summer or will the Utah heat be too much for them to handle?

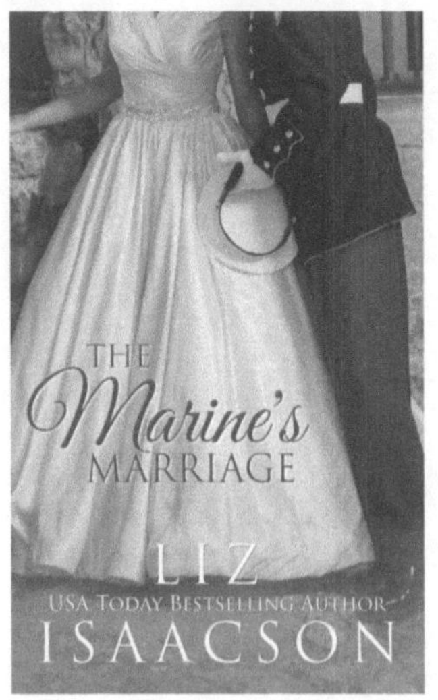

The Marine's Marriage: A Fuller Family Novel - Brush Creek Brides Romance (Book 1): Tate Benson can't believe he's come to Nowhere, Utah, to fix up a house that hasn't been inhabited in years. But he has. Because he's retired from the Marines and looking to start a life as a police officer in small-town Brush Creek. Wren Fuller has her hands full most days running her family's company. When Tate calls and demands a maid for that morning, she decides to have the calls forwarded to her cell and go help him out. She didn't know he was moving in next door, and she's completely unprepared for his handsomeness, his kind heart, and his wounded soul.Can Tate and Wren weather a relationship when they're also next-door neighbors?

The Firefighter's Fiancé: A Fuller Family Novel - Brush Creek Brides Romance (Book 2): Cora Wesley comes to Brush Creek, hoping to get some in-the-wild firefighting training as she prepares to put in her application to be a hotshot. When she meets Brennan Fuller, the spark between them is hot and instant. As they get to know each other, her deadline is 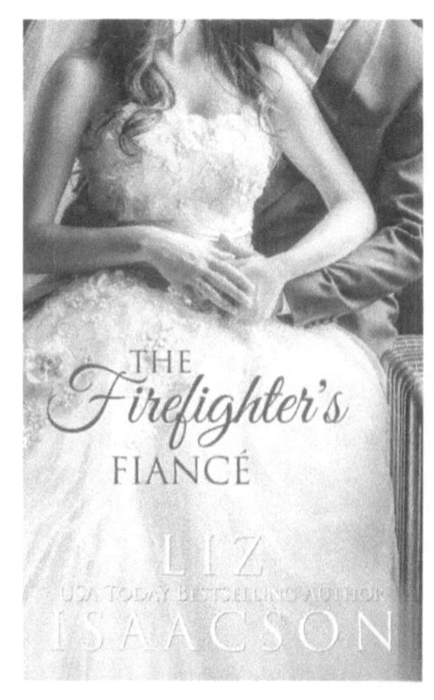 constantly looming over them, and Brennan starts to wonder if he can break ranks in the family business. He's okay mowing lawns and hanging out with his brothers, but he dreams of being able to go to college and become a landscape architect, but he's just not sure it can be done. Will Cora and Brennan be able to endure their trials to find true love?

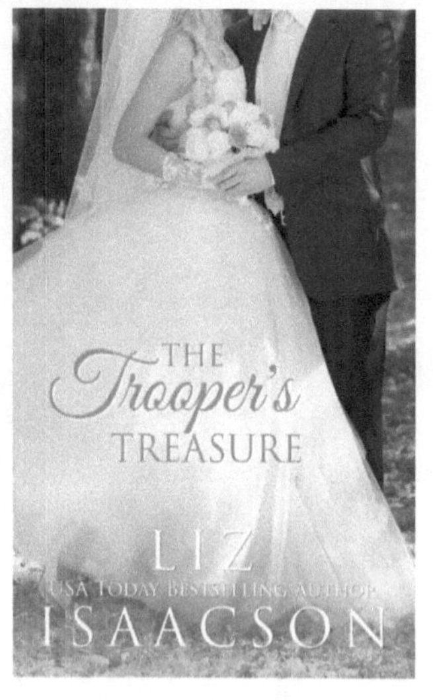

The Trooper's Treasure: A Fuller Family Novel - Brush Creek Brides Romance (Book 3): Dawn Fuller has made some mistakes in her life, and she's not proud of the way McDermott Boyd found her off the road one day last year. She's spent a hard year wrestling with her choices and trying to fix them, glad for McDermott's acceptance and friendship. He lost his wife years ago, done his best with his daughter, and now he's ready to move on. Can McDermott help Dawn find a way past her former mistakes and down a path that leads to love, family, and happiness?

The Detective's Date: A Fuller Family Novel - Brush Creek Brides Romance (Book 4): Dahlia Reid is one of the best detectives Brush Creek and the surrounding towns has ever had. She's given up on the idea of marriage—and pleasing her mother—and has dedicated herself fully to her job. Which is great, since one of the most perplexing cases of her career

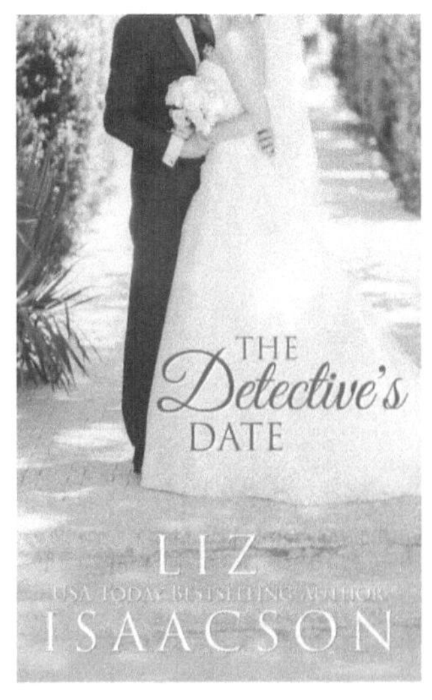

has come to town. Kyler Fuller thinks he's finally ready to move past the woman who ghosted him years ago. He's cut his hair, and he's ready to start dating. Too bad every woman he's been out with is about as interesting as a lamppost—until Dahlia. He finds her beautiful, her quick wit a breath of fresh air, and her intelligence sexy. Can Kyler and Dahlia use their faith to find a way through the obstacles threatening to keep them apart?

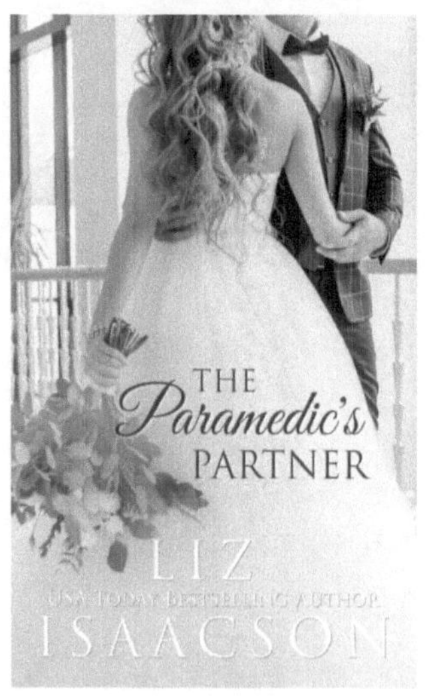

The Paramedic's Partner: A Fuller Family Novel - Brush Creek Brides Romance (Book 5): Jazzy Fuller has always been overshadowed by her prettier, more popular twin, Fabiana. Fabi meets paramedic Max Robinson at the park and sets a date with him only to come down with the flu. So she convinces Jazzy to cut her hair and take her place on the date. And the spark between Jazzy and Max is hot and instant...if only he knew she wasn't her sister, Fabi.

Max drives the ambulance for the town of Brush Creek with is partner Ed Moon, and neither of them have been all that lucky in love. Until Max suggests to who he thinks is Fabi that they should double with Ed and Jazzy. They do, and Fabi is smitten with the steady, strong Ed Moon. As each twin falls further and further in love with their respective paramedic, it becomes obvious they'll need to come clean about the switcheroo sooner rather than later...or risk losing their hearts.

The Chief's Catch: A Fuller Family Novel - Brush Creek Brides Romance (Book 6): Berlin Fuller has struck out with the dating scene in Brush Creek more times than she cares to admit. When she makes a deal with her friends that they can choose the next man she goes out with, she didn't dream they'd pick surly Cole Fairbanks, the new Chief of Police.

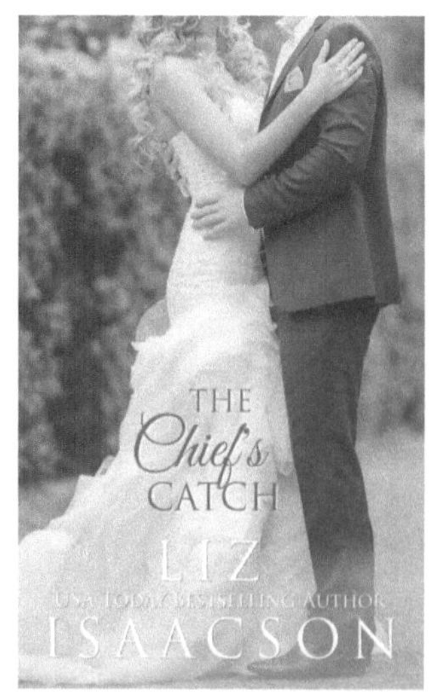

His friends call him the Beast and challenge him to complete ten dates that summer or give up his bonus check. When Berlin approaches him, stuttering about the deal with her friends and claiming they don't actually have to go out, he's intrigued. As the summer passes, Cole finds himself burning both ends of the candle to keep up with his job and his new relationship. When he unleashes the Beast one time too many, Berlin will have to decide if she can tame him or if she should walk away.

About Liz

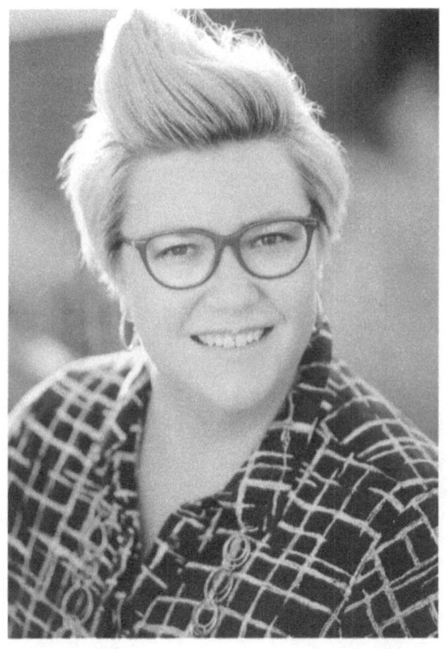

Liz Isaacson writes inspirational romance, usually set in Texas, or Montana, or anywhere else horses and cowboys exist. She lives in Utah, where she writes full-time, walks her two dogs daily, and eats a lot of peanut butter M&Ms while writing. Find her on her website at lizisaacson.com.

www.ingramcontent.com/pod-product-compliance
Lightning Source LLC
Chambersburg PA
CBHW061204190726
48288CB00001B/53